Playboy Billionaire's Fake Marriage

An Enemies to Lovers Romance

Judy Hale

Contents

Playlist

LISTEN ON SPOTIFY

Often— The Weeknd
Mercy— Shawn Mendes
Shallow— Lady Gaga, Bradley Cooper
Hrs & Hrs— Muni Long
Somewhere Only We Know— Gustixa, Rhianne
Falling Like The Stars— James Arthur
All That Matters— Justin Bieber

Chapter One

STELLA

"YOU'RE IGNORING YOUR DATE. Again." I nudge my friend Bonnie, as she takes the empty seat beside me for the third time during this wedding reception.

"I could say the same for you, Stella," Bonnie retorts, staring pointedly at Greg, my own date, who is way across the room with a group of guys, laughing and arguing over something.

The man is great for booty calls, he's just not the attentive date type, which works for me.

Although the bride and groom have long disappeared, the party shows no signs of slowing down with music from the string quartet blending into the laughter and chatter.

I take a deep breath and the smell of the white roses I'd splurged on hit me again, drawing my attention to the large arrangements on each table. *The dent in my savings is so worth it.*

I release my breath on a contented sigh, glad that the day turned out even better than I'd hoped. "I'm the maid of honor, Bonnie, I'm busy."

Well, I was busy. Not anymore though. Now that Brooke and Xavier have finally jetted off on their honeymoon, people are starting to really let their hair down, moving between tables and indulging in food, wine and lively conversation.

I turn to Bonnie, "What's your own excuse for leaving Sam by himself? You said he was 'great arm candy' when you met him three hours ago." I air quote, mimicking her.

"Yeah, he is, nothing wrong there." Bonnie pinches her thumb and index finger together and squints, "He's just a tad boring."

I notice however, that Bonnie isn't looking at her date when she says that last part. Instead, she's glaring daggers into the back of Ethan's head.

"Besides," Bonnie continues, no doubt satisfied that she has now annihilated Ethan with her laser gaze, "Sabrina's keeping him company." She nods to where Sabrina, our other friend, smiles then shakes Sam's hand before sauntering away.

"Nope, Sabrina's not keeping him company. She's just offered the man a modeling job at her gallery."

Bonnie reaches out and plucks a white rose from the confection on the table. "At least he landed himself a gig. What's there to complain about?"

My response gets snatched out of me because the bane of my existence, the best man of this wedding, Ryan Fairchild, leaves the group of men at the back of the room and starts to walk toward our table.

I don't plan to stare, my eyes just aren't taking instructions to look away. And it seems I'm not the only one with that particular problem. A few heads are turning around the room. The man moves like a panther – sleek and arresting.

I'd love to see his family photos because, damn, if those aren't good genes.

Easily one of the tallest men in the room, he's broad and muscular, but in a way that makes his overall look graceful rather than overpowering. With sandy blonde hair, deep blue eyes, and a jaw that seems hewn out of granite, Ryan Fairchild is one hell of a show-stopper, a fact that is, unfortunately, not lost on him.

Bonnie pretends to fan herself. "That man is smoking hot. Quick, Stella," she passes me a napkin, "catch the drool leaking out the side of your mouth before he gets here!"

I can't help the answering laugh that bubbles out of me, which is the last thing Ryan's overinflated ego needs. A couple of grown-ass women giggling like teenagers because he's on his way over.

I tear my eyes away from him to face Bonnie. "Yes, I'm sure the whole of Manhattan's womenfolk would agree he's quite something to look at, but that's where the appeal ends, isn't it?"

Unfortunately, for me, it's not. I'm intrigued by him. And I hate that he gets to me easily. That I always seem to do whatever he tells me, and while I won't admit this on the pain of death, those nights I'm seeking relief from my own fingers, it's always his face I see when I'm tumbling over the waves of ecstasy.

But more than anything, it's his smile I can't get over. The blinding smile that never reaches his cold blue eyes. Its playful edge draws me in, yet there's something equally chilling about that smile.

"Sorry to burst your bubble," Bonnie laughs again then takes a sip of my champagne. "But he's packing a lot more than looks.

He's got a name that swings all kinds of doors wide open—and slams them shut. We're talking old money here."

Although you couldn't tell by speaking to the guy just how wealthy he is. You'd be too busy trying not to poke him with something sharp out of sheer irritation. "Ugh. Well, I can't stand him. And the feeling is mutual."

"Hell no, not with the way he looks at you. Sabrina and I think he likes you, Stella. Maybe you could try to be a bit nicer."

I roll my eyes, dropping my voice to a whisper and speaking faster as Ryan gets nearer. "Bonnie, he looks at every female like they're juicy game and he's the hunter. He probably has women falling all over him with that well-practiced smolder."

Bonnie snorts into her drink. "Hey, pot, meet kettle."

"I'm so not like him," I say with a dismissive wave.

"Yes, you are. We both are, dear. We don't do commitments or boyfriends. So, you see, you and Ryan have a lot more in common than you think. Maybe if you two found an empty room and a locked door, you'd be able to resolve your monumental issues. We are, after all, in a hotel. Waste not—"

I interrupt her, scoffing. "Bonnie, I know you're not suggesting—"

Bonnie cuts in right back. "I am suggesting it, recommending it even. Anyway, here he comes. I'm out. See you later babes."

Bonnie throws him a flirtatious smile as she leaves and he responds with the subtle wink of a seasoned charmer.

"Hey, darling." Ryan drawls, taking the seat Bonnie vacated.

I grit my teeth. "What?"

His smile gets wider. "Aren't you just a ray of sunshine today? Anyway, I've been wanting to talk to you all evening."

"Why? To give me another long list of what I should do?"

The past couple of months leading up to the wedding have been crazy. I don't think I've spoken to another human being as much as I've spoken to Ryan during that time.

I now know things about the man that only a roommate should.

Like the fact that he's a morning person because he usually calls at the crack of dawn, sounding as energetic as a terrier while I feel like death warmed over.

I know he gets headaches when he doesn't get his beauty sleep. Or sex. I'm still trying to work out which one is true and which is false.

And despite pretending otherwise with Bonnie earlier, I'm well aware that Ryan comes from a family so old they still use 'lineage' to describe which side of the family tree they come from. He could probably trace his ancestors back to the Stone Age, recounting how his clan occupied the biggest cave in existence.

Ryan chuckles. "Relax, Stella. There are no more errands or 'to-do' lists. The best man and maid of honor duties are officially over. I only wanted to say that I think you're an amazing friend and you did a great job. Brooke was speechless with joy today."

A reluctant smile pulls at my lips. "Yeah she loved it, didn't she?"

"Yes, she did." He continues to look at me expectantly. When I say nothing, he raises a single eyebrow in a gesture that draws my attention to his arresting eyes.

He looks away but says, "Stella, that was your cue to say something along the lines of, 'Ryan, you too were great.' Actually, for future reference, I prefer the term 'magnificent'."

I roll my eyes, shaking my head. "First off, there's no universe, present or future, where I'd use that word to describe you. And second, you're telling me you need yet another person to inflate your ego? How is it that your head hasn't burst yet?"

"Aha, so it's on your mind, you just don't want to admit it. Come on, let it out. It's always better out than in."

"What?"

"Those feelings. And for the record, I think you're smoking hot too."

I only smile, choosing not to engage. This is our usual dance: he baits, I try to resist biting, I fail and somehow end up wanting to throttle him while he seems to get a kick out of it. Not today. "I'm sure you didn't come all this way just to flatter me."

Casting a quick glance at my strapless navy organza dress and lingering just a moment too long on the large butterfly tattoo on my back, he leans away with a smirk. "No, flattery wasn't my only agenda. I thought we agreed on a best man and maid of honor dance as the final act of the evening?"

"Yep, about that, I nixed it from the program last minute. Sorry." I'm not the least bit sorry.

Ryan chuckles. "Stella, why on earth would you run back to the printers and scrap it after we agreed to do it?"

"You make it sound like I did something scandalous or forbidden."

"I told you. It's bad luck not to do it."

"For the Fairchild ancestry maybe, but not in the twenty-first century where the rest of us live."

"So you're saying you don't want to dance with me?"

"Absolutely not." I lie. I want to get lost in his embrace, yes. Just not while everyone is watching.

"You don't know how to dance." It's not even a question. "It's okay darling, it doesn't matter. We're not competing in 'Strictly Come Dancing.' I'm only going to move your body wherever I want while you're going to look pretty and let me do it."

I'm already shaking my head. "I don't want to dance." Is it me or is what he's describing sounding like something else?

"Stella Marsh. You know you can tell me what you really want," he says with a playful smile, though there's an undertone of something else. Something dark and provocative, and so hard to resist.

I shrug, hoping to play it off as unaffected by him. "Fine, I'll tell you what I want. Just as soon as you start showing me more than one type of emotion."

Shit. Where did that come from?

"Meaning?"

I might as well forge on since I've put my foot in it. "Meaning more than your standard cold-eyes-warm-smile, Ryan."

He pauses, looking at me in consternation. As if he's just seeing me for the first time.

"Come with me." Suddenly, he stands and takes my arm, urging me out of my seat. As soon as I'm up, his hand spans the small of my back, and he turns us away from the tables.

"Whoa" *Okay. Was it what I said?*

"Come on, let's go," he starts leading me to the middle of the room.

I knew he was strong, but that took no effort from him. He's doing it so smoothly I doubt anyone can tell he's practically manhandling me.

Just like he did the day Xavier was going to confess his love to a pregnant Brooke and I wasn't buying it. Ryan had carried me from the room like a sack of potatoes.

And I absolutely hated how much I loved it.

"Where do you think you're dragging me off to now?" I ask, although I can tell because he's already signaling to the band. *Oh crap, he's going to make me dance.* A flutter of excitement begins low in my belly.

"Here, the dance floor." Ryan murmurs. "I imagine the only way we can talk and not argue is if we're choreographed. There now, smile; people are watching." He pulls me into his arms, holding me tight against him as though I might bolt.

"Relax," he whispers against my ear. "I won't bite you. Not here anyway."

I try to ignore how his words are making my belly flutter worse. "I have a date, you know. And I'm pretty sure he can see us."

"Greg will be alright. I already told him I needed to do this." Ryan starts to move slowly taking me with him.

"What? You told him you needed to dance with me?" I can't believe the man's nerve. What's more annoying is that I know Greg probably gave Ryan his blessing too. Too bad I can't play it off like Greg and I are a thing.

"To hug you, yes. You've been amazing the last couple of months. You've surprised me, actually. We hardly saw each other while planning this, yet we pulled it off. And it's mostly because of you."

Refusing to let his sweet words dissolve my irritation, I tilt my head back in defiance. "Really? You were surprised? What, you didn't think I was capable of anything besides looking pretty?"

Again, he gives me that brief look. I wonder if it's annoyance, but I can't be sure since he's still smirking and never makes eye contact for longer than two seconds.

"No, Stella, you surprised me because despite all the times you scoffed and rolled your eyes while planning this incredibly romantic event, you've done a phenomenal job. Take the decor you designed, for instance." He gestures toward the exquisite arrangement of fresh flowers on the now-empty couple's seat. "It's breathtaking."

"Breathtaking! Wow, we're showering each other with compliments today, Ryan. Do you want something?"

Again, that look. "Now that you mention it, yes. I do. I always have. And it's the same thing you've wanted since the day we met."

"Oh, so now you're psychic. Well, I'm not, so I don't know what you're talking about," I retort, though deep down, I know exactly what he means. Ryan and I have been walking a tightrope of intense sexual tension for months now.

He fits my type perfectly: a charming playboy with a trail of broken hearts behind him. In theory, I should indulge in what he so generously offers, but something about Ryan keeps me from giving in to the temptation.

"You do Stella. Actually, it's interesting how very similar we are. Ask me I'll say yes."

"You'll say yes to anything?" I tilt back my head to look at him.

He pulls me closer. "Because I already know what you'll ask for. Just try it."

He's daring me. Pushing me. His hand moves from my waist to my naked back, his thumb subtly tracing a pattern on my skin. Like an ever-expanding ripple, the tingles spread wider until my body is awash in sensation.

Would it really be so terrible if I did something as clichéd as joining the long line of women that have slept with this playboy? After all, there's no unwritten rule against crossing that line when our best friends are married, is there?

A reckless part of me argues that it might actually do me some good. Perhaps it would quiet my overactive imagination when I find that Ryan is all bark and no bite in the sack.

With my decision made, I lift my arms and wrap them around his neck, relishing the sensation of his warm skin and the silky strands of hair slipping through my fingers. His cotton-covered chest feels solid against my cheek as the scent of musk and pine envelops me.

He bends toward my ear and gruffly commands, "Ask me, Stella. Now."

I take a breath as though bracing to take the plunge into icy water. Then I close my eyes and jump. "Okay. Fine. I'd like you to fuck me. Tonight."

He lowers his head further and grazes his lips on my exposed shoulder, causing a shiver to run down my spine. "Done. Room 1320. One hour."

Heat engulfs my face. How unoriginal. Total fuckboy vibes. Talk about a forgone conclusion.

Well, you made your bed, you better lie in it.

"Don't be late." He steps back and bows with a flair. I roll my eyes, knowing he did that just to irritate me.

Ryan sometimes talks and acts like he's a hundred years old. "Back to the twenty-first century, Romeo. You're already making me regret this. I bet you'll have a gramophone playing in the background."

He chuckles wryly. "Well, you'll have to show up to find out, darling."

He saunters away, clapping Greg on the shoulders as he comes to take his place on the dance floor.

"Interesting guy, that Ryan." He turns back to watch Ryan's retreating back.

"You could say that again," I respond.

"Do you guys have an open relationship or something?"

"A what?" I ask, unsure if I heard him right.

Greg only shrugs, "He says you're his 'person.'"

"What the hell does that mean? I'm not his 'anything.'" I huff.

"Maybe you should ask him because he made it sound like you belong to him."

I shudder in mock revulsion. "Oh, I plan to." He'll be explaining what he means by that later tonight. In precisely one hour.

When you meet him in his pre-approved den of sin.

I ignore the snarky voice in my head and the annoying fluttering in my belly, and tell myself I'm only going to do this once. Just enough to get him out of my system for good.

Chapter Two

STELLA

THE RECEPTION IS STILL not showing any signs of winding down when I break away, hoping my absence wouldn't be noticed by Bonnie.

I've already dismissed Greg, taking a raincheck on our planned after-party activities. He'd only smiled, as if he knew I was going to spend the rest of the evening with Ryan. Or perhaps that was just my imagination.

I step out of the elevator onto the thirteenth floor, my heart pounding harder with every step.

"Okay, calm down, Stella," I mutter to myself, wiping my slick palms on my dress. "You've done this before."

Actually, I haven't. I'm usually the one who calls the shots and waits for men to show up, not the other way around. That must be why I'm so nervous. I hate not being in control. It feels like everything in me is unraveling and spiraling out.

I take a deep breath. *In. Get him out of your system. Out. Stop obsessing.*

I stand at the door and hesitate again.

This is such a bad idea.

My fist rises of its own accord and knocks on the door with a confidence I don't feel.

"It's open," I hear a voice call out from the small square vent near the door. A female voice.

What the hell? I look up to check the room number again — 1320.

"I'm looking for Ryan," I answer, feeling all kinds of stupid.

Maybe I got the room number wrong? I'm about to reach for my phone to call Ryan when the guy's baritone comes through.

"Come on in, Stella."

I freeze. He's in there.

Dear God. That woman in there had better be Room Service.

Did I interrupt something? He told me one hour. Did that mean he had someone else scheduled before me?

Is he just finishing up with her?

Oh hell no. What sort of things is this guy into? Steeple chases?

Suddenly, I want to run.

But I'm too curious at this point not to depress the handle, push the door open and step inside.

It's a luxurious hotel room, as I've come to expect of any piece of real estate belonging to Xavier, my friend's husband.

As my eyes adjust to the darkness, I see that the room's thick curtains are drawn, and it is furnished in deep rich browns and velvets. Dimmed golden lights peek from recesses in the walls and ceilings. A huge four poster bed that screams of decadence dominates the center.

I take my time looking around, because it's easier than dealing with the scene playing out before me.

There's a dark-haired woman kneeling on the floor with her head bowed. She's naked.

My gaze finally comes to rest on Ryan. He's sprawled over the plush chaise by the wall, his shirt fully open to reveal tanned skin and abs I might be tempted to go over and run my hands all over if I wasn't so shocked.

He's on the phone, speaking in low tones, and appears to be giving the person on the line some stern instructions. A glass of dark liquid hangs carelessly in his other hand.

I notice how the bulge in his pants grow the more I stare, until it tents his pants obscenely.

Oh dear. He likes this. He's into threesomes. *Fucking kinky bastard.*

I'm not a blushing virgin, but I prefer my men one at a time, thank you very much. I want all of my partner's attention focused on pleasuring me, and only me.

I take another discreet glance around. Could there be even more women or men lurking around? Any more surprises here today?

I finally glance at the woman on the floor and then back to Ryan, a wordless question in my eyes.

Ryan finishes the call and with an impatient flick, tosses the phone to the side.

"Come here, Stella."

Say what? "You have got to be kidding me. What the fuck is this, Ryan?" I wave my hand back and forth between him and the woman on the floor.

"Ask her to leave if you don't want her here, although I'd very much prefer if she stayed," his voice is thick with arousal.

My mouth opens, and a million questions pop into my mind. "As what? A spectator? A chaperone?"

The corner of his mouth lifts in a playful smirk. "It's really not a big deal, Stella. I won't touch her if you don't want me to."

If anything, that sounds even more annoying. "How very charitable of you," I spit. I can't believe this guy.

Ryan is silent for a beat, a muscle ticking in his jaw. Then his tone hardens. "Alright. He addresses the woman. "Cathy, you may leave." Cathy nods quickly, but sends Ryan a look I can only interpret as utter longing, then she scrambles to her feet to do his bidding. I ball my hands into fists as the reality of what is happening dawns on me.

So Ryan is a dom. The woman is a sub. And what the fuck does that make me?

The village idiot? The snarky voice in my head suggests, and unfortunately, I have to agree with her.

"Hey," I say to the woman. She turns but doesn't look at me. She's a good few inches taller than me yet adopts a subservient role for me.

A general sub? Is that even a thing? Okay, I've seen enough. I need to get the hell out of here.

"I think you'd better stay and...continue whatever it is you two had going before I interrupted." I cock my head in Ryan's direction.

Cathy looks conflicted, her gaze flitting toward Ryan and back to me. She badly wants to stay. Good, which is why I should let them carry on their party.

"This was a mistake." I spin on my heels. "Excuse me."

"Stella."

I stop. There's a wealth of need, of authority in that one word that makes my nipples bead beneath the tape I wore to keep them invisible under the gauzy material. I want nothing more than to turn and crawl to Ryan.

The thought alone is enough to shake me out of my sensual haze and I bolt out of the room and toward the bank of elevators like the horde of hell is at my heels.

It's not until the doors close in on me before I finally allow myself to release the huge breath I hadn't realized I was holding in.

My heart is still pounding, my face aflame. And I'm supposed to return to the party and act like nothing happened?

I pass by a small seating area facing a window and wearily drop into one of the modular chairs to gather my wits.

That man is such a jerk. Could he not have asked about my preferences instead of shocking me like that?

But if I'm being honest, the most confusing part was how badly I wanted to stay and do whatever he wanted.

I wasn't interested in a threesome. I wanted the man all to myself. But if that was what Ryan needed from me, watching as he sat back on that opulent couch like a king, watching his erection thicken in his tan pants the moment I stepped into the room, I was willing to give him that moment.

I'm so glad shame and common sense won out. It's just as well that the wedding is over. That should bring an end to our tête-à-tête. I don't ever have to speak to him again. Or see him.

Although something tells me it's wishful thinking. Because our best friends have just gotten married and are expecting a baby in a few months. I'm the godmother. He's probably the godfather.

Crap. My life just got a lot more complicated.

Chapter Three

RYAN

FIVE MONTHS LATER

I stare at the amber liquid in the tumbler in my hand, refusing to process what the eagle-eyed man opposite me is saying. "McGrath, you're telling me you spent weeks poring over these policies, and all you could come up with is the reason I needed a loophole in the first place?"

"Unfortunately, Mr Fairchild, your company policies are airtight. There's no getting around it, not if you want to retain controlling shares of Ocean Gate in the coming months. You need to get married."

My lawyer's words trigger a surge of bile up my throat, and I almost taste the acrid bitterness. I drain my scotch and slam the glass on the polished wood of my library desk.

McGrath doesn't even flinch. Instead, he keeps his eyes trained on me, letting me see how serious he is. McGrath is one of the best corporate lawyers I know. He has been the head of my personal legal team since I became Chief Operating Officer. And in all the legal skirmishes we've fought, we haven't lost any.

Except this one battle. Ocean Gate versus my freedom.

My father is the CEO and lives in Seattle, where Ocean Gate's headquarters is. But he's only an administrative head. New York is the heart and soul of the ship-building company, and I've been heading the New York branch for four years. I might as well be the CEO.

It galls me that, despite wielding so much power over the company, its thousands of employees and clients, I have so little control over my own life.

I'm being led to the altar like a lamb to slaughter, and there doesn't seem to be a damn thing I can do about it.

McGrath interrupts my morose thoughts. "The good news is, it need only be for six months. We can begin divorce proceedings by the fourth month. It will be an uncontested divorce anyway. That's the only way you'll gain everything and lose nothing."

Fuck. Marry now, get separated in four months, and cleanly divorced in six months. It shouldn't be too hard a sacrifice for Ocean Gate, the one thing I've wanted to do since I could count.

"I'm sorry, but this is the only way," McGrath says gently as though talking down a bristling horse. He's no doubt seen the irritation furrowing my brows and how hard I'm clenching my fists on the table. "I'll draw up an ironclad prenup." He continues, "All you need is to find a wife. As long as no child is born during the six-month period, you'll have all your shares back as well as your independence."

Not to mention cinch my position as CEO when Dad retires in a couple of months.

I nod, partly to reassure the man I'm not losing it. I'm surprised McGrath is unfazed by my odd reaction. Perhaps he's used to grown men having meltdowns at the thought of having to get married.

McGrath leans forward. "Mr Fairchild, can you think of any women who would be willing to take a slice of your fortune in exchange for discretion and six months of their life?"

I fall back into the leather chair and fold my hands behind my head. That's the problem there. Not only do I need a wife, I also need an actress, and a darn good one. Someone who can pull off being happily married to me enough to convince the entire Fairchild dynasty.

Someone who wouldn't turn around and ask for more. More time. More of money. Or God forbid, fall in love with me.

Dammit. I never imagined I'd ever be in this position. I was sure I'd find some loophole or excuse before the time came. I thought I would have made CEO before turning thirty-one, and kicked out the outdated company policies, consequences be damned.

"Mr Fairchild?" McGrath seems to be waiting for a response.

"Fine," I grind out. "I'll work on getting a wife. You have the legal jargon ready."

"Of course." He stands to leave. "I'll get back to you in a few days."

After he leaves, I contemplate what my near future would look like. And I immediately sense a headache coming on.

Living with a woman for months. Talking over dinner, arguing, looking after her when she's sick—

An unwelcome flash of light signals the start of my cluster headache as my left eye waters. I grind my teeth and brace myself against the wave of intense pain until it passes. But I know it will return in a few minutes.

I pick up my glass and automatically wipe non-existent spills with a cloth. Then, I leave the office, longing for my bed.

Unless I have late afternoon meetings, I'm usually home by four pm and in bed by six or seven. This routine accommodates my unusual sleeping pattern and reduces cluster headaches.

I head to my kitchen sink to rinse out the tumbler, then place it in the dishwasher. I grab a bottle of water from the fridge and drink the whole thing in a few gulps. Then, I lean against the marble counter and weigh my options.

There's only one woman on earth I could remotely endure being within a meter distance of me when I'm in my personal space.

Stella.

Sassy, cynical, and saber-tongued. She probably hates the idea of marriage more than I do, going by her reaction to both our best friends falling in love and getting married. Although, right now I think she hates me more.

I know she's open-minded with sex, she likes to be in control, and she prefers her men docile. I thought the only way we could get on in bed was if someone were to submit.

Yet, watching the play of emotions on her face in that hotel room tells me I was wrong about her. She would have submitted to me. She'd hated that someone else was in the room.

Ever since that day, she's been avoiding me like the plague. When she can't, she turns into this gigantic thorn in my ass.

Instead of putting me off her, her attitude has only stoked my desire for her. Tempting me to capture all that crackling fire beneath me. To feed it with mine and take us both to a place where we can both crash and burn. Then do it all over again.

I pick up my phone and dial her number. It rings off. Of course. Stubborn woman. The last time she picked up my call was on the morning of Brooke and Xavier's wedding. That was five months ago. A lifetime ago.

My phone vibrates with a text. Although I shouldn't be looking at the screen during my headaches, I can't help thinking it's Stella responding to my missed call. But it's only a text message from Wyatt, one of my friends.

> Are you still coming out, or is it past your bedtime yet, Ryboy? Cathy and a few others are here. And we all know who they're hoping to catch a glimpse of. Wouldn't look at the rest of us mortals.

Fucking hell. I may have agreed to hang out at the club tonight. With Xavier off the market, the boys have recruited more single guys into our group. We've talked about having the originals, or OGs, show up on clubbing nights to encourage the rest.

Another wave of headache hits, but I manage to type a quick response:

> Bed.

I throw the phone down in disgust and walk into my dark bathroom to rummage for my Zomig spray.

A couple of sprays up my nose and within minutes the vice-like grip around my head and sharp pain behind my left eye eases into a dull throb. Still, with the lights off, I strip and step into the shower. I set the nozzle to full power, mostly because I need the hot spray to massage my skull until it stops pounding.

By the time the water cools, the headache is completely gone but I'm exhausted. I crawl into bed, ignoring the incessant beeps. Most likely it's my friend Wyatt cursing me out for bailing on them again.

I'll deal with all of it tomorrow. Starting with that sexy, stubborn, green-eyed witch who won't pick up my calls.

Whatever else she is, Stella is a businesswoman. And this offer, she'll most likely be unable to refuse. I just need to get her to see me first.

Chapter Four

STELLA

MY FOOT TAPS ON the worn gray carpet of the waiting room of the child welfare agency. As usual, my nerves are threatening to ruin everything again. Despite my many visits here, the pervasive silence and grayness never cease to unsettle me.

My anxiety also stems more from the fact that I never come out of these meetings with the Administration of Child Services with a positive outcome. Something tells me today won't be different.

I failed the last apartment inspection because the elevator in the high-rise building I live in chose that day to break down again. And of course, my ever-leaky kitchen faucet decided to rear its ugly head.

"Miss Marsh?"

My head snaps up, and I flash a tremulous smile at my niece's caseworker before rising to follow her into the small office.

I smooth down the simple green dress I chose for today. I'm usually more comfortable in tank tops and jeans, but I need to make the best impression. I thank her and sit stiffly in the proffered chair.

"Right, Miss Marsh," Anita Brodkin begins, shuffling papers on the desk. "I know how passionate you are about adopting Harriet, but there are some realities we must consider." She pauses while I brace myself for rejection. "Given that she is already settling in with her foster family, and compared to the setup you have right now, it seems sensible to let things remain as is."

My heart sinks at her words, but I'm determined to push for what I want. Harriet is my only family, my late sister's daughter. Her deathbed wish was that I raise Harriet as mine.

"But I'm her aunt. Her only family. Surely that has to count for something?"

"Family isn't always enough in the eyes of the law, especially in this case," Anita states, not unkindly.

She goes on to list the financial stability and housing requirements. The real kicker, which Anita is too kind to mention, is that Harriet's current foster parents, the DuPonts, are a young, affluent married couple residing in the Hamptons, epitomizing stability.

I, on the other hand, juggle styling and makeup gigs, event planning, social media influencing, with attending night school. I can see how I measure up—or don't measure up—to the DuPonts.

I huff out a sigh of frustration as I stand to leave. How the hell do I compare with that, with my meager savings and unpredictable income as a stylist and social media influencer?

Ever since Brooke moved in with Xavier, I've had to pay the whole rent myself. She didn't get why I couldn't just find a cheaper studio apartment. I couldn't tell her it was because I was hoping to get Harriet in the second bedroom.

I haven't told my friends about Harriet. If I do, I'll also have to talk about my sister and what happened to her the day she turned eighteen.

What I let happen to her.

No. I swallow the lump of guilt in my throat and take deep breaths. I can't tell anyone that. Not yet. Maybe not ever.

I thank the caseworker and leave, disappointment weighing heavily on me. All through the bus ride home, tears threaten to spill, but I don't let myself go. I fist my stress ball tightly, mentally holding myself together.

There's only one place I let all my grief out. Under a scalding hot shower.

It's been six years since I held my baby sister's hand. I watched the light fade from her eyes, promising to look after her newborn.

After I lost her, I spiraled into a darkness filled with guilt and pain. The only thing that kept me going was the thought of fulfilling my promise.

I learned to stuff all my self-hatred and hate for men into a dark place. I kept it hidden deep under my bright smiles and bold flirting. Only events like these case worker meetings force me to remember how much I'm failing Vivian and Harriet with every passing year.

I grip the stress ball tighter.

Finally reaching my fourth-floor Brownsville apartment, my phone rings. I groan when I see it's Greg. I'm so not in the mood but I pick up.

"Hey Greg, how are you?"

"Great, I just got back from Italy." Greg had gone to Italy for a three-month modeling contract.

"Awesome. How did you find it?" For Greg and me, it's out of sight, out of mind. As soon as he'd left, we stopped speaking.

"Unbelievable!" Greg gushes, "Everything is amazing. The food...the language..."

"The women..." I add, letting out a humorless chuckle.

"You said it, not me. But I agree wholeheartedly. I'm actually trying to wrangle another contract with the agency, and hopefully a longer one."

"I bet." I kick off my heels, smiling in spite of my dark mood.

"Listen. Are you still with that guy? Ryan?" Greg asks.

That brings me up short. "Greg. I told you, I'm not dating the man. He's just a friend's friend."

"I see."

"What's that supposed to mean?"

"I have eyes, Stella. And seeing you two together at that wedding. I don't know, I thought there was something there. Besides, I like the guy, he's cool."

I roll my eyes. Everybody just seems to love the guy, don't they? "Well, I don't like him."

Liar. That inner voice accuses.

"O-kay." Greg drawls, "Well in that case, what are you doing tonight? Why don't we catch up?"

By "catch up," he means hook up.

"No, I'm good, Greg, I'm not really in the mood to go out."

"I can come over," he offers.

I should be down with this, considering I've not had sex with another human being in months.

My trusty vibrator, on the other hand, should have packed up, given the kind of workout it's been getting recently. Lately,

I've been too busy trying to work hard enough to save for Harriet to meet guys.

"Sorry Greg, not tonight. I've got a lot of things on my mind. "Give me a call next week, okay?"

I think I hear him whine, but I don't bother waiting for him to finish. I disconnect and leave my phone on the dresser, then strip off my clothes.

Only a hot shower and a good cry will make me feel better. I set the power as high as it can go and let the punishing heat and the roar of the shower drown out my wrenching sobs.

I'm trying, I really am. Saving as much as I can and putting my dreams on hold. I should be providing the little angel with a home. She should experience the joy of being raised by her relative. This was something Viv and I never had.

Images of Harriet's adorable blonde curls and chubby arms fill my head, fueling my desperation. She looks just like me. Like Vivian.

I leave the shower, my eyes red and skin wrinkled, but feeling so much lighter.

I wipe the fogged mirror, and for a moment, through the distorted image the steam makes, it seems like Viv is staring back at me.

Vivian and I could pass for twins. I gently finger-comb my thick, blonde, almost silvery hair, then grab a towel to dry it in a way that retains the natural waves.

I force my thoughts to more pressing needs, declaring my pity party now over.

I say to my reflection. "Stella, you're going to get a new apartment and in a better neighborhood. It's never going to be the Hamptons, but hell if you're going to let that cow you."

As I leave the foggy bathroom, I wonder whether it might be worth getting a regular-paying job. Bonnie has started working in Ethan's company, and she doesn't seem to be regretting it so far, despite the man being a bosshole.

I'm about to pull on my favorite silk robe when my phone vibrates on the dresser.

It's Ryan.

I let out a huff of irritation, ignoring the way my heart skips a beat. Again? He's been calling me every day for the past week now. What's crawled under the guy's ass?

The last time the guy called me this frequently was five months ago when I stormed out of his hotel room, wishing I would never lay eyes on him again.

Of course, that notion was laughable. Short of moving out of New York, I was unlikely to get that particular wish granted.

We ended up meeting again and again, and every time, I came away hating him a little bit more.

Craving him a little bit more, that snarky voice mocks.

I decline the call with a savage flick of my thumb and fling the offending phone on the bed. Then I whip off the towel on my head, drying my hair in vigorous jerks, something I tell my clients to never do. But I need to dispel these horrid thoughts.

What could he possibly want from me this time?

I remember those early morning calls just before Brooke and Xavier's wedding. How I managed to come away from that with my sanity intact is beyond me. The man just gets under my skin like no one ever has.

I enjoy teasing men and calling the shots, but Ryan is like uncharted waters, wild and unpredictable. I hate the way something inside me trembles when he's near. I tell myself it's the sheer size of him, but I know better.

I glare at the phone until it finally stops vibrating. Then, I head to the kitchen to fix myself a much-needed sandwich. I'd skipped breakfast because my stomach was in knots this morning.

I'm just settling at my kitchen table and loading up my laptop, ready to power through some client bookings when the doorbell rings.

Awesome! Must be the delivery for the new makeup brushes I speed-ordered yesterday.

I refasten my robe's belt, take the towel off my head and fluff out my hair. Then, I quickly pad across the living room and pull the door open without even checking the peephole.

I'm shocked to see it's Ryan.

He fills my doorway, tall and imposing. His hair is sexily mussed, like he's been running his fingers through it. This time his eyes aren't cold. They're scorching. Helplessly, my own eyes rove over his tailored black shirt. It contrasts with his tanned skin and lovingly molds to his torso.

I catch myself and yank my gaze back to his before it has a chance to descend even lower. And I find his own eyes haven't quite made it back to mine because they're busy roaming all over my silk-clad body.

Shit. I thought this was a quick delivery.

I jerk the edges of my robe more firmly together. "Ryan?"

His smile widens. "Stella." My name sounds like a prayer rolling off his lips.

The last time he was here was the very first time I saw him in person. He'd drenched himself trying to help me repair my leaky faucet.

That seems like ages ago. Before I got to know the real Ryan. The bossy one.

The dom with the big ass dick.

I feel my face flaming, and I immediately want to kick myself for going down that stupid lane.

"Why are you here?" I snap.

"If you'd picked up my calls, I wouldn't be here. You look good, by the way. Very good." He gives me another slow once-over, and I want to grit my teeth against the ripples of awareness coursing through my skin.

"I would think you'd take the hint and stop calling."

He loses the teasing smirk. "Stella, I need to speak to you. It's important."

I cock my head in disbelief. "What could you possibly need to talk about? What, you're tired of recycling all the floozies in Manhattan?" At the rate Ryan goes through them, it's a real possibility since he has a habit of doing more than one woman at once.

"Can I come in, or do you want to talk out here?"

"Whatever it is you're selling, it's a no from me, so I don't see the point of us talking."

"Jesus, woman, give me a break. You should hear me out on this."

"I'm not sleeping with you, Ryan Fairchild."

Ryan laughs. Actually holds his belly and laughs. I'd love to say that I hate the sound tickling my ears, but that would be a lie. "That is a very easy yes since I have no desire to sleep with you, Stella."

Some of my animosity melts away in surprise. And a little bit of hurt. "You don't." It's more a statement than a question.

"Me, you, and a bed? Hard pass. Not even if you say please. Can I come in now?"

I grudgingly move away from the door and turn to the living room, leaving him to follow. I go to sit on the couch.

He follows me, shutting the door behind him. Immediately, my tiny apartment feels even more constricted. As he moves toward me, my eyes are again drawn to his body.

Why does everything about Ryan have to be so sensual? Like he does everything in slow motion so you can take in every nuance of his movements. I shake myself out of my mental fog and wait for him to join me.

He drops onto my couch and faces me, and I try not to notice how his tight shirt stretches against his broad chest.

"So, what do you want?" I want to get this over with as quickly as possible.

He glances at me, and unlike his usual behavior, he doesn't look away. Instead, he stares. And I soon get why Ryan doesn't look at people for long. Someone must have warned him it's too intense.

I break eye contact, suddenly uncomfortable, but not before I see his brows furrow in concern.

"Have you been crying?" Ryan asks.

"No, I haven't." My foot taps against the thin living room carpet.

"Yes, you have. What's the matter?"

I can't believe this. The last thing I want is for Ryan to see me vulnerable. I leave my seat, needing to put some distance between us. "Really Ryan? You know, it actually sounds a bit strange coming out of you. Almost like you care."

His smile falters. "I do care, Stella. Why would you think I don't?"

I roll my eyes. "Of course, you do. I've got a vagina."

Ryan rears back, his smile now completely wiped off his face. "Okay, listen. We aren't going to do this anymore. However much you can't stand me, you're going to be civil and respectful. So, Stella. That was your last free pass. Open your mouth and talk to me like that again, and I'll spank you."

I gasp in outrage and blink in rapid succession, unable to believe his audacity. "Not unless you'd like to leave here without your balls, you wouldn't dare lay a finger on me, jackass."

"As long as we understand each other." We stare at each other until he looks away, gritting his teeth. "Look, what I want to propose isn't going to work unless we find a way to get along."

"I highly doubt that I can see eye to eye with you on anything." I snap.

"You managed okay before, Stella, I'm sure you can figure it out again, just as soon as you let go of your rage. Why are you so angry anyway?"

"I don't know what you're talking about." I turn away, suddenly finding the view of the brick wall opposite my apartment very fascinating.

"The look in your eyes just now tells me you know what exactly I'm talking about. God, Stella, can you fucking hold a grudge. I already apologized. Squash it already and move on."

I don't realize he's left the couch until I feel his heat on my back mere seconds before his hands circle my upper arms. He bends toward my ear and whispers, "Let it go."

My lids flutter closed. Goosebumps, unlike anything I've ever felt, cover my entire upper body, and my nipples harden to achy points. If I turned around he'd see them poking through my silk robe.

"I'll think about it." I'm proud of how steady my voice is.

For a few moments he simply waits. Then he says. "No."

"What?"

"No, this stops right now. It's been five fucking months Stella. I'm sorry I shocked you. I misread what I thought you would like."

A flash of irritation hits me. "So just because we exchanged a bunch of calls you thought you knew me? There's nothing to apologize for. Absolutely nothing. I was the idiot. I was horny and drunk so at that point anyone would do. Even someone like you."

Okay. I probably should not have said that. The tension crackling from him tells me he didn't appreciate that comment either. But what can I say? The guy makes me nervous and I run my mouth.

"I see." Ryan's arm suddenly circles my waist and pulls me flush against him. He spreads his palm on my lower belly, holding me in place. I feel his arousal digging into my butt and resist the urge to move against the hard bulge.

"What do you think you're doing?" I have to fight to keep my voice even.

"What I promised I'd do. I'm going to spank you. Then you'll get on your knees and apologize. On my cock."

Chapter Five

STELLA

I GASP FOR THE second time, shocked by his boldness but even more so by how I'm reacting to it.

I can do nothing about the heat creeping up my face. I don't blush. Ever. Not even with the crudest form of language. But having this big blond smirking man talk about his cock in my mouth and suddenly it's the most scandalous thing I've heard.

"You wouldn't dare." I can't believe how breathless I sound.

He bends his head to my ear and says in a gruff whisper. "Spread your legs."

Oh God. My heart lurches to a stop. Gone is the raging spitfire ready to crush his balls. Now I just want to beg him to let me go. The plea doesn't make it past my lips though.

"Ryan?" I croak, throat suddenly dry.

"Do it now."

It's not the hand on my belly or even the whispered command that makes me obey. It's my own traitorous body giving up fighting this insane attraction that has been raging between us. I'm well and truly caught in the sensual web he's woven around us.

The moment I move my feet apart, he loosens the belt at my waist and my robe falls open.

"Wider."

Oh fuck. I should say something. Turn around and slap him. Knee him in the balls like I threatened. But my mouth feels like lead. Quiet as a mouse and red-faced, I spread my legs further.

"Good girl. Feel free to scream."

"I hate you." I whisper, face aflame.

"I know." He opens the flap of the robe, exposing my pert breasts, with nipples hard and straining, but he doesn't touch them. Instead his hand trails down my abdomen until his thick fingers slide into my slick folds. I grit my teeth against the sensation but a moan escapes me.

He rubs on my swollen clit and my vision goes dark as my head falls back on his shoulder, unable to resist burying my face in the warm scented skin of his neck. He doesn't let me. Instead, he moves his neck away the moment I try to push my face toward him. Still chasing that contact with him, my hands start to lift. They're about to curl around his nape when I hear his gruff voice again.

"Give me your hands."

Without thinking I hold out both my arms. He grabs my wrists and holds them together in one of his, trapping them against my belly. Then his other hand leaves my pussy, only to return in a sharp stinging slap.

"Ryan!" I cry out in shock and pleasure.

He doesn't respond. He just holds me firmly against him and does it again. And again. Until my knee threatens to buckle under me and I'm twitching like mad.

I think by the tenth slap I feel my own wetness on his palm and the sound it makes as it connects against me drives me mad with lust.

"Please…" the word leaves me before I realize it.

He pauses, waiting for me to say more.

"I want… make me…" But he knows what I want because his fingers return to my swollen, sensitive clit. I gasp, and beyond shame now, my hips move against him in a mindless need to come.

Two fingers slide deep inside me and pump while his palm still strokes my clit. In less than a minute, my body tenses, and my eyes roll back in pleasure.

"Oh fuck. I'm going to—"

He removes his fingers from me and delivers a final spank right on my clit. I scream as lust explodes in my pelvis. I come hard, trembling and moaning. Right in the middle of my orgasm, he suddenly lets me go. Without his arm holding me up my knees slowly buckle to the floor.

Still eerily silent, Ryan steps around me, then cradles my head against his crotch almost lovingly.

The smell of his skin hits me hard and I take lungfuls of it, wanting more. Without thinking, my shaking hands go to fumble at his belt, but he holds them still.

I look up at him but Ryan looks away in that moment. Still, without speaking, he slowly unbuckles his belt and lowers his zipper.

I don't care that this is a different Ryan from the smirking, boisterous guy I like to rile up. He's cold and detached. But then I stop thinking altogether because his cock springs out huge, hard and uncut.

I gasp, loving his size and feel. I wrap my fingers around his girth and stroke until I feel his hand tighten in my hair. Taking it as a cue, I open my mouth to lick his engorged crown when a loud ringtone pierces the silence.

And instantly, the sensual fog in my brain evaporates in a mocking hiss.

What the fuck am I doing kneeling before this jackass and fawning over his cock? I jerk back in alarm, almost falling back on my ass but he catches me.

"Easy darling."

"Get your fucking hands off me!" I scramble to my feet. The loud ringing continues. It's not my phone so it must be his, but he doesn't make a move to pick it up. Instead, he comes toward me.

"Stella."

"Stay the hell away from me Ryan!" I pull the flaps of my robe together and tie my belt with a forceful yank. Breathing hard, I rush to my room, desperate to put a wall between us. I shut the door behind me and lean against it, drawing in huge breaths.

What the fuck just happened here? I let Ryan spank me, came all over his hand, and all but begged to suck his cock just now. Why would I let him do that to me?

Because a part of me that I could no longer deny always wanted to.

As the shock of what just happened recedes, I realize my phone, too, is ringing. I lean over the bed to grab the phone from where I tossed it earlier.

It's Xavier.

"Hey, what's up Xavier?"

"Stella!" His deep voice is rich with excitement. "I've been calling you for ages! Lily Rose is here."

"No freaking way! I squeal. "Are you serious?" I can't believe
my friend has just had her baby.

"Would I joke about this? I mean it, get your ass over here!"

"Oh my God! How? When? Congratulations! Shit, Xavier,
you're a dad!"

"I know, right? It's the best fucking feeling in the world. Lily
Rose is beyond beautiful, Stella. I cannot believe how fucking
perfect she is. It blows my mind. And Brooke... Brooke is so
amazing."

A smile splits my face. Yeah, Xavier gets so sappy when he's
overwhelmed with love. I've seen it so many times with my
friend, and now I know it'll be worse with his baby girl. "I can't
wait to meet her. Is Brooke doing okay?" I ask.

"She's a little exhausted but couldn't be happier. I'm so fucking proud of how strong she is. Come over, she'll want to see
you. Some of our folks are already here."

"We'll—I'll be there soon." I quickly amend, not wanting
Xavier to know his best friend is with me.

Most likely it was Xavier's call that interrupted us. Talk about
being saved by the bell. I might have had my face stuffed with
Ryan right now.

I change into jeans and a T-shirt and give a quick fluff to my
now almost dry hair. I put on a fresh coat of lip gloss, dabbing
an extra coat on the raw area where I must have bit myself not
too long ago.

I hesitate as my hand rests on the doorknob and I listen. Ryan
is talking and laughing. Judging by the excitement in his tone, I
know he's likely getting the same news from Xavier.

I pull open the door just as Ryan is getting off the phone and
I brace myself for awkwardness as he turns to me. My eyes focus

on a spot just above his shoulder, but I can still see his blinding smile. This time it's a real one.

He's back to playful bubbly Ryan. I wonder where he stashed the cold dominant lover I caught a glimpse of just now.

"Did you hear about Lily Rose?" He approaches me, and I tense.

"Yes, Xavier just called me. You need to leave. Go see your friend and the baby."

"Of course, we're both going there. Are you all set to leave then?" He eyes my outfit and then puts a hand on my elbow to urge me toward the door, but I snatch my arm from him.

"We can't go together. I don't want anyone getting ideas of something happening between us."

"Giving you a lift is hardly a relationship, darling. And everyone will be so taken with Lily Rose that they'll have no time to wonder why we showed up together."

He has a point. I let him lead me to a sleek white Bugatti, which looks so out of place in my neighborhood that it might have been painted in gold.

"Wow. Are you trying to get me burgled? Don't you have a regular car you could have brought here?"

"This is my regular car, darling. I'll bring the motorbike instead next time. Or we could bump up your security. Actually, we should sort out your security anyway."

"Um, let me stop you there, Ryan. First, don't call me darling. Just because that happened doesn't mean you get to call me pet names..."

"I call you darling all the time."

"Well, now's a good time to stop. And there's no 'we,' okay? And you shouldn't come around here again."

"Okay." Ryan nods, a serious expression that I'm not sure I can trust on his face. He opens the passenger door and cocks his head, motioning for me to get in.

The moment he shuts my door I smell him. Leather, pine and musk. The interior is finished with luxurious hand-stitched black leather and black chrome accents. They contrast with the almost snowy white exterior.

Hell. This car packs its own share of sex appeal even without its owner inside.

"Don't be an idiot, Stella," I mutter. But it's unbelievable. How in twenty-six years, this is the first time I'm getting into a man's car?

Sure, I've been friends with and dated men who owned cars. I just never got in their cars or let them take me anywhere.

Not since Vivian.

Ryan rounds the hood and then gets into the driver's seat. "You okay?"

I realize how rigid my posture is and make myself loosen my muscles, leaning against the backrest of my seat. "Yep."

"Any more laws you need to lay down?" Ryan asks blandly. He starts the car and merges into the Brooklyn traffic.

I watch his profile, unable to tell if he's joking, but I declare with all seriousness. "As a matter of fact, Ryan, there is. If you ever touch me that way again, I swear..."

Still, with that expression, he says softly, "You don't have to swear, Stella. I won't. Not unless you beg me to."

My mouth falls open as my mind unhelpfully reminds me of how I begged moments ago. Angrier with myself than with him, I snap, "Don't fucking hold your breath, you've got half a snowball's chance in hell of ever getting to spank me again."

Ryan chuckles wryly. "Don't speak too soon. You haven't heard what I want to propose. It may yet come to that again, given the way you speak to me sometimes." he murmurs the last part under his breath.

"I can't think of anything in this world I'm less interested in hearing than your so-called proposal. If you're looking for a fuck buddy, don't bother with a grand proposal, the answer is hell no."

He only huffs a breath, "You think that's all I could ever want from you? Sex? You know, Stella, I can get a fuck buddy anywhere. And contrary to your earlier comment, there are a great many women in Manhattan I've yet to touch."

"*Yet to.* Your arrogance is off the charts. Ryan, why are you such a–" I was going to say whore, but I think better of it.

"What? Say it." He taunts.

"I meant you have quite the appetite for sex." I amend finally.

"You and me both Stella."

"I only do one person at a time."

"Oh, and here we are back to that. You're telling me you've never had a threesome before?

"Er, let me think about that... No," I snap.

He looks genuinely surprised by my admission, but he recovers quickly. "But what was so horrible about the setup? She's obviously a sub, and we're both—"

"Excuse me. If the word you're about to utter is 'dominant,' I'm getting out of this car. Are you kidding me? I'm not into all that shenanigan." I mentally sift through all our conversations, wondering what would give him that idea.

Ryan chuckles. Stopping at a red light, he turns to me. "No. I was going to say that we both like to have control. I wanted you badly. But I worried that if I made you give up control, it would turn you off. So Cathy was there to even out the scales."

"Oh wow, how very thoughtful of you to have gone to the trouble," I snark.

"I try." He focuses once again on the road. "So did you enjoy being spanked?" He casually asks.

I feel my face flush. "Ryan, what did I just tell you? I swear I will strangle you if you ever try that on me again."

He shrugs, his posture relaxed, eyes still on the road with one hand lightly gripping the steering wheel while expertly maneuvering the powerful car through traffic. "You know Stella, I didn't actually do anything. I simply told you what *I* wanted you to do. You could have said no. Why didn't you?"

Yes, why didn't you? My inner voice mocks.

I sputter. "Because I was... curious! And now I know that I hate it."

He laughs out loud. "No, you don't. You came so fucking hard you lost your mind and forgot who and where you were."

I blush furiously, glaring daggers at him. I'm this close to doing him grievous bodily harm.

"Don't worry, your secret is safe with me. Now, if you truly don't want any more of that, be civil to me, nice even. Otherwise, I can promise you'll get another dose."

The way my core tightens as his words annoys me. I want the blinding pleasure but not the mindless submission that comes with it. So I'm going to try and be nicer to him.

"Agreed. It won't happen again," I say quickly. "And I won't hold what happened back at the hotel against you anymore."

"Good God, finally." Ryan muses, "Remind me never to get on your bad side ever again."

His teasing smile is infectious and I find myself smiling at him too. Then he looks away and back to the road. "So," he continues, "are you going to tell me why you were crying earlier?"

"Okay, don't push your luck here. I agreed to let that night go, not that we'd be best buddies. And, I want nothing to do with your proposal. I'm not interested in hearing it, Ryan."

With his talk of control and submissives, I can't help thinking his plan must be something kinky. A fetish of some sort.

He takes a parking spot, and I'm surprised to see we're already at the City Memorial.

"You're not even the least bit curious about what I want from you?"

I consider that. "You promise it has nothing to do with sex?"

"Not precisely, no."

"Hmm," I throw him a skeptical look. "Anyway, we're here." I'm about to leave the car when something occurs to me. "Listen, let me go in first. Give me ten minutes before you follow so they don't think we came here together, okay?"

I push the door open and climb out but then lean back in. "Actually, make that twenty because I need to swing by the ground floor shop to get some balloons, okay?"

His brows furrow in displeasure, and he seems about to argue. But I shut the door, and I'm already striding across the lot before he can get a word out.

I buy a stuffed teddy and vinyl balloons from the shop. I feel a tad guilty about getting Lily Rose her first gift from the hospital shop rather than a proper toy store. *There'll be plenty more opportunities for that,* I tell myself as I hurry through the hospital corridors to Brooke's private maternity suite.

I breeze into the room, delighted to see that Bonnie and Sabrina are already here. So are Xavier's parents, his grandmother, and his friends.

"Congratulations!" I beam, dragging the vinyl balloons into the room. "Brooke, sweetheart, I've heard how amazing—"

The door opens behind me, and I freeze mid-sentence. Ryan comes in and stands next to me. "Sorry we're late, guys. We were held up by..." He pauses and throws me a suggestive look "traffic."

Is he fucking kidding me right now? He agreed to wait! I shoot him a death glare, to which he responds with a self-satisfied smirk.

I grit my teeth into a smile then return my attention to the room which has suddenly grown silent. Xavier throws a meaningful glance at Brooke. Bonnie and Sabrina grin like a couple of cats that just gobbled up all the canaries in Manhattan.

And just like that, I know all our friends suspect that something went down. The one thing I asked him not to do.

Well, there goes your truce, jackass.

Chapter Six

RYAN

Two Weeks Later

Richard Fairchild levels me with his pale blue stare, his face a stern mask of composure and authority. My father is thought to be a hard but fair man, but for me, he's always been a few laughs short of being normal.

"I know all about your deal with Marine Safe, son. You already sent me the report last week. That you still felt the need to lead with that begs the question of why you're avoiding the real reason why you're here."

I drop my glass of scotch on the coffee table and lean back on the plush leather seat.

The library in the west wing of the Fairchild mansion is where my father calls his office. It looks more like a museum though, with its high arched ceilings and walls lined with thousands of books.

I'd finally flown into Seattle this morning, after weeks of my father's repeated summons.

"Since you didn't specify the reason, Pop, I can only imagine you needed me to explain in person how those deals came by. You're coming to the end of your term, you might be getting cold feet, thinking I'll tear the company apart."

He doesn't like to be called Pop, but, seeing as Mom calls him DILF, he can't complain too much.

"Son, I have no doubt you'll make a phenomenal CEO. You've been trained for it since you were in diapers. You eat and breathe ships and Ocean Gate. There's no one more qualified in this world to take the reins."

"Wow, thanks, Pop." I beam at him, the exaggerated widening in my eyes letting him know I didn't hear it often. Not that I need to. Ocean Gate is my passion. And in the last ten years, it's the only thing I've spent my waking moments living for.

"Yes, well. Whether you will actually become CEO is another matter." My dad grumbles. "You've done everything else but the one thing you need to cement your position."

I lean forward, resting my forearms on my knees and steepling my fingers. "Father. About the marriage thing..." I begin, letting my voice trail off.

"What about it?" he feigns an air of boredom.

"That's the reason I decided to come to Seattle today. It's not happening."

He raises an eyebrow. "Really? Son, your ability to negotiate deals in record time is uncanny. Are you then telling me there's no woman in the entire city of New York who will have you?"

"You know that's not it." I look into his eyes and let my nonchalance fall away. I let him see my pain and fear, in hopes that he'll scrape together any remaining dregs of sympathy within him. "I don't want to do it, Dad. You're the CEO, you can make an executive decision to delay this a few more years, hell, you could throw the dated policy out altogether."

For the longest moment, Richard Fairchild only stares back at me, and I see something shift beneath the icy shards of blue. He huffs out a breath, making me think I've finally gotten through to him until he slowly shakes his head.

"Son. I hate to say this, but it's just the truth... I doubt that you have any room in your heart for a woman. Ocean Gate is your only priority."

"Dad—"

"Ryan Richard Fairchild," he calls me by my full name and I know he's about to make an unshakeable pronouncement. "Are you telling me you're not prepared to marry a woman you can't love in order to win a company you can't live without?"

I chafe. My father is even more infuriating when he's right. "But why that clause though? It's archaic, ridiculous. Not fit for purpose."

Ocean Gate is an old ship-building company, but beats its newer competitors by miles in innovation and modernness. And that's where its façade ends. At heart, it exists on the most archaic principles.

"Dad," I continue, using the term he prefers in hopes of getting him to relent. "Being required to marry by a certain time might have been acceptable in the nineteenth century when this company started. But right now? I'm ashamed to have to abide by those rules because you wouldn't change them."

"Every family has its skeletons. Embrace yours." Dad shrugs.

"Really? That's your excuse for not getting rid of it?"

Dad smiles wryly, "No, the reason I didn't touch it is because of you."

"What?" My brow furrows in confusion.

"Because that's the only way to safeguard your inheritance. The Reuben-Fairchild lineage can't hold down a marriage to save their shares." He replies, referring to our fiercest rivals. "As it happens, we Richard-Fairchilds can. Without the policies on our side, they'd do anything to wrest power from us. From you. And you know they fight dirty."

"I know." The creepiest sons of bitches I know happen to be my cousins.

"Good. So I would, for the sake of your children, keep the clause in. Teach them to learn to live with their partners instead."

I'm afraid this nugget of wisdom is completely wasted on me. I might be the one to break this lineage. Because if I can't stand being married for six months, how will I endure it for life?

"So, speaking of wives," Dad continues, "are you going to come up with one in the next couple of months, or do I have to find you one?"

I throw my head back on the sofa and stare at the intricate carvings on the ceiling.

Fuck. There's really no way around this. Unfortunately, I've managed to piss off the only woman I can see myself doing this with. What the hell did I do this time? It wasn't the spanking two weeks ago. She had it coming. And she fucking loved it.

I close my eyes and let my mind recall how her green eyes grew bright with anger and then darkened with desire. The smell of her creamy, almost translucent skin. The way I grinned like a fool the rest of the day even as she glared daggers at me.

"Ryan?"

"Yes, I... er, have someone, Pop. We're not at any commitment stage yet, but given the timelines, I should be able to hurry things along."

"Well," he beams. "That's what I'm talking about! I knew you had this in the bag. Your mother would be pleased to hear this, I tell you."

"Pop. Listen. I do not want a ceremony. I'll get it sorted in New York; you guys don't need to bother; you'll meet her at some point later."

"Fine, Son, you can do what you want this time. And as long as you produce a wife that you're legally married to, you can do the ceremony in your kitchen for all I care."

"Great." I stand to leave, suddenly feeling claustrophobic. I've failed in my last-ditch attempt to get the archaic clause removed. I now have six weeks to get Stella to marry me.

My dad falls into step beside me, his hand on my shoulder as we leave the gloomy library. "You don't have to love her, just do right by her and make her happy. That way, she wouldn't file for a divorce."

"Uh-uh, sure," I murmur.

As we reach the top of the long curving staircase, the sight that greets me below draws an amused chuckle out of me. On the couch sit my mother and my baby sister, heads pressed together. Mom's dark tresses mingle with Gina's mass of blonde ringlets, and they appear to be engrossed in a magazine.

Somehow, in the hour Dad and I have been in the library, they've managed to convene like a covert operations unit.

Gina lives right across the city yet she's here. And so is Mom, who's more likely to be spotted at her daily social luncheon than lounging at home at this time. It's clear they're not just catching up on celebrity gossip. They're on a mission to extract every piece of info about my upcoming nuptials.

"They're done!" Gina exclaims. "I came as soon as I heard you'd touched down in Seattle, Ryan, I even ditched a meeting at work so I could see you before you jetted back to New York. I've really missed you."

"I've missed you more," I respond, and she smiles wider. Gina is twenty-six, only four years younger than me but, the whirlwind of drama that surrounds her often makes me feel decades older. Especially with her romantic entanglements. Most of the brawls I've been in my life had to do with prying some creepy fucker away from her.

My mother stands and approaches us, all smiles. "Let's see, no bruises or blood stains, Richard. I dare say it went well."

"Oh, better than that," Dad announces. "We have a Fairchild wedding in a few weeks."

Mom squeals, a spring appearing in her step as she hurries up the stairs. "Well done, Ryan!"

"Don't get too excited, Di; we're not invited. It's just going to be a small kitchen ceremony."

"Really! Why bother with a ceremony at all then?" My mom gives me a stern look but hugs me firmly. "You might as well exchange your vows on the bed while consummating the marriage."

I bend to air kiss her cheeks. "Oh, that's a brilliant idea, Mom. I don't know why I never thought of it."

She only shakes her head and tsks.

"Mom, you'll still get to arrange the big Fairchild welcome to the family party."

She huffs, "Well, I suppose that's something to look forward to. Anyway, when do we meet her?"

"When I bring her home." I state firmly.

"Don't you think we should meet her before?" She counters

"How will that change anything, Mom?"

"Di, the boy has a point there." Dad states. "He'll marry her and be committed to her forever. That's the bottom line."

Gina coughs subtly and I throw her a sharp look. A lawyer herself, she knows my exact plans.

Mom, apparently not satisfied, continues. "Can we know her name at least? And is she fully on board with the rushed timeline?"

"Ha, Mom. I don't think you need to worry about that," Gina pipes up. "Ryan's problem has never been getting women to agree. It's always been how to peel the women off him."

Except for the ones I really want.

Gina stands and approaches, throwing me a meaningful look. I know she's concerned about what would happen if the woman doesn't want to leave. After six months, she becomes entitled to half of everything I own.

After another quick hug Mom moves to Dad, offering her lips for a quick peck, but someone goes in for more, and their lips end up locking.

Gina, who is behind them, rolls her eyes. "Typical."

For all his stuffiness, the moment Mom walks into a room, our dad becomes a hormonal teenager.

"Way to go, DILF," we hear Mom murmur as they come up for breath, and Gina gags.

I don't even spare them another look. I take Gina's elbow and we start back down the great curving staircase. Those two can deliberate on my upcoming wedding once they've had enough suckface.

"So, spill, Ryan," Gina pokes me in the side, blue eyes twinkling, "who's the unlucky lady?"

"Not a chance." I steer the conversation to her on-off boyfriend instead. "Guess who I met in New York last week?

Chad. He's doing some pro bono work for some women's charity. And killing it in the courtroom, I bet."

She rolls her eyes. "Wow, Ryan, you should get a medal for
being subtle."

"He's a good guy, Gina, and you like him. What's the problem?"

"I told you, he's boring."

"So you'd rather have the bad boy that will break your heart,
or one I'd have to break his nose for being an asshole?"

"Xavier isn't breaking Brooke's heart, is he?"

She sees the look on my face and laughs. "What, he was my
first crush. We tend not to forget things like that."

"You love Chad, Gina," I insist, hoping I'm right. "You just
love drama more."

She shrugs. "I dunno. Maybe I do, maybe I don't."

"He won't hang around forever."

"Speaking of," she smoothly deflects, "who is this woman
you're planning a drive-through wedding with? I can't imagine
she'd be okay with her 'forever' starting like that."

"Let's not talk forever here—" I begin, already wincing at her
mention of that.

"Well for you, six months of marriage is forever, isn't it?"

"Agreed." I try to change the subject again, but this time she
digs in, nagging me for the next hour, until I feel the life draining
out of me. I finally cave and I give her a name.

Gina still doesn't relent in her quest for more details about
Stella, so I show her a photo on my phone just to make the
hounding stop.

The moment she sees Stella, she gasps, then snatches the
phone from me, peering closely. "My God, Ryan, she's gorgeous. Shame you're only marrying her for power."

"Technically, she will also be marrying me for money."

"It's still unfair since she's going to end up falling in love with you. You on the other hand would be chomping at the bit to kick her out." Gina stares for a few more seconds, then suddenly shouts at the top of her lungs. "Mom, I've got a picture of the incoming wife of Ryan Richard Fairchild the sixth!"

"Gina!" I hiss as she dances just out of my reach. "So help me, if you—"

She takes off like a jackrabbit with my phone, presumably to find Mom.

She returns after a good ten minutes, with a huge smile, and not at all fazed by my glare.

"Analyzed to your heart's content?" I snap, holding out my hand for the phone.

"We can't wait to meet this Stella. I can tell we'll be besties. Your union might be temporary, but Stella and I will remain friends for life."

"Hold your horses with the declarations. How do even you know you'll like her?"

"I just know."

"The way you knew with Brooke?" I tease and snicker at her injured look.

She'd had such high hopes that she and Brooke would become 'soul sisters' or something wack like that. Unfortunately, her pipe dream didn't even take off. I suspect it has to do with Gina having no filter when she speaks.

Something she has in common with Stella. Come to think of it, they might actually get along.

I just need to find a way to propose to Stella. *Fuck*.

Chapter Seven

STELLA

"You need a haircut, Bonnie." I stare pointedly at my friend's signature asymmetric curly pixie cut with its purple highlights. "Your curls are growing out into a bob."

We're sitting at my kitchen table, and our knees are almost bumping with how small the table is, but any bigger, and it wouldn't fit in my cramped kitchen.

Bonnie only runs her hand through her hair, then flicking the curls away from her eyes, she pins me with a look that tells me she has major tea to spill. "Stella, I've been rather... preoccupied lately."

"Preoccupied with what?"

Bonnie takes a deep breath. "See, I have no clue how it happened. Somehow, I went from hating Ethan to... well, the opposite of that." She pauses, not daring to look up from her coffee.

I sit up straighter. "What the hell are you saying, Bonnie? You're in love with your bosshole?"

She nods, screwing her face in a part-mortified, part-euphoric expression. "We've been dating for a bit. And doing a lot of other things I don't even have a name for."

I hold up my hand. "Back the hell up! When did this happen? This is Ethan fucking Hawthorne we're talking about here!"

Bonnie nods. "Maybe three or four months now? It's been a blur. But one thing that's certain is this: I'm so fucked."

"Why do you say that?"

"Because I've started obsessing about when he'll ask me to marry him."

My eyes and jaw appear to be competing for which can open wider. "Jesus! This–" I poke the table repeatedly for more emphasis. "This is the Stockholm shit we talked about back then. Bonnie, I fucking warned you not to take that job!" I finish on a near yell.

"I know. Only it feels like the best thing I ever did."

I incline my head as if to peer at her from a clearer angle, "Who the fuck are you right now girl?"

"I stopped asking myself that question weeks ago." She takes a sip of her coffee while I just stare at mine, untouched and cooling on the table.

I take a calming breath. Seems like I'm the only one freaking out here. Bonnie looks as zen as ever. "Does Sabrina know?"

"I haven't told her yet but Ethan and Jordan are practically brothers. And you know Jordan can't keep a secret to save his life. So, my bet is yes, Sabrina already knows but she's too busy with the gallery to grill me out."

"And Brooke?"

"Not yet. But it's only a matter of time. I mean, if Ethan asks me to marry–"

I don't let her finish. "Oh God, will you listen to yourself!"

A part of me feels betrayed. Bonnie and I are usually on the same page about love, relationships, and men. None of my other friends get me like Bonnie does. Now it seems Bonnie has joined Brooke and Sabrina in their hearts-and-flowers mindset.

Bonnie suddenly starts to chuckle. "You should see your face, Stella. You look like you're about to cry. I promise you it's not the end of the world."

I gesture with my palms up, imploring her to listen. "I'm just really concerned. What if he breaks your heart Bonnie? You know he will, don't you? They always do."

She shrugs, "You think I want to be in love with him? I'm telling you I can't help it."

I sigh, dropping my hands in defeat. "That sounds so fucking depressing."

"Trust me, babe, it's not. It's the complete opposite. Anyways, moving on. Ethan is only part of the reason I came down here you know."

"Oh yeah?" I shake off my lingering unease in anticipation of some good gossip. "Spill then."

"Oh no. You're the one with all the tea. What's up with you and Ryan? You both want to do each other so bad, yet you seem not to be able to. It's frustrating to watch. I can't imagine what it must feel like for you guys."

I give an answer that sums up just about every vague and confusing relationship. "It's ...complicated."

"No, I think it's pretty simple. Look, if you're worried that Brooke won't approve of you doing the dirty with Ryan, you're right, she won't. So don't tell her. Sabrina and I both give you our blessing."

My breath comes out in a shaky sigh. "We sort of, already–"

She screeches, practically bouncing in her chair. "Really! Oh shit. I knew it! Let me guess, it was the day Brooke had the baby? I'm sure you've done it tons after, but I will put good money down to bet that he fucked you just before you two arrived."

"Bonnie! Calm down. Things didn't go that far. Besides how could you even know that? Aside from his announcement that we arrived together."

"Oh, it was all over you, babe, not to mention the look of pure joy on Ryan. I mean, he was in higher spirits than Xavier who'd just had a baby."

"He was just being an ass."

"He likes you, Stella."

I scoff "Of course, he likes me. Haven't we established how much he likes women in general?"

Bonnie cocks her head at me in disbelief. "Sweetheart, I love you, but that's rich coming from you. Stella, the man works like a horse and he deserves to play just as hard as he wants. And, he's the male version of you."

Ryan said the same thing but I don't see it. Yes, I like to pick my men and kick them out the next day but that doesn't make us identical. "I thought opposites should attract."

"Sometimes love doesn't obey any laws," she says with a wistful look in her eyes.

"Whoa, speak for yourself. I don't do love."

Bonnie only smiles, then stands to take her empty mug to the sink.

"Do me a favor and don't touch the faucet, babe." I quickly warn her of the leaking sink.

Bonnie chuckles when she sees the faucet I've bound up in rubber bands like some kind of voodoo artifact. Then, she bends to pull the under-sink cupboard open, spotting the bowl

I shoved in there to catch leaks. "My goodness, even the under-sink pipes have joined the drip team."

"Welcome to my life," I muse.

"Why is this still leaking? I thought the super had it repaired?"

"Yeah, he had it patched up for the third time. What it needs is a whole unit replacement, but I know that's unlikely to happen."

Clucking her tongue, Bonnie grabs an empty bowl and replaces the overflowing one.

"Thanks, babe. It's a slow drip, nothing that is likely to flood. Besides, I'm going to move soon. I need a bigger place." I immediately close my eyes in regret, wanting to kick myself for saying that.

Bonnie, of course, doesn't let it slip. "Stella, why would you need a bigger place? Already this apartment is large enough for two people."

Guilt eats away at me, and I wonder if it might be best to come clean, too. Bonnie will get why I've not mentioned Harriet to anyone. Also, she's the most secretive person I know and so unlikely to fly off the handle at me.

"Bonnie," I begin.

"Yeah?"

"I–ah..." I clear my throat and try again. "I have a niece. My sister's daughter. Her name is Harriet. She's six."

Bonnie looks at me like she's not processing what I'm telling her. "You mean you have a sibling? I thought you were an only child, like me."

"No. I had a sister. Vivian." My heart breaks again, thinking about her. "She died."

"Oh my God!" Bonnie's eyes go wide. "I'm so sorry. That must have been horrible for you."

When I remain silent, she gently prods. "What happened to her?"

"She, uh, died in childbirth. She was only eighteen." My throat clogs with unshed tears and I clench my fist, wishing for my stress ball.

"My God, Stella. I can't–" Her hands cover mine. "Eighteen?" I can see the wheels turning behind her dark brown eyes, still wide with shock. "Douchebag boyfriend?"

"Um, yeah, no...worse. She was um... She was drugged, I think. I'm really not sure, to be honest Bonnie."

"Jesus." Bonnie covers her mouth. "Stella, I– I have no words."

"Yeah, it was such a mess." I see Bonnie's soft gaze, and I make myself rehash the painful details. "She went to a college frat party with her boyfriend. The next morning, she couldn't remember much."

Bonnie goes deathly pale, her eyes taking on a faraway look as she puts her suddenly trembling hands into her lap.

I know it's a lot to take in. I've lived with this harrowing reality for seven years now. And still, I feel like my heart is being gouged out with a blunt knife every time I think about what happened. So, I suppose for someone else it would feel worse.

Suddenly I feel guilty for piling my baggage on her. "Bonnie, are you okay?"

She blinks and fixes me with a wan smile. "Of course, it's just, shocking. I never imagined... I mean, gosh. Was it only the two of you?"

"Yeah, our parents died when we were really young. And can you imagine, they were both orphans too. Viv and I grew up in group and foster homes. It was terrible, and we swore never to let it happen to our children."

"So where is Harriet now?" Bonnie asks.

I close my eyes in defeat. "In foster care. I've been trying to adopt her for close to a year now but I'm not... I don't have enough to do it yet."

Bonnie leaves her seat and comes to put her arms around me. "Oh sweetheart, you are amazing for even trying this hard. And you'll get Harriet, I know you will." I accept her comfort, grateful for her love and friendship.

"One of the reasons why my application keeps bouncing is because of this place." I spread my arms wide, looking around the apartment with slight disgust. "And apparently this neighborhood."

Bonnie nods in understanding. She lives in Long Island, and never fails to secure her motorbike with chain and lock when she comes around here.

"It's probably no use. Bonnie. I mean, what do I know about being a parent anyway?" My shoulders slump as I feel Bonnie's arms tighten around me.

"Come on Stella. Of course, you'll make a great mom. You're fiercely protective and loyal. You're fun to be around, yet you manage to keep everyone in line. You're practically a mother hen."

I sigh, feeling some of my self-doubt melt away. "Thanks, babe."

"Of course." She waves off my gratitude. "And don't worry, you'll make it happen. Does Brooke know?"

I shake my head. "I haven't told anyone."

Bonnie looks like she might cry. "Oh, Stella, thank you for telling me. I would totally understand if you want to keep this to yourself, but you know, between us girls, we could work out a plan to get Harriet back. I think you should tell Brooke and Sabrina. Brooke especially. You've been friends the longest."

Brooke and I met in our first year at Brooklyn College. Although I dropped out right after what happened with Viv, Brooke and I never lost touch and eventually, we ended up sharing this apartment.

Bonnie is right. I've been doing this on my own for too long, and it's clear I need some help now.

"Okay, I'll tell them."

"Sweet," Bonnie smiles, returning to her seat.

Eager to lighten the mood, I say, "Time for a fun discussion topic, babe" I'm about to launch into a fun story when Bonnie immediately suggests, "Let's talk about Ryan shall we? Has he finally told you what he wants yet?"

I groan. "No. I have too much going on in my life right now for some bored, rich boy games."

"You don't even know what the man wants to talk to you about." Bonnie chides gently.

"I'm pretty sure it has something to do with sex."

"Oh God I hope it does," Bonnie rubs her hands together in glee. I'm about to respond when she puts her hand up to stop me. "I know you don't want a relationship. Ryan doesn't seem to want one either. So what's the problem with him giving you a little sex therapy while you smooth out the kinks in your life?"

Speaking of kinks... My mind serves me a vivid picture of Ryan aroused and sprawled on that couch, but this time it's with whips and gags in his hands.

I shake my head in a bid to dispel the heated thoughts, but Bonnie already sees my flushed face.

"Wait, Stella," Bonnie suddenly goes serious. "Are you worried you might fall for him?"

"Don't make me laugh," I scoff. "Lightning doesn't strike twice. And it's already struck you."

"Exactly. So what harm could there be in hearing him out? And if you don't like it, you can simply say no."

But isn't that the problem though? I haven't yet seen anything about Ryan I don't like. And I'm terrible at saying no, especially when he goes all alpha on me.

Chapter Eight

RYAN

THE BUZZING IN THE pit of my belly escalates with every minute this two-hour-long meeting draws closer to a satisfying close.

My excitement is not so much to do with finally getting the elusive Aqua Balance Inc. to collaborate with us. It's due to the fact that right after this meeting, I'll be seeing Stella. Finally. She's probably already on her way up.

I suppress the urge to glance at my watch. Instead, I look around the sleek conference room as our lawyers discuss liabilities and contract specifics with the AquaBalance lead reps.

This month alone, I've closed deals with three large clients and still have a few more lined up. The ocean liner model I insisted we build last year seems to be massively paying off now. It couldn't be happening at a better time, laying to rest any lingering doubts about my capability to take on the CEO role. Doubts raised by my cousin and fiercest rival, Don Fairchild, and his minions.

The edge of my vision catches a muted notification that moves across the screen of my phone.

I'm here.

Fuck. My heart pounds, and suddenly the hardest thing I've ever done is remain seated. My fingers start drumming on the oak desk, and I quickly clench them into fists to avoid drawing any attention.

Get it together, Ryan. You're jittery like someone desperate for their next fix. Your clients might start suspecting you're into drugs.

The connection between the shipping industry and the illicit drug trade is well-known, and a few Fairchilds have dipped their hands into these murky waters.

I let my lawyers answer the reps' questions until at last, they face me with satisfied smiles. I bring the meeting to a quick close and watch as they pile out, barely able to wait until the last one leaves.

The moment our guests are gone, I spring out of my chair and leave the rest of the team to debrief without me. "I'm afraid I need to run, guys." I address my head of finance, who also happens to be my older cousin, "Roman, meet me at lunch tomorrow with an update will you?"

"Certainly, boss." He replies.

"Awesome." I stride out, tearing off my tie as I take the elevator to my office on the top floor. I think of the ten-carat diamond sitting in the top drawer, feeling like a clown. Why did I think the size of the diamond mattered? I'm convinced she'll refuse.

Then where would that leave me?

I have a month until my thirty-first birthday, and I move to Seattle as acting CEO in two weeks, provided that my marriage is imminent. Fucking company policy feels like a noose tightening around my neck.

I enter my expansive office reception, spotting her immediately. She's standing by the panoramic windows, sipping on a glass of water but she turns as soon as I enter the room. Need slams into me, and I tell myself it's because of the way she left me the last time I saw her. Hard and throbbing for her.

Ada Patson, my receptionist intercepts me, her seasoned gaze flitting from Stella to me as she almost reluctantly informs me. "Mr. Fairchild, Mr. D. was just here—"

"What did he want?" I bark, impatient to get to Stella and not at all in the mood for the crafty bastard. Don Reuben-Fairchild is not only my cousin and rival, he's also next in line for CEO should I fail in my duty to marry in the next four weeks.

"He asked to see you before you leave today. What time should I tell him to come back?" She shoots Stella another slightly puzzled look. I've never had a woman visit me in all the years she has worked for me. And while Stella is dressed for a business meeting, Ada knows this is personal.

"Tell him I'll call him when I'm ready. Thank you, Ada." I dismiss her gently.

I go to Stella, a smile on my face as my eyes roam over her delectable form. Her tucked-in shirt emphasizes her small waist, and her grey skirt molds to her curves in a way that makes my mouth water, ending just above her knees. My gaze follows her shapely legs right to her black heels. I don't remember anyone looking this tempting in work clothes. "Stella. Thank you for coming here."

She shrugs with an air of boredom, "I thought I'd put an end to the constant nagging and just hear you out."

That makes me chuckle because she's the furthest from bored. I knew asking her to meet me here at Ocean Gate would pique her curiosity and it's worked. "Well, that's very kind of you."

I take her elbow and lead her into my office. The moment we push through the double doors and step into the room, she halts in her step. "Oh wow," she breathes, taking in my corner office. She looks around the space. It's my second home in Manhattan because I spend so much time here.

The way she stares at the space makes me feel like my soul is being bared to her and I feel the first stirrings of discomfort.

The unusual polished oak flooring and wall paneling lend warmth to the otherwise impersonal office. Recessed lights in the ceiling and floors complete the modern look. Everything else is in beige. The plush rug, the executive desk and swivel chair and the cozy sitting area at the back. Wall-to-ceiling windows offer a view of the Empire State Building and the Manhattan skyline.

"Hmm." She muses.

I instantly want to know what she thinks. Is she impressed? Does she like the decor, or think it's pretentious? I want her to like it, although why on earth that should matter is beyond me. She'll never have to come here again. Besides, if all goes to plan, it won't even be my office for much longer.

"Is there a problem?" I ask.

She makes a sweeping gesture. "No, it's uh, really nice," she turns to face me, and while I enjoy the feel of her eyes on me, that knot of discomfort returns to my belly. "It's not what I was expecting. I mean, of course, it's a corner office. It's just…"

"Let me guess," I interject, "you were expecting a boudoir sleigh bed with velvet bars, whips and clamps?"

She chuckles and playfully nudges me.

"This is a place of business, Ms. Marsh. Sorry to disappoint but we try to keep it classy here." I lead her toward my desk rather than the seating area.

"I guess I deserved that. I'm sorry. I should have reined in my reaction. I suck at hiding my feelings."

"Nor should you Stella, at least not when you're with me." I see the moment she tenses that, so I lighten the mood again "In any case, the room you're looking for is in my home."

She gasps. "Are you serious? You actually have one of those... what's it called? Playrooms?"

"Of course not," I laugh gesturing to the chair opposite my desk.

She sits, then I take my seat, facing her. Then I allow myself the pleasure of simply looking at her for a moment. Her dewy skin, expressive green eyes which for the first time aren't filled with irritation.

God, she's fucking beautiful, this woman. In an understated way. I imagine she'd be breathtaking wearing nothing but her large butterfly tattoo and the pink flush of arousal. If I'd bothered to watch the last time in her apartment, I would know exactly how she looks when she's coming.

"So, Ryan, who was that Mr. D?" Stella's voice pulls me out of my thoughts.

The smile falls off my face, and I recall Ada mentioning that Don had come looking for me. "Did you see him?"

"I sure did," she says, and the excitement in her tone makes me tense. "He was nice. And you know, he looks a bit like you."

I ignore that and ask instead, trying to keep my voice level, "What did he say to you?"

Her smile widens. "Not much. We just flirted a bit, and I asked him out."

My eyes widen in disbelief, "You did what?"

Stella only shrugs, "What, he's hot, and I'm not one of your employees. Why, is there a problem?"

My scowl darkens as I grapple with how to respond, but before I can gather my thoughts, she drops another bombshell.

"I'm meeting him later tonight."

"Like hell you are!" I roar, leaping to my feet.

It's only when the angry haze settles that I notice Stella is chortling. "Jesus, Ryan, calm down. I'm kidding! Gosh, Manhattan is brimming with bossholes, isn't it? Somehow, I thought you'd be one of the nicer ones, but you're probably worse than Ethan!"

"What are you talking about?" I drop back to my seat, striving for patience.

She waves off my concern. "Never mind. It doesn't matter. Why did you ask me to come here?"

"First, tell me what Don said."

She rolls her eyes. "He gave off the typical rich, entitled vibe. Rude too. And he looked at me like he didn't believe I had an appointment with you. As if I could crash into the CEO's office. This place is like the Titanic of office buildings."

"COO," I correct her.

"What?"

"My father is the CEO, and our head office is in Seattle," I explain before getting back to my question. "So, what did you two talk about?"

"Ryan, you're like a dog with a bone." She throws up her hands, in exasperation. Then pausing for effect, she narrows her eyes and smirks, "If I didn't know better, I'd think you were jealous."

"Of him?" I shake my head dismissively, a wry smile playing on my lips. Leaning back against my seat, I lift my hips to readjust, rolling the tension out of my neck and shoulders with practiced ease. Stella's gaze flickers towards my movements before she quickly averts her eyes. "Stella, tell me what was said."

She sighs. "Alright! He said something along the lines of the position I'm vying for not being open to strays and walk-ins."

I ball my fist in anger. One of the downsides to a family business is that employees are so hard to get rid of, much less senior partners. But one of these days, I might have to find a way to cut him out.

Don is well acquainted with company policies, and he's actively finding a loophole out of his own sticky marriage situation. He knows that if I'm not married in four weeks, he becomes CEO. "And what did you say?" I fight to keep my voice even.

Stella only shrugs, looking somewhat sheepish, which tells me she's done something. "Stella? What did you tell the man?"

"Don't be mad, it was annoying how he looked down on me, so I sort of claimed we were dating."

I sit forward in my chair. "Really!"

Her hands come up in a defensive pose "It came out of nowhere. Sorry," she adds quickly.

"And he believed you?"

"I can be convincing when I want to be. And I know enough about you to pull it off. It's actually weird how many random facts I know about you." Stella remarks with a seemingly nonchalant shrug, but her foot is tapping nervously against the floor.

I cock my eyebrow at her, unable to stop the smile tugging at my lips. Stella is just so effortlessly brilliant for this.

She looks confused at my reaction. "You're not mad?"

"Not at all. On the contrary, I'm pleased."

"You are? Why? What's the deal with him?"

"He's my cousin." I say, as if that should explain everything.

Stella blinks in surprise, more interested in the cousin part. "He's your cousin?"

"Yes. Don Fairchild. Why are you surprised we're related? You said he looks like me."

"Yes, a little. But, wait, you mean you have a cousin that works for you?"

I huff out a laugh. Ocean Gate is crawling with Fairchilds. "I have twenty-eight cousins that work for me."

"Jesus! What the hell is this place?" She scans the office again as though searching for clues.

I find her reactions amusing. "It's an ocean of sharks."

"What? What does that mean?"

"I told you, this company has been in my family for two hundred years." Suddenly, I want to tell her everything about my family.

"Yes, but Ryan, I had no clue it was such a large family. I thought it was just you and your parents and then a few distant cousins. I didn't know you were literally on top of each other. How did I not know this about you?"

I only laugh at her genuine puzzlement. "Because it never came up."

"But seriously, Ryan, twenty-eight cousins," she breathes, "It must be so nice to have such a huge tight-knit family."

I can't help noticing her slightly awestruck look. She's suddenly acting like I'm a celebrity." I scoff. "Did you not hear the part where I called them sharks?"

"I don't care if they're rattlesnakes. I would kill for a family," she blurts out, and immediately, looks like she regrets it. "I mean, a large one like this—yours."

I want to probe into her slip-up, but something tells me she won't budge. Getting information out of her is like pulling teeth.

"No, Stella, not if they were anything like mine."

"Why do you say that?"

"Because we're rivals. Our ancestors made it so when they pitted us together with certain outrageous but binding laws that we have no choice but to adhere to."

"What kind of rules?" She asks almost before I've finished speaking.

For someone who doesn't like talking about herself, she's mighty curious "I'd rather not bore you with history."

"Well, you're in luck because history is my favorite subject," she returns.

I hate rehashing these details but, seeing as I want her in my family, I might as well tell her. "Alright. Two hundred years ago, the Ocean Gate was split between five Fairchild sons: Reuben, Russel, Reid, Ralph, and Richard. The chunk of assets owned by each family line over the past two centuries have depended on how many of them stayed married or got divorced."

"Oh wow. Okay." She rests her elbow on the desk as she leans in and prop her jaw on her hand. If anything, she's become even more interested.

"The Richard-Fairchilds have a zero incidence of divorce in two hundred years, so hold the largest company shares.

Our most formidable rivals are the Reuben-Fairchilds. They're shrewd and arguably the best in business, but unfortunately, they're terrible at holding their families together."

"My goodness, HBO should take a look at your family, Ryan. Now let me guess, you're a Richard-Fairchild, which makes Don a Reuben-Fairchild."

"Exactly." I knew Stella would get it. "And he's next in line if I mess up. So you see, there's no love lost between us, yet no one can ever turn their back on the family."

Her smile falters, "No one leaves the company?"

"No, because our entire livelihood is more or less tied to being a working member of the Fairchild family."

"Are you saying you're all stuck?" She dubiously eyes the opulence in my office and back at me. "You don't like this life?"

"Don't get me wrong. I love what I do, and my lineage is lucky to have been right at the top of the Fairchild food chain for the last forty years. But it's also a source of constant stress."

"Because the other Fairchilds want a shot at CEO too."

"Yep. In one month, my father retires, and I'm to take his place."

"Ah, I see," Stella smirks, "You worry that you might be the one to let your lineage down."

"It's part of my concerns, yes."

She leans back and folds her arms. "Wow. Talk about rich people problems."

I shrug, "It's true. It reeks of privilege, but they're real problems."

She rolls her eyes. "Oh no, I completely understand. I get how depressing it must be knowing you'll be CEO, the top dog of this multi-billion-dollar empire next month. On top of the fact that you can literally get everything you want. It must really suck to be you right now."

I narrow my gaze at her sarcasm but I choose not to pursue it. Because I sense the perfect opening to deliver my pitch now that she's hooked.

I lean forward, ensuring I have all her attention. "I don't get everything I want, Stella. And whether I become CEO depends on how well I can play the game. If I lose, my lineage loses out, and Don gets the position."

She shakes her head in confusion as her curiosity wins. "What game do you have to play?"

It's now or never. I knew all the talk about my family would bring us here. That's why I didn't shut down her questions.

I stand, then round the table and go to her, perching on the edge. I usually don't make eye contact with women, but this time, I need to see what her expressive green eyes are doing when I say, "Something happened to me ten years ago. I won't bore you with details. But in order to deal the winning hand, Stella, I need to be married before I turn thirty-one."

Her eyes get luminous but I don't think she sees where this is going yet.

"How old are you now?"

"I'll be thirty-one in four weeks."

"Really! So who will you marry..." her voice trails off as her head snaps back to me in shock and disbelief when she gets it.

"Ryan?"

"Now, now, Stella. Listen." I murmur in my best soothing tone.

"Are you fucking kidding me?"

"No, Stella. I need you to marry me."

Chapter Nine

STELLA

I STARE AT THE crazy man who just asked me to marry him. If he hadn't been telling me about his family mere seconds ago, I would be inclined to think he was playing a prank. But the earnest, solemn look in his eyes tells me Ryan isn't joking.

"Why on earth would you want to marry me?"

"I don't want to marry you. I need to. Or else I'll lose the only thing I care about. This company. I'm asking you to help me ensure that doesn't happen."

"Wow." *You really are an asshole, Ryan Fairchild.*

I didn't expect declarations of undying love. But, the casual way he just told me he didn't care about anything except his company stung more than I care to admit.

I muster a nonchalant response. "Why on earth would you think I'd want to get married, least of all to you?"

"Because I'm prepared to pay you."

My eyebrows fly to my hairline and I huff out a disbelieving breath "You couldn't pay me enough to—"

"Twenty million."

I gasp, "Twenty million dollars?"

He nods.

"Like twenty, and then six more zeroes behind it?"

"Yes, Stella." He confirms, apparently not seeing the big deal about that figure.

What was that idiotic thing someone just said about not being able to pay me enough? Because it sure wasn't me talking. For twenty fucking million, I wouldn't only be his wife; I'd be his hitman. Half a million dollars alone would make all my problems disappear, and then some. Multiply that by forty times!

Come to Mama, Harriet darling!

Ryan's chuckle, no doubt at the stars now shining in my eyes, yanks me back to reality. His proud, satisfied smirk is that of someone who knows his money or body can buy him anything.

His blue eyes twinkle in warm humor and a subtle challenge. They draw me into their depths. I notice that his blue irises have dark spots within them. *Fascinating.*

When he suddenly breaks eye contact, I realize I've been staring too long. Although the man doesn't maintain eye contact for very long, does he? Almost like he has something to hide.

I wonder how he sells his ideas to clients if he won't make eye-contact?

"So?" Ryan prompts, snapping me out of my thoughts.

I'm sorely tempted. I can't even recall a single reason why this would not be the best idea anyone ever came up with. I'm sure there must be plenty of reasons; they just happen to have taken off like a flock of spooked birds, save for one lone beacon of sense.

The fact that he can throw that much money around and make me instantly rethink my very strong feelings against getting married raises some alarm bells.

"You want to pay me twenty million dollars to be your wife?"

Ryan nods, speaking in a warm and coaxing tone. "Only for six months. We could even get separated at the end of four. You'd have ten million at the point of signing the marriage contract. And ten million on signing the divorce papers. Six months, and you have your life back. It'll be like it never happened." He finishes with a practiced wrist flick.

How does anyone ever refuse him anything?

He must have mistaken the awe on my face as disbelief because he straightens, goes back to his side of the desk, and takes a black box from his drawer. He pushes it across the table. "Your engagement ring."

My heart skips a beat. This man is serious about this. With shaky fingers, I reach for the box and flip it open.

And gasp.

It's huge. A breathtakingly beautiful diamond ring that seems to sparkle with a life of its own.

"It's custom-made, and you can keep it. It's not part of the contract. I bought it with you in mind." Ryan says.

Despite myself, the toughest parts of me begin to melt. Still, I manage to snap myself out of it. *This isn't a romantic proposal; it's a business deal! He's just thrown in a little extra to sweeten the pot.*

I snap the box shut and push it back. "That ring was made for me?" I scoff. "Is that what you've been telling everyone who's been turning you down? "

He levels me with an almost wounded look, which is so out of character for the usually cocky and self-assured Ryan I know.

"Stella, I have only ever considered you for this. Why else do you think I've been hell-bent on speaking to you? You're the only one I want to do this with."

Okay, that sounded a bit sweet. "And what if I say no? Where does that leave you?"

"Funny, I've been asking myself the same thing. I guess I'll have to extend the invitations elsewhere." His voice hardens. "Stella, one way or another, I will be married in the next four weeks, and I'd rather it be you than anyone else."

Lord help me, but I believe him about only wanting me for this. But I can't figure out why. "Why me, when there are many women– *many subs–* who actually want to be married. I'm clearly not one of them."

He totally ignores the sub comment. "I want you because you're not boring, you're not clingy, you're unlikely to demand more or fall in love with me. And most importantly," he adds, putting a finger up for emphasis, "you're very nice to look at."

"Wow, Ryan Fairchild, you inspire me with how deep you are sometimes."

He flashes me a grin, "I knew you'd get me. Most people don't think there's more to me than the pretty face." Without missing a beat, he continues. "Now, there are just a few things to consider," He brings out a leather document folder and passes it to me. "But before then, would you like something to drink? Something strong, perhaps?"

"Why would I need a strong drink?"

He goes to pour himself two fingers and does the same for me anyway. Then he again perches on the edge of the desk beside me as I open the document folder.

Uh-oh. I think the other shoe is just about to drop.

I start reading the terms and conditions.

I haven't gone through the first page when my head snaps up. "You expect me to delete my social media handles? I have ten thousand followers!"

"You'll have new accounts set up for you, and people to manage it."

I shake my head. "No fucking way."

"Stella, you'll be grateful for it."

"Oh, will I?" I scoff.

"How do you think your followers will react to you becoming Mrs. Ryan Fairchild? Because they will find out. Fairchild business never stays under wraps."

True. Ryan is often photographed with multiple women and sometimes in compromising positions. And I am the most vocal about feminism and being a liberated woman. I'd be trolled and dragged through the streets of social media for doing something as hypocritical as marrying a spoilt, promiscuous, and sexist rich boy.

"But if I lose my online presence, how will I work? And if you say I don't need to work—"

He interjects. "No, I wasn't going to suggest that. But tell me how you work. What's your setup like?"

"It's a cross between model photoshoots and personal styling. Clients around Brooklyn come to my apartment. For those around Manhattan, I usually rent a space in an upscale salon."

"Okay, I'm afraid you can't freelance anymore. Especially not in Seattle."

I rear back in shock. "Seattle! You expect me to move to Seattle?"

"That's where Ocean Gate headquarters is, so yes. I move in two weeks, but after our wedding you can take some time to tie things up here before you join me."

I take a sip of my scotch, needing more courage to keep going down this crazy lane.

Ryan continues. "I'll buy you a few salons you can manage while we're married. You can be as hands-on or off as you want. But this isn't negotiable."

I'm still thinking about moving away to Seattle. I haven't even been to the city before. Ryan would be the only person I know there.

"How many can you handle? Four? Five?" Ryan asks.

"Whoa, what do you think I am, a robot? One is fine."

"Two then. One that is very well established and another that needs a bit of TLC. It'll help you understand the industry there quicker."

I can't resist rolling my eyes at his high-handed attitude but chalk it off to him being used to pushing people to their limits at work. "I really don't see the logic in that since I'm only going to be in Seattle for six months, tops."

He shrugs like it doesn't matter. "No experience is a waste. You'll want to start up your own business when you return to New York won't you?"

When I'm twenty million dollars richer. Okay, he's right,

I scan the next page, then again look up. "It doesn't say here, Ryan, are we going to live together?"

"Yes, we are."

"And... be exclusive?" I don't imagine I'll start picking up random men when I get to Seattle. It would also be nice to know that my contractual roommate won't be bringing home screams and pounding headboards.

He pauses, steepling his fingers together, and I don't think I've ever seen Ryan this serious. This side of him is a bit jarring. And I hate to admit also very hot. "Stella, first off, if I'm in a relationship, I don't cheat. Ever. If in the coming months you see a photo of me naked and wrapped around a woman, I'm either dead, drugged, or we're divorced. Okay?"

I nod. "Okay. What's the other thing?"

"Nobody can know about this arrangement," he points back and forth between us.

Because I have no family, I assume he means my friends. "I don't see how I can move to Seattle or live with you without my friends getting to know." I already feel bad for not telling them about Harriet.

"Oh, of course, they'll know we're getting married, but nothing about the restrictive clause or company policy. Can you do that for me?"

"Two of my friends are married to yours, Ryan. Brooke to Xavier and Sabrina to Jordan. Does that mean your friends won't know about the marriage clause either? They'll believe you just woke up and decided to marry me?"

Ryan chuckles. "Stranger things have happened. People go to Vegas and wake up married."

"Um, sure," I say, already thinking how hard this is becoming. "But what about your own family?"

"My parents and sister think we've been dating a while, so it just makes sense to hurry things along for the sake of the company."

That perks me up. "You have a sister!" And then it hits me. "You told your family we're dating?"

"Yes, I have a younger sister. Her name is Regina—Gina for short. Everything else you need to know about everyone in my life is in that file. Listen, for this to work, we need to appear head over heels in love with each other. Touchy-feely, PDA, googly eyes, whatever else—just channel Bonnie and Ethan."

"Eww..." I grimace.

"I couldn't agree more."

Bonnie and Ethan's mutual fascination is so palpable that you could almost reach out and feel it. At least he finally proposed to the girl.

"Ryan, I don't do besotted. But you're good at it, going by your antics at the hospital the other day. Maybe you can try to be all over me. I'm sure no one will notice my subtle gags and eye rolls."

Ryan laughs. "I knew that's what pissed you off! By the way, that wasn't me being besotted. I just found it amusing that you desperately wanted to hide the fact that we'd been together."

"And you on the other hand did everything but shout it from the rooftops. Bonnie thought you acted like you'd just found the key to life. So did Brooke."

"Hardly," he scoffs, and I'm not sure if I should be offended. *Was I really that forgettable? Was it not good for him?* He'd been so cold, so controlled. I, on the other hand, still can't believe how unhinged I was.

"Anyway," Ryan says into the sudden awkward silence. "I won't do all the heavy lifting; you should pull your own weight to convince everyone. There will be a welcome party when we get to Seattle. We must be perfect."

I'm starting to wonder if I'm not in over my head. *His family is like an ocean of sharks.* "They'll probably hate me and call me a gold digger." I force a light-hearted chuckle telling myself that it won't matter what anyone thinks because I'll only be there for six months.

He watches me for a few moments, his expression unreadable. Then puts a single knuckle under my chin and raises my face up to meet his. "Stella, I'm going to be the king of that pack, and you'll be my queen. They might hate you, but they wouldn't dare disrespect you."

Slowly, his large hand cups the side of my jaw, his fingers wrapping around my neck. His hold is light, but it might as well be steel manacles for the effect it has on me. His thumb grazes the rapidly beating pulse in my neck, his gaze holding me captive as his words resonate in my head like an endless gong, bolstering my confidence.

I imagine being like this for hours. Letting him touch me like this. Making me feel needed. Seen.

And I'm an idiot because this is Ryan Fairchild.

I snap out of my daze, breaking the spell. Suddenly needing to do something, I grab the tumbler and throw back the rest of the scotch. Then I flick the pages over to the part I'm really looking for. *The sleeping arrangements.*

There's nothing about those in there.

"Ryan?"

"Hmm?"

"This isn't complete. What about sleeping arrangements?"

"What about them? We'll be married."

I throw my hands up like it should be obvious. "Yes, since there won't be anyone checking in to see if we're actually sleeping together, do we have to?"

"Considering neither of us would be fucking anyone else, I say we'd better make do with each other."

Okay. "And is that going to be enough...for you?"

Ryan laughs. "Stella, do I detect you fishing for compliments there?"

"No, I'm serious. You didn't seem to be into it much the last time when it was just you and me."

"Really? What gave it away?"

I shake my head, feeling like I said too much already. "Never mind. What kind of sex do you have anyway?"

"The normal kind I imagine." He chuckles. "Is there any kind you don't like?"

I lick my suddenly dry lips. "Threesomes."

He throws his head back and laughs. "I wouldn't dream of it. Anything else?"

"Anal."

His face falls. "Really?"

Oh wow. He likes anal. "I've not let anyone do it to me before, so it's a no."

"Can I touch you there though?"

My face heats, and I hate my sudden indrawn breath. *Calm down. You're Stella, you can talk about sex with a guy.* Or so I thought. Ryan on the other hand, looks like he's discussing one of his ships.

I hazard a look at his pants. *Yep, no boner.* "I guess?" I finally reply.

"Okay. Any other restrictions I should know about?"

"Like what?"

"Like light bondage, spanking, toys... just anything you consider off-limits?"

I clear my parched throat. "Um, no, not really. What about you?"

"I'm pretty good with everything–"

"I bet–" I snort.

"–except I can't fuck in a bed."

"What? You can't have sex lying down?" Is there any end to this guy's ability to shock me?

"Any surface, horizontal or vertical is fine, just not in a bed." Ryan clarifies.

I'm just wrapping that around in my head when he delivers another shock.

"And another thing. I don't kiss."

"You don't kiss," I repeat inanely, too surprised to say anything else.

He simply shakes his head.

"What's wrong with kissing?"

Ryan shrugs, "I just don't do it. Not unless I'm pissing drunk."

"On the mouth?" My eyes train on his lips. They're well-defined, and his top lip curves gracefully, softening his otherwise rugged features. His bottom lip is full, almost pouty. *It's too bad, he appears to have a mouth made for that sport.*

"Not anywhere." He clarifies.

"You don't know how to?" I smirk, remembering how he teased me about not wanting to dance six months ago. "It's not rocket science you know, all you need to do is to relax, look pretty, open your mouth slightly, and let me—"

"No." He interjects, as though he can't stand the thought of what I'm describing.

"Well, you were sober when you kissed my shoulder." I challenge, unsure how I managed to remember that detail.

"When?"

"At Brooke's wedding. When we were dancing." *After I asked you to fuck me.*

"Huh." He cocks his head as if he has no clue how that happened. "In any case, I thought I might warn you. Will that be a dealbreaker for you?"

"I just don't see how we can be intimate without kissing. Everything kind of starts out with that, doesn't it?"

He just continues to level me a bland look, making me feel like I'm explaining advanced biology to a brick wall.

"You did pretty well the last time, in your apartment." Ryan counters.

True. He didn't actually kiss me. He didn't even look at me, and I came harder than I've ever done.

"I promise you won't miss it," he coaxes.

"Well, now that I know it's off the table, I'm sure I will."

"Come here then. Tell me if this feels any different." He pulls me from my seat and then leads me around to his side of the desk.

I watch as he takes off his suit jacket, puts it on a nearby coat hanger, then rolls up his sleeves. My eyes eagerly roam over his crisp white shirt and the muscles clearly delineated under it. "What are you doing?"

"Offering you a test drive."

Chapter Ten

STELLA

RYAN DROPS INTO HIS chair and gestures for me to sit on his lap.

"Ryan, we're in your office!" I protest.

"I'm aware of that. Come here, Stella. Let me show you something."

When I don't move, he gently pulls me onto his lap, facing his desk, my back against his chest.

"Tell me if you don't like anything."

Heart in my throat, I can only nod.

In a smooth motion, he spreads my thighs apart to straddle both of his, then drags up my skirt, bunching it at my waist. His fingers trail over my thighs higher and higher toward to my already damp core.

My breath hitches with anticipation as he reaches the top of my thighs. But, instead of pulling the crotch of my drenched panties aside, he changes course. His hands go to untuck my shirt and then slowly start work on the buttons while I work hard to control my breathing.

When my shirt falls open, his fingertips run over my lace-covered breasts and follow the dip of my waist and belly as if he's trying to commit my curves to memory without looking. It feels like live wires are being dragged against my skin.

It's been months since I was touched like this, and I can't even remember it feeling this good. "Too slow" I complain, reaching for his hands to pull them over my achy breasts.

He drags down the lace of my bra and pinches my hard nipples and I gasp, heat pooling in my core. I start to rock my hips against him, forgetting my earlier misgivings about being in his office. "Faster." I moan, needing to get off right now.

"Rub your clit," he commands.

I don't want to touch myself. Over the past six months I've been dreaming of the way his fingers felt on me, inside me. I'd much rather he touch me. "I thought you wanted to show me something." I whine.

"Do it, Stella."

I close my eyes and grit my teeth against the overwhelming need to obey him. When I hesitate Ryan gently pulls and rolls my nipples between his thumb and index finger, making me moan. This time I can't help doing as he says, I need to come now.

The moment I reach into my folds, he spreads his thighs, and mine, wider. Then he starts to pinch my nipples hard and fast sending bolts of pleasure to my clit. I stiffen and cry out, my core rippling against nothing. Unable to clench my thighs to chase the feeling, I rub my clit faster, needing the relief of an orgasm so bad I sob.

He doesn't stop his torture on my nipples until I start to jerk in climax. "Please fuck me, Ryan" I beg, feeling empty even while coming hard.

Suddenly he stands, taking me with him and bending me over his desk. I whimper as my over-sensitized nipples drag across the polished surface. He pulls off my shirt and then his fingers run all over my back.

"Gorgeous" he marvels, admiring my tattoo. "You're fucking made for me, Stella." He keeps my legs far apart so that every clench of my pussy drives my relentless need to feel him inside me. The sound of his zipper makes me tense with anticipation.

If all his twenty-eight cousins walked into the room right now, I don't think I'd care.

He fists on a condom, grasps me by my nape then, and notches himself against my entrance. I realize I'm shaking with need, goosebumps all over my skin. I just had an orgasm, yet I've never wanted a man inside me this badly.

Still, he waits. "Stella, are you—"

Ready? Sure? "Yes! For God's sake will you just fuck me!" I snap, unable to keep it together any longer.

He laughs. I'm about to send him a snarky retort about his laughing, but my mind goes blank as he surges into me all the way to the hilt. I bite my lip to hold in what would have been an embarrassingly loud moan. My fists clench repeatedly, mirroring what my pussy is doing around his girth right now. "Ryan, oh God," I shiver.

"What is it?" His steady, detached voice irritates me.

"What, are you waiting for the lights to turn green?" My voice comes out breathy and not the snap I was aiming for.

Again, he chuckles. "Here we go then." He pulls out most of the way then drives back in. Hard. I gasp. He does it again and again, picking up speed. In a few moments, I can no longer catch my breath in between thrusts.

I hear myself crying out but I can't seem to stop. He feels too good. God, I really hope this room is soundproofed. "Oh, please," I babble, unsure of what I'm begging for. I thought I wanted it fast, but if he doesn't slow down right now, I might die of pleasure. I try my best to keep my voice down, but I can't do anything about my legs which have started to tremble. Still, he fucks me hard.

As I near orgasm I start to crave more. I cry out his name, begging for something that even I don't understand. My subconscious knows, though, because I reach upward to my nape, where his hand is holding me down, and grab at him, my fingers not quite encircling his wrist. That little bit of contact warms me, feel and thickness of his wrist. My fingers greedily trace the veins and muscles of his forearm and suddenly everything feels a hundred times more intense.

At the first ripple of climax, I slam my palm on the desk, gritting my teeth against the deluge of pleasure. He only grunts, thrusts a few more times deep and hard, and then he still as controlled as ever, plants himself deep.

"That's it Stella. Let go. Come for me."

I've never wanted a man's weight as much as I want Ryan's right this moment. His smell surrounds me but I want more. "Ryan," I gasp, my other hand blindly reaching behind me for him, catching nothing but the tails of his shirt.

"Please. Touch me." I whisper.

"What?" As he bends over me, a cool drop of liquid lands on my bare back. His sweat. It's too much, the needing; I clamp down on his big cock, and I come. And come. Screaming.

I'm still twitching madly when he curls his arms around me and pulls me from his desk and right back into his lap without withdrawing from me.

What the fuck just happened?

I craved him so much that the feel of his skin and his sweat triggered another climax? I've lost my fucking mind. I already feel my face heating up in mortification.

"Do you want more?" He whispers, still hard inside me.

More!

I shake my head frantically even as my traitorous pussy clenches again. "No, I'm quite alright," I croak.

"Okay, Stella." He pulls out of my still-clutching core. Then, he stands me up so he can slip out from beneath me. He heads across the room to where I think the bathroom is, leaving me to collapse back into his chair.

I try like hell to process how I feel about what just happened.

I rake my hands through my messy hair. Then, as if just realizing I'm half-naked in a man's office in Manhattan in the middle of a workday, I replace my bra cups back over my still-sensitive breasts and look around for my shirt. I freeze when I see the shirt, huffing out a sad laugh.

That right there is the problem I've been trying to wrap my head around.

My shirt is not crumpled on the floor, or hanging ten feet away where Ryan carelessly flung it. No. It's neatly laid on the far side of his desk. While I was unraveling like a fucking tornado and begging for his touch like an addict, he might as well have been folding the laundry. I didn't even hear him make a sound. Except when he laughed.

Now I understand why he would rather be with two women at once. He doesn't do intimacy. Does the man even enjoy sex?

What happened to him? I like to think I know men. But this one throws me.

On the surface, he seems like a passionate, outgoing guy, but Ryan Fairchild is a broken man who won't make meaningful eye contact, touch, or kiss. And I'm supposed to spend six months as his wife?

He returns, shirt tucked back in. He comes toward me, again perching at the edge of his desk. "Are you alright Stella?"

I raise my eyes to his smiling face, but this time I see beyond the façade. And I know, twenty million or not, I couldn't live with six months of him doing this to me. I would go insane. "Yeah, I'm good."

"Now that *that's* out of the way, do you have any more questions about our contract?"

"Um, actually, yes, about that. Yeah, I don't think we'll work out after all, Ryan."

His brows rise in surprise. "You're telling me you didn't enjoy that?"

"Oh, don't get me wrong, it was a slice of heaven... but also a bit of hell because it left a horrible aftertaste in my mouth." The confusion on his face tells me he doesn't fully grasp what just happened. "I couldn't imagine having to live the next six months on that. Thanks for considering me, but my pride and dignity are not for sale. I'm going to have to pass on your offer."

I think of Harriet and tears spring to my eyes. I was close. So very close. But now we're back to square one. I discreetly catch the stupid tear hanging on to my lash and tell myself I'm crying because of how close I came to achieving my dreams.

A muscle ticks in his jaw. "Stella. I realize this is a big ask— putting your life on hold to cater to mine—and I know you don't like losing control. How about this; we don't have to have sex if you prefer not to, or we could work out something else within each other's boundaries."

I shake my head no. My thoughts are all over the place, and now would not be the time to make rash decisions. I need to leave so I can process this properly.

As if reading my mind, Ryan says, "I'll understand if you need some time to think about it."

That was a reasonable suggestion, but somehow, I allow the proud and stubborn part of me to respond. "Ryan, I don't need time. The answer is no. Like I said, I'm not the woman for this."

I stand, turn around on admittedly shaky legs, and leave him staring after me, too mortified to explain the real reason why I'm turning him down.

Chapter Eleven

RYAN

"SOMETHING'S EATING AT YOU, Ry." Xavier drops into the seat beside me. I turn to face my friend, watching as the strobe lights of the nightclub dance off his face.

"Is that so?" I grin. "How do you know that?"

"Come on, man," Xavier chides. "You really think you're an enigma because everyone else is fooled by that thousand-megawatt smile? You're not right, man."

It's annoying when your friends know you that well. Xavier and I practically grew up together in Seattle, and our families are still close. "I'm still waiting for you to enlighten me, genius. What makes you think I'm not right?"

"For one, I don't see you bringing in the women."

My friends and I make it a habit to celebrate small milestones with a night out. The definition of a small milestone ranges from closing a deal to tearing off a hangnail. So, my send-off to Seattle would be considered a legit reason to get all the boys out.

"It's my fucking party Xavi, you'd think someone else would be doing the honors for once?"

"Pulling women? No Ry, that's your specialty," Xavier cocks his head toward the rest of our friends. "Wyatt is all mouth; he might as well be an altar boy; Ethan and Jordan are retired, and so am I. That leaves you man."

I snort. I look over to the far side of the VIP lounge where the boys are arguing over a pool table. "Ethan's getting hitched to Bonnie in less than a month, and Jordan—"

"Can no longer recognize a female species that isn't Sabrina" Xavier finishes and we laugh.

Jordan and Sabrina have been married the longest among us and we declared that he lost his edge ages ago.

"That leaves you, the life of the party. And you've been quiet as a mouse with that strange look on your face since you got that phone call. So, before I freak out and imagine the worst, spit it out."

I lean back on the box sofa and sigh. "It was my cousin. The guy just undermines me at every turn. What the hell does the fucker want from me?"

Xavier laughs. "Same thing they all want. A piece of you, Ry. Or rather, you, in pieces. Which one of them was it this time?"

"Don."

"Which one is Don?" Xavier scratches his stubble. "The one whose wife disappeared? Or the one who married his stepsister?" Xavier has always found the Fairchild family's dynamic extremely entertaining.

"The one missing a wife."

Don's wife left him four years ago. Word in the Fairchild grapevine is that he killed his wife to avoid losing his shares through divorce. It's not true, but as that narrative is more sensational, the gossip-mongers prefer to run with it.

I'm one of the four people in the world who know where she is right now.

"What did he want?" Xavier presses.

"To know if I'm getting CEO or he is."

"Wait a minute. Aren't you next in line? You've been the de facto CEO for the past four years!"

"There's just a small detail in the fine print." I say to the ceiling. "Legal constraints I can't get around."

"Which are?"

"It all boils down to the fact that I need a wife."

"Get the fuck out of here! What does that have to do with running Ocean Gate?"

I run my fingers through my hair, tightening my grip "I'm almost thirty-one. It's been ten years. You know how the shares work."

"Root of all the Fairchild excitement, yes, but I didn't think it was applicable to you since you have already—"

I wave him off impatiently. "It does, Xavi, it fucking applies."

"I see. That's a tough one man." Xavier muses.

It occurs to me that Xavier might be able to help me out of this tricky situation. I sit up and lean forward to get his attention.

"Anyway, I managed to find a way around the restrictive company policy. The loophole involves a 6-month arranged marriage which needs to happen in the next three weeks. And it needs to look real."

Xavier's eyes widen in shock. He knows how much the idea of marriage puts me off.

"Hell. Ryan, you realize your entire family will be watching? You'll be under a microscope."

I nod. "I know."

He looks almost worried for me. "You'll also need someone who will not fall for the very shiny outer shell. No offense."

"None taken, dumbass. I am very much aware of that. Which is why Stella would be perfect."

Xavier looks at me like I've gone mad. "Excuse me?"

"Yeah, Stella. She's single and not looking to settle. She's very passionate about her work. And the money I'm offering will do wonders for her business."

Xavier is already shaking his head. "Bro, bro. You're talking about my wife's best friend here."

"Stella has a mind of her own; she can do whatever she wants."

"Are you crazy? That woman is like a sister to me. Remember how you almost killed me when you found your sister in bed with me?"

My stomach lurches at the memory again. In our senior year of high school, I'd come home to find fourteen-year-old Gina in my bed, wrapped around Xavier. That was enough to break our friendship for years. It didn't matter that Gina confessed that Xavier had been fast asleep when she stupidly decided to slip in next to him.

"Come on Xavi, it's not even the same thing. Besides, Stella and I, we have a special connection."

"A special connection?" Xavier scoffs. "I suggest you take your special fuckery far away from that woman, Ry. She's not your plaything. She seems super tough on the outside, but she's really not. Brooke is even way tougher than her."

"I bet." Of course, since Xavier's balls are firmly ensconced in Brooke's fist, he's bound to think of her as tough.

"You act like I mean to scar the woman."

He huffs out a breath. "Ry, I don't know what you do to them. But, every time you're with a woman for longer than a month, they end up so screwed up I have to get them into therapy. I love you like a brother, but I cannot let you near my wife's friend."

I raise my hand in surrender. "Geez, I'm not that bad." *What am I, contagious?*

"Really? What about India?"

I recall the doe-eyed brunette. "You know she had daddy issues."

Xavier goes a little green.

"What the fuck, man, you used to get through just as many women as me and now you're suddenly acting like a saint."

"For one, I never put any of my exes in a shrink's chair, you twisted fuck. Now, get this; you're not playing games with Stella. I don't care if she tells you she's up for it."

I shrug. "She said no anyway."

"Smart move." Xavier's deep scowl disappears in relief. "So, where does that leave you?"

I'd been hoping to steer the conversation along the lines of Xavier putting in a good word for me, but I see that has zero chance of happening. Shame. I was starting to get excited and yes, more than a little nervous about living under the same roof as Stella. She does something to me. Arouses me to no end and threatens my iron-clad control.

And there's the other matter of her eyes. Christ. They feel like lasers burning into me, leaving behind the most delicious sting.

And the way she responds to me like she's made for me. Her flawless skin and that sexy butterfly tattoo. As if she knows how I like to fuck, and got that tattoo just to drive me crazy as I slide in and out of her tight, clutching depths.

When she left my office last week, I'd caught the sheen of tears and the slight tremor in her voice. She'd been hurt. Was it something I said? Something I did? She'd been crying the other day in her apartment, too.

Perhaps Xavier is right. Stella might not be as tough as she looks.

"Have you considered asking Vanessa?" Xavier suddenly asks. "I know she'll be more than happy to help you."

I frown. Vanessa is a mutual friend from college and an old flame of Xavier's who had a bit of trouble letting him go. "I don't want to marry Vanessa."

"We both know you don't want to marry at all, Ry. It's only a transaction. Vanessa is an attractive woman, and I've not known you to be choosy; you do friends and foes alike."

"Fuck you."

He only laughs. Xavier has climbed this disgusting high horse since getting married. The jackass probably gets laid several times a day but somehow is still above reproach because he happens to be married.

"Ry, I mean it. When you're done throwing a fit, you'll see I'm actually handing you a lifeline here."

I shake my head. "It's no use. Vanessa won't cut it because I already told my family I'm marrying Stella."

Xavier rears back in shock. "You told them about Stella without first asking her? Have you lost your mind?"

I shrug. "I must have."

"Unbelievable. Well, you could tell them Vanessa's middle name is Stella. Or perhaps see if Vanessa wouldn't mind being called Stella for six months."

"Such a genius idea," I mutter.

Ignoring my sarcastic reply Xavier continues, "Ry, you know Stella could even be an endearment, it means star, doesn't it?" He murmurs as if testing it, "My star. My Stella. Could work."

Xavier is trying his hardest to push this. I imagine it'd be nice to be able to tell Brooke that Vanessa is now being shipped off to Seattle, where she is unlikely to be making eyes at her husband.

I shake my head, feeling somewhat sheepish to admit the rest. "Save it, Einstein; they know what she looks like. Gina nagged a photo of me and ended up showing it to everyone."

The two women couldn't be less alike. Vanessa is a tall brunette. Stella is petite and blonde. *And so fucking beautiful.*

I don't see how that last part was called for, but my mind thought it necessary to throw that in just to torment me.

"Oh, you showed them photos!" Xavier chuckles, leaning back in his chair as if he needs to observe my stupidity from a different angle. "Well, seems you've dug a nice fat hole for yourself there. Perhaps Vanessa would consider wearing a wig?"

"I should deck you for suggesting that." I laugh in spite of myself.

Xavier gets serious again. "Bottom line, it's either Vanessa or you're on your own because you cannot go near Stella. If you choose Vanessa though, I'll do everything to see you hitched in three weeks. Possibly two."

If I didn't know my friend was whipped before, now I have every doubt laid to rest. He's desperate to get rid of the woman. Seeing no other choice, I throw back my drink and pin him a glare. "You have a deal jackass."

"You're welcome, dumbass." Xavier grins, knowing he's won this time. "We've been through so much shit together. What's one more sewer?"

Chapter Twelve

STELLA

I FINISH TRIMMING BONNIE's hair with a final flick of my wrist. Her wedding is in a few days, so it needs to be perfect. I also managed to convince her to change her highlights from purple to gold, and judging by her expression in the mirror, she loves it.

I'm at the upscale salon I rent once every other week so I can serve my Manhattan clients. I'm getting more interest in the city, but unfortunately, I'm unable to afford to pay for more space to be able to give that many appointments.

"Oh, Stella!" Bonnie gushes when I finally pull the apron off her. "This is amazing. Why did I never think of gold?"

"Because purple makes a bolder statement, which is what you like, isn't it?"

"Yeah," she agrees, "but my God, I love this."

"The gold really brings out your skin and eyes." Bonnie has Irish and Samoan roots which gives her a distinctively warm tone.

"Yeah, I know, my skin seems to glow these days."

"There's a reason they call it pregnancy glow Bonnie." That was something else Bonnie tried to hide from us girls.

Bonnie hums in agreement, preening at the mirror. As though reading my mind, she suddenly asks. "Stella, have you told Brooke and Sabrina about Harriet yet?"

I bite my lip, shaking my head no.

"Stella!" She scolds. "I keep telling you, between us and the guys, we can work something out. Ethan for sure will find a way. There's no problem on earth that man can't solve."

"Whoa, whoa, sappy much? Do you want to reach over and grab a tissue to wipe the drool off your face?" I tease, turning her words back on her.

Bonnie giggles. "Gladly. If only drooling was all the man made me do, I'd be a way more productive person."

I wrinkle my nose. "Eww, TMI babes! But seriously, Bonnie, six months ago, you were this cynical, hard-ass dominatrix, and now... I hardly recognize you."

"I know Stella. Something has changed alright. I didn't realize what I'd been missing all this time, always wanting to be in control. It's so much more fun to let Ethan take the lead and work to make me happy, and boy, does he! Totally recommend it babes."

"Really?" I lift a disbelieving eyebrow.

"I'm not saying get ordered around like a farm animal, but you could just try letting down your guard just a little."

I'm too busy trying to block out my own heated memories with Ryan's domineering attitude to reply, so she carries on trying to explain the novel concept to me.

"Okay, so instead of dwelling on who is calling the shots, just focus on what feels good. I promise the pleasure is just mind-numbing."

"I bet." I focus on getting my area cleaned up before my next client arrives. But Bonnie is not to be deterred.

"So you've never tried that with any guy?" Bonnie presses.

"Nope."

Liar. You have. Twice. And you almost blacked out in ecstasy.

"Interesting." She muses, a thoughtful smile playing around her lips.

"What's interesting?" I snap.

"Nothing." She shrugs.

"Out with it, Bonnie!"

She hesitates. "I only assumed Ryan was, you know, a bit like Ethan."

"Brooding and darkly magnetic? Nah, Bonnie, your husband-to-be is the undisputed king of grumpy land."

She laughs. "Oh, I know that. I meant like super bossy but you can trust him to look after you. God, if anyone ever suggested I'd be crazy about a man like Ethan Hawthorne, I'd slap the silly out of them. Now, the way he makes me feel scares me sometimes."

I just roll my eyes. "Puh-leeze. It's the pregnancy hormones talking."

"A little. But it's mostly love, Stella. I needed to get out of my own way and let it happen. It's unbelievable how much I love that man."

"Okay, I think I just threw up a little in my mouth. Keep going, and you could end up with some in your hair."

Bonnie chuckles. "Oh, you wouldn't dare!"

I wonder how all my friends managed to get so lucky with their men without even trying. Like they closed their eyes, pointed, and hit the jackpot, leaving the creepy, psychotic jack-holes roaming around. I'm not naive enough to expect to get that lucky. Most men I meet are only good for a few hours at a time, and then the toxicity starts to set in.

You mean the fear and guilt.

If only I'd believed Viv instead of trying to convince her she was seeing things, she might be here today.

I wave the unwelcome thought away as Bonnie hops out of her chair and then comes around to give me a hug.

I give her a good look. "Your cup size is different. Bonnie, how could you not have mentioned this? Your dress is all set for Saturday."

She looks apologetic. "Honestly, Ethan and I have been so busy with work..." She trails off.

"Never mind, but we need to refit you ASAP; we can't have you ripping through your wedding dress."

We make plans to book a final refit, then she throws me a final warning glare. "Tell the girls, Stella. Especially Brooke.

"Sure, I promise." Delaying isn't going to make things any easier.

As soon as she leaves, my phone vibrates on the beauty counter.

A quick glance at the clock, and I know it's Anita from the child welfare agency. I'd missed her call yesterday, and she left a message that she would be calling back today. Something about an important development on Harriet's case. My heart skips a beat as I wipe my sweaty hand on my apron.

It's never good news with that woman.

I grab the phone and stride across the busy shop floor, heading for the break room in the back area. Relieved to find the room empty, I move to the far corner and connect the call.

"Hi, Stella here."

"Hello, Stella, thanks for taking my call. Is this a good time to talk?"

"Oh yeah. I'm at work, but it's fine."

"I'll make it quick." She pauses, then says, "The paperwork is coming soon, and this is off the record."

"Okay." I wait for the news with bated breath.

"The Duponts are planning to legally adopting Harriet."

"What?" My pulse roars in my ears.

"I know. I'm sorry because adopting her means a lot to you. But our priority is to think of what is best for Harriet. The DuPonts love her and want to provide for her on a long-term basis."

No. This can't be happening. "Do I not get a say in this? To ask for a review, make another application?"

"Of course, you could do that, Stella. But ultimately what we all want is to see every child settled permanently. And remember that whatever happens, you are and will continue to be a huge part of Harriet's life."

She seems to be preparing me for the worst. And I get it. It's her job to get children adopted as fast as possible.

I start to imagine all kinds of scenarios. "But—what if somehow, I can't see Harriet anymore? What if the DuPonts leave the country?"

What if they decide to get her away from the psychotic aunt who visits every day? They are certainly wealthy enough. They can afford to move to an exotic country. Then Harriet will grow up not knowing who her mother was. Who I am.

A wave of panic so strong hits me that I suppress the urge to gag.

Anita's voice is gentle, "Stella, that's very unlikely as they haven't expressed any desire or reason to relocate."

"Okay, but what happens if they choose to leave?" With my rotten luck, I'm sure it could happen.

She sighs "Hypothetically, if the DuPonts choose to relocate after adopting Harriet, then she goes with them. But that is a very unlikely—"

I can't hear anymore. "Please, Anita. She's my sister's daughter. She's like my daughter. I'm trying hard here, jumping through all the hoops. I just need a little more time..." my voice breaks.

"Stella, please calm down. This is just a heads-up. The DuPonts haven't made a formal application yet. Even then it could take months to finalize things. In the meantime, once your social or financial circumstances change, then the changes will be taken into account. Since you've been trying for a long time now, I thought it would be unkind if you suddenly got blindsided by this."

I sniff, rubbing my itchy nose on my sleeve. Anita didn't need to let me know. She might even be risking her job doing this. "Yeah, I understand... and I'm grateful you contacted me."

"You're welcome, Stella, good luck."

I click off the call and take huge breaths through my mouth.

I can't lose Harriet.

Which is what would happen if the DuPonts get her. The pinched look Faith DuPont gets every time I visit tells me I won't be welcome once they get full custody and parental rights.

There's only one thing left to do if I want to block this adoption.

Every pulse in my head seems to be beat double time, even as I return to the shop floor to meet my next client. I paste a plastic smile on my face and power through the rest of the client list despite my shaky hands. Eventually, I make it through the day.

As soon as my last client leaves, I return to the break to call the man I've been avoiding for the past month.

Ryan answers on the first ring.

"Hey, Stella." He sounds surprised. "How are you?"

"I'm alright, Ryan."

He pauses, waiting for me to say what I need, while the words get stuck. Finally clearing my throat, I say, "Can I see you?"

I hear his breath rush out of him. "Of course. When did you want to?"

"Now?"

He chuckles. "That's going to be tricky since I'm in Seattle."

Oh. He did say he was going to be CEO in a month. That was a month ago. "Congratulations."

"Thanks, Stella."

"Are you still having the congrats-on-making-CEO/welcome-to-the-family party?"

"Hell yeah, my mother is knocking herself out planning that one." His tone is warm with affection.

He's close to his mom. Probably his sister too. I remember what he said to me when I fretted about facing his extended family. How he looked into my eyes and called me his queen.

Would it really be that horrible being his wife? So he doesn't kiss; big deal.

His voice brings me back to the present. "I'll be in New York for Ethan's wedding. Why don't I swing by your place on Friday evening unless you prefer to meet me somewhere for drinks?"

It's probably too late to change anything. For all I know the guy could already have struck the deal with another woman. "Okay. Whichever is fine with me," I say.

"Are you okay Stella? You don't sound like yourself."

"I'm good."

"Have you reconsidered my offer? Is that why you're calling out of the blue after ghosting me for two weeks?"

"I didn't ghost—" I begin

"Answer me," he interrupts.

"Okay, fine." I snap. "Yes, I've changed my mind."

"Fuck."

"Although not everything in the contract works for me," I quickly add. "That's what I wanted to see you about."

"Stella, you do know my wedding is in two weeks, right?"

"And I know you don't give a fuck who the bride is," I retort.

I hear his deep chuckle and immediately hold the phone away from my ear. I can't stand his laugh. Certainly not the way it makes my toes curl.

When he settles, I hear him say, "She's already signed the contract."

"But she's not fulfilled the requirement; you've not said the vows yet."

"Wow, you're suddenly so eager to get hitched to me." he drawls, "I thought you found the idea revolting. What changed?"

Do I detect a note of hurt? It's hard to get beyond his playful exterior especially when I'm not looking at him. I'm not sure if he's mocking me or if he was stung by my rejection.

"Out with it Stella"

"I can't tell you now, not over the phone."

"But are you okay?"

"I don't know; it depends on if we marry," I admit in a small voice.

"Whoa. You need money."

"Not per se."

"Damn. Stella, I told you to always talk to me if you want something."

"I thought that was a sexual thing."

"No, survival before sex. So, you're telling me that all the time I was hounding you because I wanted something from you, you were stranded?"

"Stop talking." Humiliation washes over me.

"Is that why you were crying the other day?"

I can't believe this guy. "Ryan, that was months ago. And not everything is because of money!"

"I know that. And I hope you know you don't have to marry me for it? That ring sitting in my desk is yours with no strings attached."

He didn't give it to his new fiancée. "It's not just money I need." I admit

"What else do you need then?" He asks warily.

"It's complicated. Can we get married or not?"

"I'm afraid we can't."

I suck in a breath and release it slowly. For months, the guy pursued me. Even bought me a fucking gigantic ring. And now it's too late.

I just can't seem to catch a break with bad luck and worse timing, can I?

"I'll tell you what, Stella, I'll try and finish here a day early and pick you up at eight or nine on Thursday, and you can tell me all about what you need."

What's the point? But I force a smile and agree to meet him. "Okay. I'll see you Thursday."

Chapter Thirteen

STELLA

One Week Later

"I need you guys to leave the bridal suite right now and let me focus, or we'll run late," I urge Hana, Bonnie's mom, Sabrina, and Brooke out of the room. I've spent the last hour styling them and am finally about to start on Bonnie.

"We'll be swearin' to be quiet and not disturb ya. I mean to watch me darlin' turnin' into a beautiful bride, Stella," Bonnie's mom states in a heavily accented Irish brogue.

I get the gist of what she's saying, and so do Brooke and Sabrina, because they nod emphatically, promising not to make a peep. But I know better; they'll make her talk, laugh, and possibly cry, and I need her face still as stone for most of the bridal makeup.

"Nope. Trust me, Hana, the effect is better when you don't see the process. And I'm recording the process for you, okay?" I point to the ring light and tripod set up for that purpose.

Taking no more excuses, I shoo them out of the makeshift bridal suite. The wedding is in a huge conference hall at The Reed, Xavier's beachfront hotel. The hall has a circular lobby, great for pictures and confetti. It also has several anterooms. Xavier had this remodeled into a bridal dressing room complete with mirrors and a wide counter for makeup and hair accessories.

As soon as the ladies head into the lobby and toward the main hall, I start to close the double doors to the bridal room. Then I spot Ryan coming up the wide staircase and into the lobby. He reaches the top of the stairs and turns back, holding his arm out for someone else.

I didn't, in fact, get to see Ryan the whole week. He was stuck in Seattle for days due to a storm. He'd kept calling and texting, but I assured him I could wait until he got back. He got into New York this morning, having flown overnight. But you couldn't tell by looking at him how stressful the past day had been for him.

I'm already moving toward him when I realize that the person he's holding out his arm for is his date. She's stunning. A tall and willowy brunette. Her ice-blue dress molds to her perfect curves, and her long hair tumbles down her back in soft waves.

Vanessa. Xavier's ex.

Right, now they're talking and smiling.

I've seen photos like this, but watching it play out in real-time, Ryan with another woman arm in arm is jarring.

An unpleasant and unfamiliar gnawing starts in the pit of my belly. Accompanied by a desire to tear the woman's arms away from Ryan. I recognize the alien feeling as possessiveness. Jealousy.

What the hell is wrong with me?

He notices me from afar and immediately says something to Vanessa. She nods, continuing into the hall, while he turns and approaches me. I step out of the dressing room and close the door behind me.

He looks good. He always does, but perhaps not having seen him since that day in his office, he looks even more attractive in his blue suit and snow-white shirt.

"Stella, great to see you." His hand gently encircles my upper arms, rubbing up and down and he holds me at arm's length while his eyes rake over me. I'm still in my jeans and T-shirt and haven't even changed into my bridesmaid dress.

"Hi, Ryan."

"You look lovely."

"Thanks."

Ryan drops his hands from me. "Do you want to go somewhere to talk after the wedding?"

"What will your date say?" I can't resist asking.

"Oh, Vanessa is just a good friend."

"Are you sleeping with her?" The words are out before I can stop them, and I wince. "I'm sorry, it's none of my—"

"No, I'm not sleeping with her. But I'm marrying her."

Oh crap. That awful gnawing returns, and this time it seems to be chewing right through me. "It's her then. She's the one you're marrying," I repeat stupidly.

He shrugs in resignation. "Yes."

It's the slump in his shoulders, the tightening around his mouth, the muscle ticking madly in his jaw, subtle signs that make me know. He doesn't want to marry her. He wants to marry me.

He doesn't want to get married at all, silly, my rational mind screeches at me. But I can't listen. I'm going with my gut now.

"Do you wish it was me, Ryan?"

"Stella... tell me why you've suddenly changed your mind. You said it's not just about money."

I shrug. "I, ah, I've simply had more time to think it through. It's an amazing deal. I'd be a fool not to take it."

He looks somewhat disappointed, and I know he saw through my blatant lie.

"We would be divorced in no time," he reassures me, and I huff out a derisive laugh.

"Oh, are you asking me to wait my turn right now?"

"Right, that came out wrong. But Stella, can you just tell me what you need?"

"Okay. I need the money, yes... and need the status too?"

His brows knit in confusion "Status?"

"You know, a wealthy man's wife. Nothing beats marrying into old money."

"You're saying that you, Stella Marsh, want to be the wife of a spoiled, sexist rich boy for the sake of it?"

I have the grace to blush. Yep, he's not buying it. I should really learn how to lie better. Still, I say nothing.

He watches me for a full minute while I look anywhere else but at him. Then he clips, "No can do."

"What?"

"It's a no, Stella."

"Ryan, I..." I clutch as straws, "I could be pregnant."

"Excuse me?" His face pales in horror.

"I'm not saying I am, alright," I amend quickly, "but it's a possibility."

He looks around to ensure we're not being overheard, then pulls me to the corner.

"Ryan, wait. I should get back to Bonnie." He doesn't seem to hear me.

Once he's satisfied we're out of earshot, he whispers, "Are you serious?"

I scan his face. His initial response was shock, which I could deal with, but now it's just mild curiosity. I shrug.

"How do you know? Miss a period? Did you take a test? "

"No, not yet."

"I used a condom."

"And I'm sure you don't need a lecture on the failure rates of those."

"So, take a test!"

"It may be too early to tell as I haven't missed a period yet. What if you go on and marry her next week, and then, a month later, bam, I find I'm pregnant—"

"It's been three weeks since I fucked you, Stella. It's not too early to know if you're carrying my baby using an early response kit."

"Hmm. Is it a little strange that you know so much about a woman's cycle? Why do I feel like you've been in this situation many other times—"

He simply scoffs, then spins on his heels.

What did I say now?

"Ryan!" Where is he going?

He stops but doesn't turn back. I go to him, suddenly unable to take his coldness.

"Take a test, and let me know." He clips.

"And if it's positive?"

He turns to look at me, his playful smirk now returning. "Well, if it turns out you're pregnant with my child, Stella, you're fucking marrying me." He leaves me standing in the middle of the lobby.

Oh, shit. Okay. I better be pregnant then.

Chapter Fourteen

RYAN

"YOU OKAY, RYAN?" VANESSA's lilting voice floats toward me, and in seconds I feel her hand on my shoulder. I resist the urge to shrug off her hand and make myself accept her comfort.

I open my mouth to respond, but Xavier beats me to it.

"He's not okay, Vanessa," he scoffs. "He's getting hitched."

Vanessa knows she'll be paid ten million for marrying me and the remaining ten after our contract ends. She also knows I don't want to be married. Plenty, in my opinion; she doesn't need to know the rest of it.

It was only Stella I told everything about my family and company policy. And if she asked me for more, I would tell her.

"Yes, I know, poor baby," Vanessa smiles. "Since the Reverend arrived, you've been as jumpy as a cat. Think about how much more credible you'd be as the head of Ocean Gate once we're married."

"Hmm," I grunt distractedly, barely hearing her words.

She's not pregnant. That must be why Stella hasn't called all week. She must have taken the test. I should be relieved she's not pregnant. Instead, I'm irritated she didn't call to give me an update on the test, instead of leaving me to wonder.

And what about her need for money? She could at least have called to ask for her ring.

Or maybe she is pregnant and doesn't want me to know.

Or she doesn't want to be pregnant.

Oh shit. I break out in a cold sweat, trying to wrack my brain if we ever discussed dealing with accidental pregnancies.

Okay, this is getting bizarre. Suddenly annoyed at myself for letting the woman twist me into knots, I snap myself out of out of it and turn away from the window I've been staring into. I put my arm around Vanessa's waist and say, "I'm ready when you are, 'Nessa."

I lead Vanessa into my library where the minister is waiting for us. He stands as soon as we pile in.

"Is everyone here?" He asks, looking from Vanessa to me.

"Yes" I reply.

Xavier comes to me and gives me a friendly pat on my back. "You'll be fine, brother."

"Piss off," I snap.

Vanessa looks between us, shaking her head. "Good to know I've got more of these loving sparring sessions to look forward to for the next six months."

"Actually, no, 'Nessa, you'll have him all to yourself." Xavier is positively beaming. No doubt he feels like a genius, having accomplished in a single stroke, a way to get my paws off Stella and also get rid of Vanessa.

"What do you mean I'll have Ryan all to myself?"

"Well, you're moving to Seattle," Xavier explains. "Oh wait, he didn't tell you? Typical man."

Vanessa whirls toward me. "Ryan!"

"Asshole," I mutter.

"Exactly that was such a dickish move. Why wouldn't you mention that?"

The minister discreetly clears his throat.

It was in the contract if you'd bothered to read it. In a soothing tone, I say instead, "We can negotiate how many days a week you'd be willing to stay. Let's talk about it later."

She relents, but her mouth is still tight with irritation.

"Okay, if everyone's ready," the minister begins, "we shall start by—"

Three firm raps on the door interrupt us, and my heart lurches.

"Mr. Fairchild," Mabel, my housekeeper's calm voice floats through the heavy door. "I'm sorry to interrupt."

Mabel isn't only a trusted staff; she's become more of a friend. She used to be part of the Seattle house staff, but when I moved to New York, she asked to join my household staff. Mabel knows I'm getting married today and would never dream of interrupting unless she had to.

I leave Vanessa's side, and in the next few seconds, I'm throwing open the door.

Beside Mabel's wiry frame is none other than Stella.

The feeling is indescribable. Bubbling softly behind my sternum and threatening to pull my mouth into a goofy smile. I resist it.

"Mr. Fairchild, I'm afraid she—" I hold a hand up, not wanting to hear anything Stella might have said to get past Mabel's incredible bouncing power.

"It's alright, Mabel, I was expecting her."

Stella's raised eyebrows is the only reaction I get from her.

I step back to let her in, and as she passes by me, I catch her scent. It's not cologne. I smelled it on her in my office four weeks ago. It's her skin.

And since when did I become this person who can tell someone's distinct smell?

"Stella?" I hear Xavier's puzzled tone. "Is everything okay?"

"Hey, Xavier," she greets with a too-bright smile.

Vanessa looks from Stella to me. "Okay, what's going on here?"

The minister continues, "Alright, if we're not expecting any more persons—"

"I'm afraid we can't go ahead," I say to the minister. Turning to a shocked Vanessa, I take her elbow. "I'm so sorry for wasting your time."

"What the fuck, Ryan? Who the hell is she?"

If I wasn't trying to stamp the hint of joy still bubbling inside my chest, I would be surprised at the hurt lining Vanessa's face.

"Stella?" I prompt, not even looking her way. There seems to be an invisible thread binding us. We're in this together. I don't know what she's come up with, but she arrived in time to crash a wedding I didn't want. She's right up there with my favorite people in the world right now.

"I'm pregnant," she says into the room. I release a breath I didn't realize I'd been holding, my earlier irritation dissolving into relief. Whatever her excuse today, I was going to take it. But she's come up with the best-case scenario. The most irrefutable.

The silence that follows is deafening. When I face the minister's questioning gaze and incline my head to indicate that it's true, he simply gives me a reproachful shake of his head, packs up his stuff, and leaves without a word.

"Thanks, Mabel." I catch the excited glint in her eyes before she sees the minister out, and I wonder what on earth Stella said to her.

I face the room. "Guys, I'm sorry about this mess."

"Somehow, you don't strike me as surprised, man. Did you know about this?" Xavier finally finds his voice.

"No. Not exactly."

"And you believe her?" Vanessa's screeches. Gone is her usual lilting tone.

"I've got the stick if anyone wants to see." Stella offers with a shrug.

"You little—" Vanessa spits, advancing on Stella but Xavier smoothly catches her.

"Okay, okay. Calm down." Xavier coos, and gently leads her toward the door. "Let's give them time to hash this out, shall we?" He shoots me a "you're a dead man" glare before shutting the door behind them.

I'm confused by Vanessa's reaction. She's carrying a torch for Xavier, not me. It's not about the money; in any case, she still gets two million for even signing the NDA and prenup. And she owns a very successful business, a millionaire in her own right. It probably boils down to not wanting to be upstaged by another woman.

As soon as the duo leaves, the silence and tension in the room become palpable.

I finally turn to her; she's leaning with her back against the wall and seems to have been watching me the whole time.

"So. You took a test." I begin. "When?"

"It was taken a week ago."

"The same day I told you to. Why did you wait to say any-thing then?"

"I wasn't sure it was the right thing to do."

"What, crash my sham wedding?"

She shrugs.

"Could you not tell that I wanted you to do it?" I ask.

She gasps. "Why?"

"I told you. I prefer to be married to you. You're not clingy, you're not boring, and you—"

"Yes, caveman, I got you the first time. Why did you need me to do it? You could have put Vanessa out of her misery much sooner."

"Oh, 'Nessa will be fine, don't worry."

"I'm surprised she's that upset over it. I thought she wanted Xavier. Or..."

I see the questions brewing in her eyes, but I don't want to talk about Vanessa right now. "She and I don't have history, if that's where you're going with that. However, I do have a serious question for you."

"What's that?"

"Are you a fan of shrinks?"

She chuckles. "Why are you going to make me see one?"

"No, the reason I turned you down was because of Xavier. He's convinced I'd put you in the shrink's chair. And I like you too much to do that. So you have to promise to stay away from them."

"Noted. Funny, Bonnie too worries for us. Thinks one of us should tone down their inner control freak and let the other lead. She had the nerve to suggest that person should be me."

"Interesting. And what do you think about that?" I approach her slowly, a predatory gleam in my eye, already warming to the thought of showing her what that would look like between us.

She smirks, then as if reading my thoughts, smoothly deflects. "I think both our friends are right to be concerned about us. Don't you?"

"Absolutely." Finally giving in to the urge beating down on me since she walked in, I turn her toward the panoramic view of Manhattan and wrap my arm around her waist, roughly dragging her back into my front.

Fuck, she feels good. Small-boned, petite, but also tough and resilient.

"Are we like... hugging? Because it feels weird." She snarks.

"Shut up. This is a thank you for crashing my wedding."

"Hmm. So how does this work?"

"Well, I recommend you read the rest of the document."

"That sounds ominous. I wonder if that was why you distracted me with sex before I could get through the damn thing."

"No, that was why I offered you a stiff drink before we started."

She laughs, the sound washing over me and making me smile.

"We'll need to apply for a new license, I'll need a new witness since we've pissed off Xavi."

"We'll need another officiant too." She points out cheekily.

"True. The minister was quite put out by my philandering ways wasn't he?"

"Ryan Fairchild, you know I hate it when you talk like that."

"I love the way you hate it."

"Good thing we're getting divorced in a matter of months then."

"Now, about the baby—"

"Ugh. I can't do this with your sweaty arm wrapped around me and you breathing down my neck." She pulls out of my arms and faces me.

She might not realize that what she's doing right now feels more intimate than me holding her. I've never met anyone whose look I could *feel* like Stella's. Her eyes are like lasers. "So, about the baby."

She smirks, "What you want proof? I told you I brought the stick." She rummages in her purse. It's somewhere here..."

"You mean the stick you peed on from a week ago? Not unless I'm drunk, I don't fucking wanna see it."

She roars in laughter, and I can't help but join after a moment. When she catches her breath, she gasps. "I promise I wasn't trying to gross you out. I just thought since I was coming here to cause chaos, I'd arm myself with proof.

"The proof is in when your belly swells with my child. Speaking of, it'd be so hot to see."

"Um, no way. Not at six months." Stella counters

"What, are you four or five weeks already? You'd be showing plenty by then. Sooner if you're carrying twins."

Now it's my turn to guffaw at the horrified look on her face.

"Why do you even know so much about women anyway... Oh, I forgot, you mentioned having a sister." A cold sweat runs down my spine, but I grunt noncommittally and dive for a change in the subject.

In a more brusque tone than I intend, I say, "So, the earliest we can wait is twenty-four hours. We're doing this tomorrow—I'll send a car for you. Nine in the morning okay?"

Stella shrugs, "It'll have to be."

"Great. Someone will come by your place later today to hand in the prenup and other paperwork and I'll be available to talk you through any part you may find confusing."

"Hey, excuse me, it's not advanced calculus." She quips, "I'm sure I can manage."

I pause. "Sure. Tomorrow then." I bend to the intercom. "Mabel?"

"Wow. If I didn't know better, I'd think that was my cue to get lost." She looks at me like I've sprouted a second head. "Remember to hand me a fucking neck brace before you switch moods on me next time." She starts toward the door and then stops. "Happy Birthday, jerk."

She storms out without a backward glance, muttering about 'stewing in a foul mood.'

That actually makes me smile.

Chapter Fifteen

STELLA

I TAKE A LONG, noisy slurp out of my icy margarita, not oblivious to the three pairs of narrowed gazes aimed at me. Okay, two pairs, since Bonnie is on my side, literally. She sits next to me while my other two friends, Brooke and Sabrina, attempt to castrate me with their eyes.

We're at the VIP section of Empire, Xavier's swanky nightclub, and as it's our ritual, we meet once a month to catch up on each other's busy lives.

I'd been absent from the last two meetings. Two months ago, I was out of town on a last-minute gig. And last month... Well, last month, I made up an excuse because I couldn't face these ladies and lie through my teeth. They'd smell bullshit from a mile off.

"So, Stella," Brooke begins her eyes like gray flints, "What's up? Anything new happen recently?"

"Oh God, you guys, just let me off the hook already! I know I messed up."

"Really?" Sabrina cocks her head in disbelief. "Considering the last time one of us did what you're doing right now, you cut them no slack."

"Okay, ladies," Bonnie throws her hands up in my defense. "I get it, Stella fucked up, but I've been there, and I can tell you sometimes some wounds are so deep it's hard to talk about them. Brooke, I know—"

"Hold up, hold up," Sabrina says. "What's so wounding about marrying Ryan Fairchild?"

Bonnie whirls on me, her body turning so fast I almost hear the air around us whoosh. "Back. The. Fuck up. You what?"

I put my head on the table, knowing there's no easy way out of this. I didn't tell Brooke or Sabrina about Vivian or Harriet. And I didn't tell Bonnie, my new best ally, about my wedding.

Brooke supplies, her voice tight with hurt. "Two weeks ago, Stella crashed Ryan's wedding, and they ended up getting married the following day."

Sabrina's black ponytail swishes as she shakes her head in confusion. "I'm lost here. I didn't even realize Ryan was getting married, and I saw him at your wedding Bonnie."

Bonnie and Ethan had settled straight back into their lives claiming they were "too swamped" for a honeymoon.

"Yeah, Ryan was engaged to Vanessa at the time," Brooke replies, "Their wedding was meant to be the week following yours Bonnie."

Bonnie half yells, "To Vanessa! The bitch that wants to bang Xavier?" I swear the woman has no filter.

Brooke gives Bonnie a stink eye. "Thanks a lot, Bon, but yeah, the same one. Anyway, Stella showed up, and bam, Ryan made his choice, because isn't that what you do when you have two women vying to marry you?"

The look Brooke gives me says she knows about the pregnancy but she's choosing to be quiet. I throw her a grateful look but she instantly looks away, a sign that she's not ready to forgive me yet.

Sabrina is still slowly shaking her head. "But Stella, why would you even want to marry Ryan? You guys can't stand each other." Out of the four of us, Sabrina is the one with the least amount of information. Probably because, between her twins and her busy gallery, she spends the least time catching up.

"Yeah, they've been 'standing' each other lately," Bonnie answers for me, having gotten over her shock pretty fast.

"'Stand' him as much as you like, Stella, why on earth would you marry him?" Brooke's tone is a mix of worry and irritation.

"And you of all people, Stella." Sabrina pipes in. "You never stop reminding us how you can't imagine yourself in a long-term relationship."

I shrug, trying to diffuse the mounting tension with humor. "And you all never stop raving about how great it is to be married; maybe I just decided to take your word for it and give it a go?"

"Stella," Bonnie says from beside me, her voice now soft. "I'll put my hand up and admit that I did push you toward Ryan. But in reality, this is happening way too fast, not enough time for the guy to change. You know Ryan is a game player. He probably got married on a dare or something like that."

"Exactly! Why on earth would you agree to be his plaything?" Brooke knows the reason why Ryan needs to marry, but doesn't know why I need to marry him.

"Maybe I'm the one playing with him."

A quick look at their faces, and I see they're not buying it.

"You're so not taking this seriously, Stella." Brooke's voice breaks. "It's not a joke. We are really worried about you. Do you even know Ryan? Really know him? Did he tell you the real reason he wanted to marry in the first place?"

I can't take it anymore, so the words spill out of me.

"Yes, I know he's marrying to further his business; he was upfront with me. I agreed because I need his help, okay? But I can't say more than that. I signed an NDA."

Bonnie snorts into her drink. "Holy shit. It's more fucked than I thought. Whips and gags and things?"

When I say nothing, Sabrina too puts her drink down and tries to set Bonnie straight. "Girl, nobody needs an NDA for spanking or gagging. That's normal territory. Heavy bondage, swinging, sharing, for sure..."

"Role-playing, choking–" Bonnie continues.

"Enough guys!" I interject.

Bonnie and Sabrina chuckle while Brooke just looks alarmed.

For some reason I can't bear my friends thinking the worst of Ryan, so I quickly tell them the rest. "It's nothing like that, girls. He's from an old rich family. I'm sure even the paperboy signs an NDA."

"We see," Sabrina replies, "Anyway, you said you need his help? What for?"

I take a deep breath before answering, "I need money and stability."

Brooke pauses her drink in mid-air and carefully puts it down "Come again?"

"I know, ludicrous coming from me, but I need to adopt my niece."

"What!" This time Sabrina and Brooke yell.

Now that I've started talking, I can't stop "My sister—Viv, she died giving birth to her, and I promised her I would look after her."

Brooke's face has gone pale, her eyes glassy. "You had a sister, Stella?"

"Now Brooke, Stella was going to tell you this ages ago." Bonnie interjects.

"You told Bonnie about this?" She swings accusing eyes to me.

"I swear I only got to know recently," Bonnie backtracks. "Literally a few weeks ago."

A sob escapes Brooke as she dabs at her eyes. "I can't believe you wouldn't tell me. We lived together for two years. I thought we were best friends. I told you everything."

"I—I didn't mean to not say something. It was just hard and painful." Tears fill my eyes too and I start to cry softly. "Brooke, I'm sorry."

Brooke is still shaking her head, hurt and disappointment warring in her features, "So back then when you dropped out of your design program and started modeling... this was what you were dealing with?"

I hang my head and sob harder, feeling awful for hurting her, but also wishing someone understood what it meant to have a pain so deep you couldn't share it.

Bonnie wraps her arms around me while Sabrina does the same for Brooke.

"Stella, what happened to Viv?" Sabrina asks.

I take a breath. "Viv would often sneak out to hang out with her friends. She had this boyfriend who was in college— NYU. He was an exchange student from South Africa. She was still in high school at the time. He took her to one high-class party that he'd somehow got tickets to attend. A Greenhouse party, she called it."

Brooke looks up sharply. "That was Xavier's society, college frat thingie too."

"Yeah, the Greenhouse was the 'it' thing then, made up of the high and mighty, according to Vivian"

"So what happened to your sister?" Sabrina prompts when the silence stretches.

Brooke takes my hand in hers as if she expects this part to be difficult. She's right. I accept her comfort gratefully.

"I returned from work the following morning to find Tyrique—her boyfriend—pacing our small apartment, and Vivian scrubbing herself raw in my shower. Her skin was red and wrinkled, and she had huge welts and scratches from where she'd taken the sponge to her skin. Her eyes were haunted, bloodshot, and almost swollen shut with tears."

Bonnie's grip tightens almost to the point of pain. She's heard some of this story before yet she seems to hit her afresh. "Are you okay Bonnie?" I ask.

She nods tightly. "Go on Stella."

Okay. "Anyway, I dragged her out of the shower and wrapped her in a towel. She wouldn't say anything, so I got the story out of Tyrique. They'd gone into one of the rooms in the Greenhouse, got high on some sort of aphrodisiac, had sex, then got into a fight. Tyrique had left in anger but went back for her in the morning. She was in the same spot he left her. Only, she was still out cold, her lip was split, her face bruised, and she wouldn't speak to him."

I can still see Vivian. Distraught, scared and confused.

"Jesus, what happened to her?" Sabrina's voice sounds far-away but draws me back to the room.

I continue with a deep sigh. "After Tyrique left it took a good two hours to get Viv's version of events out of her. She couldn't recall much but swears someone else, not Tyrique, had slept with her that night."

Brooke who had been silent before now, gasps, "She was sure it wasn't her boyfriend?"

I shake my head, feeling chills race down my arms again. "She swears this man was much bigger and blond. He'd hit her a lot, then tied her, face down to the bed."

I pull Bonnie into a hug, because I need the comfort and I can see that she does too. But I need to finish this. Talking about it feels like a cathartic release. Painful but also relieving.

"Viv couldn't remember the man's face but there was one thing she couldn't forget."

"What was that Stella?" Sabrina asks.

"He wore a ring. A large tri-stone ring on his index finger. She recalled the ring in startling detail. It's no surprise, since she felt its impact a few times and it was all she could stare at as the man took her."

"Did you find the bastard? Bonnie grits out.

I shake my head. "Sadly no. The police checked all the CCTV feeds, asked around, but there was no such man. All they found was she and Tyrique getting hot and heavy in the common room before taking things to one of the bedrooms there. No one was seen entering or leaving the room. Also, their argument was caught on camera, how her boyfriend left and how she tripped and fell on her face shortly after. Evidence that Tyrique was right and Vivian was likely hallucinating from all the alcohol and drugs she took."

"What happened then? Was that the end of the investigation?" Bonnie presses

"Yes, they closed the case and she Viv even got booked for underage drinking. The next few weeks, Vivian withdrew into her shell, and all she did was sketch and paint obsessively."

"What was she sketching?" Sabrina asks.

"The ring. I was concerned about the drugs' lasting impact on her. They made her see things. I begged her to get professional help but she flatly refused. Six weeks later, Viv turned out pregnant."

I hear their collective gasps of pain. Their sympathetic looks and although it was difficult, I know I did the right thing speaking up.

"Tyrique swore they never had sex without protection, but come on, it fails, right? Besides, they were stoned. Anyway, he had really strong views on abortion and insisted she keep the baby even though Viv didn't want to. They got engaged at his insistence too. I thought Tyrique was a bit over the top, but he was such a massive support system for Viv I just let them be. I even encouraged her to keep the baby too. Before long, she stopped the obsessive sketching."

I shut my eyes, my heart bleeding all over again. "I thought everything was going to be alright from there on out. But I couldn't be more wrong."

"I'm so sorry you lost her, Stella," Brooke whispers.

"I got the shock of my life when Viv's baby came out blonde and blue-eyed. The doctors weren't obliged to explain, but I tried to figure it out. It happens, right? Maybe there was some Caucasian in Tyrique's lineage. Viv had taken one look at Harriet and told me I should have believed her. Harriet wasn't Tyrique's. She belonged to the man with the ring. And I didn't believe her."

Tears are streaming down my face now, and through my blurred vision I see my friends in a much similar state. Sabrina is sobbing gently. Brooke is still as pale as a sheet and Bonnie is holding on to me like her life depends on it.

"I tried speaking to Tyrique, who was livid, but the man walked out of the delivery room and never returned. He wouldn't hold Harriet or even take another look at the baby he'd loved up till she was born. I don't even think he knows Viv didn't make it out alive. I never saw him again. And can I really blame him. She's not his baby, right?"

Apart from losing Viv, Tyrique walking out on his fiancée and Harriet was the most painful part.

"Vivian had been telling the truth. There'd been someone else with her that night, but I never believed my sister. I pushed her to do the thing that would eventually kill her. And all for a man who couldn't love an innocent baby because of how she looked...or didn't look."

Sabrina comes over to my other side and puts her arms around me. "Goodness, Stella. I'm so sorry. What happened was beyond awful. You're so strong."

"I'm not strong. I'm really not. And I feel really alone most of the time." I sob.

"Oh, sweetheart, you're not. We're here for you, and we've got your back." Sabrina replies, hugging Brooke and I tightly.

Brooke is still sitting shocked and red-faced, across the table, her arms folded tight. Sabrina leans over then then pulls Brooke around to where the rest of us are huddled.

Sabrina throws her arms around Brooke and me, and then we cry some more.

⊷◆⊶

In another hour, our mood gets considerably lighter. I see the shock and grief gradually lift but the concern and questions remain. I am after all still married to Ryan Fairchild.

Sabrina is the first to bring up my marriage again. "Stella, I'm beyond heartbroken to hear about what happened to Viv and your struggle with adopting Harriet. It's beyond painful and I can't imagine having to carry that burden around for years."

I already sense the "but" coming before it lands.

"But are you sure you need to marry Ryan and move all the way to Seattle? I mean, if it's stability they want, like a regular income, a big house, whatever it is, girl, come on, we can make it happen, can't we? I mean, I could employ you in one of my galleries..."

"And Ethan and I could pitch in with a house or land if you prefer to self-build," Bonnie adds.

Brooke just looks at me like I killed her dog. It's not until Sabrina nudges her with an elbow before she says something.

"Um yeah, anything Stella."

"Brooke?" I push, knowing she has a lot more to say. "Spit it out."

She takes a deep breath. "Stella, I won't lie to you. Ryan likes you. I've picked up enough from the bits and pieces I hear when he talks to Xavier. But he's... well, he can be a lot to handle."

"I know that, Brooke. I know he's moody and infuriating and has huge commitment issues." Except he's also kind, funny, and sometimes, surprisingly sweet.

The only problem is, sex with Ryan flips a switch inside me, lighting up this intense and absolutely terrifying need for him.

Brooke looks like she's on the verge of saying more but stops herself, so I jump in, "Thanks for the heads-up, really. But I've got this. I actually did want to marry him."

At first everyone stills at my admission. Then Sabrina exclaims, "Oh shit, it's happened! Stella is in love with Ryan."

"Don't make me laugh, Sabrina." I scoff.

"It's alright, babes," Bonnie smiles, nudging my shoulder. "There are worse crimes than falling in love with your husband."

I shut my mouth and shrug, knowing that the more I protest, the more they'll dig into the narrative.

"Well, hell. Never thought I'd see the day this would happen." Sabrina muses.

Brooke sighs "I kind of saw it coming and dreaded it. From the very day he almost drowned you trying to repair our broken kitchen faucet."

We laugh, but I notice Brooke's strained smile and pale face. She's still hurt. But beyond that she looks concerned, almost afraid for me.

What the hell does she think Ryan will do to me? I remember Ryan joking about a shrink.

The man can't be all that bad, can he?

Chapter Sixteen

RYAN

THE BEEPING OF MY phone pulls me from sleep. A smile stretches my lips when I see it's Stella. I've not seen her since we got married a month ago.

"Hello, wife."

"Yuck. Try again."

"That reminds me, I'm going to need to call you something other than 'Stella' when we're in public."

"Why?"

"It's standard couple behavior for some reason. Even my parents do it."

"Really?"

"Don't ask. Actually, on second thoughts, I should give you fair warning about what my mom calls my dad."

"What does she call him?"

"DILF."

She gasps. "In public?"

"Not at business lunches or dinners, but yes, pretty much everywhere else."

"Oh my God. Now that is something I can't wait to see." The excitement in her voice is palpable but I feel the old twinge of anxiety in the pit of my belly at the thought of her living in this house with me.

It's got to be done. Stella will be moving to Seattle soon. It's been four weeks already.

I force the thoughts to the recesses of my mind and focus on the present. "So, tell me why you've woken me up."

"I've woken you up! You're three hours ahead of me; it's ten p.m. in Seattle."

"I'm usually in bed by seven and up by one a.m. My routine is not fixed, and I'm a light sleeper, so feel free to wake me up if you need."

"What? Why would you go to bed at seven in the evening?"

"It's just the way I am. Like I said, my routine isn't set in stone."

"I'm still waiting for you to tell me why you called." I say when the line goes silent.

"Oh yeah, I've been going through the Fairchild history, by the way, that's some family tree. Anyway, I have a few questions."

"Shoot. Although I have to say that I'm impressed by your dedication. Studying like you have an exam."

"More like a job. You want to be sure you're getting your money's worth. And since I'm the world's highest-paid actress, I can't be fumbling my lines."

"You know you'd be forgiven if you don't remember the names of every single member of my family and their little quirks."

"Which is exactly what I don't get; why the hell do people's names change every five seconds? Is that another ancient quirk?"

"Unfortunately, yes."

She groans. "No don't tell me..."

"First son adopts father's name after his father dies."

"Oh my goodness. There's no end to this is there? So, you mean to tell me that Ryan is just a placeholder; you will eventually be called Richard?"

"Yep. And thank you for that deafening eye roll. We should make that a spankable offense, actually." I hear her breath hitch, and I smile.

"You don't even know if I've done it." Her voice comes out breathless.

"I'm willing to bet anything that you did."

She giggles. "But honestly, what did you expect after dropping that on my head?"

"If that shocked you then you're not ready to hear my children's names."

"Hell no. Fucking hell no. Your kids have names already?"

"Afraid so, like hurricanes, the name precedes the child."

"I think I'm starting to see that shrink's chair somewhere in my near future."

I smile, "If you're thinking of having a meltdown then let me help you get there faster. It's Rex and Ronin for boys. Ramonda and Roquette for girls."

"Get out of here! You're making that up!"

"Appendix 5," I simply say.

I hear rustling as she quickly flips the pages.

"Oh shit, it's true! There is no way I'm letting you name my child any of those."

My cock twitches as her words seep into my pores. The thought of my child growing in her belly makes my loins tighten. "Speaking of, are you feeling okay, Stella?"

"Okay, as in?"

"Your pregnancy symptoms. You're what eight weeks right?"

"You know, I'm actually surprised that the idea of becoming a father doesn't send you running for the hills after your independence."

It takes long before I can form the words. There was a time I would have done anything to have a child. I shake off the dark memories, and instead imagine Stella as she is now. I wonder what she wears to bed. Silk and lace? Something ratty like me? Suddenly feeling too hot, I reach behind me and yank off my twelve-year-old holey PJ top.

"It wouldn't be my choice to get you pregnant, no, but now that you are, I need to make sure you're both fine."

"Hmm. I see. To answer your question, I feel good." She pauses. "Very good, Ryan." Another meaningful pause. "It's almost as though I'm not pregnant at all. I have no changes whatsoever. Zero changes. You get?"

She sounds like she's talking in code but I'm too tired for her riddles right now. "No, I don't 'get' it since I've never been pregnant."

And I know she's rolling her eyes again, meaning she's thinking of some scathing reply. Which makes me wish she would run her mouth so I can spank her when next I see her. "So, now if you don't have any other issues to raise, shall we talk about sex?"

"What about it?" She asks warily.

"You said it was horrible for you the last time."

"Oh God, Ryan, your ego is unbelievable. You still remember after all this time?"

"What do you mean 'all this time'? It's only been a couple of months, and I remember because it was a blatant lie." I palm my cock.

"How are you sure of that?" she purrs.

"Because I was there, Stella. I was inside you."

"And you're not aware of the proportion of women who fake orgasms?"

"There's no actress on earth as good as that. You fucking loved it."

"I've had better."

"In that case, I won't touch you anymore, not unless you beg me."

She makes a gagging noise. "You're so obsessed with begging. A snowball has a better chance in hell, Ryan."

"I've heard that before. Anyway, are you ready to move next week?"

"I've pretty much wrapped up here so yes."

"Whirlpool and BodyLift staff are eager to meet you. I've had your managers prep the staff."

"Prep, how?"

"I had them tell them you're a she-dragon. All your staff, as of right now, are shaking in their shoes."

"Are you kidding me?"

"No."

"What, why on earth would you do that Ryan?"

"Stella, it's better for them to think you're a fire-breathing dragon. Then they'll get their act together long before they realize you're a soft, pudgy iguana."

I hear a choking sound. "Are you okay there? You sound like you're trying to cough out a ball of hair."

"You're a jackass, Ryan."

"I know." I chuckle. "Stella?"

"What?"

"Thank you for doing this."

"Whatever." She disconnects the line, leaving me the way she always does. Rock hard and throbbing.

Chapter Seventeen

STELLA

I WAKE UP TO loud squawking. My eyes fly open in panic. I think I'm being attacked by geese. Then I realize it's my alarm clock. I chose that specific ringtone because I needed drastic measures to get me up at this ungodly hour.

It's 4 a.m. Looks like I have a good chance of catching the man before he leaves this morning.

Living with Ryan Fairchild has been impossible. It's like the guy doesn't even exist.

He's usually off to work before dawn, and by the time I return from work, he's asleep. Or at least in his bedroom. He must have a fully fitted kitchen in there because he doesn't even come out to eat or drink anything after seven.

It's been a month of hardly setting eyes on him, only seeing his hilarious scrawled notes. And the gourmet dinners he makes for me.

I drag myself off my plush bed and pad to the bathroom. I should ideally be sprinting out to see if he's still here, but after almost a month of not setting my eyes on him, I'm not going to leave my room with bed hair and an unwashed face.

When I'm ready, I step into the expansive open-plan living space of the penthouse and I immediately spot him in the kitchen.

I halt in my steps, my heart lurching. He's standing by the breakfast bar, holding a glass of orange juice and peering into a large sheet of paper.

He's wearing the oldest, rattiest gray T-shirt I've ever seen, one that's as thin as a wet tissue. What's more, I'm pretty sure he's wearing it back to front because the neck looks awkward.

The shirt might be old, but what Ryan does to it should be labeled a crime. The stretchy material pulls tautly against his muscles, begging for fingers to stroke along its ebbs and dips. His bottom half is covered in my personal kryptonite, tight grey sweatpants with a mouth-watering imprint of his cock.

This view is definitely worth waking up early for; the man is beyond gorgeous.

He looks up as I resume my approach.

"Hey Stella. You're up early today."

When I reach the breakfast bar and take a stool, I see the faded inscription on his shirt that reads **'Ryan.'**

"Oh wow, that's an interesting PJ choice. Is that in case you forget your name in your sleep?"

His lips twitch. "You're bright-eyed and bushy-tailed this morning. Everything okay?"

"No, everything is not okay. Ryan, what's with the skulking around?"

He cocks an eyebrow. "I don't skulk around."

"You're awake at freaking 4 a.m.! And peering at..." I move closer to see. It's a drawing plan or blueprint, but in the shape of a ship.

"Work." He states.

I sniff. "Wow. Work at four a.m. I, on the other hand, can barely hold my lids up before my second cup of coffee at nine. Which reminds me where do you hide all the coffee? You don't even have a machine. I've checked everywhere."

My assistant has been my lifeline this past month. She already knows to have a steaming one ready for me first thing.

Ryan throws me an unreadable look. "I don't drink coffee, so I don't have it. Besides, you should limit your coffee intake."

My heart skips a beat. He still thinks I'm pregnant. How many clues do I need to drop this guy before he gets it?

I should just come right out and tell him, although he seems a bit grumpy this morning.

I take a breath but what comes out of my mouth is, "Why don't you drink coffee?"

Ryan doesn't answer me, instead he moves to the refrigerator.

I'm still staring at his backside when he asks, "Would you like some orange juice instead?"

Not waiting for me to respond, he grabs a large jug of freshly squeezed oranges.

I grumble. "So not an alternative to coffee, but I guess it'll have to do for now."

He reaches for a glass, pours the juice and pushes it across the counter to me. "What about tea?"

"Nope, it's got to be coffee. No cream or sugar."

He simply grunts and continues staring at his 'work'.

Okay. I can't fault the guy— it's four in the morning. Stimulating conversation is a bit much to expect at this hour. "Anyway there's one brand a client gave to me. I don't think I've tasted coffee so good. Such an exotic flavor. It almost tastes like... wine."

"Which brand was it?" He pours himself another cup of juice and returns to his blueprints, making notes.

"It's um something... 'gold'." I wrack my brain trying to remember the actual name. "Gold Label? No Medal I think it was. Yep, that's the one. Gold Medal. Lucinda- my assistant says I have to order it from the website. Which reminds me..." I grab my phone. "I might as well look it up now."

I notice Ryan go still just before he looks up sharply. "Why do you like that brand?"

I shrug, "It's something about the taste. Why, do you know it?"

He inclines his head. "Most people I know hate that particular one. It's a medium roast blend from Ethiopia."

"Really! I thought you didn't drink coffee? How do you know so much about it?"

Is it me or has the air suddenly gone chilly around here? He straightens to his full height and says. "I know the person that owns that company."

"And did he beat you at a poker game?"

"What? No." His brows furrow in confusion.

"A business rival then."

He takes a deep breath and releases it slowly, almost like he's striving for patience. Then returns to the darned blueprint.

"You sound really pissed about something Ryan. Is it the really coffee you hate or the man?"

"I don't hate coffee."

"It's the man then, I get it. Makes zero sense of course since I don't know the context, but I get it. Sometimes I can't stand people for no reason."

He sighs, "Can we talk about something else? Or better still not talk at all?" He adds wryly. "It's usually very quiet here at this time of the day."

"Sorry to disturb your peace. No one warned me coffee was such a sore topic around here. I mean it's just coffee—"

"Stella!" He barks.

I raise both my hands in surrender. "Okay! Fine. Jesus." I mime zipping my lips.

Grabbing the empty jug and his glass he moves to the sink. I glare at his infuriatingly gorgeous back, wishing my eyes were daggers. And that's when I see the rest of the faded words in front— the back of his PJ top. I squint my eyes to read,

"**If found, return to Ivy League**.'" I roll my eyes. "Geez, could you be any more pretentious? You know, University of Washington, your alma mater, isn't even an Ivy League college—"

He suddenly reaches back, grabs a fistful of his shirt, pulls it over his head in one smooth motion, then drops it to the floor.

"Whoa! Blind me, why don't you?"

He wipes his hand on a dish towel and returns to the counter. "It's old. I need a new one."

I can't even pretend not to look. "I agree. It had nine lives but is currently on its twelfth one. But you deciding that right this minute is the time to get rid of it? That's just you wanting to show off your torso."

I'm still staring. The sight of his bare chest is doing all sorts of things to my ovaries. My fingers itch to trace the golden expanse of his skin, smooth and taut, almost like warm, polished stone.

My eyes feast on his sharply defined muscles, from his pecs and obliques and down his... I do a quick count...dear God, eight packs.

My gaze follows the path lower, beyond the delectable vee of muscle. Ropes of veins fan upward from his low-riding waistband. Once again, my gaze drops lower to the imprint of his cock. Which has now lengthened considerably since the last time I peeked, and is also now... twitching.

Holy mother of fuck.

I tear my gaze away as my mouth goes dry.

"Feel free to show off yours too," he says in a voice like warm honey. "I promise you I'll be just as impressed."

"Uh, no thank you."

"Go on, don't be shy."

The throbbing in my pelvis turns to an ache I can't ignore. I'm so wet right now and tempted to do what he says because I know it'll end with me bent over this counter. Losing my mind and begging for his touch. While he might as well carry on studying his blueprint.

It'd be too humiliating. "No, I'm good, thanks."

With a slight smirk, he shrugs, then returns to his paper while I change the subject.

"Why are you even awake at this time Ryan?"

"I told you what my routine is like."

"Yes. Knowing about it and living the reality are two different things. Ryan, do you have any idea how it feels living with you?"

He looks up from his work and gives me his attention. "How does it feel?"

"It's like living in a haunted house, and you're the ghost I've been trying to catch."

"You could have said something."

"I'd have to see you to say something."

"You could give me a call. We talked a lot last month."

"Yes, that was when you were here, and I was in New York. I didn't actually think I'd have to carry on with that while under the same roof. I mean, you're so distant... and...and so clean."

"Clean!" He laughs.

"Yeah, like it doesn't even feel like you live here."

He only shakes his head in amusement then comes round to stand beside me. "Stella, I told you, I'm here if you need me. Just knock on my office or bedroom door. My sleep pattern is unusual, but feel free to interrupt as often as you want."

"What time do you wake up?"

"I wake up around two in the morning. Hit the gym, then breakfast."

Figures, I steal another look at his ripped torso. "And what about when you go out at night?"

He shrugs. "Like I said, it's not an issue. I'm a light sleeper. And if I want to go hang out with friends, I'll let you know."

I smile, "By leaving me one of your chicken scrawly notes?"

"Exactly."

I tense as he bends to my ear and whispers, "Next time you need me, Stella, just wake me up." He runs the tip of his nose along my temple. Goosebumps cover my skin, and my nipples bead painfully. To make matters worse, he notices. He traces a finger down my arm and murmurs, "Fascinating."

I concentrate on keeping my breathing even.

"You know, Stella, you only need to ask. I won't hold it over you or gloat."

"Ask you what?"

"Ask me to fuck you. You may need to say it a few times, though, but you'll eventually get what you want. Over and over."

I wonder if he can smell my arousal. "Ryan?"

"What?"

"You're in my space."

"We're married, of course, I'm in your space." He takes a step back, though, and I instantly miss the warmth radiating from his naked chest.

"But I mean it, if you're bored or you want to talk, just knock on my bedroom door, okay?"

I scoff. "So you think I'm that woman who will wake you up because she's lonely for a chat?"

No, but you're the one who'll set an alarm and sprint out so you can speak to the guy.

"I wouldn't mind either way, as long as you do what makes you happy. Done?" He gestures to my barely-touched orange juice.

I nod, watching as he picks up both glasses, rinses and places them in the dishwasher.

"I'm leaving for work in thirty. Have some French toast." He points at the smart oven. He starts to leave, then turns back. "By the way, we have dinner at the Richard-Fairchilds this weekend."

A wave of panic hits me. "And you tell me this on Thursday!"

"Relax, it's not the sharks. It's just my parents, Gina, and her boyfriend. Or ex, depending on how she's feeling at the time. You don't need to break out the scripts. They already love you."

"They do?"

"Yes, and my parents believe we've mated for life, so you're good no matter what."

"And Gina?"

"Piece of cake. She's desperate for a 'sister'. Her last venture didn't quite work out, so you're her last chance."

"What do you mean?" I call after him.

"Brooke. Only God knows what she did to piss the woman off."

Yep. Gina and I have that in common. And I'm not the only one who can keep a grudge. Brooke is still not speaking to me, which I totally respect because if the shoe were on the other foot, I'd be doing the same.

Chapter Eighteen

STELLA

"STELLA, I HEAR YOU now own Whirlpool and BodyLift." Diana Fairchild remarks as soon as we settle down to eat. "I'm curious: why did you choose those two?"

Ryan and I had arrived late, deliberately, he'd said, to avoid any messy grilling his mom and sister had in store for me.

I wouldn't have minded getting questioned. In fact, I think I would actually have loved to talk to them, but since Ryan and I aren't seeing each other much these days, there was no way to tell him that.

I stubbornly refused to get him out of his bedroom, resolved not to be the needy type of woman but it's getting harder to stay away.

I catch the look Ryan sends his mom, but before I can open my mouth to tell her it's okay to ask, Gina who is sitting right beside me, steps in. "Whoa, Whirlpool and BodyLift? Savage, girl. Talk about a fucking entrance into the Seattle beauty industry!"

Richard Fairchild raises a single eyebrow at Gina, which earns him a pout. He briefly glances at me. Then he continues cutting into his tenderloin, a smile playing around his lips.

"Why did you choose those salons?" Diana pushes.

I throw a quick glance at Ryan. He seems more interested in catching the chef's attention for more wine so I take that as green light.

We'd agreed on the way here, no reaction or lack of eye-contact meant I was safe to answer in any way I liked. A non-committal gesture while looking at me, meant I should under no circumstances, answer truthfully.

"It wasn't my choice. We thought it'd be better if I started with a curated client base. I didn't want to build one from scratch, since I don't know the Seattle market. But I left the choice of salons to Ryan."

"That makes a lot of sense," Richard smiles. An older version of Ryan, Richard has a distinguished look, his hair is thick but almost fully gray, his deep-set blue eyes cool and assessing. He's not overpowering but possesses the air of a man used to calling the shots.

Diana nods in agreement, "Very ballsy move but yeah, I agree with you, DILF,"

I almost spit my wine out, but I manage to catch myself in time. I don't dare look anywhere but my plate. Ryan warned me but hearing his mom say it sounds so much dirtier.

Gina leans toward me and whispers. "I wish I could tell you you'd get used to it, but no, you won't."

Somehow that makes me want to snicker even more, but I hold it in.

"...would you say you are Stella?"

Shit. I have no clue what Richard asked me.

Ryan puts a hand on my thigh. "Oh, I think Stella is big on taking risks, aren't you baby? Which is why I thought those two businesses were perfect for her."

Richard considers this, a twinkle appearing in his eyes. "Incredible." He muses. "You'll fit right in."

Somehow, I sense this is high praise from my father-in-law.

Diana adds, chuckling, "Maybe you'll even turn some of the sharks into guppies."

"Is there something special about those salons?" I venture, peering around the table.

"You could say that," Diana replies. Her voice is tinged with a mix of amusement and pride. "They're the most sought-after in the whole city. The very establishments Leanne has been lobbying Reuben to buy for her. But he keeps refusing."

Leanne Fairchild is Reuben's wife. Don's mother. I look at Ryan, who just shrugs.

"Why has he refused?" I ask Diana.

"Because Reuben for all his faults has compassion for the women of Seattle. If Leanne took over, she'd ruin the salons. Then where would the high-society ladies go?"

Ryan leaves his food and puts his arm around my shoulder. "I thought Stella could show the Seattle folk how we New Yorkers do business. It's only been a few weeks, but Stella is already doing amazingly well."

I shoot Ryan a nervous look. First of all, I'm just a stylist from Brooklyn. I don't jump into rings with sophisticated, wealthy women and compete with them for what they want.

Ryan continues, "A couple of years ago, Stella arranged a makeover for five homeless men. Two ended up with modeling contracts."

"Wow, that's incredible!" Gina gushes.

I turn to Ryan, beyond shocked. "You... knew about that!" That was way before we met.

"Didn't you know I was one of your ten thousand followers?"

I don't even know how to respond to that.

He bends to whisper in my ear, "I've been watching you for a long time Stella. You're fucking incredible."

A warm sensation envelopes me and my cheeks flush. That would have to go down as the hottest thing anyone has said to me. And that he chose to do it while we have company only makes me hornier. If he'd said that while we were alone, I might have jumped him.

Like a switch was flipped inside me, the pent-up tension of the last few weeks slowly starts to uncoil. I become hyper-aware of his fingers drawing lazy circles over the skin exposed by my off-shoulder cashmere top. I bite my lip and suppress a shiver. As of right now I'm no longer acting; I just can't tell if he still is.

He continues touching me until the servers clear the table of dinner and replace them with dessert. Ryan pulls away and digs into his blueberry ice cream. But, as if he can't help it, in less than a minute, his arm is back around me.

Across the table, Diana and Gina are exchanging loaded glances. Richard just carries on as if oblivious.

"Actually, Ryan is right about Seattle." Diana says, now looking at me anew with a mix of fascination and respect. "New York is light-years ahead of us in the high fashion and beauty industry, for sure. Did you also get your college degree in New York?"

Without thinking to check Ryan's reaction, I blurt, "Um, I don't actually have a college degree. Not yet, anyway. I'm halfway through my online design tech program."

Ryan freezes next to me, and Richard and Diana exchange a look.

Great, I've really stepped in it now.

Their surprise at my admission is palpable, but then they smile, sensing there's more to the story.

Diana leans in, her curiosity sparking. "Do your parents live in New York too?"

"Well, I actually never met them. We grew up mostly in a children's home," I share, feeling a bit like I've just exposed a piece of my soul.

If Ryan goes any more rigid, he'd be splintering apart.

"We?" Gina picks up on the plural, a note of surprise in her voice.

Ah, shit. Another bomb unwittingly dropped there. I can't bring myself to meet Ryan's eyes any longer. Since the gate is now thrown wide open, I simply plod on.

"My sister and I."

"Oh, you have a sister!" Gina gushes. "Older or younger?"

"She was younger by a year. But she died six years ago."

"That's terrible!"… "I'm so sorry!"… the sincerity in Gina and Diana's voices wraps around me like a warm blanket.

"It's okay," I shrug, trying to keep the mood light. "I had the chance to say goodbye, and now, I'm living for both of us by keeping her dreams alive."

"What. The. Hell?" Ryan's growl is so low I almost don't hear it.

"That's really touching," Diana stands and comes round to my side. "May I?" She asks, holding her arms out.

Standing, I lean into her and accept her hug. For a brief moment, I think I might cry. It occurs to me this is the first time in... forever, that I've been held by a mother.

Everything goes on autopilot from there on. Ryan remains as stiff as ever, his smiles no longer reaching his eyes with the more I reveal.

Diana, Gina and I, on the other hand, are having the night of our lives. Richard too seems captivated. He occasionally adds his own comments and questions, adding to the lively banter.

Somehow, I end up telling them all sorts of stories. Funny experiences with clients in Brooklyn, encounters with annoying celebrities, and even the bittersweet memories of Viv. Thankfully they don't press too much about Viv, sticking to topics I'm comfortable with.

Ryan remains a silent, attentive presence, only that I can feel him vibrating next to me. I can't work out what he finds most unsettling about the situation but I suspect it's how well his family and I are getting on considering we'll be divorced in a matter of months.

As the night wears on, despite chatting away, I start to get even more aware of Ryan. His nearness, the way he keeps holding my hand, touching my thigh, his fingers stroking my shoulder, and playing with the hair at my nape.

By the end of dinner, I'm more than ready to leave. I need to find out what his deal is. And tear him out of his clothes.

"What the hell was that, Ryan?" As soon as we're off the driveway, I snatch my hand away from under his and push his palm off my thigh.

"Why didn't you tell me about the way you grew up? About your sister, dammit." His tone is hard, laced with accusation and a tinge of hurt.

The topic is a minefield I've long avoided. "It never came up." I hedge.

He gives me a look that tells me what he thinks of that excuse.

"I don't talk about it," I try my standard defense.

"Oh indeed. Which is why you saw fit to tell my family your entire life story on the very day you met them."

His tone, equal parts sarcastic and hurt, hits a nerve. I can't very well tell the man that I was so excited to be around his family that I couldn't stop talking. So I respond with a nonchalant shrug.

He heaves a sigh, then reaches over and takes my hand. "Stella, I had no idea that you lost someone so close to you." His voice softens, a stark contrast to the earlier tension.

"Hey, I don't need your pity, okay?"

"Pity is the last thing I'm feeling, right now."

We fall into another tense silence, until Ryan says gently, "You know, you don't have to answer questions you find difficult."

"But wouldn't it be rude not to answer?"

He shakes his head, "Not at all. If anything, it makes them feel bad for asking." His explanation feels strange, yet oddly comforting.

"I don't understand," I admit.

"That's just how it works with my family. Because anything you say could be twisted into gossip fodder or used against you, it's more than okay not to answer a question."

"Okay." I file that bit of information away. "I really didn't mind telling them though. I mean, they're good people, right?"

"Of course. But Stella, I really had no clue things were that tough for you."

My face heats up with embarrassment. "That was a long time ago, growing up. It's not who I am anymore. That's why I don't talk about it; it changes how people see me."

"You think knowing your past would change how I see you?"

"Well, it certainly did something to you. For four whole weeks, you couldn't bear to be in the same room with me. Then I tell my 'sob story,' and of a sudden, you were all over me at dinner. I thought you said we didn't have to put on a show."

"It wasn't a show."

His denial sparks an unexpected warmth in my chest. "Oh, really? The touching wasn't a show?"

"You took me by surprise tonight. And turned me on. The way you trusted my family enough to bare yourself that way... They were honored. You've won their loyalty."

"Let me get this straight. Me opening up to your family turned you on?" His admission fuels my own desire, and the relentless throbbing in my core surges again.

His hand returns to my thigh, heavy and warm "Not that exactly. But how you owned your past, how strong you've had to be after losing the one person you had in the world. That's what got to me. And somehow, it led me down the path of wanting to bury my cock in your tight warmth and fucking you until you're limp."

"Ryan" I gasp, his words are clouding my brain with a fog of arousal. I resist the urge to pull up my skirt so he can reach my bare skin.

"You were in a similar state all evening Stella. You want me. And you know what you have to do to get what you want."

"Why do I have to be the one to ask though? Why can't you do it?"

"Because I didn't run my mouth saying how bad the sex was when you and I know it wasn't.

"It just doesn't seem fair that I have to beg."

"No?"

"I say we choose who begs based on who needs it more. And before you say anything, I'll have you know that I have perfectly working fingers."

"I've got a good gripping hand as well." He shoots back. At his words, my gaze immediately flies to his large hand gripping the steering wheel as he swings the Maybach into our underground parking lot.

I dimly register that we're home even as my imagination kicks into overdrive. I remember how his hand felt holding me down by my nape. Spanning the small of my back. Slapping my pussy. How would it look wrapping around his cock and stroking himself? A fresh burst of wetness drenches my panties.

He shuts off the ignition, the corner of his lips lifting in a knowing smirk. Without even looking at me it's as if he knows what I'm thinking.

I grit my teeth in frustration. It's too late to back out. While I'm determined not to go to bed in this state of arousal, I'm also not prepared to lose to him by begging.

I lower my voice to a throaty whisper "How nice for you. Well, I also happen to have a nice fat vibrator."

He goes still.

Good, that got his attention.

I dig in. "I mean, it doesn't feel half as good as your cock. For instance, it doesn't throb or twitch or always hit the right spot, but that's where my imagination comes in."

"Stop it." He snaps.

"I'll just think about your big hard veiny cock pounding my soaked pussy into submission, dragging against my G-spot as I come all over you, screaming."

"Fuck Stella" he growls, clearly at breaking point.

"Anyway, you get my drift, so I'm good tonight, thanks." Reaching across the center console, I pat his abs, and I swear his cock fucking leaps in his pants. I can't resist stroking lower until I palm his hard length along his inner thigh.

"What are you doing?" He bites out in a voice as rough as gravel.

I give him a quick squeeze and whisper, "I'm just giving you a neighborly warning. In exactly thirty seconds from when I shut my bedroom door, I'll be screaming out your name with or without you inside me. You decide."

Ryan snaps. Like a coiled snake suddenly striking he flies out of the car and heads to my side.

Uh-oh. I've done it now.

He looks wild. But I can't help the bolt of excitement that streaks through me. Not only for winning our little game but because, finally, I'll get what I've been dreaming of: Ryan, unhinged.

Chapter Nineteen

RYAN

FROM THE FIRST MOMENT I met Stella, I knew the green-eyed witch would be the death of me. I just didn't envisage death by blue balls. Which is exactly what would happen to me if I'm not buried inside her tight heat in the next few minutes.

I just need to get her upstairs.

I step out, round the car, and throw her door open, but I don't bother helping her out of the bucket seat. She can find her own feet without me fucking pulling her out.

Frankly, it's because if I touch her right now, I'll take her here in this parking garage.

I could practically smell her arousal all evening. Yet she's spun some magic on me. I feel my hands trembling. I've never ever been this close to losing control like this.

"You have ten seconds to get yourself out before the doors lock."

I spin on my heels, ignoring the look of confusion on her face and storm off toward the bank of elevators. I only said that because I need her upstairs asap.

"Fine. Alright!" She calls after me.

I don't respond.

I hear the car door slam so I know she's left the car. I glance back to see her walking toward me, her heels clacking on the concrete. My eyes drink her in– toned legs and shapely calves I'd like to take a bite out of, her white outfit draping and clinging to her body in way that makes my balls ache even more. And that sexy mouth that can make a guy's ears bleed or make the most erotic sounds when I'm deep inside her.

She stops halfway. "Ryan?"

"What?" I snap.

"You're mad."

Mad with lust. Insane. "Your powers of observation are legendary."

"Well, don't throw your toys out of the pram yet."

I huff out a laugh. "What does it look like I'm doing?"

"Leaving me. Going to your room to touch yourself" A look of disappointment crosses her face.

I shake my head in disbelief. "Stella I'm this close to–"

"Please." She interjects. "There, I've said it. Please."

Lust slams into me. I stalk back toward her and crowd her until I'm backing her into the car hood.

"Please what?"

"Do it. Fuck me."

Before the words are fully out of her mouth, I spin her around and bend her face down onto the hood of the car. I put a hand down on the warm black shiny paint and push her cheek onto the back of my hand. The heat from the engine heightens the sensation in my groin, along with the knowledge that I'd rather my flesh cook than let her skin touch the still-warm hood.

"Ryan," She squeaks, "I didn't mean right here!"

"You're getting me right here baby. I can't make it upstairs in this state." I unzip my jeans and free my aching cock and balls.

"Someone could see."

"Us fucking and hear you screaming, yes. But otherwise, nothing else. Now, show me where you want me," I command.

She flips up the back of her skirt without hesitation, and I see she's already soaked through the crotch of her silk panties.

Christ. I imagined she'd be this wet, but seeing it hits differently. I hook my hand into her panties, and the material gives with a sharp tug.

I wanted a quick fuck, but I now can't resist running my fingers over her plump ass cheeks then grazing my thumb back and forth over the pucker of her ass.

"Ryan?" Her tone is both pleading and apprehensive.

"You have a gorgeous ass. But not now and not here okay. My fingers continue downward and between her legs until they're running through her folds. I watch her back arch in response.

"You're going to show me how you fake your orgasms, Stella. First around my fingers and again on my cock."

"Deal. Keep going" she moans.

I sink two fingers into her slick pussy. Her long, keening moan echoes in the car park, making me feel superhuman for getting her to make that sound. Stella is such a dream to touch.

"You are so fucking drenched baby. So tight and hot." *Shut the fuck up* I tell myself, but words of adoration keep pouring out of me as I work my fingers in and out of her. I add a third finger, and she groans loudly, slapping her palm on the car hood.

"Careful now, the mask is slipping, you should only be pretending to enjoy this."

"Shut up and let me act." She snaps.

I chuckle even as I change the angle, hitting that bundle of nerves on her front wall that makes her crazy. I feel her muscles contract hard around my fingers, her thighs shaking as she begins to come.

She grits her teeth, groaning as she rides her orgasm. I pull out my fingers from her twitching, sopping pussy, line my cock up against her entrance, and thrust into her tight heat.

Her scream is music to my ears while I hold myself against her still jerking hips to let her ride out her the rest of her orgasm on my cock.

The moment she becomes aware of herself again, she freezes as if I've just doused her in cold water.

"Ryan?"

"Yes," I pant, my hips already starting to rut into her, past the point of holding still while her walls squeeze my dick.

Christ, she feels so good. It's been too fucking long. I must be insane to have stayed away this long.

"You had better be wearing a condom there." Her voice cuts through my euphoria and it takes a while to process what she said.

"Excuse me?"

"I'm pretty sure you heard me, Ryan."

"No, I don't think I did."

"Are you wearing a condom?"

I huff out a laugh. "You tell me. Does it feel like I'm wearing one?" I pull out partway and slam back inside her to emphasize my point.

Her eyes roll back and she moans. Still, she says. "I'm serious Ryan go put it on."

"Are you kidding me? What am I going to do, knock you up twice?"

"Well...actually, about that..." She trails off.

And that's how I know.

"Oh my fucking days. You're not pregnant, are you?"

"Not technically...I mean... not yet."

"You. Little. Liar." I withdraw and step away from her as if she's on fire then shove my still-hard cock into my jeans.

She straightens and comes toward me while I hold up a hand to ward her off.

"Ryan wait, in all fairness..."

I don't want to hear it. I turn away from her. For the second time, I stride toward the elevators. But, this time, with far less grace. I'm rock hard, and my balls ache.

Why are you so angry? Because she lied or because you're not going to be a father after all?

I slap the call button repeatedly, in a bid to shut off the taunting voice in my head.

Although if I'm being honest a part of me knew she wasn't pregnant. All the clues were there.

She'd been eager to get married, desperate almost. And I told her in no uncertain terms that the only condition under which that could happen was if she wound up pregnant. And she did.

But it's been two months since then, and she didn't say anything to stop me from thinking... *hoping*...that it might be true.

With a vicious shake of my head, I dispel those thoughts and step into the elevator.

Once in the penthouse, I head straight to my office, pour myself a scotch and drop into my chair. And fight the urge to turn on the security feed to the parking garage to see that she's made it inside and she's okay.

I down the drink and relish the burn all the way to my stomach. If only that were a path of fire burning away the forbidden emotions roiling in my belly.

I never let myself feel anything for a woman except for detached amusement. I don't remember ever being this angry. Or aroused. Or wanting to look after someone this bad.

I hear a hesitant knock. "Ryan?"

When I don't respond, she pushes the door open and steps in. She takes in the room then her eyes come to rest on me while mine helplessly move over her.

She's changed from her dress into a plain thin shirt and shorts. Her blonde waves are artfully tousled. She looks like the sin I'd very much like to indulge in. And a sinner needing to be punished.

"Ryan I'm sorry. I didn't know you would be upset. That you'd be this upset, I mean. I have no excuse, but we kind of stopped talking when I got here, and it didn't really come up..." She trails off running a hand through her hair and licking her lips.

When I still say nothing, she continues. "I'm not proud of lying. I was...desperate. It was last minute, and I thought the only way to get you to marry me was a reason as compelling as that."

I watch her for a beat, then calmly move my desktop monitor further down the desk to make more space. "It's not the only time you've lied to me, is it?"

"What?" Her brows knit in confusion.

"You still haven't told me the truth behind your desperation to marry me. You're going to tell me tonight, but first, take off your clothes."

"What?" She gasps.

"You heard me."

I continue to stare at her, watching as her breath catches, and her face flushes because of how much being ordered turns her on. Her hard nipples are visible through the thin material of her top. She grasps the hem and slowly peels it off. She drags down her shorts and panties and steps out of them. Naked, she lifts her gaze to mine. Full of defiance, lust and something else. Trust. And a plea. I'm not sure what for.

I let myself drink her in. From her silvery blonde hair, her high cheekbones and full lips. To her pert breasts topped with prominent nipples, and the tiny waist that flares into generous hips. If I were prone to waxing poetic, I would write an ode to her almost otherworldly beauty. But I'm not. I'd rather make her feel.

I push myself away from my desk and undo my belt, pulling it out in one long strip and tossing it on the desk. She flinches at the jarring sound the buckle makes on connecting with the wood and stares at the belt like it might be a snake.

"Eyes on me Stella."

Her eyes snap to mine as I take my shirt off. She watches me, pulling her lower lip in between her teeth. When I undo my fly, she starts to rub her thighs together, cupping her breast in her hand and pulling hard on her own nipple as if trying to relieve the ache between her legs.

I take the hand she's worrying her breast with and lead her to the desk. She comes willingly, shaking with desire. The way she stares at the belt on the desk tells me she knows what's coming.

With my hand at her nape, I bend her over for the second time tonight. She keeps looking at the belt but doesn't say anything.

"Only my hands will touch your ass tonight, Stella, no matter how much you want that." I swipe the belt to the floor.

I run my fingertips over her butterfly tattoo which stretches from her shoulder blades to her waist. She shivers at the first touch. I continue trailing my hands over the delectable curve of her ass and right into her drenched folds.

She cants her hips higher in a silent plea for more.

"You don't lie to me. Ever again, do you understand?"

She stays silent, no doubt loving and hating my hard, authoritative tone.

I draw back my hand and give her a hard smack on her ass.

She jerks and gasps. "Ryan!"

I deliver another smack. "Do you understand?"

"Yes!" She yells.

I slap her ass over and over again, on the same spot until she's crying out and mumbling something.

"Use your words, Stella."

"Harder. Please."

My erection swells and twitches against the too-tight team of my jeans. I unzip my fly and release both cock and balls so I can focus back on Stella.

"You said what?"

She grits her teeth as if mortified. I knead her smarting, red ass cheek until she can't take the aching pleasure and pain.

"Spank me harder. Right where you're touching."

"Why?"

"Because I love it," she admits in a small voice.

I laugh. "You won't be able to sit tomorrow you know that?"

"I figure I'll...use the other side."

And so, I give her what she wants, spanking her ass until she's a moaning, trembling mess, her palms opening and closing reflexively. I dip my fingers between her legs and find her dripping, strings of wetness clinging to her pussy lips and running down her thighs.

"Christ, Stella. You're unbelievable."

I reach into my drawer and bring out a strip of condoms, throwing it meaningfully on the desk. "You wanted one of these? Take your pick."

"Please."

I'm not even sure what she's begging for at this point. "Shh." My fingers return to her pussy to gather her moisture then I slide my wet thumb back over the tight ring of her ass. I trace the bundle of nerves until she starts to whimper.

"Ryan, Oh my God"

I breach the ring, and she jerks. "Please Ry."

"What are you begging for?" I chuckle darkly.

"I want you inside me."

"I am inside you." I slowly slide my thumb in and out, teasing and stimulating.

She reaches for the condoms and tears one open, pushing it toward me. "Fuck my ass."

My eyebrows fly up in surprise. "You're not ready for that yet."

She bristles, "You don't get to tell me what I'm ready for."

I withdraw my finger and give her a smack that makes her gasp.

"Yes, I do. You on the other hand will trust me and take what I give you like a fucking queen."

She lifts her head to look at me, anger and arousal warring in her eyes.

"Liked the sound of that, didn't you?" I tease.

Suddenly, she swipes all the condoms off the table, flinging them across the room and onto the floor. "Only if you can dole it out like a king." She snaps.

My cock goes even harder as a feral need to possess her overtakes me. I let go of the beast inside that's demanding to claim, to tame this wild, strong, beautiful woman.

I hold her down by her nape, line my cock against her then enter her in one savage thrust.

Her scream of pleasure mixes with my animalistic groan as I slam into her over and over, not giving either of us space to adjust to the sudden blinding pleasure.

"Oh please...so hard... too good" she moans.

It's about to get better baby.

I knead her plump, sensitive ass as I angle my cock to hit that spot that makes her shudder and her eyes roll back.

"Ry, oh my God, Ry, you sound so sexy."

What the hell?

That's when I realize I'm actually being louder than she is. The more I try to stop the raw sounds tearing out of me the louder they get.

What the fuck is she doing to me? And then I can't think anymore as I feel her inner muscles clamp down on my cock. Her fingers curl around the hand I've splayed over her nape, her nails digging into my wrist, while her other hand reaches behind her, blindly seeking for any part of me.

"Ryan," she pleads.

I freeze. She's done this before. And this time I understand what she's asking for. Something I never ever give.

But this is Stella. My wife.

As I resume thrusting, I pull her up from the desk while I curve my torso around hers. Without even thinking about it, drop my face into the crook of her neck, and suck on the fragrant skin there while my other hand goes between her legs to stroke her clit.

She cries out as her orgasm hits her in a series of full-body jerks, so strong it immediately triggers mine out of nowhere. With a roar, I collapse back onto the desk, and I barely manage to brace myself on my forearm so as not crush her delicate frame, then withdraw my already spurting cock out of her before descending into a vortex of pleasure, rutting into her ass and smearing the rest of my cum all over her.

"Christ woman. You're so fucking sexy when you come," I manage amid gasping breaths.

She's still trembling and breathing hard. "And those sounds you were making Ry..."

"Believe me, I would have gagged myself if I could."

"No Ry you were magnifice–" she snaps her mouth shut.

I start to chuckle. "Am I going crazy, or were you about to call me magnificent?"

She flushes scarlet. "Um... It's my postcoital brain trust me."

"In that case, I'd love to keep you permanently in this state."

"I'm sure you would."

I swing her up into my arms and return to my desk, arranging her on my lap, her back to my front. I lightly run my fingers over her ass. "How sore are you?"

"It's just hot and it stings. Keep doing that," she shifts to give me better access. I oblige her and within a minute of stroking her ass cheek, I swear she starts purring like a cat. At least her breathing changes. She fucking loves being touched.

Then it dawns on me that this is her first time here. My library is a replica of my Manhattan one except for the tall shelves of books here.

"Gosh Ryan, do you actually read this much or is it just decor?" She stares at my book collection.

"They're mainly books on business, engineering, and poetry. I've read most of them, it's the fiction part I'm working on reading, I'm told it expands the imagination."

"Do you need that to build ships?"

"Yeah, I do, for design and innovation."

"And you have so many awards, too" Her slightly awed look makes me smile.

"They've piled up mostly because I don't throw them away." She looks about to dig in more so I steer her to the reason we're here in the first place. "Now let's come back to the question of why you were bent on marrying me."

"It's because of Vivian." She murmurs. "You know when I said I was keeping her dream alive?"

I nod "What did you mean by that?"

"She has a—" She breaks off abruptly, and then sits up straighter on my lap "Hey, what the fuck is that?

"What is it?"

She goes eerily still, face as white as she stares at the wall of plaques and awards. She points and I follow, half expecting to see a ghost but it's only a shelf. On it sits a lone trophy from the Greenhouse fraternity.

Chapter Twenty

Ryan

"Why do you have that?"

I cock an eyebrow. "Why do I have a trophy on a shelf full of trophies?"

"I'm serious." She springs out of my arms and pads to the shelves on the far side of the wall.

I know she's delaying the inevitable, and it makes me think of the worst.

Before I can say anything, she picks up one of my oldest trophies, one I got from college. It's one with the model of a classic greenhouse with a pointed roof encased within a spherical frame, with green leaves peeking out from behind it.

"Ryan, is this yours?" she asks in a slightly shaky voice.

What's upset her now? "Does it not have my name on it?"

"It does. But... it says 'The Greenwich Society.' Is that not the same as the Greenhouse, an NYU fraternity?"

"It used to be. You know about it?"

"I've heard a lot about it."

Figures. It was an exclusive group made up of heirs to billion-dollar empires and trust fund babies. The parties were some of the most sought-after in colleges from within and outside New York.

I huff out a breath, striving for patience with her as she looks over the award, her eyes wide with emotion. She seems lost in thought for a while, then suddenly puts the trophy back and returns to me.

I pull her onto my lap. "What just happened right now, Stella? You look pale."

"Ryan, I thought you attended the University of Washington. Brooke mentioned something like that. About you and Xavier having a huge fallout and then getting separated during college. I assumed..."

I fight to tamp down the surge of panic inside me. "Yes, I had my first year of college at UW, then moved to New York—"

"Why did you move colleges?" She interjects, twisting back to look at me.

I keep my expression bland. "To reconnect with Xavier." *And escape the ghosts.*

After a moment, she nods, then leans back into my chest. "That award was for Social Navigator."

"Some stupid shit, a euphemism for helping people and partying a lot."

I'm not sure why we're still discussing my college days but chalk it up to her not having an experience of college life.

"What were the parties like?" Stella asks.

"Wild, I guess. I was almost always drunk in those years in college. I hardly remember graduating college, much less getting that award."

If it hadn't been for Xavier, I probably would have flunked out or even wound up dead during those dark days.

She takes several deep breaths. Again, I'm puzzled by her reaction and something occurs to me. "Stella, did you ever attend those parties?"

She shakes her head. "I'm just curious."

"Okay, enough about my college life. Tell me why you lied to me."

"Am I allowed to put my clothes back on?"

"Are you cold?"

"No, you're like a furnace."

"So no, not until you tell me the truth."

"It's... personal."

"Good thing you're naked and in my lap, wife. It doesn't get more personal than that. No more running from this."

She takes a deep breath and releases it in a rush. "I was desperate because I'm trying to adopt my niece."

"Your sister had a daughter?"

She nods. "Her name is Harriet. She's the most adorable little girl. I've been trying for the past couple of years. For the first few months, they wouldn't even look at my application."

She burrows closer to me, folds her legs in my lap, and buries her nose into my chest, letting my warmth seep into her skin. I would never have guessed how big of a cuddler Stella is.

Holding her this way triggers frissons of unease down my spine, but I'm not about to interrupt what she's saying. Besides I made her do this by not letting her get dressed.

"I was so close last time Ryan. I'd already got a financial adviser to help me straighten things out, and things were looking up, and I had finally saved enough to move to a better neighborhood. That should have cinched things for us."

"So what happened?"

"Harriet's foster parents decided they want to adopt her too. And they are wealthy, married, and she's settled in with them, so their application would be stronger."

"Ah hell. Is that why you were crying the other day?"

She nods. "I'd just been to the agency that morning."

"I see. And now that you're married, have you contacted them again?"

She shakes her head. "I've only told them to give me some time, that my circumstances might be changing soon. But I've been terrified of reaching out. I fear that they'll see through this marriage. And this might be the final refusal."

I hold her tight against me, feeling her pain, angst, and sense of urgency.

Something stirs deep in my chest—in that cold, dark place that I never let anyone reach. My first instinct is to get her away from me. Put the distance of the past month between us again. But Stella needs me and I know she's too stubborn to ask.

Before I realize what words are coming out of my mouth, I say. "Do you want me to help you get her Stella?"

She twists to look at me, surprise and hope in her features "You could? You would do that?"

"Of course. I'm still your husband. We should leverage what you have now."

She bursts into tears, sobbing into my neck.

"Is that a yes then?" I murmur in confusion.

"Oh God yes! Yes. Thank you, Ryan."

In the next moment, she raises her head and looks at me with those gorgeous green eyes luminous with joyful tears, and I know she's about to kiss me. The knot of unease tightens, and I tense, fighting to hide my irrational urge to push her away. She bites her lip and desire wars with apprehension, tempting me to taste her lips.

She leans in, and by reflex, I rear back. That makes her pause, a furrow of confusion appearing between her brows before smoothing out as she no doubt recalls my hard limit.

She flushes, but manages a lovely smile. "Thank you, Ryan."

"Sure." My response is more clipped than I would have liked. "I'll get Gina on it ASAP. She snacks on cases like this and will get it done in no time. Shall I talk to her, or would you prefer to do it yourself?"

"I'll, um, I'll speak to her. Thanks again, Ryan."

"Anytime, Stella." My voice is softer now but still strained.

As if aware of my unease, she disentangles from my lap and pads across the room. I watch her put on her clothes, wanting her to leave but wishing she would stay wrapped around me.

"Goodnight," she whispers softly.

She closes the door softly behind her, leaving me stewing in the cocktail of emotions she just roused inside of me.

Chapter Twenty-One

STELLA

I FINGER MY DIAMOND teardrop earring, savoring the cool, smooth surface as Ryan guides me into his now-familiar family home.

The lounge, unlike my last visit, is bathed in light, the heavy drapes thrown open to reveal French windows and a garden teeming with guests. A sea of blond heads bobbing under the sun draws a nervous chuckle from me—I've never seen so many in one place. The Fairchilds. There are at least sixty of them, and all of their eyes will be on me.

Ryan's grip tightens at my waist as he murmurs. "Baby, stop fidgeting."

Baby. It sounds strange, but not in a bad way.

He turns to face me, takes both my hands in his and strokes his thumbs along my knuckles in a way that sends a shiver down my spine. I in turn, take a breath, square my shoulders, and shoot him the sultry, heavy-lidded look I copied from Bonnie.

"What the hell is that?" he asks, a playful smirk on his lips.

"What?" I ask, still anxiously glancing out into the garden.

"That look you just gave me."

I glance around again as if to remind him of where we are. It's the Fairchild welcome party, and we're supposed to be playing the besotted couple. "It's the 'I'm so in love with you' look. What else would it be?"

"It looks more like the 'I'm trying to take a difficult shit' look," he snickers.

Jackass. "You just ruined it. And I've been practicing that for days."

"And yet, you failed to nail it, sadly."

A ball of irritation tightens in my gut. "You wouldn't recognize 'being in love' if it stared you down, Ryan."

"That's where you're wrong," he retorts. "Here, let me teach you. Think of that gooey feeling you get when I give you something you want."

"Like when?"

"What do you mean 'like when'? Just imagine it, and give me the look. Now," he commands when I hesitate.

"I need a frame of reference; it's never happened before."

"Now you're just messing around."

"And you're bold to assume you've ever given me 'gooey feelings.'"

"So you'd rather lie than admit you like me, even a little bit?"

"This is hardly the time or place for you to fish for compliments. Ryan, we've got work to do." I cock my head in the direction of the garden.

"Oh, I know. The only way to get compliments from you is to fuck them out of you."

I flush, his words equally irritating and arousing. "Has anyone told you lately what an unmitigated ass you are?"

He shakes his head, grinning. "I love it when you use my own words against me."

"And now we're arguing where everyone can see." I huff.

"Just like an old married couple," he observes. "And you're less tense now. Nothing like an argument to get the adrenaline flowing."

"Oh, fantastic. Should we schedule our next public spat or do you prefer to keep everyone guessing?"

He only chuckles. "Don't look now, but Gina's on her way. She's caught up talking to someone, but she'll be here soon."

"Okay," I say, pulling myself together for the performance. Not that I need to, it's only Gina, but I can't help it.

"By the way, I really love your hair up like that. It's stunning. You're stunning." His eyes linger on my upswept hair with silvery tendrils framing my face.

I know he's not pretending because it's the same scorching look he was giving me just before he spanked me in his library. That feels like ages ago. "Thank you, Ryan."

And like that, my anger dissipates, replaced by a warm flutter in my stomach. Whoever gave him the playbook on me did their job well—he knows how to push my buttons.

He helps me take off my coat, then does a double-take, his eyes widening. "Christ," he breathes out.

"What?"

His gaze trails down the back of my dress, his hand following the curve of my waist and the nearly bare expanse of my back. "Stella, this dress is insane. You need a scarf."

I chose a silver-gray, form-fitting mermaid dress with a modest v-neck and delicate spaghetti straps. The back plunges to a deep vee at the waist. It's adorned with crisscrossing silk ribbons that tie into a bow at the center, giving it a daring, almost backless look.

"You don't like the dress?"

"It's classy, but too... distracting."

"For you, maybe," I smile.

He takes another glance at my back, probably at the tattoo beneath the straps, but remains silent.

"What?"

He simply shakes his head, a mysterious smile playing on his lips. "You may be right. I'm realizing I have such a thing for butterflies," he murmurs.

My cheeks flush with the memory of how his fingers traced the ink on my back the last time I was bent over his desk. "Do you now?" I reply softly.

Since that day in his office, we've defaulted back to texts and scrawly notes. Ryan has buried himself in work and allowed his crazy schedule to keep us apart. And I refuse to chase after him—I have my pride, after all.

I know the distance between us isn't about his workload; His shift in attitude has everything to do with that almost kiss.

"Finally! You're here. I've been on pins and needles, waiting for you Stella!" Gina's voice carries through the lounge. She engulfs me in a bear hug as soon as she reaches us. "I feared you might skip your own congratulatory party."

"No way," I reply, matching her enthusiasm.

Then, with all the subtlety of a town crier, she leans back and bellows toward the east wing, "Pop, Ryan and Stella have arrived!"

"Jesus, Gina, could you maybe turn up the volume? I'm not sure they heard you in New York," Ryan quips.

She gives a nonchalant shrug at her brother. "Dad wanted an update the second you two showed up, and, well, before you dive into the ocean." She cocks her head toward the garden. "He's in a meeting and wants you there."

"Why?" Ryan questions.

"I haven't the foggiest clue," she shrugs again, not meeting his eyes.

"Let me see what he wants." Ryan is already moving away. "Baby, give me a few minutes. I'll come and find you as soon as I'm done and then we'll join everyone in the garden, alright?"

"Sure," I say with a smile.

The way Ryan almost sprints for the curving stairs, especially after Gina's too-casual tone tells me there's more. It seems the siblings have their own secret language, not unlike the one Ryan and I are perfecting.

Before I can ask her any question, Gina links her arm to mine, her voice laced with excitement. "We have so much to catch up on, Stella. Let's go to my old room."

I follow Gina in the opposite direction thankful for the delay before having to face the crowd in the garden.

Gina eyes my earrings as we go up the stairs, beaming like a Cheshire cat. "By the way, those diamonds are an absolute crime... talk about a masterstroke."

"You don't think they're over the top?" Ryan laid the blue diamonds on my dressing table this morning with a note—**Do me a favor. Wear these tonight**

"Over the top?" Gina snorts softly, her approval unmistakable. "Ryan's playing four-dimensional chess with those. They're not just jewels; girl, they're armor."

I can't help but feel the undercurrent of tension. "In essence, you're saying I'm dressed for battle?"

"You've got that right," she affirms. "But here, you're no pawn. You're the queen, gunning for a checkmate."

"So if I'm queen, what does that make you then?"

She winks, mischief dancing in her eyes. "Oh, I'm only a chess square. Except that this square is rigged with a few hundred landmines."

We both laugh and some of my nerves settle. "I've missed you, Gina."

"Hear that, Ryan?" She yells, though Ryan is well out of earshot and on the other side of the huge mansion. To me she says, "He says I'll talk your ear off, but I think he just doesn't want to share you yet."

"Nonsense," I mutter, not daring to believe her. "Anyway, how've you been?"

"Busy juggling two jobs. I thought Ryan becoming the boss would mean less demand on me."

"And that hasn't been the case?" I prod. I know Gina is one of Ocean Gate's litigation counsels, but I was surprised to learn that she also offers free legal aid to those in need.

She shakes her head in exasperation, "Ryan's an even bigger pain. Don't get me wrong, he's great, but could stand to dial back the bossiness. You probably know him better."

"Oh, I know that Ryan," I confess, feeling my cheeks warm. "One minute you're under his spell, the next you're ready to throttle him."

Gina smirks, her gaze sharp. "You really do know him."

I clear my throat, suddenly self-conscious. As if seeing my discomfort, she lets me off the hook and changes topics. "So, you know what you're in for tonight, right?"

"I have a vague idea." *I think.*

"Think of it as a tactical formation. The front liners are all sweetness and strategy, softening you up for the Reubens, who are more like snarling guard dogs."

I didn't expect less, given what Ryan has already told me. "What's your advice then?"

"Be yourself. I know it sounds cliché, but honestly, you're amazing," Gina reassures me. Seeing my skeptical look, Gina presses, "Lucinda's my close friend you know."

"My assistant?" I clarify, again masking my surprise. I don't think Gina is a snob but I'm still slightly taken aback that a high-profile lawyer and billionaire heiress would have regular friends.

"Yep. We got into a bit of gossip the other day. Apparently, the folks at BodyLift were all really intimidated by you in the beginning."

"Really, why?"

"She says you have a unique way of doing things, and coupled with your straight-talking and no-nonsense attitude, most of them thought they wouldn't last. But they're now getting to know how sweet you really are."

"Cue the pudgy iguana phase," I mutter, allowing a full grin to spread across my face.

"What was that?".

"Just some inside joke," I wave it off, reluctant to steer the conversation to Ryan again.

"So, you see, I don't doubt for a second you'll have the Fairchilds wrapped around your finger in no time. You're a force," she says with a conviction that's infectious.

Overwhelmed by her faith in me, I envelop her in a grateful hug. "Thanks, Gina. That means the world."

She gets a glint in her eyes. "How about we seal that gratitude with a little glam session and some insider intel on the who's who tonight?"

"Sure. What do you have in mind?"

"Makeup," she gestures to her face. "Yours is flawless, by the way."

"Thank you, Gina."

We enter her room and head for the walk-in closet that is set up like a beauty salon. I see a slinky black dress showcased like a piece of art. It's gorgeous but unwearable for anyone over a size two.

Catching my look, Gina chuckles from her vanity seat. "Oh, that old thing? It's my muse. I'm on a mission to fit into it again—just need to downsize a little here," she motions to her breasts.

I eye her full D cups. "I wouldn't touch those. Heck I might even kill for them."

"No, you wouldn't. You're the poster girl for 'petite and chic'. Besides, your ass is giving the Kardashians a run for their money."

I cast a glance over my shoulder at the mirror, mirth bubbling up inside me. "You think this is something? You should see Brooke. She's got the monopoly on curves." Then, realizing what I just said, I let out a small gasp "Oopsie."

Gina feigns a wounded heart. "Yeah, go on, twist the knife, why don't you? Remind me how sexy Xavier's wife is."

I chortle "Gina, that was ages ago!"

She waves it off, but not without a dramatic eye roll. "Yes, but I was desperate to be friends with her. I opened my big mouth and told her that, at fourteen, I jumped into bed and wrapped myself around her nearly unconscious husband."

"Ouch." I wince. My ears bleed just to hear it.

"Precisely. And at the Bennett's dinner table no less. I'm sure they regretted inviting me."

Knowing Gina, they probably didn't invite her. Most likely she twisted Ryan's arm to take her along so she could meet Brooke.

"Real smooth Gina," I tease, "that story makes for such a lovely taboo sisterly bond, don't you think? No wonder Brooke adores you."

She narrows her eyes at me in a mock glare. "I think another free makeover just got added to your tab, just for that dig."

"I completely agree, if purely on compassionate grounds. For fuck's sake, Gina you crammed that sweaty foot so far inside your mouth I bet you can probably still taste it."

"Actually, you're right. I still fucking can," she deadpans, and we both dissolve into laughter.

"At least I didn't send you running in the other direction Stella. I've always wanted a sister, you know. What was yours like?" Her curiosity is kind, but it tugs at old wounds.

"Er..." I pause, letting memories of Viv filter through the good before the bad.

She backpedals with a wince when she sees my hesitation. "Oh, listen to me pry. It must be painful. Sorry."

"Um... actually, it's okay."

"Really?"

"Uh-huh." I grab the powder brush on the counter but find its bristles as stiff as straw. "Do you mind if I use my own?"

"Oh, yeah, go ahead, do what you want with me," she says, eyeing my own face with envy.

I turn the swivel chair away from the mirror. As I deftly apply her makeup, I share light-hearted chapters about Vivian while she tells me hilarious stories about growing up with Ryan and Xavier.

We're still laughing when out of the blue, she hits me with, "Do you love him? I know you guys were casually dating before he told you about the marriage clause, but do you see yourself loving him?"

I hedge, not quite ready for this level of interrogation. "Well, marrying him wasn't on my bingo card for this year to be sure, but I dropped everything to do it so..." I let that hang in the air.

"I ask because Ryan is in love with you, Stella," she states.

My heart thuds painfully. *Impossible.* "Um. I know he's very fond of–," I try to lie but I can't even get it past the lump in my throat.

"You don't get it. Ryan doesn't do love. He was never ever going to settle down, not after—"

"Baby?" Ryan's deep voice floats into Gina's bedroom, cutting through our conversation.

"In here!" I call out, a little too quickly. "Just finishing up." I spin the chair around to face the mirror. "Take a look."

Her reaction is genuine, pure delight. "Oh my God, this is incredible. Stella, you have magic hands!"

"Right?" I smile. "Although your skin is beautiful, it made my work easy."

Ryan pokes his head in. Satisfied he's safe to proceed, he enters the closet.

"Is it time to go down?" I ask him.

Gina's eyes widen as if suddenly remembering. "Oh crap, we didn't even get to the Fairchild dynasty gossip."

"Don't worry," I say, "Ryan actually gave me a pretty good run down on everyone."

"Did you at least get to gossip about Harriet?" Ryan questions, and I cut my gaze sharply to him. He's just blurted out what might have taken another few weeks to work myself up to telling Gina about.

"What?" Ryan sees my apprehension. "Baby, Gina's a kickass lawyer. She and her friends will throw some weight and legalese around, thump their chests and scare the shit out of those people. Before they know what's up, they'll be handing the kid over to you." He says more to rile Gina up than anything.

"Oh wow. Thank you, Ryan. We really love being compared to apes."

"That's a high compliment, and you know it. Anyway, if you're all set here, Gina," Ryan's tone becomes more teasing, and his eyes twinkle with a hint of an inside joke. "There's someone's here for you."

The resigned look on Gina's face says it all. "Don't tell me–"

"Yep, Chad is here." He nods at Gina in quick succession like a puppet, and I can't help laughing. To me, Ryan says, "I do believe trysts under the bushes are in store for tonight."

"Oh, shut up. I don't like the guy." Gina complains.

"Good, he's asking to see you. Go and show how much you don't like him."

"Seriously, he puts me to sleep."

"And isn't that's how it all begins?" Ryan returns.

Gina tries and fails to repress a chuckle. "You're so annoying, Ryan."

"Hmm, sounds like there's a lot to unpack there, girl." I probe, curious despite myself.

She rolls her eyes, a clear sign there's more to the story. "There's nothing to unpack. At all."

Ryan guffaws. "Just go. I have a wife to attend to."

She huffs, but I see her trying not to hurry. *Was that why she wanted help with her makeup?*

"Stella, how about I swing by BodyLift next week, and then we can see what we've got?" Gina's question is casual, but I know she means to talk about Harriet.

"Sounds good," I manage, still reeling from the sudden detour our conversation took.

Gina gives me a quick hug before stomping away, not even bothering to change from her furry flip-flops. It doesn't matter; she's dressed in a simple floor-length sheath dress that hugs her curves in the right places.

Once Gina's gone, I blurt, "What was that about, in the library with your dad?"

Ryan's demeanor shifts. The playful façade falls away, leaving something more somber behind. "Just a business partner who wanted to congratulate me in private."

Why would he request a private audience instead of attending the party like everyone else?

"Ship-building too?" I press. I know I'm being nosy, but somehow, I can't help feeling it's important.

"No, he imports coffee. I do the shipping."

I gasp as it dawns on me. "Oh my gosh. The Gold Medal guy! I would have wanted to meet him! I'm such a fan of his coffee."

A wan, almost sad smile crosses his lips then he abruptly changes the subject. "You seemed a little taken aback there. Didn't you want to tell Gina about Harriet?"

"No, it's alright, I'm glad it's out of the way really." I'm still thinking about his meeting with the coffee mogul, but I don't press my luck, considering how he got the last time we talked about the man.

"So, who is this Chad?" I ask instead, filling the silence.

"Gina's on-again, off-again boyfriend, and the only man who seems capable of surviving her for longer than a month."

"Really!" I smile, intrigued. "What does she do to them?"

"I don't want to know. But the guy must be a glutton for punishment. They've been at it for years, even I am now a believer in his staying power. If only she'd remain in the relationship long enough to let the guy propose."

"I can't wait to meet him then."

"That's highly unlikely. Not tonight"

"Why?"

"He won't get any further than the front door. She'll ditch him post-haste, post-tryst."

I laugh. "That sounds... dramatic."

He smirks, a fleeting gesture. "Drama's their middle name."

"And what about us?" I venture. "What's ours?"

"Smoke and mirrors. Ready baby?" His smile is sharp, yet there's an overwhelming chill beyond the usual. *Something upset him.*

I nod, letting the moment pass. Now's not the time for probing questions. The show must go on.

Chapter Twenty-Two

STELLA

Maybe it was all the prep work or the adrenaline, but walking into the Fairchild gardens felt like diving into a snake pit. As we step out through the French doors, applause fills the air.

Thanks to Seattle's love affair with rain, there's a huge marquee set up in the back just in case. But the weather is holding up, so most people are out enjoying the autumn sun.

Ryan gives the small of my waist a reassuring squeeze, his way of telling me to smile. Not that I need the reminder—I know how to handle a crowd. After all, dealing with high-maintenance models and demanding directors in photo shoots shouldn't be too different from mingling with the elite, right?

We're quickly swallowed up by a flurry of hugs and air kisses. Ryan introduces me to his uncles Russel, Reid, and Ralph, and their families. They're actually his cousins many times removed, but for simplicity he calls them his uncles and those who are nearer Ryan's age, he calls cousins.

Although I've not met most of these people before, I feel like I already know them. I notice Ryan does the introductions like he's ticking off some sort of official checklist, moving from the oldest to the youngest.

After the last cousin disappears into the crowd, Ryan hands me a champagne flute. I try not to preen under the look of pure admiration he levels at me.

"That wasn't too shabby now was it?" Ryan breathes. "You aced the introductions, remembering just enough to tickle even Uncle Ralph."

"You told me he's passionate about sailing."

"Yes, but I didn't tell you he has the disposition of a stone wall. And I certainly didn't mention that he once won the regatta. That was all you, baby."

"A stone wall!" I groan, "And there I was laying it on thick, practically flirting!"

"You simply reminded him of a time when he felt most alive. You made him blush with pride. It's something we've not seen him do in years."

Okay, I preen a little bit.

Just then Ryan's mom emerges from the marquee and approaches us, her face a picture of pride and excitement. "Stella, you are a vision!" She pulls me into a firm embrace, one I'm coming to love so much.

"So are you Diana, your dress is lovely," I return her effusive greeting. She's wearing a one-shouldered, rust satin dress with a sweetheart neckline.

"Thank you, darling," she beams.

"Mom, I see you've been busy," Ryan observes.

"Well, since you decided to arrive late, and your father is holed up in the library, I've had to be the entertainment. But now that you're here, you both can take over," she says with a playful nudge at Ryan.

She bends forward and kisses my cheek. Which seems odd since we've just been hugging. I realize why when she whispers, "Powerful earrings Stella. Great choice," she straightens and shoots me a conspiratorial wink before disappearing into the crowd.

Again, I wonder what is it about these earrings considering everyone else is draped in diamonds too.

After Diana leaves to mingle, I scan the crowd as bright smiles and soft murmurs of 'congratulations' pass by.

"Who are you looking for?" Ryan asks.

"I don't see any of the Reubens yet."

"Good eye," he drawls, nodding toward the marquee. "They'll be right there, trying to look busy but really just setting up a lair for you to walk into."

I smile, feeling emboldened by my success so far. "Shall we get it over with then? I hope they're worth the hype."

"The first thing they'll do is pull you away from me. Then they'll try to wring juicy info out of you which will end up getting fed into the elite gossip circles."

"Okay. I think you've armed me well enough," I say, fingering the earrings again.

His smile widens as he leads me toward the tent. The reassuring pressure of his hand on the small of my back both grounds me and sends tingles through me.

"The diamonds speak a language only Fairchilds understand," Ryan replies.

My curiosity spikes "What do they signify? Everyone else seems to know what they mean except me!"

He shrugs. "Let's just say, it's a two-hundred-year-old expression for 'don't fuck with me'."

Oh wow. Alright then. Now, I want to hear the whole thing. He sees the wheels turning in my head and smirks, "You'll get the long version later. Come on," he motions to the white marquee.

I hesitate just as we're about to go in. "What if I say the wrong thing in there?"

"You're my wife, Stella; you'll do fine." My heart races because, God help me, I really, really like the sound of that. Ryan continues, "Just remember, you don't have to say anything if you don't want to, and I won't be far away, okay?"

As soon as we enter, I spot Leanne. She's tall and regal in a long peach gown. Her dark hair in an elaborate updo. She's surrounded by a group of her friends, much like ladies-in-waiting. Reuben, Don, and a few others are deep in conversation. The older man seems to be muttering angrily, a deep scowl etched onto his lined face while Don responds with an insolent smile.

Don notices us first and breaks away from the group to greet us. He might be a cunning snake, but I can't fault his blond good looks and blue eyes, a Fairchild trademark.

"Look who it is, Stella! And the boss."

Ryan accepts his hug, patting him on the back a few times, "Don, my man. Looking great as always."

Don's smile is more a baring of teeth than a warm gesture. "Well, what can I say? Good genes, right? Stella would agree, wouldn't you?"

"Sure," I manage, though my own smile feels strained. Something about the guy just rubs me the wrong way. And his rudeness from our first meeting still grates on me.

Don addresses Ryan, "Well, I suppose congratulations are in order. It felt like a crazy game of musical chairs for a while there, but who knew you had an ace up your sleeve? Speaking of," he turns to me, his eyes like icy flints.

Ryan steps behind me and pulls me into him, wrapping both arms around my waist. "What can I say, Don? Can't reveal all my secrets."

Before anyone can say more, Reuben, a slightly older version of Don, reaches us. I'm surprised how much the Fairchilds look alike despite their fair coloring. Almost all of Ryan's cousins are blonde, too. I'm the furthest from a genetics expert, but I thought blonde was meant to be recessive?

After a congratulatory back thump for Ryan and an air kiss on my cheek, Reuben puts his arm around Ryan's shoulders. Leanne leaves her group and approaches us with a haughty grace that's hard to miss. As if on cue, Reuben mutters something about some blueprints he sent for Ryan to look over, stealthily dragging him away just as Leanne arrives.

"Don, stop hogging the lovely Stella. Let her get to know the rest of our family and my friends." I see the moment her gaze locks onto my earrings, her spine stiffens, and her smile falters.

"What exquisite earrings, my dear. I'm Leanne." She looks like she might cry. Or claw them off me.

"Thank you. Yours are pretty stunning, too." She's decked in glittering diamonds- a full set of earrings, necklace, and bracelet. Why would a pair of blue diamond earrings upset her so?

She hooks her arm through mine, ushering me toward her intimate circle. It's like deja vu, watching the social dynamics unfold. I'm quietly impressed by Ryan's knack for predicting their behavior. After the introductions, Leanne leaves her minions to pump me for information while she hangs back, observing me with hostile curiosity.

When the inevitable questions about my background and education come up, I take Ryan's advice and turn the conversation back on them. I thought it would be odd but it turns out so very effective.

Finally, having my fill of forced grins, I make my excuses and escape. I deserve another drink, a small celebration for acing yet another milestone without falling flat on my face.

Right on cue, as I step into the now dimly lit garden, Don appears with two flutes in hand, as if he'd planned this moment all along.

I accept the drink he offers with a grateful smile.

"So, Stella," he drawls, "you've, ah, changed quite a bit since I last saw you in the New York office."

I take a sip of the bubbly champagne, "How so?"

His gaze trails up my dress, lingering in a way that makes my skin crawl. "Well, you've somehow shifted from job seeker to star employee."

His words hit me like cold rain. I was more than ready for Leanne's unpleasantness, but Don has caught me off guard.

"Excuse me, I should find Gina."

I make to leave, but he smoothly steps in my way. "Gina's off with her date. Those two should be giving the Fairchilds another spectacle to swoop in on but Gina won't do it. Whatever made that girl so wary of commitment is a mystery to me, especially when the man is obviously the best she'll ever find."

My hand clenches into a fist, the urge to punch him as strong as it was the last time I actually followed through. It was back in high school, and some jerk made the mistake of calling Viv a crude name.

What an asshole. I grit my teeth, reminding myself that this isn't the place for bloodying people's noses, however much they deserve it. I take a calming breath instead and ignore him. He's no longer in my way now but I've changed my mind about leaving. I want to hear everything he has to say.

"So, what's the plan then Stella? Marry him, make him CEO, then divorce him in six months? I know he's found a loophole in the company policy, which explains your sudden employment."

"Excuse me?" I counter, channeling my inner shocked and loving wife.

"Hey, I'm on your side, believe it or not. You do know you'll walk away with nothing if you don't give him a brat right? And from the look of things," he glances at my flat belly, "it ain't happening before your time is up."

No doubt seeing the confused look on my face, he presses on. "Oh, he didn't tell you that, did he? Bet he promised you a lot of money to put your life on hold. How much? Two million? Five?"

Twenty, you rotten cheapskate.

"Don," I say acidly, "I find it incredibly insulting, not to mention presumptuous of you to suggest that my husband would pay me to marry him."

He chuckles. "I love the act; it's brilliant. You've even managed to get the great Leanne to back off with those diamonds. But drop the pretense and listen. You might actually learn something."

His blunt words render me speechless.

"Good," he says, satisfied he has my full attention. "Now listen, whatever he promised you is tied up in company funds, which can only be released if you give him a child within wedlock. He, on the other hand, will have no further use for you in a few months and will divorce you swiftly."

"And why are you telling me this? Are you that bitter he edged you out in the race for CEO?"

"Hell, yes I'm bitter. Ryan has always been one for cheap tricks. Anyone can pick up a woman off the street and put a ring on her finger."

I inhale sharply, the rebellious part of me itching to put this privileged brat in his place. But I hold back for Ryan's sake. And for Gina, Diana, and Richard. I'm about to walk away, but I can't resist throwing in a biting remark. "Yes, but you seem to lack the skills to actually keep the ring on a woman's finger. Remind me, did Carmen leave you for a real man, or did you offer her a pair of concrete boots?"

Don steps back, clearly taken aback. "Whoa, he's picked one with claws."

I mask my sneer with a sweet smile. "I'll retract them if they frighten you, but only if you sheathe your fangs, Don."

He tones down his bitterness but still hits back. "For someone who's just passing through, you're making yourself comfortable. In any case, enjoy your brief moment of fame, luxury, and my house before you're sent back to where you belong."

His smile widens, his first genuine smile of the evening, when he sees my brows knit in confusion. "Oh, you didn't know? The house you live in is mine. My deck, my pool, my lake, my views. Hell, you're probably fucking in my bed because the wretch didn't bother to change the furniture."

"Yeah, right," I scoff, refusing to engage with his nonsense. The man's clearly lost it.

Just then, I feel a strong arm slide around my waist. Ryan. God I've never missed his solid presence like I have in the last half hour. I grab onto that arm like a lifeline. He's right. There are sharks in this ocean.

"You two seem to be getting along like a house on fire." I hear the smile in Ryan's voice as he pulls me even closer. "Can I have my wife back now?"

"You sure can," I reply, sick of being civil. I turn into Ryan's embrace thus dismissing Don.

An awkward silence falls over us, and though I don't see it, I sense the two men exchanging unspoken words through their glares. I just take deep breaths, letting Ryan's warmth and scent envelop me. Eventually, Don walks away.

"He upset you," Ryan observes. "From across the garden, I could tell you were a second away from tackling him to the ground."

I laugh. "You're not wrong there."

"What did he say to you?"

"Just the usual intimidation tactics. But I'll tell you this, Ryan, that man despises you."

Ryan lets out a deep sigh. "I prefer to call it profound envy; otherwise, it just gets depressing."

"How so?"

"He's my COO and first cousin. I can't exactly get rid of him."

"If I were you, I'm sure I'd find a way."

His laughter vibrates against my cheek. "Don takes rivalry to a whole new level. He can be a real nightmare if you're in his way, but aside from that, he's a sharp businessman."

I'm surprised that Ryan is actually defending him. "You almost sound like you admire the guy?"

"He's family," he shrugs, a hint of resignation in his voice. "And it's my responsibility to look out for him. To be able to do that, I have to see the good in him, even if it means squinting through an electron microscope."

I realize Ryan now carries the burden of being the head of this family. And once more, I'm proud of myself for maintaining my composure with Don.

"Did he try to say something to you?" Ryan asks again.

"He's full of it, but really, he was more interested in undermining you."

"Typical."

"Gosh, Ryan, staying classy can be so dull you know. How do you manage it?"

He gives me a look, then chuckles. "Isn't that what true friends and siblings are for? Loving and sparring."

I sigh, "Nah. My friends and I keep it classy and respectful. Anyway, Don knows about the loophole."

"Of course, he does."

"You knew! Why didn't you give me a heads-up?"

"He won't say anything so don't worry. He's too busy looking for a way out of his own marital maze."

"But I'm curious, after four years and with billions at his disposal, how is it that he still hasn't found Carmen?"

He shrugs, a twinkle appearing in his eyes. "Maybe she doesn't want to be found."

"Wow. The plot thickens."

His silence is confirmation that he knows more about Carmen Fairchild's disappearance than he's letting on.

"Ryan?" I prod.

"What, you think I'm hiding treasure here, Stella?" His tone is defensive, but his eyes are twinkling with...something.

"Holy shit, Ryan, you know where she is, don't you?"

He gives me nothing but a silent stare in response.

"Oh, I get it. This is one of those 'say nothing' situations. I wonder, do you try it on Xavier and your other friends too?"

"No, they'd just think it's some weird shit. But you're a Fairchild, you understand."

His words warm me, but I continue to press. "So, are you ever going to tell him?"

"And why the hell would I do that?"

"But if she remains missing for another couple of years, she would be ruled as dead, and then he's free to re-marry."

"Yes, but you do know–" Ryan begins.

I interject, "Oh shit! Unless there's a credible witness or a body, company policy doesn't accept that the spouse is dead."

So unless Don Fairchild finds his wife, alive or dead, he can't get back what he lost.

"Why Mrs. Fairchild, you never cease to impress me with your knowledge of these ancient policies."

I wave off his teasing. "Ryan, I think you may just be the great white among those sharks."

"Nah, that title belongs to Leanne."

"No, it's you. You're the apex predator that no one sees coming."

He gives me a look that's half admonishment, half amusement. "Let's not overdramatize. Come here," he says, pulling me into a hug.

As if on cue, and perhaps because the musicians see us swaying together as we speak, a string quartet begins playing in the background.

"By the way, speaking of unforeseen disasters, if you're ever in trouble and I'm not there, Alex Price is your man. I'll send you his details."

My eyebrows furrow, I'm not sure who Alex is. "The guy who had the big wedding in Cancun? He has a liquor company, doesn't he?

Ryan laughs. "Yes, but he's also very good at making problems...and people disappear."

My eyes widen when I get his meaning. "Carmen? He arranged it didn't he?"

He only inclines his head, again not saying anything more. But he doesn't have to. I already know. And plan how to drag every juicy detail out of him.

I lose track of time as we stand there, my arms around his neck and his face buried in the crook of my neck. We continue talking and laughing, unaware—or perhaps indifferent—to the curious glances thrown our way by the entire Fairchild clan.

Chapter Twenty-Three

STELLA

WHEN I REACH THE breakfast counter the next morning, I find Ryan's note on top of a folded newspaper. Beside it lies a single white rose.

There's something charming about his preference for handwritten notes over texts. I love the challenge of his lazy handwriting; it makes decoding his messages feel like a treasure hunt. I inhale the scent of the rose and squint at his note.

> *Morning, Stella. I wasn't sure of your news preference, but I thought we'd kick it old-school. Bottom line: you were amazing last night.*

I bite my lip. *Last night.* If I didn't know better, I'd think we had sex. Ignoring the flutter in my stomach, I pick up the Seattle Post and see Ryan and me featured on the front page.

The article reads:

Yesterday's inaugural party wasn't just a celebration of the new CEO of Ocean Gate Enterprises, but a testament to the deep love between him and his wife. The event celebrated the Fairchild tradition of intertwining significant wealth with robust family values. As the couple embark on their new roles, the Seattle community anticipates their continued success, and a marriage that lasts, epitomizing the Fairchild legacy's true spirit.

Hmm, not bad. Sounds like we fulfilled the assignment then. Next up is dissolution in a few months. A pang of sadness strikes, but I quickly dismiss it. Ryan isn't made for marriage. A glance around the empty penthouse at 7 a.m. is reminder enough. And marriage isn't in my game plan either.

Yet, the poached eggs and hashbrowns waiting in the oven suggest a different story. Ryan insists on making breakfast for two, claiming he couldn't possibly prepare his without doing mine as well.

Approaching the fridge, I spot another note scrawled in his unmistakable handwriting.

Why settle for OJ when you can have coffee?

With a squeal of delight, I dash to the cupboards, somehow already knowing I'd find my Gold Medal brand waiting for me.

Several boxes of coffee beans greet me, along with a sleek new coffeemaker on the black marble countertop.

My God, this man. A warmth spreads through me, ending in a slow smile.

I feel the goofy expression lingering on my face even as I enjoy my breakfast, each sip of the aromatic coffee followed by a contented sigh.

I just hope like hell I won't end up in the famous shrink's chair when this is all over.

—⊰✦⊱—

I've just finished getting ready for work when my phone buzzes on the dresser. It's Bonnie.

"Hey babes," I greet.

"I knew you'd fall for him!" Bonnie yells into the phone

"Calm your horses down. First off you didn't 'know' anything of the sort. And what the hell are you even talking about?"

"What happens in Seattle doesn't stay in Seattle, babes. It gets splashed all over New York."

"Wait, what? You saw the Seattle Post article?"

"Yep, but it's not just there. It made the Metro Tribune too. And don't get me started on the online news blogs!"

"How? You don't read the news, and you're too slammed for internet deep dives. Let me guess, Ethan tipped you off, right?"

"Nope. Sadly, Ethan wouldn't feed me a drop of gossip if I were dying of thirst. I have to resort to my own sleuth services to keep myself going there."

I laugh. Ryan's the total opposite. He'd compile information in a binder and insist I read it.

Although he won't look at me for more than five seconds. And hasn't made an attempt to touch me since that day in the library.

And I'm still determined to give him space since that unwanted almost-kiss.

"So. How did you know about the party?"

"'Cause I have alerts set on all of my friends. Your names come up online, and I get notified. Pretty cool huh?"

"Really?"

"Yes, you should try it too. Anyway, back to you, are the papers correct? Is what they saw real?"

"Not even close. They saw exactly what we wanted them to see."

I can hear the disappointment in Bonnie's sigh. "Damn. Okay, but you're happy, right?"

"Well," I pause, thinking it over. "I wouldn't say I'm unhappy. Could be happier, sure, but living with him isn't as bad as Brooke made it out to be. Maybe you could pass that along; she might believe it coming from you."

Brooke has been distant since I moved to Seattle, but I know Ryan and Xavier catch up a few times a week.

"She's worried about you. She feels guilty for pushing you into this. Something about if she'd been a better friend, you might have told her about Harriet. Then you wouldn't need to broker yourself into marriage."

"Oh God. Now I feel guilty that she feels guilty. For fuck's sake she didn't push me into anything. Bonnie, I literally used your urine to trap the guy into marrying me."

"Whoa, don't drag me into this, perv. You asked me to pee on a stick on my wedding day; how was I to guess you were plotting something? Speaking of, how's that going? Hit up any prenatal classes yet, you little felon? Got yourself a fake baby bump yet?" Her laughter rings through the phone.

"That? It sort of imploded last week."

"Oh shit, how did he take it?"

I feel a blush creeping up my cheeks as I recall that evening—the last time we were together. "Um,—" I hesitate, fidgeting with the buttons on my blouse. "He took it... okay, I guess."

"That sounds suspiciously vague. Care to expand on that?"

"Actually, I've got to run. I'm late for work." I gather my phone and purse, hurrying out of my room.

Bonnie hoots out a laugh. "I'm seriously loving you right now, Stella."

"I don't know what you mean."

"Oh, you know. And you know that I know that you know." Bonnie sounds like a demented robot.

"What the hell are you talking about?"

"Okay. I'll clue you in. Remember when you promised that Ethan was going to... let's say, 'discipline' me when I returned from Vancouver?"

"I'm hanging up on you now."

Bonnie's laughter fills the air, an annoyingly loud cackle for someone so petite.

"Bye, Bonnie."

"Wait, hold on! You can't blame me for putting two and two together. Ryan seems like the type to have a... special room. And then you and your big mouth and even bigger butt have been living under his roof for months. It's bound to happen."

I stop short as the thought suddenly strikes me.

Actually, I wouldn't know if he's got a room of that sort. I've never once seen his bedroom suite.

She exhales loudly, resigning herself to my silence. "Fine, keep your secrets. I've got to run, too. But let's video call later. I need to show you this line on my belly. I've tried all sorts of scrubs, but I can't seem to get rid of it. It's driving me mad."

"Ugh," I shake my head, finding her lack of basic knowledge endearing. "It's normal." Bonnie is one of the smartest people I know, but sometimes she has no idea of the simplest things.

"You don't even know what I'm on about, and no, it's not normal. Brooke or Sabrina didn't have it. I've not shown anyone yet, except Ethan, of course, and he thinks it's sexy; otherwise, he doesn't care."

"Bonnie, you've got a darker skin tone than Brooke and Sabrina," I explain patiently. "You'll get linea nigra."

"That's a super convenient diagnosis, smartass."

"Fine, we'll check it out later—I really have to go now."

"Love ya."

After we hang up, I pause to really look at the penthouse in a way I never have in all the time I've been living here. It's large, with sleek, modern furnishings. The living room is surrounded by wall-to-ceiling windows. It has everything you'd expect in a luxury penthouse.

Beyond that, I notice the odd things. The house is bare. Sterile. There's a stark lack of personal effects, which is so unlike Ryan's personality. He presents himself as warm and outgoing on the outside. I would have thought his living area would reflect his outward warmth—full of life and color, leaving the coldness to his office and bedroom.

The exact reverse might be happening here.

Ryan's office is a beautiful place, a treasure trove bursting with books of every genre, surrounded by beige leather furniture and dark, polished wood. The shelves are crammed with awards and knick knacks from way back in college days.

Ryan is a pack rat, a collector at heart. He holds onto memories and achievements. If this is the vibe of his office, I can't help but wonder about his bedroom. What would I find behind those doors?

He's not even living up to his playboy persona. Instead, he shows such sexual restraint unlike anything I've ever known a man to possess.

Why have I never realized that I've been living with a shell, and the real Ryan keeps himself locked away?

Suddenly I have the urge to run into his bedroom.

Glancing at the large digital clock on the sleek console across the room, reality pulls me back. I have a meeting with a high-profile client at Whirlpool in forty minutes. Fred, my chauffeur, has a knack for weaving through Seattle's traffic, but even he can't work miracles if I wait too long.

Today's not the day to explore. I'll have to find another opportunity to nose around. Specifically, inside that bedroom, which seems to be marked 'off-limits' in bold, invisible ink.

Chapter Twenty-Four

RYAN

"I'll be in New York today," I tell Xavier as I navigate through Seattle's morning traffic.

"Really! Are you sure?" His voice comes through the car speaker, tinged with surprise. "It's... today."

I shake my head, even though he can't see me. "And?"

"Nothing. I just thought that today, of all days, you'd be in Seattle."

"Stella has a meeting with Harriet's caseworker. I'm coming with her." Stella's lawyer— one of Gina's contacts in New York arranged a last minute meeting with the adoption agency. Stella immediately reached out to the DuPonts to arrange a visit with Harriet.

Xavier goes suspiciously quiet.

"If your mouth is open, man, I suggest you close it and help me gather everyone tonight."

"Does that mean you'll be Harriet's adoptive father then?"

I shrug. "That's Stella's decision, but considering the circumstances, yeah it's possible."

"Ryan. Have you thought about the fact that you'll be divorcing her? In six short months you'll be making her a single mother of two."

I haven't told Xavier that Stella isn't pregnant. "Are you then suggesting I turn her down if she needs me to be Harriet's adoptive father, genius?"

Xavier sighs, "I just don't want her hurt, man. She was single, and then all of a sudden, you're all over her."

"She's my wife, you idiot. Of course, I'm all over her." Why does everyone think I'm out to hurt Stella? "Just gather everyone and let me worry about my marriage." I pause for a beat, then add, "*And children,*" just to get under his skin a bit more.

"Fine, dumbass." Xavier snaps. "I'll get everyone and their dog."

"Stella will definitely want to see Brooke. Things have been off between them since our wedding."

"I know. They need to hash out things." Xavier agrees.

After giving him the rundown of tonight's plans, I hang up and park the car, heading upstairs. I had hoped to work a few hours this morning before our flight to New York. I left the house at dawn, asking Stella to meet me on the tarmac. But, all I managed to do was what feels like a hundred thousand phone calls trying to make sure everything goes smoothly for tonight.

I sent Stella a text about half an hour ago telling her I would swing by and pick her up myself.

My phone buzzes again, this time with a notification from McGrath. I glance at it as I approach the elevators.

> **Just checking we're on track to begin the process of separation at the four-month mark.**

Fucking hell. The man doesn't miss a beat. How are we at almost four months already? I mentally count. Yep, she spent the first four or five weeks of our marriage in New York before moving in with me.

Stella and I haven't even talked about whether she'd like to return to New York or stay in Seattle. She's doing extremely well with her businesses here, but her friends are in New York, not to mention Harriet.

I have an inkling of what she would choose to do and it leaves a bitter taste in my mouth.

Resolved to delay things a bit, I start to craft a response, but another call comes in. It's from Rob, my New York fleet manager. "Fairchild," I give my standard greeting for official calls, something Stella finds amusing since there are so many Fairchilds.

"Boss, I missed your call earlier."

"I need the new twin hull ready to hit the water tonight," I say as I step into the elevator heading up to the penthouse.

"Sure thing, boss," Mike responds. "The hundred-footer?"

"Yeah, and make sure she's looking sharp. I'll be in New York tonight. Once she's ready, talk to Xavier."

"Cool. Engines and system checks too?"

As the elevator doors open into the penthouse, I instantly lower my voice. I half-expect to see Stella at the breakfast counter, iPad in hand, sipping her second cup of coffee. But she's not there.

"Yes, get those done, too. If you run into any issues and can't reach me, just call Xavier."

"Will do, boss."

I hang up and pause. Stella's luggage and handbag are neatly placed in the corner. Good, she's packed. She's probably still getting ready. Glancing at my watch, I note it's only 7 a.m. We have an hour before we have to leave, which is reassuring.

Deciding to give her more time, I head to my office while finishing off my text to McGrath. To my surprise, I find the library door wide open.

"Stella?" I call out and step inside. The room is empty, save for the lingering scent of her peach and jasmine perfume.

She's been here recently.

My gaze sweeps the room. The desktop monitor is off, and it feels cold to the touch, indicating it hasn't been used. Everything is in its place, undisturbed. Perhaps she was looking for a book?

I stroll towards the towering bookshelves. Nothing looks out of place, although there are that many books I probably wouldn't know if she took one. I move over to the second column of shelves, which houses awards, ship models, and micro Lego action figures.

A memory flashes—her last visit here, her intrigue with the Greenwich Society trophy. Oddly, it's now resting a couple of shelves lower than I remember from yesterday. She must have come back for another look. I reach out and finger the pointed end of the glass trophy, wondering about her fascination with the Greenwich Society.

Dismissing my curiosity with a shrug, I exit the library and move toward her room. I knock lightly.

No answer.

"Stella? We should be heading out soon." Silence greets me again.

I turn away and decide to give her a few more minutes while I get changed. But, a sound stops me. It's the soft click of a door closing from the direction of my suite.

What the hell? Is she in my bedroom?

A wave of unexplained anger washes over me as I stride towards the room. I burst through the door of my spacious master suite and sure enough, I find her there. She's half-dressed—barefoot, with the shirt she's thrown over her short black skirt unbuttoned and her black lacy bra peeking out temptingly.

She stands at the foot of my bed, absorbed in the oil painting above the headboard, but jumps when I burst in.

The first thing that strikes me is how stunning she looks against the backdrop of the Seattle cityscape visible through the glass wall on the far side of the room.

"What are you doing in here, Stella?"

"I—" Guilt colors her face. "Ryan...you're back home! I thought you'd be— that is, I was to meet you..."

I close the distance between us. "What the fuck are you doing in here?"

"Um—" She fidgets, picking at her fingernails. "I was just looking for, um..."

"What were you looking for?" I growl.

"I thought..." She glances around, her gestures now more frantic. "I mean, the door was open, and..."

I feel my patience fraying. "If you want something, you ask. You don't just snoop around like—" My hands clench as I struggle to maintain control.

"I'm sorry—" And unbelievably, her gaze returns to the painting as if drawn by an invisible magnet. "It's... the painting—"

"Get out!" I bark, louder than intended. She flinches, skirts around me, and then darts out, her quick steps silent on the warm marble. I instantly regret my harshness. Yet, the anxiety over the fact that she's invaded this space overwhelms me.

After she leaves, I look around my room. My safe place. Where I am under no compulsion to make everywhere clean and spotless.

Now I'd never be able to not picture her in here, touching my things, probing. I look down at the unmade bed and the scattered knickknacks on the shelving. The adjoining study is overflowing with personal designs for yachts and the model of the one I just built from scratch. For her.

She didn't break in; you left the door open.

I silence that voice of reason with a burning question.

Isn't it enough that she dissects me with her eyes, her words. Her touch. Her need for me? What did she want to know so bad that she couldn't just ask?

The one thing you haven't given her: You.

The thought terrifies me yet fills me with hope. But hope is a feeling I don't have the luxury to indulge in.

I go to the foot of the bed where Stella stood just now and stare at the painting that embodies my grief and pain. Beyond showcasing exceptional talent, I never thought it meant more. But, the raw emotion on Stella's face just now tells me I may have been wrong all along.

Suddenly, I'm seized by an overwhelming urge to pull her back, to ask her what was going through her mind at the moment she was looking at it.

To wrap my arms around her and tell her it's okay. To feel her body respond to my touch. It's been way too long since I held her.

Before I fully grasp my own intentions, I find myself heading towards her room. I'm about to knock when a soft sound halts me—sniffling.

Damn. She's crying.

I'm an absolute jerk.

Retreating, I spend the next half-hour in my office, wrestling with my thoughts. By the time I muster the courage to return, it feels too late to reconsider our departure plans. New York is five hours away, and three hours ahead of Seattle. If we wait any longer, we'll be late for our meeting with Anita Brodkin.

I approach her door again and knock.

"Yes?" comes her steady reply, stronger than I anticipate.

"We should head to the airport soon."

"I know. I'll meet you there. Fred will take me."

She's opting for a separate ride instead of joining me, a choice I would typically challenge. This time, however, I decide to respect her wish for space.

Chapter Twenty-Five

STELLA

"Thank you, Fred," I say, flashing my driver a grateful smile. I leave my Bentley and stride across the tarmac to the waiting aircraft, crushing the stress ball in my hand repeatedly.

Ignoring the surprised look on the ramp agent's face, I start mounting the steps. I'm sure he wasn't expecting me to show up alone.

"Mr. Fairchild—" he begins.

"Is on his way," I interrupt, throwing the comment behind me as I continue up the steps.

The pilot and crew don't look surprised, so I know they have already been updated about Ryan and me arriving separately.

I was not going to get into the same car with him after his epic meltdown. From his reaction, you'd think I unearthed the corpse he was hiding in there.

I heave a sigh of relief when I see how spacious the aircraft interior is. We're taking the bigger jet. All the better to avoid speaking to the man. I find the spot furthest from the door, all the way in the back, and take one of the large seats.

What was it about his room that was so off-limits?

So, his room is a tad messy, big deal. He should see mine.

Although that in itself is telling, considering he keeps the rest of his home freakishly clean and organized.

And he must have a thing for grey tops with inscriptions about Ivy League colleges. Maybe the man's dream was to attend one? Why didn't he?

And what the hell was that old painting?

It was a hauntingly beautiful one. An oil painting of Ryan's muscled back with a woman hugging him from the front. Except that his torso completely blocked out the woman, so only the woman's pale, tattooed delicate hands on his back were visible.

It represented both tender intimacy and painful detachment. Instead of hugging the woman back or even looking at her, Ryan's arms hung free at his sides while he looked back over his shoulder.

I feel the stupid tears threatening to return. How many women have desperately clung to him not realizing he can't be held down? Am I a fool for believing that he has more to give?

Ryan chooses that moment to arrive.

"Welcome, Mr. Fairchild," the crew greets while my knuckles whiten against the squishy stress ball.

I look through the windows, fighting back tears as he slowly makes his way down the cabin. Thankfully, he takes one of the seats furthest from me, right across the cabin, and doesn't say anything to me.

When the plane takes off and there's nothing more to see outside, I sit back stiffly. I smooth the prim black skirt I'd chosen to make a good impression on Anita Brodkin. Then I fish out a style magazine I brought along for the sole purpose of ignoring Ryan and try to lose myself in it.

Usually, Ryan and I would chat, laugh, and argue nonstop, instead an awkward silence stretches in the cabin. When it becomes too oppressive, I hazard a look in his direction and see him sprawled on his seat, watching me with an unreadable expression.

I quickly return my attention to my magazine, but knowing he's staring at me from across the cabin is more than a little unnerving.

"Mr. Fairchild... Mrs. Fairchild," a crew member comes in with a trolley, and I almost sigh in relief. "What would you like to drink?"

"Baby?"

I grit my teeth against his melting tenderness. "Nothing, thanks."

"Nothing for me too," Ryan declines.

She's about to leave when Ryan stops her. "Annalise? Tell the crew under no circumstances should we be disturbed, alright?"

"Understood, Mr. Fairchild." She scurries off.

Ryan stands and slowly stalks toward me until his shadow falls over my magazine.

I look up.

"Did the DuPonts finally confirm for how long you'd be able to see Harriet today?"

My lips twitch as I desperately try to kill the smile threatening to escape.

The sneaky man knows the one way to ensure I won't be able to ignore him is to mention the fact that I'm seeing Harriet today. I'd messaged Faith DuPont as soon as we knew we'd be going to New York today.

"Yes, they said from three till bath time," I hesitate but can't resist adding. "Which is a long time compared to usual. I might be able to take her somewhere besides the park near the house."

"Of course, you'll have a car and a driver at your disposal when we get to New York, so it won't be a problem."

"Thanks." My face settles back into a cool mask. I'm otherwise not ready to speak to him just yet.

"When did you last get to visit her?"

He's really going for it, isn't he?

I watch as he takes the seat directly opposite mine. Seriously? "Ryan?"

"I know you didn't have time to buy anything with the unplanned visit, but I thought you might want to get her a few things. What do you think she'd like?"

"Ryan?"

"Yes?"

"What are you doing?"

"Is it not obvious? I'm trying to apologize to you."

"For what?" I scoff. "Shouldn't I be the one apologizing for trespassing and desecrating your 'inner sanctum'?" I finish in air quotes.

He raises a single eyebrow. "Alright." He leans back. "Go on then, apologize."

"Are you kidding me?" I almost yell. "You roared at me like a freaking monster because I went into an unlocked room, and you expect me to say sorry?"

"You were in my bedroom!"

"I went into an unlocked room in my house! I live there, Ryan. I appreciate you may have many other homes, but that place is the only home I have on earth right now, and you made me feel like an unwanted guest."

"You're right. Like I said, I'm trying—"

"To apologize, but all you've done is talk," I wave my hand in a gesture of impatience. "I haven't actually seen you do it yet."

A muscle jerks in his jaw, and he takes a breath, releasing it slowly.

"I agree, I was unfair. I may have overreacted."

Some of the tension leaves my spine, and I cross my legs. "Go on."

He leans forward and palms my knee, rubbing circles around it.

"I'm sorry," he rumbles.

My lids flutter shut. God, I love the sound of that. His hands on me make it even better.

He reaches down and takes off one of my shoes, then lifts my foot onto his abs. *Ah, a foot rub too, yes please.*

I guess it wouldn't hurt to take some ownership of my actions, too.

"I, uh, I probably shouldn't have been snooping. I could have asked you instead why you're so secretive about your room."

He nods, making a noncommittal sound, then moves my knee to the side. Blunt fingers stroke upward under my skirt, making me catch my breath as my foot involuntarily flexes against his abs.

"I should have handled my shock better." He reaches the apex of my thighs, hooks his fingers into my panties, and moves the crotch aside. He stares at me, the look in his eyes like that of a starving man.

I start to pant.

He licks his lips. "I'm sorry I made you cry."

Suddenly he takes my foot off his stomach and falls to his knees in front of me.

I gasp, electricity zapping through me. Surely he's not about to go down on me? The man who refuses to kiss?

"Ryan are you doing what I think you're–"

He drags my butt to the edge of the seat and then spreads me open like a meal.

Oh shit. He is.

My hesitation disappears in a cloud of lust. I want his mouth on me so bad I can taste it.

"Fuck Stella, you're gorgeous," he stares for a full minute as I get wetter under his intense gaze. My heart is beating out of my chest and I'm dying with anticipation.

"Keep apologizing," I whine.

His burning gaze snaps to mine,

"Please?" I add.

He bends and plants an open-mouthed kiss right at the crease of my thigh, and I moan.

"You promise not to make a sound?"

I shake my head in assent before realizing I should be nodding it, then I try doing just that, thinking I must look like a crazy puppet, but the moment he puts his mouth on me, my mind goes blank with pleasure.

I grab the arm rest, my nails digging reflexively into it and bite my lip hard to keep from making any noise. But when his tongue drags against my folds I can't help moaning.

"Ryan. Oh, God." His name slips out of my mouth in a desperate whispered plea to end the torture.

He doesn't. He eats me like I'm his last meal, spearing his tongue repeatedly into my quivering depths, then sliding it through my folds and ending at my clit, which he sucks on.

I lose my mind and start to cry out. There's no fucking way every single person on this flight will not know what's happening right now. The thought further spikes up my arousal, sending heated tingles racing across my skin.

He suddenly lifts his hand to my face, inserting two of his fingers into my mouth and I gratefully suck on them, muffling my cries. Still, his mouth continues to drive me to madness.

His golden head between my legs, his dark bronze lashes fanning over his flushed cheekbones, and the rapid strokes of his wicked tongue against my clit becomes too much to contain. Even before he slides his fingers from my mouth and inserts them into my core, going straight for my g-spot, I'm already cresting the wave of orgasm.

"Oh fuck, Ry!"

It's blinding hot, a sharp twisting pulse of pure pleasure engulfing my pelvis and radiating up my spine and down into my cramping toes. I slam my hand against my mouth to stifle the scream threatening to escape, but it's too intense. I give up trying and just let go. My back bows as my hips shamelessly rock against his mouth, chasing my orgasm until I'm limp and breathless.

He tears his mouth away from me and kisses a sensitive spot high on my thigh, then he digs his teeth into the soft flesh, gently nipping. And unbelievably, I clamp down hard on his fingers.

"Hmm. Interesting." He does it again, and the same thing happens, accompanied this time by a long moan from me.

Sweet Jesus, what the hell was that biting thing?

"Oh, we are going to have so much fun with this little quirk, baby." I see the lower half of his face glistening with my juices. He still looks just as hungry as he did before he went down on me, although that might just be me projecting.

Without thinking I blurt. "I thought you didn't kiss?"

He shrugs. "I don't. That wasn't a kiss. That was just me saying I'm sorry for being a jerk."

I nod as if it makes perfect sense.

He stands, pulls out a handkerchief from his pocket, and wipes his face. Then he bends over me and proceeds to blow my mind again.

Bracing one arm by the headrest beside my head and staring deep into my eyes, he slowly wipes me up.

It's achingly sweet and so very intimate. And the fact that it's Ryan who doesn't make eye contact for more than a few seconds at a time makes it feel like he's giving me something precious.

I'm unable to look away, I can't even muster a snarky comment. Instead, I let myself drown in him.

It's the little things he does without thinking. The way he looks out for me. The chicken scrawly notes. The flowers. The opening of car doors even when he's boiling mad.

Something shifts in my chest. Something that puts me on this man's side. Behind him, rooting for him in spite of his flaws.

When I'm dry, he repositions my panties and then smooths down my skirt. I see the enormous bulge in his pants before he lowers himself into the seat opposite.

"Don't you want me to... reciprocate?" I gesture at his crotch.

"Later, if you want to. This was for you. I told you I wanted to apologize."

Well then. I smile, "Apology fucking accepted."

He chuckles, and again I see he's not quick to look away.

Chapter Twenty-Six

RYAN

STELLA SITS NEXT TO me, her posture stiff as she picks at a manicured nail. I don't recall ever seeing her this anxious. Gently, I cover both her hands with one of mine, halting her fidgeting.

"Mr. and Mrs. Fairchild," starts Anita Brodkin, Harriet's kind-faced caseworker. "Ms. Finch has briefed me about your plans, and the paperwork looks good so far. Harriet has been with the DuPont family for nearly a year now and has settled in quite well. We typically avoid disrupting this settling-in phase. However," she looks at me, a small, respectful smile on her lips, "your wife has been a consistent presence in her life, and Harriet is very attached to her auntie. You'd undoubtedly offer her stability and a loving home. This is a positive development, one that Stella didn't hint at."

I slip an arm around Stella. "Yes, we've always been close friends. We just didn't realize how in love we were until recently. And with a baby on the way, we've decided now's the best time to become a real family—with Harriet and her soon-to-be baby sister."

Stella's shocked gaze meets mine, and I respond with a re-assuring smile and a wink. "It's okay to share the news with Harriet's caseworker," I assure her in a low voice, then look back to Anita. "We're still keeping it under wraps for now. Large family and all."

"Of course, I completely understand," Anita gushes, her en-thusiasm palpable. "Congratulations to both of you. We will need to arrange an updated home study, but I'm pleased to say we will be considering these very strong points to move the adoption forward for you."

Stella beams, her joy infectious. "Thank you!"

"Thank you for providing a home for Harriet." Anita smiles.

I guide a somewhat dazed and grinning Stella out of the office and into the empty waiting room.

"Did that just happen? Is this really happening?"

"Oh yeah." I lean in to whisper, "Congratulations. You did it."

She throws her arms around my neck. "Oh my God, Ryan, thank you! So much."

I pull her flush against me and bury my nose in her fragrant hair as her breath warms my neck. We stand like that for minutes because I'm reluctant to let her go. The last time I held her like this was at the Fairchild party. It feels like forever.

I move my hand to the small of her waist but can't resist cupping the curve of her ass and gathering her against me. She gasps as she slowly looks up at me and I let myself get lost in her green gaze. My eyes invariably drift lower and lock on her moist, parted lips. Putting my mouth on her earlier ignited a raging fire that has burned through all my apprehension and restraint. In moments, the warning bells in my head fade, drowned out by the driving need to taste her again.

She leans toward me, aiming to kiss my jaw but I turn my head at the last minute so our lips collide instead. My mouth has barely touched hers when she jumps out of my arms.

"Shit. Ryan, I'm so sorry!"

I tilt my head, observing her flushed face, and wonder if she didn't realize I was the one who went in for the kiss. "It's okay, Stella, really."

"Um, we should head out." She glances at her watch. "I'll just about make it to the DuPonts by five-thirty if I leave now."

"Jerry will take you there," I say, referring to the chauffeur.

"What about you?"

"I'll catch a cab back to the penthouse, and when you're done, you could join me for dinner. Mabel's been looking forward to seeing you again." I pause, thinking, "Or, I could take you out for dinner."

She smirks, "You mean like an actual date?"

"Hm-hm."

"I can't believe we've never actually been on one before."

"It sounds almost criminal, doesn't it? We've been too busy with laws and contracts to have a proper date. So, what do you say?"

"I don't know, I've always been a stickler for laws," she replies playfully.

"Well consult the rule book and let me know in the next two minutes."

"Two minutes to decide? Where are we going? A take-out drive-through?"

"That's a brilliant idea actually." I ignore her mock-glare as I escort her to the car where Jerry waits. I get her settled in the back and I'm about to shut the door when she asks. "Do you want to meet her?"

"Harriet?" The surprise in my voice is unmistakable.

She gives a nonchalant shrug, as if to say, 'Who else?'

I pause, taken aback by her offer to introduce me to her niece. I knew I would meet Harriet at some point, considering I may be named as her legal guardian, but Stella actually looks like she wants me to meet her niece.

"If you're sure?" It's one of those rare times I feel out of depth and willing for someone else to decide.

"Of course." Stella affirms. "She's an enchanting little girl. And I'm sure she'll like you, too."

"Then, I'd be honored to meet your niece. Thanks, Stella."

"I just need to call Faith and let her know I'm bringing someone along."

As I get into the car, Stella dials the DuPonts, but she only manages to reach their answering machine. She leaves a few voice messages and sends texts, hoping they'll be received in time.

"Sometimes it's hard to reach Faith, but hopefully, she'll get my messages and won't mind you coming," she says. I'm somewhat puzzled by the fear in her voice.

Half an hour later, we arrive at the DuPonts' sprawling mansion. No sooner than we step out of the car, Harriet darts out of the house like a ball of energy, pigtails flying, her laughter filling the quiet afternoon air.

"Auntie Stella, you came!" she squeals, her small legs propelling her across the driveway until she launches herself straight into Stella's arms.

I instinctively move behind Stella's delicate frame, fearing they might topple with the impact of Harriet's momentum.

But, Stella, clearly used to Harriet's effusive greetings, stands her ground firmly.

"I missed you so much, Auntie Stella." Harriet cries, "Faith and Mal said you went to Seattle and I was worried you wouldn't come back to see me."

"Of course, silly sausage, I'll always come back. And I've got someone here I'd like you to meet."

Harriet lifts her gaze from Stella's shoulder, noticing me for the first time. Her blue eyes go round in wonder.

"Harriet, this is Ryan," Stella introduces.

"Hi, Harriet," I say, offering a smile and a small wave.

She pins me with the serious look of a judge in a cookie court, weighing her verdict. "Are you Auntie Stella's boyfriend?"

My smile broadens. "I'm her husband."

Harriet gasps, bringing her small hand to cover her mouth, "Auntie Stella," she whispers in awe, "you had a wedding!"

"I did, but it was a really small one, sweetheart, we couldn't even have kids there," Stella explains, and Harriet nods as if this makes perfect sense.

Harriet gazes at me for what seems like a full minute, then looks back at Stella with an impish grin. "Can I call him Uncle Ryan then?"

My heart skips a beat. I'm so fucking out of my depth here although I can't say that I'm uncomfortable. It's an unexpected but not an unpleasant feeling.

Stella shoots me an uncertain glance, and I wonder if she's regretting bringing me along. She finally says to Harriet. "Why don't you go ask what he'd like you to call him, sweetheart."

Harriet nods, wriggles out of Stella's arms, and approaches me with a hint of shyness. "Can I call you Uncle Ryan?"

I gaze into her slightly smudged, lovely face, noting her round cheeks flushed with excitement. Her light blonde curls are neatly divided into pigtails—a mirror image of Gina at that age. The resemblance is uncanny. She could easily pass as my own daughter.

I squat down to her level. "Yes, you can call me Uncle Ryan, Harriet." Her joy is palpable as she bounces on the spot, then, as if unable to contain herself any longer, she wraps her arms around my neck.

Initially, I'm taken aback, frozen in place by her sudden affection. *Aren't children usually hesitant around strangers?* Encouraged by Stella's reassuring smile, I gently hug Harriet back, then stand, lifting her up in the process.

"Come on," Stella urges, "let's go say hello to Faith and Mal."

As we approach the house, Harriet's foster carer, Faith, appears in the doorway. Harriet, still clinging to me, excitedly proclaims, "Look, Faith, I have a new uncle!"

Faith steps onto the porch, eyeing me with a blend of curiosity and caution. "Your uncle?"

"Yes, Uncle Ryan," Harriet chirps, bouncing in my arms, barely containing her excitement. I put Harriet on her feet, and she skips to Faith, explaining. "Auntie Stella went to Seattle to get married, but kids weren't allowed, so I couldn't go. But he's here now."

Faith manages a smile for Harriet, then turns her cautious gaze back to us. "Hi, it's been a few weeks. How have you been?"

"Hi, Faith," Stella says, "I've been very well, thanks. I wasn't sure if you got my message about bringing someone along today. This is my husband, Ryan," The word 'husband' hanging awkwardly between us.

Faith gently nudges Harriet. "Harriet, darling, why don't you go wash your face then I'll come and help you get ready for the park with Auntie Stella."

"Alright!" Harriet squeals, darting inside.

Faith's smile is polite but doesn't reach her eyes. "Yes, I got your message. Harriet and I were baking cupcakes, so I didn't see it right away." She hesitates, then adds, "But, husband? That's, uh, quite the development."

Mal, Faith's husband steps out, having caught the tail end of our exchange. His eyebrows arch in surprise, mingled with something bordering on disdain. "Sounds like congratulations are in order, Stella. We hadn't heard."

I step forward, offering a handshake. "Ryan Fairchild. It's a pleasure to meet you both. I've heard a great deal about Harriet."

Faith pauses, a flicker of recognition crossing her face, while Mal does a double-take and clarifies, "Fairchild... of Ocean Gate Enterprises?"

"Correct," I confirm, feeling the weight of their recognition and the sudden shift in the atmosphere.

Faith's voice becomes cold, dripping with insinuation. "This must be quite a change for you, Stella."

"Excuse me?" The words escape me before I can rein them in, my tone sharper than intended. The undercurrents of judgment and the veiled skepticism annoy me more than I want to acknowledge.

Feeling my unease, Stella loops her arm around my waist and replies in a saccharine sweet voice, "Absolutely Faith, it's a wonderful change. For Harriet as well."

The atmosphere grows tense as Mal's tone hardens, his voice filled with concern. "For Harriet? Meaning?"

I don't hesitate. "Meaning that we're here to support Harriet in every possible way."

Faith's response is terse, her words revealing just how much Harriet means to them. "Look, we've been her family for a whole year, and she's happy here—"

I cut in, striving to keep the irritation out of my voice. "We're not here to turn her world upside down. We're simply looking out for her best interests."

Mal crosses his arms "And you think this sudden change is in her 'best' interest?"

"Harriet now has even more people to love her. That can't be seen as anything but positive, right?" I point out.

They fall silent, unable to argue with the logic, but the air is heavy with unspoken objections.

I choose my next words deliberately, wanting to make Stella's intentions clear. "We should all work together to ensure this transition is smooth for Harriet."

Mal's acceptance of the situation grudging at best. "We need to think about the legal implications—"

I cut in again, my tone firm "We have. We're committed to doing this the right way after all, aren't we, baby?"

I glance at Stella, half expecting her to be seething at this point since I've taken control of the conversation. She nods, the smile still on her face, so I continue speaking. "Now, regardless of our views on this, the last thing Harriet needs is to see discord among us, right?"

"Sure," Faith concedes, though her agreement feels hollow. Mal merely shrugs, a reluctant acknowledgment. "She's what's important."

"I'm glad we're all on the same page," I respond, feeling a mix of sympathy and indignation. It's obvious they love Harriet, however, the fact remains—Harriet is Stella's niece. But despite knowing Stella's desire to adopt Harriet, they were prepared to take that chance away from her.

Was it because they didn't think Stella stood a chance against them? Or because they felt Stella wasn't an appropriate choice for a parent?

Faith huffs, then turns to head back into the house. "I'll go and get Harriet ready. At the threshold, she pauses, looking back. "Do... you want to come in?"

I glance at Stella to see what she wants to do.

She shakes her head. "Oh, no thanks. The weather is so lovely, and your grounds are beautiful. Would you mind if we took a little walk around?"

"Not at all, please feel free," Faith responds, stepping inside. Mal follows her in shortly.

Once we're alone, I can't help but ask, "Was that as painfully awkward as I thought it was?"

Stella gives me a small smile. "Oh, it went a lot better than most days, so it wasn't unexpected. I actually think they were nicer today and I dare say it's because of you."

"Nicer? How so?"

"Well, because they invited us in!"

I struggle to keep my irritation in check. "That wasn't nice. That was rude and condescending." The thought of that sweet girl being raised by those people unsettles me deeply, strengthening my resolve to help Stella get her niece.

"They can't help themselves," Stella shrugs. "And I really don't like to antagonize her foster carers; after all, they're doing what I can't right now, and I'm grateful to them. But thank you for putting them in their place, even just a little. Sometimes they can be a bit much to handle."

"What, you're not going to bite off my head for speaking for you?" I fully expected her to give me an earful about what happened on that porch.

"Not today, no. I can't lie, I'm glad you were here Ryan," she admits.

Soon, Harriet emerges with Faith in tow, dressed in a pink flowery blouse and jeans. Harriet approaches, extending her hands to both of us. I envelop her small hand in mine, feeling an unexpected warmth spreading through me.

"We'll bring her back by bath time," Stella assures.

Faith offers a tight smile, her eyes lingering on us a moment longer than necessary, probably understanding that her role in Harriet's life is nearing its end.

Chapter Twenty-Seven

STELLA

"ARE YOU UP FOR a quick detour? If you're not too tired, I'd like to show you something." Ryan weaves through Manhattan's bustling streets. We've just left Romanos, the five-star restaurant where we had dinner.

"No, I'm not tired. But weren't you planning to meet the boys after dinner?"

"I can catch up with them later. Our nights don't start until much later anyway."

I glance at the timepiece on the dashboard, "Ryan, it's nine, and you haven't slept all day. I refuse to be stuck with a grumpy and exhausted co-passenger tomorrow."

He chuckles, brushing off my concern. "I'll be fine. And you won't be stuck with me because I'll be asleep during the flight back."

"So it's going to be a silent and boring flight then." I pout.

"Do I detect a compliment hidden somewhere there?"

"Maybe," I smile. And then I can't resist adding, "I've had the best day, Ryan. Thank you."

"You're welcome."

"So, what is it you want to show me?"

Ryan's face lights up with excitement. "We're launching a new yacht model, but I've designed an ultra-exclusive subset of it, each made to order with custom finishes."

"That sounds fascinating," I reply, my curiosity piqued. "Are we going to see one of these custom yachts tonight?"

"Yes, and this one's a masterpiece. But I want to know what you think."

I'm excited and humbled that he'd want to show me his latest work. "I don't know if I'm qualified to judge a yacht."

"Which is why you'd be perfect." He pulls into the Cove Marina, parking the car on one of the 'Captain's View' spots, a huge, raised viewing platform with railings. As soon as he helps me out of the car, I see a white silhouette in the distance. "Is that it?" I squint, rushing to the railings.

"Hey, don't throw yourself over in a bid to see, we're going down to the docks, so we'll get much closer."

"Okay!" Excited, I take his hand and we start the walk. After a few minutes, we hit the walkway, right in the middle of the Hudson River and so close to the waters to touch.

And then I really see it.

"Oh my God." I stop, my eyes widening in disbelief.

It's huge and sleek, spanning well over fifty feet in length and double-decked. The yacht gleams in the moonlight, its sleek, white exterior standing out. Two symmetrical and gently curving hulls extend gracefully from the central structure, giving it the shape of a long butterfly.

Ryan stands behind me, his arm slipping around my waist as I take it in. "So, if someone were to order this; what do you think they would use it for?"

"What would they use it for? Why the possibilities are endless! I mean, I haven't seen the inside yet, but I bet it's huge. Perfect for parties, honeymoon cruises, bridal showers," I ramble on excitedly. "Oh, and music videos, photoshoots. Hell, I'm sure some of my clients would rent it just for the fun of it! It's beautiful, Ryan; you've designed a bestseller here."

Ryan laughs softly, a sound that warms me. "Ever the businesswoman. Let's move closer, shall we?" He takes my hand as we start to walk again.

The yacht looms larger as we approach. After a minute he asks me again. "I was thinking more about personal use. If you were the client, what would you use it for?"

"Oh." I let the question sink in. "Well, I guess birthday parties, especially in the summer. Maybe my friends and I could take it out on a weekend cruise..." My voice trails off as my eyes catch the name of the yacht.

"The Stella" it reads, the letters elegantly adorning the hull.

I freeze in shock. "Ryan? What the hell is that?" I point to the name in disbelief.

"It's yours," he says simply, as if presenting someone with a yacht is an everyday occurrence.

My mouth flaps open and closed in shock. "W-what?"

"I built it for you."

"I... But— but why?" The question tumbles out, my mind racing to catch up with the reality unfolding before me.

"What do you mean 'why'?"

"I just don't understand why you'd build me something like this."

He smiles, a hint of mischief in his eyes. "Consider it a wedding gift, then."

"But—but it's not even a real marriage," I protest, the words feeling hollow even as I say them.

"The papers would prove otherwise," he counters.

"I can't take this!"

"You damn well can take it. It's all in your name. Like your ring, there's no strings attached, Stella. You inspired the design."

"I did?"

"I started working on it the day after we met in your apartment."

We'd gotten drenched when he tried to repair my kitchen faucet. I'd changed into a tank top and he couldn't stop staring at my tattoo. It was almost like he'd been poleaxed.

My heart pounds and my tears well up as it hits me. The shape mirrors my tattoo, a symbol so deeply personal to me, and now etched into the sleek lines of this yacht.

"I—I don't know what to say. It's just... too much."

"I'll give you a hint. It starts with 'M'," Ryan teases.

Laughing through my tears, I turn and wrap my arms around him, burying my face in the warmth of his chest.

"Say it," he coaxes.

"Thank you," I whisper, my voice muffling against his skin.

"Pfft. Not that."

"You're insane," I say, half-laughing, half-crying.

"Geez, what does a man have to do to hear that word?"

Magnificent

"You have a fetish for it or something?"

"No. It's just a word I chose for you."

I chuckle, shaking my head, unable to wrap my brain around his logic. "You're strange." *And wonderful.*

We stand together, my gaze drifting back to the yacht. It's hard to believe he built it inspired by my ink.

"I got the tattoo for Viv, you know. After she passed."

I feel his nod against my hair. "It's a beautiful work of art."

"Do you have any tattoos?" I suddenly realize I've never seen him fully naked.

"No. It doesn't quite fit with the schedule of a regular blood donor."

This is something else I didn't know about my husband. "Regular donor? How regular are we talking?"

He shrugs nonchalantly. "About six times a year. You have to wait a few months to donate after getting a tattoo."

"That's... impressive. Thank you for doing that."

He huffs out a laugh, amused by my gratitude. "For donating blood?"

"Yes, Ryan. I know how crucial it is. Vivian needed several transfusions, and even though we lost her, I'll always be thankful for the effort."

"You're welcome then," he rumbles.

My thoughts swirl in my head like a flock of restless birds.

Does he build yachts for all his women or does this mean he likes me a little bit more?

"So, do you like it?" He asks, and I hear a hint of concern under the teasing smile.

"Are you fucking kidding me? Ryan, it's unbelievable. Beautiful. Breathtaking. Magnificent," I whisper the last word.

He smiles widely, the grooves in his cheeks appearing. Suddenly overwhelmed, I throw my arms around him again. "Thank you."

"My pleasure. Ever been on a yacht before?"

"Just boat cruises and ferries, nothing like this," I confess. Not even on Xavier's. The girls have kept planning to take Xavier's on a spin but we never managed to.

"Well, it's about time my wife experienced her first twin hull," he says with a grin, leading me toward the yacht.

Approaching the gangway, the yacht appears even larger up close. "Come on, I'll show you around." He leads me up the short stairway to the deck.

I pause and look around again, marveling at the massive deck before focusing on the grand glass doors. It's like a floating mansion.

"Can we go in?" As beautiful as the outer deck is with its multiple seating and dining areas, I can't wait to see what the inside looks like.

"Of course, take the first look," he encourages.

As we near, the massive glass doors to the dim interior glide open. I step over the threshold, and I'm immediately blinded as all the lights flicker on, revealing over a dozen people, their faces alight with joy. "Congratulations!" they cheer.

Startled, I stagger back, but Ryan is quick to catch me.

"Surprise, baby!" His voice is warm, wrapping around me like a comforting blanket amidst the shock and sudden bursts of laughter.

"Oh my! I can't believe this!" It's not just a few friends; it's all of them, both mine and Ryan's.

Bonnie and Sabrina step forward, their grins stretching from ear to ear.

"Guys! Did you do this?"

Bonnie, sporting a belly that's starting to compete with a watermelon, shakes her head and nods at the man behind me.

"Ryan!" I spin around to catch his mischievous smirk. "You devious man!"

"I know how much you've been missing your friends, Stella." Ryan's eyes twinkle with excitement.

"And we weren't going to waste such a splendid venue," Bonnie chimes in, looking around. "I mean, look at the size of this place!"

"We might as well re-enact a wedding reception since we missed yours." Sabrina hugs me to her side.

Xavier comes forward, pushing an amber liquid into Ryan's hand and a cocktail in mine. "Mocktail, he whispers.

Oh crap. He still thinks I'm pregnant.

Xavier then cups a hand around his mouth and bellows, "Nora, Alex! Bring it in!"

My eyes nearly pop out of my head. "Ryan?" He shoots me our signature 'I'm just as surprised as you are' wink but keeps up his grin so I decide to just go with it.

Suddenly, a huge white tiered cake is being wheeled into the room by Alex, who also has a toddler balanced on his hip. His wife Nora follows with the knife, accessories, and, yep, fireworks.

"I kind of went overboard with the cake." Nora explains with a sheepish grin. "But since we've now declared it a wedding party, it makes perfect sense right?" There are several hums of agreement.

I can't believe these people. I'm overwhelmed by their love.

Brooke, who had been lingering on the side, finally steps forward. I leave the circle of Ryan's arms, and I go to her. "I've missed you so much, Brooke."

"I've missed you too." She pulls me into a hug.

"I'm sorry I didn't tell you about Harriet and the wedding."

"It's okay. I understand why you did it." She hugs me again, and I realize how much I've missed her quiet wisdom, how I could pretty much tell her anything, and she wouldn't bat an eyelash.

"Stella, this is nice though." She looks around the huge cabin. "Different from anything he's ever built, I think. A grand gesture. What do you think it means?" Brooke always cuts to the heart of the matter.

The same question I've been asking myself. I shrug. "I guess it shows his generosity?"

"Huh," her scoff tells me what she thinks of that idea. But before I can ask what she means, the room bursts into a chorus of congratulations and "Happy Married Life."

Well, everyone except Brooke and Xavier who know we'll be divorcing very soon.

A few more of my friends come around. Before long, we're deep in discussion. Most gush about how impressed they are with the yacht. They're careful not to drop spoilers though, knowing I haven't yet had a chance to see it.

"Okay, enough with the whispering and eternal group hug," Jordan, announces, breaking up our intimate circle. "I can't keep my eyes off Nora's cake if it's within a five-foot radius."

"Don't you dare touch that cake, Jordan!" Sabrina warns her husband.

"Not without the couple cutting it first!" Nora insists. "They get first dibs, plus we've got fireworks."

And so, without further ado, I'm dragged from my moment with the girls.

Ryan stands ready by the cake, having also been pushed there by the guys. He holds a cutting knife in one hand and a glass of scotch in the other. His eyes are hot and assessing, but there's also a hint of concern. He draws me close. "Are you okay?"

"Of course! I can't thank you enough—for everything. For Harriet." My voice trembles slightly with emotion. "And for this incredible wedding gift."

"Anytime, baby."

I have to tear my gaze away from Ryan when our friends start leering and catcalling, suggesting we get a room. *Geez I can't even look at the man?* It was so much easier to play loving couple with the Fairchild sharks than this bunch of horny goofs.

Nora does the thing with the fireworks, then orders us to dig in.

Ryan cuts out a piece and plates it, but instead of offering it to me, he says, with a playful glint in his eyes. "Wanna have some fun with this crazy bunch?"

He doesn't wait for my response. Instead, he picks up the cake, then feeds it to me. I do the same to him.

You'd think they were a bunch of toddlers gone high on sugar with the way they're hopping and cheering.

I have to laugh at their antics, thoroughly enjoying their joy. *Wow. Acting does give a certain rush.*

Giving in to the urge to play some more, I grab Ryan's wrist and seductively suck the icing off his fingers, giggling all through.

Suddenly someone shouts, "Fucking kiss already!" and others hoot in agreement. In a few moments, the cabin is filled with chants of "Kiss her. Kiss her. Kiss her."

I freeze. I notice Ryan has also gone very still beside me.

We don't kiss.

I turn my panicked gaze to my friends. Bonnie and Sabrina are grinning like fools while Brooke's eyes are bugging out of her head. Xavier is frantically flicking his hand back and forth across his neck, signaling to Jordan and Ethan to cut it out. But they carry on like the rest, chanting away like warlords.

Oh shit. The act just got real. How do we get out of this one?

I look back at a tense Ryan, expecting him to do something, perhaps a curt word to his friends. But again, this is his karma. Ryan is usually the one who instigates these types of games so he hasn't got a leg to stand on.

Suddenly he downs his glass, mutters, "Fuck it," curls his hand around my nape, and crushes his mouth to mine.

Chapter Twenty-Eight

STELLA

THE FIRST TIME I was kissed was by Danny Rupert in third grade. I blacked his eye. Then it happened again in middle school; that time, I initiated it. Over the following years, I've had all sorts. The good, the bad, and the downright disgusting. I like to think I've seen it all.

But now, I Stella, self-styled connoisseur of all things male, am being schooled by a simple kiss. Only there's nothing simple about it.

His mouth descends on mine in what should be an awkward clash of lips and teeth. But, as if we'd done this forever, his lips fit against mine at a perfect angle, then cling.

When I get over the initial surprise at how good he feels, I start to wonder what the man is doing when he gathers me against his hard body and coaxes my lips open.

I expected a quick dry peck that Ryan would be in a hurry to get over with, but I was sorely mistaken.

His hand tightens against my nape while his other hand leaves my waist to cup my jaw. Then he deepens the kiss and sweeps his tongue into my mouth. And like being suddenly hit by an unexpected riptide, I'm powerless against the surge of desire pouring out of him.

The room disappears as I arch into him and run my fingers up his neck and through his hair. I open my mouth wider and let him take what he needs, sliding my tongue against his and reveling in his smell, the taste of scotch and delicious cake, and something uniquely him. Something addictive

I hear a moan rumble in his chest and suddenly, I feel the wall against my back. Still, he doesn't stop, and I don't let up either.

"So fucking sweet," He murmurs against my mouth. I think I moan a response before he takes my mouth again in a drugging kiss.

The next time we come up for air, I'm more than a little dizzy. He takes a step back but braces an arm against the wall beside my head. He continues staring at me like I'm something he'd very much like to finish eating.

And that's when I remember the room. Their excited shouts float back to me.

Oh my God. That was so not fit for public. I flush scarlet. Thankfully, his shoulder blocks me from the rest of the crowd. I take a few gulps of air.

"Are you okay baby? I'm going to move away now."

Oh fuck. He knows I'm fighting for composure.

"I'm ah. I'm good." *Except I can't feel my lips from the tingles. And I can taste you.*

He turns us back to our friends, and if anything, they're even more excited, roaring and fist-pumping.

"Fucking hell Ry boy. You really went in for it there." Wyatt chortles.

"What can I say? She's delicious."

I put a smile on my face, but I can do nothing about my beet-red face. "I'm gonna get some water okay?" I say to Ryan, and before I leave his side, he presses a quick kiss on my cheek. And then pecks me on the lips. Again.

Geez. Can he stop kissing me already?

"Here," he hands me the saucer of cake. As I leave, I hear the boys already gearing up for another challenge.

I don't even know where the kitchen is, but I imagine it must be around where Alex and Nora wheeled the cake out from. With my smile still firmly pasted on I move across the room, grinning at hearty congratulations.

I step into the kitchen, considerably large for one on a yacht, then grab one of the plastic cups stacked on the glossy aluminum sink. I fill it with water then take a big gulp trying to steady my shaking hands.

Ryan kissed me.

I've been kissed before. Hundreds of times.

Never like that. And Lord, the way he tastes. Has to be the brandy and cake. No man should kiss like that.

"I think I might be in real trouble here," I say to myself, taking another gulp of water.

The door opens and Bonnie and Brooke pile in.

"Where's Sabrina?" I ask them.

"With Nora and the rest of the crowd." Brooke begins. "Now, Stella–"

"That was some fucking *Notebook* kiss, Stella," Bonnie interjects, apparently having no patience for Brooke's well-thought-out questions. "The only thing that stopped me singing your happily ever after is because I know you were both pretending, but fuck if that didn't look real. And hot as hell."

I run a shaky hand through my hair. *I know. I was there.*

"Stella?" Brooke ventures, a hopeful tone in her voice. She's probably expecting me to say we've thrown out the NDAs and prenups and decided to make it a real marriage.

"Yeah. Um." I huff out a small laugh. "It's a little confusing..."

"What is confusing?" Bonnie asks.

"Yes, it was an act. Only that..."

"What?" Bonnie snaps impatiently.

"That was our first kiss."

"What?" They both chorus, looking at me strangely.

I nod my head, and my fingers stroke my still-tingling lips.

"How is that even possible?" Brooke asks.

"I shrug. It's just not something we've... got around to doing. We're both really busy and..." I trail off realizing how weak my excuse sounds.

Brooke and Bonnie look at each other and then at me.

"If Xavier and I lived in an idyllic lake house like yours, we'd never be able to leave the bed." Brooke declares.

"Neither would Ethan and I," Bonnie chimes in.

"Bonnie, don't be greedy," Brooke scolds. "You already have a lake in your huge estate, complete with swans and everything."

"Having a lake on the grounds is so different from living in a glass house that's floating on a lake. Come on how can you beat that?" Bonnie faces me. "Yes, I snooped. I made Ethan show me your house when Brooke wouldn't stop raving about it."

I discreetly close my gaping mouth and hide my shock. I have no clue what house they're talking about but it seems like other people know. Damon mentioned something about his deck and his lake. I thought he was mad. And now my friends.

There is a lake house somewhere in Seattle.

Brooke surmises. "Anyway, back to the kissing. It may have been your first, but it's certainly not going to be your last. That much is obvious babe."

God, I hope so. After kissing me like that, if he dares to crawl back into that strange dark shell and tries to be aloof again, I think I'd strangle him.

Someone knocks and singsongs "Oh bri-ide...you're wanted at the pong game on the sky deck."

I glance at the door and groan. "No more games, please. I know Wyatt is going to keep throwing Ryan and me together."

"True. And there's only so much sexual tension we can endure before we all combust aboard this yacht! Brook adds. "Don't worry, we'll keep you away from the spotlight."

"What would I do without you guys?" I smile wryly.

"Melt into a puddle of need, I suppose," Bonnie says with a straight face, ignoring the mock glare I throw at her.

The rest of the night I feel an inexorable pull toward Ryan which I try to drown in mocktails. Bonnie keeps sneaking alcohol into my drinks because I'm not ready to tell Brooke and Sabrina that I'm not pregnant. By the fourth glass, I know I'm unlikely to last the night without somehow going to drape myself over Ryan.

The looks of pure sin he keeps throwing me from across the room don't help either.

By midnight, Brooke and Xavier suddenly announce they're leaving, and the others take their cue from them. I'd expected the party to draw on until much later going by how late the boys usually stay on their nights out.

At last, everywhere becomes silent.

I hop on a bar stool and kick off my heels. I'm still wearing the black skirt and dark green silk blouse I've had on since morning. I would have loved a chance to refresh my makeup or change, but I couldn't have hoped for a better night.

Ryan returns to the cabin after seeing the last guest off locks the sliding doors and leans against it. He stares at me from across the large cabin for a beat then slowly approaches me.

He'd long taken off his jacket, and his shirt is now untucked, with the top three buttons undone and cuffs pushed up to his elbows, typical of the roaring match they'd been at all evening. I watch him approach, letting myself enjoy the delicious tightening I feel in my womb when I look at him.

He pulls a stool and sits beside me.

"Ryan, thank you for this, for tonight. It was the best."

He smirks. "What do you say I give you a full, uninterrupted tour of the Stella tomorrow."

"Oh yes!"

He grabs my calf, stoking all the way down to my foot which he starts to gently rub.

"Ryan," I feel self-conscious knowing his penchant for cleanliness. "My feet are sweaty."

"I know. Hold still." he continues massaging my achy foot, moving from one to the other, and I try not to moan out with how good it feels.

"Ryan, can I ask you something?"

"Hm hm."

"Why does everyone think we live in a lake house?"

He stops, then lifts me to the counter, steps between my legs and buries his face into my neck.

"Because I own one. Fuck, your smell drives me crazy Stella."

I'm still reveling in how his short trimmed beard feels on my neck When he draws my earlobe in between his lips and sucks on it, drawing a gasp from me. I'm overwhelmed with sensation from suddenly having his mouth all over my skin, but I manage to stay on track.

"Is the lake house in Seattle?"

"Hm-hm." He grunts kissing a path down my neck.

"Don seems to think it's his...." I sigh, hooking my legs around his hips and reach for his shirt buttons.

He shifts the neckline of my shirt to gently nip on the ball of my shoulder, and I'm about to give up conversation altogether when he responds in a serious tone.

"It's true. It used to belong to his family. Uncle Reuben lost it to my father who then immediately passed it on to me when I turned eighteen. To rub in salt into Don's wounds, I moved into the house straightaway and threw wild parties in it. Don was devastated."

"Ryan!"

"What can I say, I was a bit of an ass then."

"But given how it all played out now, would you have handled it differently?"

"Of course. It was mean. I knew he really wanted to inherit it. It would have been a small price to pay to have gained a strong ally instead of a vicious enemy," he shrugs, "but like I said, I was an ass."

Ryan can be cold and brutal and makes for a formidable enemy himself, and one that is often underestimated. I see the envy among his cousins and uncles, but there's also a respect that borders on fear in their eyes as well.

"Why did you then move out of the place? To try to get Don back on your side?"

"To get rid of ghosts." He stills. Suddenly, he winces and then looks away, keeping his head bowed. He sniffs a few times. "Give me a minute, will you?"

What the hell is happening?

He's turning away and reaching behind him to unlock my ankles from his waist, but I tighten my legs around him.

"Wait, don't go" I plead. "Are you okay?" I wrap my fingers around his jaw and bring his face back to mine. His left eye is watering. "Ryan? Are you... crying?"

He chuckles and sniffs again. And he's still wincing. "No, of course not. It's just one of my headaches."

I know he gets headaches, but seeing one happen is a little shocking. I wipe off his tears and drop a kiss on his forehead. "I thought they were just... headaches. Caused by stress." This doesn't seem like a usual headache.

"They're cluster headaches." He winces again.

I check the wall clock. It's two a.m., eleven Seattle time. It's been nearly twenty-four hours since he last slept. "But you said you're fine with late nights?"

"I usually am as long as it's not back-to-back. But sometimes they hit me out of nowhere."

"Oh, I'm sorry. What helps? Advil? Massages?" I sink my fingers into his hair and rub his temples and the back of his head.

"Zolmig...a spray. And hot showers." His lids close and he leans into my touch. "And apparently your fingers."

Encouraged, I carry on rolling the pads of my fingers against his skull while he drops his head to my chest and purrs like a large cat.

I work silently trying to keep my breathing even and not rub my aching breasts against the head he's now laying on me.

His hands slip around my waist then slide lower until they're cupping my butt. He digs his fingers into my ass cheeks and starts mirroring my actions on his scalp.

My breath catches. I've been in an almost constant state of arousal since the flight. But now, my panties are soaked right through, and my core throbs with need. It's been too long.

"Did I tell you I love your smell?" He whispers.

"Uh... no." I'm hoping he means the smell of my perfume... my shampoo... my skin... anything but *that*.

"I can smell you right now Stella."

Well then. Done fighting the raging lust, I drop my suddenly boneless fingers to the counter then shift my butt to the edge so I can grind against him.

"Ryan, I can't take it anymore. I want you."

"I know, let's go."

"Where are we going?" I question.

"Shower. Come on."

He lifts me up and urges my legs around his waist. "I need to ask you something important."

"What's that?"

"Did you like my mouth on you?"

Ha! I raise my head to look at him. "I suppose I can live with it."

His lips spread into a knowing smile that matches mine. "Good." He takes my mouth in a hungry kiss while he slowly walks us toward one of the rooms.

I expected he'd have to put me down to fit into the doorway. But he's built the Stella with double doors, so he carries me straight through.

He takes us right into the surprisingly large shower stall fully clothed then he turns some of the chrome knobs on the marble wall.

"I should warn you, the water will be hot." He reaches up to set the direction of the spray.

"I love hot showers."

"Perfect," he puts me against the cold marble wall, covers my mouth with his then hits the spray at full blast.

Chapter Twenty-Nine

STELLA

AT FIRST, I ONLY feel hot steam since most of the spray is directed toward the back of his head and neck. Water sluices over his back trailing to his waist where my legs are entwined. After a few moments he steps us backward, drenching me too. A soft whimper of pleasure leaves me only to be muffled by his lips.

He drags a hand up to my neck and fists the hair at my nape to keep me in place while he changes the angle, taking the kiss deeper.

I'm breathless with arousal. I slowly unravel under his mastery. His silky tongue slides against mine and withdraws, only to return to tease me again. I melt into its decadence. The way he takes and gives everything, where there's no mistaking his feelings. His intentions. I didn't know a kiss could pack so much heat.

This is the reason why this man doesn't put his mouth on anyone. It's too much, too intense.. I'm perversely pleased that he's giving me something he doesn't give anyone else. His skill tells me that he did this before, but his hunger speaks of pro-longed abstinence. *For how long?*

"I could do this for hours you know." He whispers against my mouth.

His words make me hungrier, and I lean in for more. But his hold on the back of my head is secure.

He watches me through heavy lids and long, spiked eyelashes. His stare is scorching as if he wants to see into my very soul. I zero in on his blown pupils which make the dark specks in his iris much more tantalizing.

"Ryan." I moan, unsure of what I want.

"You are so beautiful, Stella." He whispers.

He's making me feel too much. Need too much. He held so much of himself away from me for months, and now, suddenly, getting it all is driving me crazy.

His fingers leave my nape to trace over my brows, down over my nose, and across my cheekbones, and finally drag over my kiss-swollen lips. My tongue darts out to lick his skin and before I process what I'm doing, I suck his thumb into my mouth.

"Fuck, you're hungry," he groans, then replaces his thumb with his tongue, and I suck on it like I'm dying of thirst.

I can no longer feel how wet I am, but my core throbs. I'm also so swollen I wonder if he would fit inside me. At any rate, if he carries on fucking my mouth, with the way my inner muscles are already twitching, he might not need to try. I'd be climaxing anyway.

He kisses me until I'm, writhing against his big body. His slick skin, the warm spray and steam feeding into my arousal until I'm caught in a frenzy.

When I feel the first ripples of orgasm starting, I tear my mouth away. "Ry," I gasp. "I can't hold on for much longer. I need to come."

He presses his forehead to mine "So, you love my mouth that much huh?" he grins.

I roll my eyes. "I think you're getting too carried away with your newly re-discovered first base tool."

His only reaction is a sharp jerk at the crotch of my silk panties, ripping them clean off. "No, it's because my greedy little pussy wants something to latch on to."

"Your pussy? You're full of grandiose ideas–ah!"

My head hits the wall as white-hot pleasure streaks through me in response to his hard slap. Right on my throbbing clit. With enough bite to drive me mad but not enough friction to send me over the edge. He slaps me again, harder and I see stars. "Ry, please"

He undoes his pants and frees his steel-hard cock which immediately surges up to hit my folds. Without thinking, my hips blindly seek to impale myself on him.

"Not so fast." He hoists me higher and out of reach. "Not until you tell me who this pussy belongs to."

"Ryan don't be annoying–"

He fists my shirt and rips the buttons apart. He frees a breast from its lacy cup, and his mouth surrounds a hard nipple.

"Oh God! Please fuck me Ry" I cry out.

His mouth is pure sin, tongue lashing repeatedly against the tight achy peak. He applies strong suction and finishes with a gentle bite that I feel right on my clit. My core clenches hungrily against nothing.

"Fine! Ryan, no more. It's yours. My pussy is yours alone, okay?"

"Good girl," he breathes.

I grumble under my breath, but he only smiles and then slides me down until his cock nestles against my folds then he pushes in slightly. I'm so swollen that he feels unbelievably huge against me, and the way he's stretching my entrance is already driving me insane. I shudder, dropping my head to his shoulder.

He chuckles wryly. "This will not take long at all. I won't last. You feel too good."

"Funny, I was thinking the exact same thing."

He puts a hand on the wall behind my head, then surges into me while his arm around my waist pushes me onto his stiff cock.

One moment, I'm empty, desperate to climax, the next he is sliding home. My whimper is broken as I writhe and clench around his invading girth. Still, he continues to fill me.

"Jesus fucking Christ, you're tight." He groans. I meet his wild, unfocused gaze, watching his face go taut with lust. "Why are you so fucking tight?" he asks no one in particular.

I can't speak, too far gone, frozen in pleasure and hanging on the precipice, my nerve endings vibrating.

"Let it go. That's your cock, baby; it's all yours." His palm covers my breast and pinches my nipple, and that's all the trigger I need. I explode on a soundless scream, my head thrown back in ecstasy. His hand protects my head from the wall while his other hand steadies my shuddering hips as he pulls out and plunges back inside me.

This time I find my voice, crying out my pleasure as he repeatedly slams against the spot that makes me lose my mind. It might have been one long orgasm. Or, many small ones. But, my full-body climax seems to go on and on until he finally covers my mouth with his. Then, he roots himself deeply inside me.

I feel his powerful shudders and his cock jerks repeatedly as he spills inside me.

We're both still panting, our hips rocking as we wantonly chase our ebbing orgasm when he drops his face into my neck and whispers. "I'm fucking wrecked. You've wrecked me. Stella Fairchild. Hell, if I'm not taking you in exchange."

My heart knocks against my rib cage as I draw in a sharp breath. That sounded a lot like some sort of declaration. Too bad all the parts of me that should have come up with a snarky comeback have melted into a gooey mess.

He takes a few steps back into the still hot water, and tilts his head back into the spray. I watch the strong column of his tanned neck, the corded veins and muscles, the pulse that beats to time with his wildly thumping chest.

He's beyond gorgeous. I run my fingers over his temples, sliding them into his silky hair then rub again in firm circles, but honestly, I just want an excuse to touch him. "Headache?"

"Gone." He stops the shower and then walks us out of the stall, still inside me, still hard as stone.

"Ryan?" I move against him "You're still hard."

"Because I'm not finished yet. Are you tired?" He grabs a couple of towels from the heated rack and gives me one. "Your hair," he says, and he uses his to dry his hair.

"Ry, you've not slept in a whole day!" *Talk about stamina.*

"Yes, which is why we're going straight to bed. I just want to kiss you for a bit, that's all."

His words make me shiver in anticipation. I thought I was the only one addicted to his kisses, it seems he can't get enough of mine either.

He drops me onto my back in the middle of the bed, then he covers my body with his, bracing himself on his forearms, links our fingers together, then takes my lips.

He kisses me as though learning every curve and groove of my lips, my tongue, and my teeth. It's raw and intimate because he doesn't let go of my hands or touch me anywhere else.

I strain and writhe, suddenly too hot, and just when I think I can't take anymore, he slides his muscled thigh between my legs. Without thinking, I ride his thick thigh, grinding my swollen clit against him repeatedly. Within seconds, I'm tipping over the edge.

I flush in embarrassment when I start to shudder in orgasm, but he groans loudly into my mouth and goes rigid on top of me. When his grip tightens almost painfully against my fingers and feel his cock start to spurt hotly against my thigh, I realize he's coming too.

I'm speechless. I'm not even sure I could speak if I had words, to describe what we just did. It almost felt like a religious experience. Also like the dirtiest kind of sex.

Especially since he's now rubbing his cum into my skin. And I'm getting an insane desire to find out what he tastes like. My cheeks flush, and I turn my back to him. Unfazed he simply drags me into his chest, spoons me, and continues his thing with my belly.

"Well, well." He drawls lazily, "Didn't know I had that in me."

"I didn't think that was possible that you could...do that without...contact. Friction"

"Now you know. And it was hot as fuck." He growls, and as if reading my mind, he rubs his index finger across my lips, coating them generously with his thick cum.

Not even waiting to see what I would do, he asks like he's just done the most natural thing in the world. "Do you sleep with lights on or off?"

"Off," I say, gritting my teeth with the effort not to lick. Not until the light goes off. I have some self-respect, after all.

"Thank fuck, I was hoping you'd say that." He reaches across the bedside and switches off the light. "Goodnight, baby," he drops a lingering kiss on my temple, then goes back to spooning me.

I lick my lips like a starving woman.

Yeah, he's not the only one that's wrecked.

Chapter Thirty

STELLA

Four Weeks Later

I step out of my office bathroom at BodyLift and catch Gina's reflection in the wall of mirrors as she tries taming her hair into a severe bun. "Zip me up, please?"

"Sure," she gives up with a sigh and throws the brush on the counter, then fluffing out her curls for good measure, comes to help me.

I've just changed out of my work attire into something a bit more elegant for the business dinner Ryan asked me to join him at.

"Stella, what do you think of Chad?" Gina suddenly asks.

"How did we leap from discussing Harriet to your ultimate raunch fest Chad?" I tease. She had come by my office earlier to talk about our ongoing plans for adopting Harriet.

"I wouldn't exactly pair 'raunchy' with 'Chad' in any context," she counters with a smirk.

"Hmm," I'm not convinced, but I don't argue. "Why do you want to know what I think anyway?"

"Because I need to decide if I should end things with him for good."

I consider that as Gina zips up my plum sheath dress, its sleek lines perfect for a business setting.

She peeks around me into the mirror. "Oh wow, look at you. Absolute knockout, she praises.

"Thank you, babes." Then I respond to her question, "Gina. If you're this conflicted about staying with Chad, you probably already know what you need to do. You're just not brave enough to follow through."

"Ouch. Stella, you sure know how to drive the nail straight in." She grumbles.

"But you know I love you."

"I know." She hugs me from the side, and I do the same, watching her through the mirror. I'm 5'4 and barefoot while she's 5'8 plus another four inches of stiletto. I can't believe how much I've come love and rely on her friendship in the past month.

My thoughts inevitably drift to Ryan, as they often do these days. The thought of being separated from him throws my stomach into knots. It's been five months, and yet, the topic of divorce remains unbroached. But the nearer the day gets, the more panic attacks I have. I'm dreading the moment I'll find out that after all is said and done, Ryan still prefers to return to being single.

"Mom thinks he's the best," Gina voice pulls me back into the conversation. "And Pop, well he only likes Chad because he's willing to change his last name to Fairchild."

"What?" I'm genuinely surprised.

"Yes, if he takes the name, he will be in line for an inheritance, which means potentially double the wealth for our kids."

"And here I thought I'd heard it all about your family's rules." I chuckle.

"Oh no, it's never-ending, I promise you."

"And what about Ryan? Why does he like Chad?"

Gina rolls her eyes, "Ryan is just...relieved."

"What?"

Gina takes a deep breath before explaining, "I'm like a bad boy magnet okay; If there's one within a ten-mile radius they'll somehow find their way to me, I swear. Over time, Ryan's had to deal with so many stalkers and crazies in my life that by the time Chad came along, Ryan was so relieved. He can't wait to marry me off to him."

"Oh, I get it now."

"So, what do you think of Chad?" Gina presses.

I shrug, "Well, I think he's a decent guy. He's not hard on the eyes and worships the ground you walk on. He's a lawyer too so you have that in common. But like I said, what really matters is what you think, Gina."

She sighs, "He's just a bit too boring."

She sounds just like Bonnie. Like me too– a lifetime ago. "Is that why you feel the constant need to push him, to create drama?"

"Stella!" Gina exclaims with a mix of mock outrage and guilt of someone caught in a ruse.

"Wasn't he the same guy who debauched you in the Fairchild gardens? How is that boring?"

"Debauched? Really, what are you, eighty?" Gina retorts, her tone light.

I can't help but laugh. "Oh my God, I can't believe I used that word. I blame Ryan. But honestly, it takes guts to make a move like that, especially at your parents' place."

"I think I pushed him past breaking point. That was the only time he's ever lost control," Gina reflects, a hint of pride in her voice, "otherwise, he might as well be made of stone."

"Gina, that man I met at last week's Thanksgiving dinner is head over heels for you."

She gasps as if suddenly remembering something. "Speaking of Thanksgiving dinner... You and Ryan are something else," Gina levels me with a knowing look.

"What do you mean?"

"You guys are just so shameless. Seriously? Spilling wine on your dress and then he 'helps' you clean it up? Classic move."

"*That* was an accident," I protest, feeling my cheeks warm. Who in their right mind would have sex in their parents' house in the middle of Thanksgiving dinner?

Gina grins, "I think you're perfect for him though. I've never seen Ryan like this with anyone, not even Ivy. You two just click, like a well-oiled machine."

I pause in the middle of applying my glossy nude lipstick the moment she mentions that name.

"Ivy?" The name triggers a vague memory. The well-worn PJ top Ryan suddenly took off mid-conversation. The identical barely-worn gray top I saw hanging by itself in his closet the day I went snooping. The one that only had 'Ivy League' inscribed on it.

Gina hesitates, realizing she's slipped. "You don't know about her?"

Taking a shot in the dark, I venture, "League?"

Gina nods, obviously relieved that I know. "Yes, the Leagues are like the Tsars of coffee. They're the producer of the Medal series."

Oh shit. Ivy League is a person. No wonder he acted weird that morning when I read out the inscription on his PJ.

"I see." I continue with my makeup, trying for casual. A part of me itches to change to subject, yet I can't resist wanting the rest of the story.

There's a pause, heavy with unspoken regret on Gina's part.

Aiming for a subject change too, Gina muses, "Anyway, my niggling worry is that Chad might be the one for me. Letting him go now might mean I'll come to regret it later—-"

"Does Ivy, by any chance, have a tattoo on her left hand?" I interject, my curiosity getting the better of me.

Gina observes me warily. "Yes, but how do you know this?"

I respond with another question instead. "Is Ivy Ryan's ex?"

Please let her be an ex.

Gina begins, "She's not exactly an ex..." Her tone sends my thoughts spiraling.

Oh fuck. Is he seeing her? Is she another one of his 'Cathys,' his submissives?

"Gina?" I prompt.

Gina's hesitation hangs heavily in the air. "I shouldn't have said anything."

"Look, I know all about Ryan's...tendencies," I state with false bravado but the words taste bitter, even as I force them out. "I'm married to the man. If he's seeing someone on the side though, I would hate to be in the dark."

"He's not seeing someone else, Stella. Ryan wouldn't—" Gina's voice softens, her eyes filled with sympathy. "Ivy was his wife."

"He was married?" I whirl on her in a near shout, my attempt to keep my composure failing miserably.

"Only for three years," She explains quickly, "They were both very young, practically just out of high school, but she died. He was not the same for a long time after."

The words hit like a physical blow. Ryan was married to his high school sweetheart. His first love.

"Stella? I'm so sorry. I thought you knew that was why he needed to re-marry."

I thought I did, too. "I thought company policy dictated for him to marry before he turned thirty-one?"

"No, the laws actually mandate marrying before thirty years of age, not thirty-one. But for anyone widowed under the age of fifty, they have to marry again within ten years. Ivy died when they were twenty-one."

I nod repeatedly, as if it all now makes sense. It doesn't. Nothing makes any sense right now.

"Are you okay Stella?" Gina asks, worry stamped all over her face.

"I'm—It's just... I'm a little surprised, that's all." But even as I say the words, tears well up and spill over despite my best attempts to hold them back.

Gina puts an arm around my shoulder, her concern etched on her face. "Ryan never talks about that part of his life. But he's over her, you know. He doesn't have room in his heart for anyone but you."

"Of course, I know." The lie tastes sour on my tongue. *He's so not over her.* "I just hate surprises, that's all."

We change the subject and I throw myself into our discussion while I finish dressing up. I even help Gina get the severe bun look she was trying for earlier, ignoring the tremor in my hands or how much my chest hurts.

By the time Fred takes me to the restaurant, I'm the picture of quiet composure.

I call on every ounce of inner strength to remain composed all through the business dinner, smiling and laughing when appropriate, even inserting my own questions and comments. But beneath the surface, my world is spinning.

As if he senses something wrong, Ryan keeps his hand over mine and maintains that contact throughout the dinner.

On the drive back home, I'm silent, responding only with a terse "I'm fine" as Ryan keeps asking to know what the matter is.

I'm the furthest from fine. Jealousy, hot and fierce, has been gnawing at my heart all evening and has now left it a painful bloody stump.

Ryan and his wife wore matching PJs.

He's stopped wearing his since that day you saw him in them. A voice in my head counters.

His bedroom was off-limits because of her.

And now he won't let you out of it.

He had a painting of both of them over his bed.

Which Ryan suddenly donated to some health charity on your return from New York.

Still, I can't get rid of my doubts and fear.

His wife is not dead to him. She's the reason he's gone to these lengths to avoid a real relationship. And the reason he'll kick me out once the six months are up. In four weeks.

Once he parks the car, I don't wait for him to help me out, but instead, I throw my door open and bolt up into the penthouse.

My heart feels too battered to hear the voice of reason in my head. All I know is that I'm in love with Ryan Fairchild. And he's in love with someone else.

Needing space tonight, I avoid his suite—-the space we've been sharing for the past month and go to my own bedroom.

I'm in my closet, struggling to reach my zipper when he walks in.

"Let me." He drags the zipper down with a tenderness that sends a shiver down my spine, then he drops a soft kiss on my back.

I step away from him, pushing down the dress and letting it pool at my feet. I step out, hang the dress, then quickly change into my nightshirt. The silence weighs heavy, his presence both a source of comfort and anguish.

"I can only ask you so many times." He whispers, "Are you going to tell me what the hell the matter is, baby?"

I want to scream at him not to call me that. "I told you, Ryan, I'm fine."

"You've been like a wall of ice all evening."

"Oh, I'm sorry, was my performance not up to par tonight?"

"Baby—-"

"It's Stella."

"What?"

"Nothing. Look, we should talk about our divorce."

"What divorce?" Ryan spits.

"What do you mean 'what divorce'? We're a month away from the end of our six-month contract, aren't we?"

He stares at me for a beat, then states "If you think for a moment I'm letting you go, you're crazier than me for setting this up in the first place."

His words hit me like a ton of bricks, and hope blooms in me, but I hide it with a sigh. "Ryan, you've made CEO, you've won, okay? You now have the life you wanted. I should also get back to my own life in New York."

He shakes his head, clearly at a loss. "Stella, what the hell is this about?"

"Ryan, it's been a long day; I'm tired..." I try to sidestep him, but he stops me, his hands firmly encircling my arms.

"Oh hell no." His tone is soft, but the command is unmistakable. "You will tell me what's gotten into you right fucking now."

"Fine! I'm sick of having to act like this relationship, this marriage is real. I can't do it anymore."

He starts to laugh.

"Care to share what's so funny about what I said?"

"I hate to break it to you, baby, you're in way over your head. We both are. We stopped pretending a while ago."

"Speak for yourself." I retort.

"Okay. I will." He slips his arm around my waist, pulling my back into his chest. "I chose you because I knew you valued your independence, that you didn't want a relationship, and wouldn't form any attachment to me. What I didn't anticipate was how much I'd come to need you. Now the thought of returning to my life before you gives me hives. I want you to stay."

I feel my resolve melting with his heated confession, but still, I dig my heels in. "So, it's all about what you want then?"

"Stella Marie Fairchild," he says, my full name grounding his confusion and plea. "You wanted my honesty, and I just gave it to you. Now tell me what's bothering you because I know for a fact you don't want to leave either."

"That's what you think. I warned you I don't do three-somes."

Shock slackens the arm around me so I pull away and head out of the walk-in closet and into my room. He follows me. "What on earth are you talking about, Stella?"

I take a deep breath, releasing it slowly. "I'm talking about Ivy. *Ivy League*."

He rears back at the mention of her name, his face paling slightly. "Did my mother say something to you?"

"It wasn't Mom, it was Gina but none of that matters since *you* didn't tell me."

"I didn't think our past relationships were relevant."

"No, you're right, they shouldn't be," I concede bitterly. "Except this wasn't just any past relationship. We're talking about a marriage here, Ryan. To a woman you're clearly still in love with!"

"Why would you think that?" He asked, his tone soft.

I scoff. "You need me to spell it out? Isn't she the reason you don't do intimacy? The reason you'd risk upsetting a two-hundred-year-old tradition? You fucking roared at me just for look-ing at her painting!"

He only shakes his head.

I fold my arms, "You want to tell me I'm wrong?"

"I'm not in love with Ivy. Yes, I loved her until she drew her last breath. I loved her with everything in me and losing her broke me. For years I wasn't functioning properly."

His words are like shards of glass slicing at my heart. *You still aren't functioning properly, and it's been ten years.*

"I never ever wanted to be hurt like that again."

I throw my arms up. "Exactly. And you have put everything in place to see that you don't."

Suddenly needing space away from him, I try to move past him, but he stops me again. "Baby, why do you think it was so hard to look at you?"

That stops me. "I thought it was women in general you didn't look at."

He scoffs, "No, that was just you."

"Why?"

"You don't know what you do to me, do you? Everything about you rips me apart and draws me in, Stella. Stirs something in me I thought was long dead."

"What's that?"

"Fear. Fear of how much it would hurt if I let myself care. But you've also become my safe place. Now I'm done being afraid. I want everything with you."

"Ryan—"

He doesn't let me finish. Pulling me close, he claims my lips in a hard kiss. I resist for a total of two seconds until my body betrays me and I cling to him with a hunger that shocks me.

Eager to feel his skin against mine, I push his jacket off his shoulders, then work on his shirt buttons. Just as desperate as I am, he bats my hands away and yanks open his shirt, sending buttons flying everywhere. He shrugs off his jacket and shirt, then his hands return to fist my nightshirt, and we break apart just enough to pull it over my head.

His mouth returns to mine with a new urgency. He curls his big hand around my nape, holding me steady as he devours my mouth like he owns it. His tongue boldly slides against mine, staking his claim, as his teeth nip at my lips. I moan as the kiss gets hotter and rougher, punctuated by his deep grunts. He palms my ass and urges me against him until he's hoisting me up and wrapping my legs around his waist.

I don't realize we've moved until my back hits the bed. He follows me down, bracing his weight on his forearm. Instead of taking my mouth again, he simply looks at me. His fingers trace along my cheekbone, then rub on my swollen lips in an achingly tender gesture that I'm coming to love. "Fuck, Stella, you drive me crazy, you know that?"

"So do you. I hate that you thought it was okay to wear those PJs around me." Granted, he'd not expected me to be awake, and we didn't at the time know we would feel this way. Still...

He trails kisses on my temple, neck and bends to lick my collarbone. "I know, I'm sorry. It was habit. One you know I've broken."

"Just because you now sleep naked?"

He growls, "Because I'd much rather wear you."

I try for a snarky retort and fail miserably. I can't even muster an eye roll for his cheesiness. Instead, say in a small voice. "I don't want to leave, Ryan."

His blinding smile is so sexy I feel the impact in the tightening of my core. "I was hoping you'd say that, Stella. I'm so fucking gone for you I can hardly think straight when I'm not around you. I love how smart and brave you are. And I can't get over how you make me feel."

"How do I make you feel?" My breath hitches with hope.

"Like I'm ten times better. So much more. I love you, Stella Fairchild."

A whimper of pleasure and surrender escapes me as he takes my mouth again. My last coherent thought is that Ryan is everything I never knew I needed, and I couldn't ask for anything more.

We're perfect together.

But I'm soon to be reminded, and in the most jarring way possible, just how twisted and imperfect life can be.

Chapter Thirty-One

RYAN

I watch my New York top executives—my cousins and uncles, really—as they line the glass wall of the Ocean Gate viewing room, holding champagne flutes. This boardroom is aptly named for its panoramic view of the waterfront and Harbor Island. It offers the perfect vantage point to watch our ships launch.

I don't need to witness this launch firsthand. The scene has played out in my mind countless times. I'd rather watch them. The awe on their faces and their acceptance, grudging or not, that I've again made the right call and secured another piece of everyone's future. That in itself is reward enough.

Besides I'm burning with a different kind of excitement. I need my wife. Having spent the past week in London and coming straight to work from the airport, I feel like I'm missing a limb. I just need to get through this final meeting and go home to her.

I inhale deeply, forcing my attention back to the New York team led by Don. God only knows what he's plotting now. If the man devoted even half the energy he spends stirring up corporate drama to actually servicing clients, his performance would be unmatched.

Instead of joining the rest to watch, Don comes to where I'm perched on the edge of the conference table. "Quite the spectacle, boss. I'll give you that," His voice drips with feigned admiration.

You're welcome, asshole. My lips stretch into a semblance of a smile. Don fought me every step of the way on this project.

"It's almost as grand as the alliances you've forged...on and off the boardroom." He remarks, his meaning clear as day.

Stella.

Marrying her was the best decision I've ever made. She's not just my wife; she completes me. Beyond that, she's also incredibly smart and talented. Given the right tools for investment, she's bound to dominate the beauty industry in a very short time.

I can almost taste Don's envy, and unfortunately, his dark fascination. Whatever he can't own or copy, he seeks to destroy.

I meet Don's gaze in the glass's reflection, suppressing my annoyance. "You should focus more on forging your own achievements rather than fixating on mine, Don."

If only he could see past his relentless drive to compete with me, he might realize he has everything he needs to outdo me in the coming years, wife or not. New York is Ocean Gate's hub of innovation, and he's currently at its helm.

Don gives me a scrutinizing look, shaking his head. "You're a lot of things, Ryan, but careless isn't one of them."

"How so?" I ask, bracing for harsh critique.

"You made a wrong move when you put your fate in the hands of a woman who has nothing to lose."

He takes my raised eyebrow as his cue to explain what he means. "When you come from nothing, you've got nothing to lose. No money, no pedigree. And still, you've kept her beyond the six-month mark. She's now entitled to a sizeable chunk of your wealth."

Don leans closer. "If she walks away now, she'll tear you apart. And weaken the company's position with investors."

I shrug with an air of nonchalance "And this concerns you because?"

"This is my company. Too." He adds the last part almost like an afterthought. "I'd rather not be left holding a bag of ashes and dust when you're done."

"I appreciate the concern, but it's not needed. My wife isn't going anywhere."

"You sure about that?" He questions. I'm about to snap back when he smoothly heads off to mingle with the rest of the team.

"Here's to the future, folks," Don raises his glass in a toast, drawing the room's attention. "Looks like we were right to trust the boss's instincts after all, weren't we?"

Glasses clink. The executives, oblivious to our tense exchange, continue to gush over the ship's design and the market anticipation.

Raymond Fairchild, ever the detail-oriented, starts off the questions. "We're still weighing in at 220k gross tonnes, correct?"

"Roughly," I respond.

Rob, my New York fleet manager, chimes in, "That's a fucking heavyweight right there! It might even give those floating cities by Royal Caribbean a run for their money. How many preorders have we lined up?"

"One hundred and fifty," Helen Fairchild, our lead engineer replies with a note of pride. Rob lets out an impressed whistle.

"So boss," Don steps in with a deceptively innocent question. "How do we ensure her stability in storms?"

I tamp down my irritation. Don knows this already. "Helen?" I prompt her to take the floor after a moment of silence.

"We have a deal with Marine Safe to access their modern navigation. And the smart ballast systems were installed by Aqua-Balance Pro. You don't get more stable than that."

Raymond chuckles, "How the fuck did you manage to bring those two giants to your dinner table and not end up in a brawl?"

"Or altogether becoming the dinner!" Rob quips, and the room erupts in laughter.

I reply, "Think of it as having a Fairchild prenup."

Again, they all laugh. Prenups are something everyone in the room understands.

Helen mutters, "Well said, boss. Nothing ever gets past that one." She is the third wife of one of my uncles so she's well acquainted with the intricacies of prenups.

Don's voice slices through the light mood. "As long as this marriage doesn't end in divorce." He returns my warning glare with an innocent smile. "What? We all know divorce is the iceberg we most dread, don't we? Hopefully, the new captain here will do us a favor and sink the dated company policies."

"Hear, hear," everyone else echoes. It shows the Fairchilds' shared frustration about the many restrictive company policies.

I'd planned to tackle the infamous marriage clause as first priority. Now, I'm beginning to see the wisdom in my father's view. Those policies might be the only shield I have, especially with a COO who'd rather see me fail. Maybe in a year or two, when tensions ease, we can revisit those policies.

"Before we wrap up here, boss," Don interjects, shifting gears. "Let's remember that New York media is all about sustainability. What the hell do we tell them about the environmental footprint of this beast?"

Don knows the drill. We've fielded this question countless times throughout the project's development. Yet, he just can't resist trying to corner me. I wouldn't put it past him to have already arranged a series of press briefings, eagerly waiting to spotlight what he thinks is a major flaw in this model.

The question hangs in the air, a seemingly innocent inquiry that sends a ripple of unease through the team. Helen hesitates, a glance at me betraying the complexity of the answer.

"Well," she begins, "it's fair to say that balancing luxury with sustainability at this scale... it's not without its risks."

Don turns to me, a sly smile spreading across his face. "Risks? Boss, do you think our stakeholders are ready for such a gamble?"

The word 'gamble' resonates, and I feel the weight of the executives' gaze and their silent questions.

I take a deep breath, choosing my words carefully. "Yes, it's a gamble, Don. But one well-calculated. We're looking to partner with the right companies to get us fully renewable energy."

Don presses, "Is there a reason these partners haven't signed on yet? Does something about this project give them pause?"

I assure the team. "The companies will want to see the vision materialize first, then they will come in droves, then we'll negotiate."

Don nods, his expression thoughtful, yet the glint in his eye suggests he's filed this information away for later use. "Just make sure you're not negotiating away your ship, captain. It'd be a shame if it eventually sailed without you."

"Good thing being a captain isn't only about navigating the ship; it's about knowing who needs to be thrown overboard."

My veiled threat hangs heavily in the now silent room. Even Don looks shocked. They know I don't make threats. I prefer to maintain an air of charm even while striking cruel blows.

Someone chuckles, and the others take their cue from that. In a few moments, the room erupts into laughter, each one as fake as the other, but it's enough to diffuse the tension brimming between the CEO and COO.

Time to wrap this shit up and go home. I raise my glass. "To new horizons."

Glasses clink again, and then the room fills with chatter, much of it from those eager for more insight into the new product launch.

I let conversations flow for a few more minutes, then decide it's time to clear the room. "Guys, give us some space, will you?"

I don't need to say more. Knowing glances are exchanged—some tinged with nervousness, others with a sense of relief. These folks have worked with me for four years; Don's leadership over them is still fresh, barely a few months old. I'd like to believe the majority are still in my corner.

Once the room empties, Don, already knowing what's coming, turns to face me.

"Ryan–" he begins.

"First off, Ronald," I cut him off sharply, using his full name to underscore how serious I am. Cross me again, or question my leadership in front of others, and I'll make sure you learn firsthand how unforgiving the corporate sea can be when you're adrift without a lifeboat."

Don protests, "Surely, I'm allowed to ask questions."

I snap, "As COO, you're supposed to be answering those questions, not undermining the very foundation you stand on. Hell, you're so busy looking for weaknesses, you don't realize you're sawing off the branch we're both sitting on.

He asserts, a hint of defiance in his voice, "I contribute just as much to this company, if not more."

"And that's great to hear. But since you've taken such a keen interest in renewable energy, I'm now tasking you with bringing two companies to the negotiating table by next month. Get me Apex Energy and Green Wave."

He chafes, shifting his weight from one foot to the other. "They're not the energy companies I would've chosen."

I raise an eyebrow. "No? Well, they're the ones I'm choosing. You have four weeks, Ronald."

He mutters something under his breath and turns to leave, but I'm not quite finished.

"One more thing," I closed the distance between us. "I've tolerated your antics for years, letting them roll off my back. But that leniency ends where Stella begins. If you ever get within two feet of my wife again or try to stir up shit, I will tear the entire Reuben Fairchild lineage apart and cheer as the pieces crumble."

The hatred in his pale blue eyes is unmistakable, but it's overshadowed by fear. Satisfied, I take a step back. "Get the fuck out of my sight."

Once he's gone, I roll my shoulders, trying to shake off the tension. Drawing this line in the sand was grim but necessary. Don is growing bolder by the day, his resentment more evident. Something tells me I might need to act on my threats soon.

I pull out my phone to call Stella, but it goes unanswered. It doesn't matter; I know she's at home. Leaving the viewing room, I head home, resolved to spend the rest of the day buried in her tight heat.

Chapter Thirty-Two

STELLA

I STRETCH LAZILY. I've been in this scented bubble bath for the past half hour, trying to pass time until I can head to Ocean Gate to see its CEO. Ryan's been in London on business for the past week. I don't think there's anything more depressing than this huge penthouse without him in it.

Even at the start, when I hardly saw him, his presence lingered in every corner. And over the past two months, we've become inseparable, doing everything side by side. I've even started waking up earlier to watch him at the gym, and he's managed to rope me into joining him.

My phone vibrates on the marble countertop, and I pick it up carefully, trying not to get it wet. It's a text from Ada Patson, his secretary.

He's free from one, but he has a meeting with the New York team at two. I'll block that time off for you.

I dry my hand on the towel wrapped around my head before texting back my thanks.

I can only hope that hour would be enough time. We've never been apart this long since things got real between us. He also doesn't know I'm coming. I make a mental note to pack myself a change of clothes, just in case something gets ruined, a likely possibility.

I wrap myself in a fluffy robe and then pad over to the vanity. Reaching under the sink for my razor, I come up empty-handed.

Shoot, I've used the last one.

I glance at Ryan's side of the bathroom, a mischievous smile on my lips. He once mentioned I could use his razor since he hardly ever does, preferring his personal groomer instead—and it's one of those fancy heated ones, too. Sweet.

Crossing to his side, I rummage through the first couple of drawers. Not finding it among the usual items, I move to the overhead lighted cabinet. I spot the shaver on its charging stand and stretch on tiptoes to grab it, but I end up pulling down a small velvet pouch as well. It hits the floor, spilling its contents.

I look down to see a tri-stone signet ring spinning by my feet, as if taunting me.

The gemstones are in three shades of blue: sapphire, turquoise, and aquamarine, each of the stones catching the light. My heart thuds painfully as realization dawns on me.

The razor clatters to the floor and drop to my knees, tears flooding my eyes. I've seen this ring too many times in Viv's drawings, and heard her describe it in astonishing detail, not to recognize it instantly.

Vivian. Oh my God. Vivian!

—⋄✦⋄—

As soon as I get back to my own room, I lock the door, go into my nearly empty walk-in closet, and call Bonnie.

"Stella, are you there!" Bonnie's worried voice cuts through, making me realize I'd gone silent over the phone.

"I'm here." I stay huddled on the floor, tears streaming down my face. I stare at the accursed ring on the thick carpet beside me. It's an heirloom of some sort, made of gold.

Bonnie squeals, "I can't believe you're calling now! Did Ethan tell you?"

"Tell me what?" I hold in my hiccups long enough to hear a drawn-out moan and then a series of panting. "Bonnie? Are you...?" I can't even finish the question as the answer becomes obvious.

"Oh shit, hang on." Then, after a full minute, she sighs and continues. "Yep, my water broke not long ago, and it hurts like a bitch, but yeah, I'm otherwise fine for another ten or fifteen minutes. I can't believe Ethan called you."

I pause, fighting back my sobs. The last thing Bonnie needs right now is me piling my problems on her. "Are you okay?" My voice comes out choked, thick with tears.

Bonnie all but screeches. "Now he's gone and made you cry! Why the hell would he tell you anyway? There's Brooke, and there's Sabrina, who's had twins, for heaven's sake!"

I manage to compose myself enough to speak. "No, Ethan didn't tell me anything. But, Bonnie, are you okay? Is Ethan with you right now?"

"Oh yeah, he's here now. He's just getting ready to leave for the hospital and taking forever. I hope he knows how to deliver a baby because, at this rate, he may well have to." She yells it loudly enough, presumably so Ethan can hear her.

My heart thumps in fear as I remember the day Vivian went into labor, her last day on earth. This time I can't hold back the sobs.

"What's wrong Stella?"

"Oh God, everything! Everything is wrong."

Her tone gentles. "Babe, I swear to you I will be fine; I'm just in a bad mood, that's all. You know City Memorial has the best doctors."

She must think my panic is all about Viv, that I'm reliving the trauma. And perhaps part of me is. "It's not that," I assure her, even as I question my own words.

"What's the matter then? Why are you crying?"

Suddenly, my reasons for calling, the ring, the revelations—they all seem trivial compared to what she's going through. "It's nothing. You're in labor. That's what matters right now."

"Don't even think about it, Stella. Tell me now!" she finishes on another near-yell. I can't tell if she's having another contraction or just being a massive grouch.

"How far apart are your contractions?"

She dismisses my concern with an impatient huff. "Stella forget that! You never cry. What is going on with you?"

She's wrong. I cry. I cry so much it's the only way to keep my tough outer shell together.

"Stella!" Bonnie's voice snaps me back to the moment. "Is it Ryan?" When I don't say anything, she panics. "It's Ryan, isn't it? Oh God, is he hurt? Has something happened to him?"

"Bonnie wait. He's not hurt okay. It's just... "I sigh again. "This is all so messed up, Bonnie."

"What is it?"

"I... I'm leaving him."

"What! But I thought you two were finally making things real?"

"We were, but..." *How do I even say this?* The tears make it hard to speak.

"But what? I swear Stella if you don't spit it out this second—"

"He's... He's Harriet's father."

"What the fuck?"

"I found the signet ring, Bonnie. It belongs to Ryan."

Bonnie shrieks, "Oh hell no! You've got to be fucking kidding me. Christ on a cracker, there is no fucking way you're telling me the truth!" I hear another string of curses, and then Ethan's strained voice comes through the phone.

"Stella?"

Feeling guilty for dumping my problems on his wife in her current condition, I murmur "Hey Ethan, I'm so sorry. I'll... I call back later."

Bonnie's shout rings clear through the phone on speaker. "Don't you dare just drop that bomb and fucking leave me hanging!"

"Baby," Ethan tries to intervene, "Stella's right. I can get her back on the phone after we get you to the hospital."

"Did you not hear what she just said? Ryan is Harriet's father!"

Ethan's confusion cuts through the tense silence that follows. "Come again?"

Bonnie's response is a string of curses, leaving Ethan to seek clarity from me. "Stella, what is she on about?"

"I found the ring," I manage to say through the tears.

"What ring?" Ethan.

"The ring! The signet ring!" Bonnie yells. "The same one from that night. It belongs to Ryan."

Another heavy silence. And then then finally gets it. "Fu-uuck! It can't be. There must be another explanation."

I hear Bonnie's voice, "Ethan, remember I told you Vivian described a big blonde guy with a very specific ring at the Greenhouse party."

"But how can you be sure it's the same ring?" Ethan insists.

I explain, the pieces connecting in a way I wish they didn't. "Vivian painted it. Hundreds of times. The ring I found matches the one in her painting exactly. It was in Ryan's bathroom,"

"He's Harriet's father," Bonnie says again, her voice leaving no room for doubt. My sobs renew at her words, the reality of the situation crashing down on me.

Ethan's voice comes through, low and urgent, "Stella, Bonnie told me Vivian was also tied up and beaten, and the man got off on her pain. I've never known Ryan to be violent, not even while roaring drunk. Do you really think he could do something like that?"

"I... I don't know," I stammer, feeling adrift. "Everything I thought I knew about him... it's all just... gone."

"He's your husband, Stella," Ethan states, and somehow, it sounds like an accusation. "You'd know if he was capable of something like that."

"Like what?

"If he enjoys inflicting pain."

"Like a sadist?"

"Yes"

My face heats. *Does holding down and spanking count? Does it matter if the bite of pain drives my pleasure to unbidden heights?* "I- I don't know."

"You do, in your gut."

Ryan craves my submission, but he also respects my boundaries. He would never force anything on me.

I sigh. "I went with my gut feeling with Viv's situation too, and I turned out very wrong."

Ethan tries to reassure me, even in the middle of their own chaos. "Listen, give me a sec. We're just heading down to the car, then I'll be right back with you, okay?"

"I feel like I'm just adding to your load. We can talk later," I offer, not wanting to burden them further.

Bonnie insists "Don't you dare hang up. We'll figure this out together."

After long minutes punctuated by groans, curses, and Ethan's calming words, I finally hear the sounds of traffic through the phone. Ethan's voice returns, steady and clear. "Stella, there has to be another explanation. Maybe the ring isn't as unique as you think."

I counter quietly. "You haven't seen Harriet. She has the Fairchild look. Ryan's eyes. How can that be a coincidence?"

Bonnie's voice filters through, her breaths punctuated by discomfort. "It's true. What are the odds?"

"You should talk to him then," Ethan suggests.

"And say what?" *By his own admission, he was practically drunk all through college; he doesn't even remember graduating.*

I consider all the scenarios of us talking about this.

If he doesn't remember does make him innocent? No.

If he denies it, would I believe him? No.

And if he remembers and admits to it could I survive the heartbreak? No

"I can't face him, Ethan" I say, my voice barely a whisper "I just can't. But I need to know the truth. Right now, I can only trust the truth."

I thought I'd gotten to know the true Ryan, the incredible person beneath that carefully crafted exterior. I fell for him, trusted him more than I've ever trusted anyone. And now, it feels like I've lost my footing and tumbled into darkness.

I should have known better. Nothing this wonderful ever happens to me. He was too good to be true.

Ethan's steady voice cuts through my pain, almost as if he's offering me a lifeline. "Stella, what do you want to do now?"

"I need to leave this place. Now." The decision cements itself with each word.

Bonnie warns, "Stella, leaving without finding out the truth will haunt you, Stella." To her husband she pleads, "Ethan, please do something."

If I didn't feel so hollow, I might find Bonnie's plea amusing. She really believes Ethan can work miracles.

Bonnie continues amid short gasps that tell me she's having another contraction. "Ethan, I know Ryan is your friend, and you will want to protect him..."

Ethan scoffs, already knowing this is boiling down to him choosing sides. "You're my priority, baby, and Stella is your best friend. There are no sides to take here, there's just the truth."

"Okay," Bonnie replies, "but you know what that means, right?"

Ethan's heavy sigh comes through the phone. "Stella, I can help you find the facts you want."

"You mean whether or not Ryan did it?"

He clarifies. "No, no one can tell you that except Ryan himself. And if you can't trust him, then you might go ahead and accuse him. What I can tell you is if he's really Harriet's father or not."

Bonnie who has seen photos of Harriet, protests. "Ethan, the girl is a split copy of Ryan. I didn't clock the resemblance before, but now I see it."

Ethan's voice grows hard. "That is still debatable. DNA doesn't lie."

"Can we do that?" I ask, barely daring to hope, feeling as though my entire future hangs in the balance of this conversation.

Ethan states. "Not without his knowledge."

Bonnie huffs, her patience clearly wearing thin. "And here I thought I was your priority! Fine, I'll handle it myself. Stella, send me Harriet's foster parents' address—"

"Siobhan!" Ethan cuts in sharply, using Bonnie's full name—undoubtedly a sign that he's serious.

"Harvard," Bonnie shoots back, "You can either get involved or get out of the way, either way, I'm helping Stella. You know how I feel about what happened to Vivian." I hear another groan from Bonnie and my throat tightens. I'm so touched by her loyalty, even at the cost of clashing with Ethan.

There's a tense silence.

"Damn it," Ethan swears, and then his tone shifts, becoming cold and detached. "Stella, take some of your husband's hair from his brush and put it in a sealed envelope. Someone will contact you shortly to collect, alright?"

"Thanks, Harvard," Bonnie says, relief evident in her voice.

"Any fucking time, Siobhan," Ethan replies with a sigh of resignation.

My heart begins to pound for a whole new reason. Okay. This all feels so covert and strange, but for Bonnie and Ethan on the other end of the line, it seems like just another day.

For the umpteenth time, I find myself wondering if there isn't more to these two than meets the eye. They're more than cyber-security experts. More than being husband and wife. They're partners in... something. It's like they're part of a secret society.

Bonnie's voice interrupts my spiraling thoughts. "Are you going to be okay, Stella? Should I ask Brooke to come see you in Seattle?"

"Um, no, no. I'll be fine. You need them more than I do right now. I just... I need to get out of this house."

Ethan tries again, "Stella, I still really think you should hear him out."

I counter, "It's better this way, trust me."

"But can you live with yourself if you don't give the man you love the benefit of the doubt?"

"The same way I've lived with myself after not believing my sister when she first told me about the assault? Yes, Ethan, I think I can."

"Okay, well get those samples, and someone will call you soon."

"Guys, I can't thank you enough. And Bonnie..."

"I'll be fine, I promise."

As soon as we disconnect, my decision weighs heavily on me, but it's too late to back out now. There is no other way to play this. I had a choice between taking Viv's word against the word of other people; I betrayed her and chose other people. I won't make that mistake twice.

Suppressing a shiver of revulsion, I force myself back into our bathroom to pluck some strands of hair from Ryan's brush. It is a betrayal, a violation of the trust and intimacy we've shared, but the need for truth drives me on.

Fifteen minutes later, my phone rings, displaying an unknown number. The voice on the other end says he's here with pizza. I'm about to dismiss him when realization dawns on me who it might be.

I swing the door open to find a young delivery boy, no older than twenty, with a bright smile.

"Hi! Are you Stella?"

"Yes," I reply, taking the box of pizza from him. I hesitate, clutching the warm box, wondering if this is just an innocent mix-up.

"Um, actually, there might have been some mistake. I didn't order—"

He doesn't let me finish. "It's okay. Sometimes glitches happen," he extends his hand.

I reach into my robe pocket and hand over the envelope, still half-convinced he's just a confused delivery boy.

"Thanks for the tip," he takes the envelope with a cheerful grin and leaves.

Any lingering doubts as to the nature of Ethan and Bonnie's plan vanish with his departure. They're orchestrating something beyond the ordinary. They're arranging for Harriet's sample to be collected just as secretly, without eventually needing an address. And all of this is happening while they're in the hospital having a baby.

Who exactly are these people?

Feeling hollowed out, I pack an overnight bag, leaving behind a note for Ryan. It's the most humane goodbye I can muster under the circumstances.

Chapter Thirty-Three

RYAN

"BABY!" I CALL OUT as I step out of the elevator and into our penthouse, dragging my suitcase behind me. The buzz of excitement at the thought of finally seeing Stella again after seven long days is almost overwhelming. Sure, we've talked every day, but phone calls pale in comparison to actually being able to touch her, to feel her around me.

"Stella?" I know she didn't have work plans today; she'd promised to stay home if I could peel myself away from the office early. An easy promise to make, considering how I struggled to focus on work, my mind filled instead with thoughts of her.

I call out again, thinking she might be indulging in one of her long, relaxing baths when something on the kitchen counter catches my eye—a box of pizza, still unopened. It strikes me as odd because Stella hardly eats pizza, but I'm game for whatever she's in the mood for.

As I reach for the box, a folded piece of paper resting on top grabs my attention. Picking it up, I unfold the note and scan the words, then read it again, and yet again, my brain refusing to process its content.

Finally, I slump into a nearby barstool, the note in hand, and force myself to read it once more, very slowly this time. A wave of shock courses through my body, leaving me numb and disorientated.

Ryan, I know it's sudden, but I can't do this anymore. You're right, you Fairchilds are a lot to handle, and I'm much too independent to want a life of dark and dirty secrets. I'm reverting to our original agreement. It's just been a few weeks over the agreed time, so hopefully, it won't make things difficult for you.

I've returned to New York. The ring, The Stella—I can't accept them. BodyLift will manage without me for now and Whirpool is practically on autopilot. Your generosity for Harriet and me won't be forgotten. Nadia Finch will be in touch to discuss changes to Harriet's adoption. Congratulations again on your CEO. There's no one else more perfect for the role.

Stella

The note crumples in my clenched fist, mirroring the tight squeeze around my heart. My head drops into my hands, and I bury my fingers in my hair as the implications sink in.

Something happened to make her leave so suddenly.

...you Fairchilds are a lot to handle and I'm much too independent to want a life of dark and dirty secrets...

My mind immediately goes to Don. He stands to gain the most from my marriage crashing. And less than two hours ago, he warned me Stella would walk out.

How could he know it would happen unless he arranged it?

I dial Stella, but her line is unreachable. The lukewarm pizza suggests she left recently.

I rush into my office. The large monitor flickers to life with a few clicks, revealing the security camera feeds. Scanning through, I find nothing out of the ordinary—just the pizza delivery boy and Stella, who had been inside until she left. The timestamp shows that she left about an hour ago, only with a small suitcase.

Pausing the feed on her image, I zoom in. The details of her beautiful face twist my stomach into knots—puffy eyes, drawn, devoid of makeup.

She looks heartbroken. It isn't fear or anger driving her away; it's pain. Something hurt my wife enough to make her think she couldn't stay with me.

I wrack my brain, my mind immediately going back to the woman who threw herself at me in the hotel elevator in London. A woman I don't remember fucking, but apparently, she did. Enough to try to follow me to my room, dressed in nothing but her trench coat.

Could paparazzi have captured us and twisted the narrative? I send her a quick text.

Baby, if this is about London, I swear to you nothing happened. Whatever else it is, we'll fix it. But if you're in danger or if it's something you can't tell me, you know what to do.

I sent the text, hoping she gets my meaning.

I call Alex to give him the heads up about Stella contacting him. Next, I dial Xavier.

"Hey, buddy!" He greets.

"Xavi," I say simply, and already he gets that something is very wrong.

"What happened?"

"Stella's gone." Saying it out loud makes it a hundred times worse.

"Gone? What do you mean gone?"

"She left a note... She's headed back to New York."

"Fuck. What happened?"

"I'm at a loss here, Xavi. No clue. We were good the last time I talked to her which was this morning. I was hoping you might have some idea, that she might have gotten in touch with you guys. "

"No, she hasn't. Hang on Brooke is here." The line falls silent for a moment, leaving me to my swirling thoughts until he returns. "No man, she has no idea. Did something happen between you two?" he asks. "You think she found out about London?" I'd been on the phone to Xavier when the woman cornered me.

"Possibly, but that doesn't seem like enough to drive her away. Not like this. I know her. Which is why I suspect she left because she had no choice."

"You think something forced her to leave?"

"Or someone." I pause, gathering my thoughts before voicing the suspicion that's been gnawing at me. "I think Don is somehow involved."

Four years ago, I helped his wife disappear, a move that dealt him a huge financial blow. Did he become aware of my involvement and decide to retaliate?

"You seriously think Don could arrange that?"

I shrug even though Xavier can't see me. It's the easiest way to cripple me. Don knew Stella was his way of getting to me.

Xavier's voice is all business. "So what's your move now?"

"First, find Stella, make sure she's safe."

"Got it. I'll put feelers out in all my hotels and places I have connections within New York."

"I also need to take the pressure off her."

"Meaning?"

"Give her some space. If Don or his minion is threatening her, they'll want to see that she's really left me."

I can hear the wheels turning in Xavier's head as the silence stretches. "Please man, tell me that's all you plan to do."

"You already know what's coming Xavi. If Don is behind this and he's desperate enough to come after Stella... He won't stop until he becomes CEO of Ocean Gate."

"Ryan—"

"He's toying with the one thing I can't afford to lose Xavi."

"So are you then just going to let him take your birthright?"

"No, Xavi" I smile in spite of myself. "I'll give it to him."

"Ryan—"

"Let him have it. I'll deal with him when the time comes. The only thing I care about right now is Stella."

There's a beat of silence, then Xavier murmurs. "Fuck me."

"What's that?"

"Nothing. I just never thought the day would come when I'd hear you say that."

"It's true."

"Okay, but just don't give in to the bastard yet. I'll do everything I can to find Stella and get rid of whatever leverage he thinks he has. If I don't locate her in any of my hotels, I'll hit Ethan or Alex up."

"Alex knows already, but I appreciate it, man."

I hang up and call Don. Looks like he was right. This ship will be sailing without its captain.

Chapter Thirty-Four

STELLA

I SIT ON MY plush bed in the Vista Astoria Hotel suite, hugging my knees and staring unseeingly at the East River through the floor-length windows out. But my focus is inward, on my swirling storm of emotions.

I chose a hotel outside of Manhattan, somewhere unlikely to be owned by Xavier, but I've ended up in a room with a view that reminds me of Ryan, though everything reminds me of him, so there's that.

It's been five days since I walked away from our home in Seattle. Twelve days since I last saw Ryan. And two agonizing days since that envelope arrived. The one currently sitting on the hallway table. The one containing the DNA report I can't open because I already know what it will say.

My phone vibrates with an incoming text. It's Brooke.

> **Bonnie told me everything. Don't be mad, she did the right thing. This business of secrets stops right fucking now. For everyone. I made Xavier tell me where you've been holing up. Queens? Really? Get out of bed and get dressed. I'm coming to you.**

Brooke dropping the F-bomb? She's pretty fucking pissed then. Well, I couldn't fucking care. I stopped giving two fucks about anything five days ago.

She's right about one thing, though. I've barely left this bed, surviving on crackers and water and self-torture in the form of hot showers. Not because of the heat but because they remind me of how we shared those showers when he needed relief from his headaches.

As for Bonnie, I stopped taking her calls because there's a limit to how selfish I can allow myself to be. She's just had a baby, yet she's made it their business to call me twice a day since I started hibernating here.

Like a glutton for punishment, I scroll over to Bonnie's text from three days ago again. It's linked to a video with the tag #playboyryanfairchild.

I've watched it over a hundred times, still the headline hits me like a ton of bricks:

"Ryan Fairchild, CEO of Ocean Gate Industries, throws in the towel."

Of course, I play the video again.

Ryan Fairchild, CEO Ocean Gate Industries has just stepped down for his long-term rival and cousin Don Fairchild. There are speculations as to why, but multiple sources point to Don being the true winner of the seat six months ago, but he was outmaneuvered by the outgoing CEO and his wife.

As karma would have it, the couple who married recently is rumored to have split up amid accusations of cheating with an ex during the ship magnate's recent London trip. His estranged wife, a high-profile celebrity stylist has now moved back to New York with her model ex-boyfriend. Score. Y'all know we love a woman who can give a good tit for tat...

The video drones on, but I'm stuck on pause, my mind racing. Social media is a cesspool of bullshit, but when more reputable sites are echoing the same story, I know there's no smoke without fire. Yet, the Ryan I know wouldn't step down for anyone, least of all Don. Ocean Gate is the one thing Ryan has always wanted.

A knock on my hotel room door snaps me out of my downward spiral. "That was quick," I mutter, expecting Brooke. I pull myself out of bed, smoothing out my ratty T-shirt, and open the door to find Xavier.

"What are you doing here?" I ask, surprised when I don't see Brooke in tow.

"Stella, we need to talk," he steps past the threshold with a look that is both concerned and annoyed.

I close the door and face him, my arms crossed. "Xavier, really, I've got my wits about me. Yes, Ryan told me you were worried I'd end up a basket case after being with him.

"Yeah, about that," he starts, his gaze searching mine. "It appears I was wrong. It's Ryan who seems to be unraveling."

My heart skips. "Oh my God, are the rumors true? He stepped down for Don?"

Xavier confirms with a solemn nod, "I'm afraid they're true. He's back in New York as of yesterday as COO."

I retreat to the bed, hugging my knees. New York suddenly feels so small now that Ryan's in it. "But—he can't just hand over his position. It's been the Richard legacy for over forty years!"

Xavier explains. "Ryan still holds the controlling shares. Technically, half of the controlling shares. The other belongs to you. Unless you guys split for real, Don is CEO in name only."

I can't grasp what he's trying to say about the shares. I still can't believe Ryan would give up his seat. "But with Don's new-found power, it won't be long before he gets enough leverage to target Ryan."

Xavier's shrug offers little comfort. "Ryan's smart enough to secure his defenses before stepping down. Hopefully."

I shake my head in frustration. "You don't get it, Xavier. Don hates him. I've felt the venom just by being close to Ryan. He won't stop until he's destroyed him."

"I agree. Which is why I'm here. Don used you to get to Ryan."

I frown in confusion. "What are you suggesting?"

"Did Don not threaten you? Made you pack up and leave Seattle?"

My mind races, "No. Did Ryan think I was being black-mailed? I left him a note."

Xavier confirms with a nod. "A vague note, raising that suspicion. Ryan has been doing everything to keep you safe. Stepping down, keeping his distance, while waiting for you to contact Alex.

"Why would I call...?" I trail off, suddenly making sense of his cryptic text.

"He even went as far as inserting plain clothes among my staff.

Of course. This is Xavier's hotel. Is there any getting away from these billionaires?

"But we've been just sitting on our hands here because nothing has actually happened from your side, Stella. You're not attempting to contact anyone. Why?"

Dropping my head into my hands, I feel the weight of Xavier's words. "He thought I was in trouble and stepped down to protect me."

"Stella, you're the one asset Ryan can't afford to lose. But he can't wait anymore. He barged into my house this morning and literally hurled me in this direction to come and get you because he doesn't think Brooke would be able to attempt a fireman's carry on you if you refused to budge."

I stand and pace to the window, unable to take Xavier's light humor.

Ethan and Bonnie didn't say anything. Ryan doesn't know the real reason I left. He's had to guess and speculate. I've cost him his inheritance.

"I wasn't blackmailed," I begin, my voice barely above a whisper. "That's not why I left."

"Was it the London scandal then?" Xavier probes. Several photos of Ryan with a half-naked woman in an elevator had surfaced online.

"Nothing happened in London, Xavier, I know Ryan wouldn't cheat..."

Xavier looks genuinely puzzled, his confusion rapidly giving way to irritation. "You weren't blackmailed by Don. You're telling me Ryan gave up his seat for nothing?"

"I didn't think he'd ever do that."

"Well, he did because all he cares about is you, Stella. And I know you love him too. So why would you walk out on your marriage like that?"

I struggle for words, "Because I couldn't face him."

"Why? What did you do?" When I hesitate, he warns, "I'm two seconds away from calling Ryan."

"Did Brooke tell you about my sister?"

"Vivian? Yes. What about her?"

I turn back to face him. "Well, she had a daughter."

"Harriet," Xavier recalls impatiently. "The real reason why you crashed Ryan's wedding. I know."

Thanks, Brooke, I make a mental note to remind myself that Brooke and Xavier tell each other everything.

"What about Harriet?" He presses.

"I–uh, had reason to believe that Ryan is her father," I admit finally and tell him about the ring.

Xavier remains silent throughout my story. Then, he wearily drops into a nearby chair, raking his fingers through his hair. He looks up at me, his green eyes filled with accusation. "I see. So that's why you left without talking to him. You believed he could have done something so despicable."

Tears spring to my eyes. "I was in shock. I wasn't thinking straight."

"You could have asked him," Xavier suggests, a hint of disappointment in his tone.

"All I could think about was my sister. I feel responsible for her death because I didn't believe her back then. And I couldn't just ask Ryan. He says he doesn't remember his entire time in college."

"One thing you should know about Ryan is he doesn't need more than a few brain cells to remember details. Yes, he had no clue which way was up most of the time, but he still graduated summa cum laude. He would have been able to tell you if he did it or not."

I nod, a wave of guilt washing over me.

Xavier probes further. "So, when was this Greenhouse party that Vivian went to?"

"November first. It was a Halloween-themed party, I think."

"Now see, that's fucking interesting."

"What do you mean?"

Xavier shakes his head, not elaborating, but continues to question, "And, the DNA test? What did it then reveal?"

Feeling awful I confess, "I... I haven't checked it."

"Why not?"

"Because I know he didn't do it."

Xavier looks at me, one eyebrow raised, his tone almost mocking, "Really! How can you be so sure?"

Ethan was right. "I just knew it in my gut it couldn't be, only I had no proof."

"I can give you the proof you need," Xavier states, rising from the chair and coming toward me. "Ryan wasn't anywhere near New York that day. He was in Seattle. Grieving."

"Grieving?" I echo, confused.

"Ivy, his former wife, was dying. Slowly and painfully. Nothing helped, and she had to be terminally sedated, it became too much for her. Too much for Ryan. It ended on November the first. Every year, for an entire week, Ryan isolates himself at the lake house to mourn. It didn't matter if the sky was falling, or in the middle of semester exams, he'd just up and leave."

The realization slowly dawns on me as hot tears cloud my vision.

Xavier continues, "He's an incredibly loving man Stella, but he was damaged goods after Ivy. He locked his real self far beyond each and offered the shell all too generously to women."

It suddenly all makes sense why Ryan was the way he was. Why he'd blow hot and cold and seem to switch off with certain topics.

"But he's healing now. And I dare say more so in the past year since he's met you."

I raised my puzzled gaze to his, a silent question in my tear-filled eyes.

Xavier shrugs. "How I know that is because last Halloween, Ryan wasn't in Seattle, was he?"

On November the first, he was in New York. Making my dreams come true. Standing up to the DuPonts for me. Throwing me a surprise party on the luxury yacht he built for me. Kissing me. Making love to me.

I collapse to the floor, sobbing. "Oh God, I'm so sorry. I had no idea. He never mentioned this."

"He doesn't talk about it. Frankly, neither do we. It's too painful."

"How... did they meet?" Despite knowing it'll cause me more pain, I need to understand.

Xavier takes a breath as if bracing himself to delve into the story. "The Leagues had just finalized a deal with Ocean Gate and invited the Fairchilds over to celebrate. That's where Ryan saw her. They fell in love despite being polar opposites."

"Opposites how?" I remember the painting; the pale, delicate hands on Ryan's large, tanned back.

"She was sheltered and homeschooled due to a condition she'd been born with. By eighteen, she was nearing the expected end of her life, but Ryan didn't care. He loved her, looked after her, and they shared precious moments together. The Leagues are forever grateful to Ryan for the happiness he brought Ivy in her final years. But we all knew their love was doomed, which made it excruciating for not only Ryan but for everyone close to them.

"Oh my God, Ryan." My heart breaks for him over and over, hot salty tears streaming down my face as sobs wrack my body."

"Come here, Stella." Xavier reaches out, pulls me to my feet, and wraps me in a hug. For long minutes, he just lets me cry, patting my shoulder. "Stella, if there's one thing I've learned, it's that pain has lousy timing. So does love."

"I should have trusted him. I never should have left. I've hurt him so badly. How could he ever forgive that?"

"You'd be surprised at how much the man can forgive. He loves you. And we all make mistakes. It's how we grow."

"I need to see him, Xavier," I wail, "Will he see me?"

"Why do you think I'm here? He sent me to bring you to him, drag you if necessary. He insisted I had to be the one to get you."

I manage a smile through my tears. "So you can carry me out like a sack of potatoes."

"I was sure it wouldn't come to that." Xavier smiles back, "but I'll have you know he gave me permission to physically remove you from here, for your own safety, of course."

"I bet he did." Suddenly I can't wait to see him anymore.

Chapter Thirty-Five

RYAN

I STARE AT XAVIER'S ridiculous text—one that he probably sent me by mistake.

> **To err is human, dumbass.**

Could Lily Rose have gotten her hands on his phone again? Which is annoying because what the fuck is he doing back home when he should be in Queens, dragging Stella here?

Just as I'm about to call him out, my phone rings. It's Mom. *Great, just great.*

I brace myself for the inevitable. My parents have just returned from their vacation in Bora Bora. I'm surprised they haven't found out I stepped down sooner. They must've ditched their phones and the TV.

"Hi, Mom!" I greet cheerfully.

"Ryan, how could you let this happen? Your father is beside himself. He hasn't slept in two days, pacing like a caged lion. Do you want to give him a heart attack? Do you want to give *me* a heart attack?"

"Mom, listen. Get Dr. Smith to do a house call. Dad may need a sedative. Once he's calmer and gets a good night's rest, he'll see it's not such a disaster after all."

I have to pull the phone away from my ear to escape her shrieking.

"Not a disaster! Ryan, have you lost your ever-loving mind? Your father spent his entire career ensuring your future, and in just six months, you've thrown it all away!—your company position, your inheritance, your wife... How could you be so reckless?"

"I'm still the COO, Mom. And my stint in New York brought some of the best deals to the company. I'm back now, and we'll do great things from here."

"Yes, that was when your father was CEO, and he let you shine. Now you're dealing with a headstrong, impulsive—"

"Leadership will temper him," I interject.

"—drug dealer."

"Now, Mom..."

"It's true. Stephanie mentioned it."

"I wouldn't listen to gossip from the tea club ladies."

"And Leonora, oh, that snotty, smug bitch. That's it! We might as well be out on our asses. You know she hasn't forgiven you for moving into that lake house."

I'd laugh if I dared to right now, but she'd have my head so I wind it in. "Okay, how about I come to Seattle later this week to see you guys and explain everything?"

"I can't believe this. Gina is beside herself, and Stella, oh poor Stella. She must be distraught. What on earth could you have done to make her leave you? I raised you better than this."

"Mom, listen. Tell Dad I'll be in Seattle soon. I need to sort things out with Stella first."

"I can't. He's got a thousand lawyers crawling the place trying to reverse this crazy move of yours."

"I signed it over myself, with witnesses present. What, are you going to put me in a straightjacket and claim I was insane?"

"If need be, yes."

A chuckle threatens to escape again but I squash it. "Okay, Mom. But I need to see my wife first. We'll talk about the company later."

The elevator dings, and I know it's Xavier. He's probably back to tell me Brooke insisted on going to Queens herself or some other excuse.

"Someone's here, Mom. I've got to go."

I hear her speaking to my father. "The boy has lost his mind, Richard. I just can't believe this."

I hang up and head to the living room.

"Xavi, I swear to God, if—" I stop mid-sentence, my phone clattering to the floor.

Stella stands there, looking like a slice of heaven, her eyes shiny and puffy. Xavier is behind her.

"Ry," she gasps, running to me. I grab her and crash my lips to hers in what is too raw and savage to be called a kiss.

I drown myself in her taste, her smell. She's mumbling against my lips, but I can't bring myself to pause or listen. I back us up until we collapse onto the sofa, our hands and mouths exploring and devouring each other with a desperation born of two weeks' separation.

"Baby, I missed you so fucking much," I manage to say between drugging kisses. "I'm so sorry. He should never have gotten to you." I bury my face in her neck, licking and nibbling the fragrant skin. I palm her breasts then bend to bite her rigid nipple through her clothes. Her cry is ragged, spurring me to take more, to give more.

I start to kiss a path down her torso, and I'm licking and biting on the soft curve of her belly when her words finally break through my haze of need.

"Ryan, can you ever forgive me?"

That makes me pause. I lift my head to meet her eyes. "Forgive you?"

"For leaving."

"Baby, I understand why you had to."

"No, you really don't... and, Xavier told me some things, and I just feel so awful for leaving."

I suddenly remember Xavier and glance around. He's tactfully vanished. "Xavier told you what?"

"About Ivy."

I go still, waiting for her to continue.

"How you loved and cared for her." She gently touches my jaw. "Ryan, that's why you keep everywhere so spotless... and why you need your own space isn't it? He told me how you grieved for her every year."

Her words are like tiny icicles on my skin. I hear her, but I don't understand why we're discussing Ivy right now. Standing, I walk to the window. It's been ages since I let myself fully remember. She'd wanted to live so badly. To be with me. She'd fought as long and as hard as she could. Until I had to let her go.

I feel Stella's hand on my back, and the tension begins to ease.

As if sensing my relief, she wraps her arms around me and presses her cheeks against my back.

"Ry, please say something. Are we... broken?"

"Broken?" I turn to face her, confused. "Why would we be broken, Stella?"

"Because I should have talked to you first. Trusted you."

"What are you talking about?" I ask, completely taken aback.

"I didn't tell you everything about Vivian."

"Okay?" I say, wondering where this is going.

"She was drugged and raped at one of the Greenhouse parties."

I feel a chill run down my spine. That explains her reaction to the Greenhouse trophy. "Baby, why didn't you tell me?"

"Because I was an idiot. I was falling for you, and I was scared. Scared of giving you something so precious in case you didn't feel the same way."

I probe, trying to understand, "You were afraid of giving me your heart?"

"Yes, but more than that, I was terrified of trusting you with my pain."

I felt the same way about what happened with Ivy. It was too deep a wound to share with just anyone. I was too used to keeping that part of me locked away, it was hard to begin to trust Stella. "I understand, baby."

An emotion very much like hope flickers in her eyes. "You do?"

I nod. Suddenly, a flash of excruciating pain hits me, and my left eye fills with water. I swipe my thumb across my eyelid and flick it away.

"Oh Ry." She cups my face. "You've got a headache."

"It's nothing. It'll pass." I drag her into my arms as she sinks her fingers into my scalp and massages. "I had the same fear so I never told anyone what I went through during Ivy's sickness. Not even my therapist. People only saw the surface."

"Xavier told me a little about that... and about how you would go to the lake house every year."

"Yes," I admit, feeling a sense of peace for the first time in a long while. "Although recently, it's been different. Instead of the old guilt and pain, I've found a sort of acceptance and even fond memories. It's incredibly beautiful there. Would you like to see the lake house?"

"Yes, I'd love to. Thank you." She rests her head against my chest, seeking comfort in the closeness. "But why didn't you go there last Halloween?"

Her question catches me off guard, and for a moment, I'm lost in thought. "I forgot. Despite having her painting above my headboard, I didn't remember until you asked me about the lake house. Being with you, Stella, is such a high. I'm consumed by you."

"You see, it was when Xavier told me that's where you went at that time every year I felt so terrible that I didn't trust my gut instinct—that you couldn't have done it."

"Done what?" And then, it hits me. I freeze. "You thought I assaulted your sister."

The pain that rips through me then is indescribable, like sharp claws tearing at my chest. My breath rushes out in a whoosh.

"Ryan—" She starts to plead, but I gently push her away, taking a few steps back.

I now understand Xavier's earlier cryptic text.

"Since when have you believed that? Was it since that night you saw the trophy in my office?"

"No, it was literally—" She tries to explain, but I don't let her finish.

"Why on earth would you think I did it? Of all the boys who were members of the Greenwich Society, and all the outsiders who attended Greenhouse parties, why would it be me? You must think very low of me, Stella."

My head pounds, threatening to split open, and I head toward my room.

"Ry, baby, please" Her anguish makes my chest tighten. I don't need to see her to know she's crying. I hate it when she cries. "Ryan, please don't walk away."

"Come with me, then," I snap, heading straight to the dark bathroom to use my Zomig spray. The relief is almost instant, but leaves me craving my bed.

She leans on the doorway, "Ry, I'm so sorry."

"Tell me why?" I ask, turning to face her.

"Viv described her attacker as a large blonde man wearing a certain ring. An heirloom. A gold ring with three gemstones: sapphire, turquoise, and aquamarine."

"Jesus Fucking Christ," I gasp, my breath hitching. "You saw that ring in my bathroom cabinet, didn't you? That's why you left."

"Yes," she whispers, her voice barely audible.

Fuck. Fuck. Fuck.

"Is... the ring yours?" she ventures, her voice laced with dread.

"Yes, it's mine," I admit. "And there's only one like it in the world."

"Dear God." Her knees buckle at my admission, and I move quickly to catch her, preventing her from collapsing onto the marble floor.

"Baby, listen if only you'd asked me, I would have told you who hurt Vivian," I say, hoping to soothe the panic I see swirling in her eyes.

"Who was it?"

"It was Don Fairchild. Seven years ago, I lost that ring to him in a poker game, the day before I left for the lake house."

Chapter Thirty-Six

STELLA

I CAN'T STOP TREMBLING as Ryan continues to hold me. My tears flowing freely, I cling to Ryan like he's the only thing that makes sense. A sense of closure overwhelms me, but so does dread, regret, and red-hot pain.

The key to finding out everything was always with Ryan. "I should have trusted you." I sob against his chest, my tears wetting his t-shirt.

He cups my jaw with both hands. "Hey, look at me. You went through something incredibly painful. I've been through endless grief too so I know what it does to you."

I let his soothing words wash over me as he drops tender kisses on my forehead, my eyelids, and my wet cheeks. "Baby, you have me. I love you no matter what. And I'll make him pay."

He takes my mouth, and I curl my hands around his wrists, returning his kiss with all I have. Tonight's revelation has gouged the scabs off old wounds and left me bleeding, but I can't deal with the hurt right now. Right now, I need to feel something else. More than Ryan's forgiveness and acceptance. More than the blinding pleasure I'll find in his arms.

"I want more," I murmur against his lips.

"I know."

No, he doesn't.

"Ryan" I moan, tearing my mouth from his and going on tiptoe, I place open-mouthed kisses on his neck and collarbone. Driven by the need for more, I drag up his shirt until he helps me remove it.

My mouth immediately returns to his pecs and I lick his nipples, loving the taste of his skin and the sexy groans rumbling in his chest. Still needing more, my tongue traces the grooves between his abs muscles, going lower and lower until I'm on my knees.

Looking up to meet his burning gaze, I whisper. "Take me out of my head, Ryan." I undo his pants button and unzip his fly, all the while rubbing my face against his steel-hard erection.

"Tell me what you want." His voice is soft, but there is the unmistakable authoritative bite.

"Make it hurt good."

He puts a knuckle under my chin and tilts my face to meet his. His eyes are assessing, I know that he gets me. "You want me to be rough with you?"

I nod slowly.

"I see. And what do you say when you can't take it anymore?"

Dear God. He's not asking me why I want him that way because he already knows. He's asking for my safe word. My heart lurches as if attempting to beat out of my chest. I know which word I want. I lick my dry lips and respond. "Magnificent."

He grins. "Good choice."

He takes his hard cock out and feeds it to me. A sigh leaves me as I taste him and my core clenches tight. I wrap my hand around the thick base and just lick the length of his big, beautiful cock. He lets me, silently watching me.

I love that he's not rushing me, that he's giving me time to get used to his size and feel. The more I taste him, the harder I shake with need. I trace the engorged veins and then tap the tip of my tongue against the sensitive underside of his glans.

"Fuck!" Ryan groans, leaking more precum. "You're making that cock weep for you. Now suck hard," he commands, and I obey, wrapping my lips around him, hollowing my cheeks and moaning at his taste.

Finally past the point of teasing, he withdraws from my mouth then fists the hair at my nape tight, making me shiver. My nipples bead in response to the burn in my scalp and I reach up and pinch one to relieve the ache. I'm so drenched right now that I'm sure if squeezed my thighs together hard enough, I'd come.

Holding my head steady, he takes my hand away from around the base of his cock then as if he just read my mind, he gently kicks my knees apart so I can't chase the throbbing pleasure between my legs.

"Hands at your back and look at me," he commands. I meet his gaze, daring him with my eyes.

"Take it like the queen you are." He surges forward, sliding his cock into my mouth and I immediately suck. His groan is long and broken as he rocks in and out, gently at first but he gradually picks up pace.

Before long he's thrusting deep, and I'm gagging. He doesn't let up, he also doesn't take his scorching eyes off me. He starts to push against the resistance of my throat.

"Let me in, baby." I open my jaw wider, relaxing my throat until his head slips in.

"Fuuuck! Stella." He holds himself against me as I swallow convulsively around his cock, my eyes watering. "You take my cock so well."

He withdraws and thrusts again and again, going deeper with each thrust. I could never take his whole length—he's too big, but he finds my limit, then starts to fuck my throat hard and fast with loud animalistic groans.

I'm so drenched listening to his basal instincts take over, to his growling and cursing, to the obscene sounds I'm making from his savage fucking. My throat and jaws burn, and I can hardly breathe, but I'm loving every second.

And finally, he stills. His hand slaps against the wall behind me and he emits a groan so feral, my pussy clenches tight and another burst of wetness seeps through. I feel his cock jerk repeatedly as he starts to come. I don't taste his cum, not until he withdraws his cock from my bruised throat and spills the rest on my tongue.

Tears are still steaming from my eyes, but they are of a different sort. Relieving, cleansing tears. I swallow his cum relishing the salty taste.

"Come here" Ryan pulls me from my knees and swings me up into his arms then walks us into the bedroom.

He lays me in the middle of the bed and follows me down. He buries his face in my neck, worrying the sensitive skin over my beating pulse and peppering my skin with tender kisses.

"You were amazing. Perfect. My gorgeous queen. My beautiful wife."

His praises are like fingers strumming over my nerve endings making me squirm until I start to crave more. I know exactly what I want. And the same way I couldn't explain needing his skin against mine, I can't explain why want to feel him in that dark, forbidden place right now.

He continues trailing kisses up the column of my neck until he gets to my earlobe which sucks into his mouth.

"I want you inside me Ry. I want all of you." I moan.

"You have all of me, Stella. I'm all yours." He strokes his fingers down my torso, pausing briefly to tweak my hard nipple through my shirt and bra then continues downward. He rears up, grabs the elastic waistband of my pants, and drags it off me along with my panties.

He comes back over me and his hand dips in between my legs.

"Christ!" He whispers against my skin. "You are so fucking wet, It's all over your thighs baby. You loved my cock in your throat that much?"

I nod, then gasp as he plunges two fingers inside me and starts to thrust. "I want more, Ry. And not there," I whisper hoarsely.

He freezes. Then raises his head, his gaze questioning as my meaning dawns on him. "Now?"

I nod my head. "Take my ass, Ry."

He shakes his head. "Baby, I've been rough with you tonight."

"And I loved it."

"It will hurt."

"Good. Do it."

He watches for a beat as if deliberating, and then in a flash, he's off the bed and taking off his clothes. Then he removes my top and bra.

He stretches beside me and braces his head on his elbow. He stares deeply into my eyes as he slips between my folds and strokes me. He gathers my slippery juices and reaches further back to rub circles around my tight bundle of nerves, then he inserts a finger down to the first knuckle, slowly sliding in and out.

I moan. It's too intimate, yet I can't look away from him. He keeps going, working me up to take the whole of his finger, then adds another while plundering my mouth with deep drugging kisses.

Sweat mists my skin and my whole body starts to tremble. "Ry, I need you now." I whisper.

He simply nods, then flips me over on to my belly. He rises then curls an arm around me and drags me to my knees so my ass is up and my cheek is on the bed. "Don't move a muscle," he says, then he goes to the bedside drawer.

When he gets back on the bed behind me on the bed I tense with anticipation, and push up my ass further, my eyes trained on him. But all he seems to do is stare and stare at my ass. *I'm about to dissolve into a puddle of need and he's taken up with the scenery.*

"Anytime today, Ryan." I snap.

His gaze cuts to me a second before I feel the slap, right on my pussy.

I cry out, clamping hard onto nothing. He does it again and I collapse on the bed red-faced and begging. "Please take me. Make me come."

"That's better," he smirks. He drags me back on my knees, squirts some lube right onto the crack of my butt, then starts to work it all around and inside me.

I whimper and spread my legs wider for him. "Ry, do it now"

"Shh, Stella, trust me you want it slow." He gently notches the fat head of his cock at my entrance and stills, not pushing in any farther, instead, he slowly circles my entrance.

Nerve endings I didn't realize I had spring to life and in moments I'm moaning, rolling my hips, and seeking more pressure.

"Fuck, you're gorgeous, Stella," his fingers tease and knead my butt cheeks while his cock continues to stroke me until my muscles relax for him.

He pushes forward and the head of his cock slips in. I stiffen, gasping at the intense stretching.

"Ah! Ah, Ryan! *Oh my God, it's fucking huge!*

"Talk to me."

"It hurts." It feels like a ring of fire.

"I know baby. Use your words."

One word. *Magnificent.* And he'll stop. "I trust you."

He releases a pent-up sigh of relief, and I realize he wants this just as bad as I do. "Breathe Stella."

I pant like I'm dying of air deprivation, but I still can't get past that giant intruder in my ass.

His arm encircles me, his fingers slide into my slick folds and he begins stroking my engorged clit.

Pleasure blooms inside my pelvis and spreads all over me. Soon I forget the discomfort and I start to move my hips, a silent plea to relieve the ache and emptiness in my pussy. He gives me more, only it's in my ass. He sinks his cock deep.

I cry out, clawing the sheets. It's too much. He's too much. I'm so full I can hardly breathe. There's no getting away from Ryan his weight, his scent. He's filling me inside and out.

"That's it," he croons, "You've got me now. All of me," he murmurs praises against my skin, and I sob. In moments my apprehension and the sharp edge of the pain dulls into an indescribable sensation.

Still, I crave more. The need to come beats down on me, and I push back the rest of the way until my butt hits his pelvis.

"Fuck, baby. You're taking my cock like it belongs in you," he praises. "You're mine. All mine. No secrets, no barriers. No holding back."

"I'm yours, Ryan. Fuck me. Make me come."

"Done." He very gently starts to rock in and out of me, rubbing my clit at the same time, and I lose myself in the mind-numbing fullness. I'm so wet, my juices are running down my thighs, and my core spasming.

And then I'm right there, cresting the waves of orgasm, the intensity of which has me screaming. He follows me over the edge, growling my name as he spills deep inside my ass.

Chapter Thirty-Seven

STELLA

I WAKE UP TO the smell of coffee, my eyes heavy with a lack of sleep. Groaning, I stretch, feeling a pleasant soreness yet deeply content.

We'd been insatiable for most of the night, an endless cycle of need and fulfillment. All I wanted was him deep inside me, his weight pinning me down, grounding me over and over again. And he was right there with me. The combination of a long separation and the revelations of last night drove our connection deeper.

I open my eyes to meet Ryan's penetrating gaze, his bright blue eyes accentuating the dark spots in his irises. He sits against the headboard, his posture relaxed and attentive, his crisp white shirt casually unbuttoned at the top showing a glimpse of bronzed skin and toned chest.

"I could get used to waking up to this view. And coffee." As soon as I sit up, the sheet slips from my breasts, catching Ryan's heated attention.

He drags a finger down the middle of my chest, making my nipples bead instantly. "Look who's talking. You're so sexy."

"And, you're so full of energy in the mornings," I gesture at his freshly showered and dressed state. "Gosh, this is you who got even less sleep than I did."

He chuckles, then passes me a mug of black coffee—my favorite brand that reminds me of his visitor at the welcome party "Ryan, it was Mr. League who visited you at the Fairchild party wasn't it?"

"Yes," Ryan absently brushes back locks of my hair and tucks them behind my ear. "We're business partners. When I mentioned your love for his coffee, he was more than happy to personally deliver it, along with his congratulations."

That surprises me. "Why didn't he stay?"

"He's well acquainted with the Fairchild dynamics. Given he's my former wife's father, his presence would spark cruel gossip and shift the focus from us. From you. It was meant to be your grand introduction to the family after all."

"Hmm. True." Feeling a growing respect for the elusive business partner, I take another sip and savor the rich taste. Which reminds me that Ryan has stepped down from his position as CEO. "About Ocean Gate–" I begin, just as Ryan also starts speaking.

"–About Don..."

We interrupt each other, then Ryan smiles, "You go first."

"Ryan, how are you going to get back control of Ocean Gate?"

His gaze searches mine. "Don't you mean how do I intend to throw Don behind bars for what he did?"

I nod, "That too. But there's no evidence. There never was, and Viv's long gone."

"If he managed to evade the police, it could mean he's perfected his crime. There's a high chance he's done it before. I'm sure he would have slipped up at some point if we look in the right places."

I take another sip of my coffee, trying to ease the growing lump in my throat. "So, how do we do this?"

"I'll start with his wife. Carmen knows him better than anyone. She might have key information we need to take him down."

Unease blooms in my belly, imagining the things Carmen may or may not know. "And will she help us?"

"She most certainly will. Carmen had been wanting to leave for a long time, but she was too afraid to do it."

"Why was she afraid?"

"Because she knows Don would rather kill her than let her leave with half his wealth."

My lips curl in distaste as I recall my run-in with Don. "And you say Carmen is somewhere in Argentina right now?"

Ryan brings out his phone and taps on it. He shows me photos of the place. "It's a small town called Mendoza. She grew up on a farm so she really loves it there. She manages a few of Alex's vineyards over there and has even acquired a small ranch by the side."

I peer at the images, each an idyllic scene of beauty and nature. "How do you usually contact her?"

"I don't. Not even Alex can reach her, and he's made it so for obvious reasons. The only person with direct access to her is a guy who works with Alex. His name is Antonio. I can get him to set up a virtual meeting with Carmen now."

Ryan moves to take his phone back, but I place my hand on his arm, halting him. "Ry, can we bring our friends into the loop on this? Keeping silent has cost me too much already. I need to start trusting and leaning on them more."

Ryan nods in agreement. "Absolutely, baby. Who did you want to be involved?"

"Everyone. Brooke, Bonnie, and the guys." Jordan is abroad on business and Sabrina's gone with him this time.

"Alright. I'll see if everyone can meet up here tomorrow night."

Ryan makes the call to Antonio while I sip the last of my now tepid coffee, a buzz of excitement in my belly.

Finally, I'm holding someone accountable for what happened to Viv.

I peer at the brunette with dark laughing eyes, one of the two other faces on the desktop monitor in Ryan's home office.

"Hey, Ryan!" she calls out, her voice warm with a distinct Spanish accent. "Long time, no see! Sorry, you caught me during feeding time."

Carmen shifts her camera to reveal two calves, one eagerly taking a large carrot from her hand. "These little ones get cranky if they don't eat on schedule," she explains, chuckling. "They must have built-in timers or something."

She pauses, catching her breath before addressing Antonio. "So, what's up Antonio? You sounded pretty ominous on the phone. But then again, when do you not?" Her laughter fills the room.

Antonio simply grunts, "It's too early for sweets, and you're overfeeding them."

Carmen rolls her eyes, "And here I thought seeing your twins again would cheer you up."

I stay out of sight, watching them with interest. When Ryan mentioned that Antonio worked with Alex, I expected a suave businessman, one with connections stretching to Argentina.

This man is the furthest from that. He exudes an air of mystery and danger. While he has the face of a fallen angel, he looks like the type of person you'd send to extract someone from hell.

From what I can see, he appears to be in a cluttered workshop, a greasy towel draped over his tattooed neck and shoulders.

Antonio's face smoothes into a professional mask, "Carmen, something's come up, You're needed back in the States so I'm coming to get you soon."

"Like hell you are." She spits, scowling deeply. "I'm not setting foot in America."

"Mr. Fairchild will tell you the rest." Antonio grinds out. Clearly not one for coaxing, or many words for that matter, he's given up. He seems to me like the type that would prefer to drag Carmen's ass back instead of reasoning with her.

"What's going on Ryan?" Carmen asks.

"Antonio is right. I need you back in New York, but first, I need to tell you some things about your husband."

"Ronald?" She questions, using Don's full name. "Is he..." She trails off, her tone somewhat hopeful.

Ryan chuckles, "He's not dead. But he's in some seriously deep shit although he doesn't know it yet. Before we go on Carmen, I want you to meet my wife." Ryan pulls me into view.

"Stella!" She squeals. "I've been dying to meet you! I've heard so much about you- from the internet of course which is hardly satisfying..."

"Hi, Carmen. It's great to meet you too. And that place looks breathtaking. And also super warm." I eye the sheen of sweat on her skin.

"I know right? I have not missed New York one bit. Except for the endless drama. How are you loving our family so far?"

I smile, "It's never dull, I'll admit."

Carmen cackles, "I bet. We Reubens have a knack for stirring the pot, don't we? And now I hear my dear husband has dug his claws into Seattle. But not for much longer, mind you." she declares with confidence. "The only thing Ronald can hold onto for long is his evil schemes."

Her frankness draws a laugh from me, and I find myself already warming to her.

Ryan leans forward, "Speaking of evil, Don's done some unforgivable things..."

"Mierda! Bad enough to drag my ass back to the States? What the hell has that man got mixed up in now?" The screen starts swinging back and forth and I suspect she's wildly gesticulating.

Antonio interjects, "You might want to sit for this one, Carmen. Besides, quit with the overfeeding!"

"Fine, cow Daddy! I'll go to the barn." She starts walking while I turn my puzzled gaze to Ryan.

"Daddy?" I whisper, my mind painting all sorts of scenarios.

Ryan scoffs, then mutes his mic. "Yeah, I believe Antonio birthed those calves. He happened to be visiting Mendoza when one of Carmen's cows was in obstructed labor. The guy is a literal grump of all trades.... master of fuck-all."

"I can lip read as well, Mr. Fairchild." Comes Antonio's grim response, and I stifle my laugh.

Ryan clicks the mic back on. "Exactly what I mean, you're a man of... many talents." It doesn't sound like a compliment coming from Ryan.

Antonio only grunts an answer.

Something tells me despite mutual respect and Ryan's gratitude to Antonio, they're not about to become best buddies any time soon. I move to Ryan's back and absently massage his shoulders.

Carmen balances herself atop what I suspect are bales of hay. "Okay, I'm ready, hit me with it."

Ryan gives her the short version of events. Her complexion pales more and more with Ryan's revelation.

Ryan's voice takes on the coaxing note I'm familiar with, the one he uses when negotiating. "So, this is why I need you in New York. I bet he's done it before and I know you know something that can help us nail him for his crimes."

"Oh, I know plenty," Carmen's voice suddenly sounds hoarse and defeated.

"What do you know?" Ryan asks.

She swallows hard. "You know, I never fully explained why I left him."

Ryan replies, "I figured it was his abusive behavior."

"Yes, that... and more. He's deranged, he took pleasure in my pain."

As Carmen reveals her ordeal, I see Antonio's expression darken with rage.

Camen pauses as if trying to recall more. Or brace herself to delve into it. "At first, I couldn't speak. Coming from a humble background and being an immigrant in need of a green card, I felt indebted to him. He belonged to a powerful family, and I didn't know whom to trust. He had me completely trapped."

My hands on Ryan's shoulder go still, and he gently reaches for me and pulls me onto his lap as Carmen goes on.

"But that wasn't the end of it. One night, I caught him in the library, watching a video. He'd been drinking and had passed out, but the video was still playing. It showed him with another woman, and let's just say, he'd been gentle with me."

Antonio's eyes close, a muscle twitching in his jaw. Ryan's hold tightens around me.

Carmen wipes away a tear. "But that was still not why I left."

"What? There's more?" I gasp.

"It gets worse. Over the following months, I started snooping around, looking for other things he could be mixed up with. The signs of drug trafficking were pretty easy to pick– having been on the streets myself. But what broke me was a stash of CDs I found."

Ryan questions, "CDs?"

"Yes, a collection. Thirty or forty, each clearly labeled by date. I thought they were his favorite albums or something. But no, turns out they were like the video he'd been watching the other night. He's a monster." She finishes in a shaky voice.

Antonio finally speaks in a cold flat tone. "He's a dead man."

Ryan's tone is equally chilly. "Death would be too merciful."

"Not the way I do it," Antonio argues.

"Baby?" Ryan nudges me to ask what I think. I can't believe he's actually asking me for permission to order a hit on Don. His cousin. A part of me desperately wants Don's physical suffering, but I can't bring myself to approve this. "I–No."

Ryan nods. "Alright. Get your head back in the game Antonio. Don will live to face the music. Looks like we will find plenty to nail him. Carmen, do you know where he keeps this CD collection?"

"There's a large safe in his library. I know the combination."

Ryan points out, "That was four years ago. He would have changed it."

Carmen only shakes her head. "That's the thing though. He has a pattern he never strays from, that's how I figured out the combination in the first place. He changes it every thirty days, but he keeps the pattern the same. I know the pattern, and I dare say I can get the combination."

"Good. Shaping up much earlier than I thought it'd be. Antonio will get you to the library safe then."

"But hasn't Don moved to Seattle?" Carmen asks.

Ryan replies, "Only about a week ago. Somehow, I doubt he's had time to transfer any 'precious' cargo.

Carmen blows out a steadying breath. "Okay. I'll come to New York."

"Thanks, Carmen. And, you can rest easy. Don is going to prison. My friends and I will see that he stays there for the rest of his life.

Antonio adds, "And mine will see that he dies there." His words carry a chill and an unshakeable resolve that even Ryan doesn't argue.

Mouth tight, Ryan only nods at Antonio, then says to Carmen "I'll see you in New York tomorrow. Best prepare to stay for a few days, a week tops. You'll need to give your statement to the police."

"Okay, Ryan," Carmen replies and then addresses the other man. "Antonio, does that mean you're coming to Mendoza today?"

"I'll be there at midnight. Be ready to leave immediately." He clips, and then his screen goes off.

Carmen shoots a nervous laugh. "Someone's mad. But when isn't he mad?"

"Don't I know it?" Ryan bites out. "The last place the man wants to go is Argentina. He wishes like hell he could point his jet to Seattle and go have a talk with Don. But he'll do as he's told. For now."

I hear what Ryan isn't saying. It's in his sigh of resignation. *Antonio will eventually kill Don.*

Carmen says her goodbyes. "Guys, I have to go pack. It's going to be fucking freezing in New York. Ugh." Her face disappears from the screen.

I'm still sitting in Ryan's lap, his hand splayed low on my belly, fingers stroking the soft skin under my shirt when he asks, "Are you still up for our friends to come in tomorrow?"

"Yeah. But I'm just thinking, Carmen will be here too? Would meeting the guys not blow her cover?"

"She doesn't need to hide anymore since Don is going down. But my worry is that Carmen is likely to show up with the tapes. So they need to know about those too."

His meaning dawns on me. "No, I don't mind us telling them about the tapes."

"Okay. What's with the frown?" He asks when he sees my scrunched up expression.

"It's just something about this Antonio guy. He seemed pretty tied up about the whole Don business. "You say the guy works for Alex? As what?"

Ryan shrugs. "I told you, he's a jack of all trades." His tone is vague and nonchalant. Which tells me all I need to know. *God, I love the way he tells me things.*

I chuckle and give him a sly look "Oh I see, he's like Alex's handyman." *More like bogeyman.*

Ryan looks back at me his eyes twinkling with humor. "Exactly. I knew you'd get it."

Chapter Thirty-Eight

STELLA

BROOKE AND I SIT together on the chaise waiting for Bonnie and Ethan to get here. Xavier and Ryan are talking in the kitchen. I suspect they're giving us space to hang out but I'm too nervous and excited to do much catching up.

Ever since Carmen called to say she got the CDs and is on her way, my anxiety has ratcheted up, right along with my anticipation of meeting Bonnie's baby.

"Why is it taking forever for those two to get here?" I scroll down my phone wanting to call Bonnie again but Brooke lays a gentle hand to halt me then puts her arm around me.

"She'll be here soon, you know they live an hour away." And as if on cue, the elevator bell chimes.

Ryan leaves Xavier in the kitchen and strides toward the entrance. "That must be Ethan. I need to punch that sucker in the face."

Brooke, soothes, "Come on Ryan, we agreed to let bygones be bygones."

Xavier quips, "After sufficient punches have been thrown. It's only fair. Ethan fucked up big time."

"Ethan was fucked either way." Brooke returns and I can't help the smile forming on my lips.

Looks like once the F-word comes out, there's no going back.

Once the elevator doors slide open to where Ryan is already waiting for Ethan. Ryan rears back when he sees them. "Oh look, he's using the wife and the baby as a human shield. Smooth, bastard."

Ethan shoots back. "Language asshole! There's a baby in here."

"Look at this fucker I'm about to deck into kingdom come. Just wait till you put Lucas down," Ryan counters, a half-threat in his voice filled with reluctant amusement. He envelops Bonnie in a welcoming hug. "Well done, Bonnie. Congratulations."

"Thank you, Ryan." She accepts his hug but then begins to confess. "Now, I know Stella covered for me, but I need to come clean. The whole DNA idea was mine. I'm sorry—"

"Actually, she didn't cover for you," Ryan cuts in with a smirk. "Instead she told me how you made her fetch my hair practically at gunpoint."

Bonnie shoots me a narrow-eyed glare. "Thanks a lot."

I just blow her a kiss. Brooke and I rush over for a glimpse of the sleeping baby strapped to Ethan's front carrier.

"Anyway," Bonnie continues, her voice softening, "Ryan, I'm really sorry I did that. My best friend was devastated, and we were both just... in shock, you know?"

"And Bonnie was in labor," I add.

"Exactly! I wasn't thinking straight," Bonnie gives us her best 'puppy dog eyes' impression.

"Yep, we forgive Bonnie," Xavier declares, "she was having a baby. But Ethan, man, not cool."

Ethan raises his hands in surrender, "Guys, come on. If I thought for a second Ryan was capable of something like that, he'd have much more to worry about than a sneaky DNA test. But, yeah, I admit I messed up. I could've handled it way better. I'm sorry, man."

"Did everyone get that?" Xavier shouts from the kitchen, unable to resist the opportunity to tease Ethan. "The great Zeus admits he was wrong."

"Shut up, Xavi," Ethan chuckles.

I sit back down and hold out my arms, my palms flexing in a wordless 'gimme' gesture, waiting for Ethan to finish unbuckling the baby carrier.

"Even gods make mistakes sometimes," Bonnie, who has now sat down on the other side of me, murmurs breathlessly. Ethan pauses what he's doing and then shoots her look which should not be seen outside of their bedroom. She reddens, biting her lip.

"Okay, I think I might vomit," I grimace. "Can you guys dial the mutual worship down a bit? You just got here."

I probably am worse than Bonnie with Ryan at this point, but that's not something I'm willing to dwell on right now.

Ethan laughs, clearly enjoying his wife's reaction to him, and then he hands me his still-sleeping son.

I rock Lucas, murmuring softly to him, smoothing the wispy dark hair on his head as I take subtle whiffs of his sweet-baby smell. Suddenly feeling his eyes on me, I look up. What I see in Ryan's gaze sends a jolt through me.

Desire. Longing. Raw need.

The room disappears as my heart starts to pound. I'm pinned to the spot, unable to move or look away from that scorching blue gaze.

The elevator bell rings again, effectively breaking the moment. "That must be Carmen." Ryan moves to toward the doors while I take a breath and collect my scrambled brain.

"Sweet baby Jesus, Girl," Bonnie nudges me, "I think you just got impregnated right there."

"Totally," I release a nervous chuckle. I can't even argue with that logic. The sight of me holding Lucas did something to the man.

Brooke who didn't notice anything looks up. "What was that?"

Bonnie waves her off. "Never mind, you missed it."

"Anyway, you're hogging the baby Stella," Brooke reaches for Lucas. Even though I've only had him for a couple of minutes, I gladly hand him over. I'm not sure how much more of Ryan's hot stares I can take. Lucas fusses for a few seconds than settles contentedly in Brooke's arms.

Ryan returns to the living room with Carmen in tow carrying a backpack. Once he introduces her to everyone, Ryan drops the black bag in the middle of the floor.

Everyone has been brought up to speed about the night of the Greenhouse party and the reason for getting Carmen all the way from Argentina. The dull thud of the backpack draws our attention as mouths tighten and postures stiffen.

Ryan says into the suddenly silent room, confirming what everyone knows, "Don Fairchild is not going to get away with what he did, and thanks to Carmen, we now have proof. This bag contains all the CDs Carmen found in Don's library safe."

"So what do we do next?" I ask, already dreading the next steps.

Ryan levels me with a look. "I'm afraid we need to know what's in it before we hand them over to the police."

My gut immediately twists into knots because I know what he means and because Viv's video might be in there. "But Carmen already said they're Don's sex tapes."

"Yes, and I think that's exactly what they are. But that was from what Carmen saw four years ago. They may be self-help videos, good old porn, or he might have erased them altogether."

"Ryan's right Stella," Carmen says. "I only checked a couple of CDs, not the whole catalog."

The room goes silent again. No one wants to do this.

"Anyway while we think about that, Xavi, is your man still expert at digging up dirt?"

"Mitch Kravinski? Yep, still sharp. How dirty are we talking?" Xavier calls back from where he's pouring himself a drink.

"Filthy. International narcotics shipping, etcetera." Ryan replies. "And, Don most likely has some chap in the NY police department on his payroll because none of the security cameras place him at the Greenhouse party that night."

"Noted Ry. Will get Mitch on it asap." Xavier says.

"Thanks man." Ryan addresses everyone, "So who's going to do it? You won't need to sit through the videos; you just need to see enough to know we're holding a smoking gun and not a bouquet of flowers."

I obviously could never do it, neither could Ryan. Xavier already looks like he would be sick.

"Ethan?" I suggest, and Ryan nods in agreement.

Ethan inclines his head, but before he can open his mouth to accept, Bonnie interjects. "Guys, um, no. Trust me you don't want Ethan to do this." She shoots her husband a meaningful look.

I might be stretching things here but because we'd just been speaking to Antonio yesterday, I immediately assume that Bonnie's fear is because Ethan might react the same way as Antonio did. A calmly murderous resolve.

"The private investigator can watch it," Xavier suggests but I'm already shaking my head, bile rising to my throat at the thought of some stranger looking through what could be my sister's video.

"I'll do it," Brooke says in a strangely cool voice. She covers my hand with hers. "Just a few seconds to confirm, right? It'll be fine, Stella; we've got you." She sends a reassuring nod to Xavier and Ryan. "The man is going down permanently."

One way or another.

Everyone seems to offer a collective sigh of relief once that choice has been made.

Carmen's voice pierces the ensuing silence. "Once we hand over evidence, I'd like to take a trip to Seattle before returning to Mendoza. I want to look into that scum's eyes when I tell him his life is over."

"Actually, Carmen, I'd like to go too," I say.

A slow smile spread on Carmen's face. "Let's make it a girls' trip then."

Ryan comes to me, pulls me to my feet and gathers me in his arms. "I need to go to Seattle as well. I've been away from my desk for too long. It'll be my pleasure to take you girls."

"Sounds like a plan," I beam.

Chapter Thirty-Nine

STELLA

CARMEN AND I HURRY through the early morning drizzle, dashing across the wide courtyard of Ocean Gate Enterprises. Too impatient to accept Fred's offer of an umbrella escort, we stride quickly across the busy Seattle street and into the glass-paneled lobby.

With Don's assistant being questioned and unlikely to show up for work today, his desk is going to be empty or manned by a temp.

Having attended business meetings and enjoyed torrid lunch dates here many times in the past two months, I've become a well-known face around here. We clear security and head upstairs, a thrill of excitement running through me as the gravity of what we're about to do dawns on me.

This is it. The confrontation, the closure I've been yearning for.

Carmen must also be feeling the same because she takes my hand as we make our way toward the bank of elevators that will take us to the top floor.

As expected, his assistant's desk is empty. It's only 8:30 a.m., HR is probably still scrambling to find a replacement.

Carmen waits outside while I push open the double doors leading into the CEO's office. Ryan's office.

Don looks up, his expression paling in shock until he composes himself, settling his face into the usual half-leer. "Stella!" He booms, leaning back in his chair and steepling his fingers. "I'm surprised to see you in Seattle, let alone in my office."

Ryan's office.

"To what do I owe this pleasure?"

"Just a bit of unfinished business," I drawl, looking around the office which bears my husband's signature of dark wood and beige furnishings.

It's very much the same. Even the crystal shark paperweight I gave him just before I left Seattle is still on his desk, making Don seem all the more like an intruder.

Don follows my gaze all around the room, and apparently, he can't resist twisting the knife. "You know Stella, I never got to say thank you. I was going to become CEO eventually—Ryan was bound to slip up and fall on his face, you see, but you made it easier by leaving."

"Did I?"

"Of course you did. So he cheated on you and fucked a model in London. And so what? What's a little bit of cheating?" He questions.

"I don't know, Don, you tell me. You seem quite at home with the subject."

He only laughs in a cruel way. "It's just as well. Ryan should have taught you that you can't make it as a sniveling child in this family. You need thicker skin, and the ability to take things on the chin. Obviously, you lack those qualities. And mark my words, Ryan will take back every cent you think you made away with. Unless I help you."

I saunter closer to Don and perch on the edge of the desk instead of sitting in one of the chairs opposite him. I want to be able to look down at him.

"I'm deeply moved by your concern, Don, but I'm not here to secure my future. I'm actually here to discuss yours."

"Oh really?" he murmurs, leaning back and linking his hands behind his head while his gaze runs boldly all over me. "I'm all ears then."

"First I need to ask you about something that happened a while back."

"What is it about me you want to know?" He slowly rocks back and forth on the ergonomic chair, clearly enjoying this.

"What were you doing at the Greenhouse Halloween party seven years ago?"

Don stills. "What are you talking about?"

"Greenhouse Halloween party. There was a girl who was half-passed out on the bed. Long silvery blonde hair... She'd just had an argument with her boyfriend..."

A glint of recognition crosses his face. Or that might be his smirk, but he stiffens even as his gaze goes to my hair.

The motherfucker remembers.

"I'm not sure what you're getting at here, but I would tread very carefully, Stella."

"Drop the fucking act, you son of a bitch. You thought you fooled everyone. You even had the police working with you.

But you and I know what you did the night after you won that tri-stone gem ring from Ryan."

He watches me for the longest time. Just when I think he won't say anything, he leans forward and places his clenched fists on the table. Then his mouth twists into something that's too cruel to be called a smile. "You know, Stella, I always thought there was something familiar about you. Does that loser know I had you first?" He lowers his voice to a whisper. "Does it still hurt?"

A strong wave of nausea hits me, I almost fan my face but I make myself act unaffected. "You could never ever have me you sick bastard—that was my sister. But it doesn't matter. You will be spending the rest of your miserable life behind bars."

"What?" His face is no longer that insolent mask. His brows arching upward in surprise and perhaps disbelief.

"Yep," I reassure him. "Incidentally, I don't think rich, entitled rapists do very well behind bars. Who knows, maybe you'll get bent over a few times, too, while you're at it. It'd be poetic justice."

He scoffs, "You have no proof."

"I didn't before," I casually slip my hand into my purse and grab a handful of CDs. They are empty CDs but the dates have been transferred onto them exactly the way he wrote them so he knows what they are and where they've come from.

"I do now." I hurl them across the desk straight at him. Some bounce against his arms and clatter to the floor, the CDs rolling around. "There's your proof!"

His eyes widen. "What the fuck?"

I stand, leaning over the table so I can get into his face. "They're copies. The originals are with the police. But you know exactly what's in them, don't you? Gosh, whatever happened plain old USB or memory sticks?" I shrug, spreading out my arms. "I mean, they are so easy to carry around and even easier to hide. But instead, you get yourself a big box and cram them all in. What are you, an idiot?"

"You broke into my home. How dare you!"

"No, that was Carmen. She broke into your safe. Opened it in two tries, too. So, you see, you're not half as smart as you think, Don."

He's gone pale as a sheet, his jaw slack. I don't wait for his response but stride to the door and throw it open.

Carmen walks into the room, her effusive presence filling the space. "Hello, dear husband." She looks around. "Fancy you making it into this office. It's all you ever dreamed about, isn't it?"

"C-Carmen," he stutters, stumbling out of his chair and scrambling back as if he's seen a ghost. "Where did you go all this time? Why would you just leave like that?"

"Well, the same reason why I've come back. For justice."

Carmen looks around the room, at the CDs on the floor, and shakes her head. "You're a sick, demented human being, Don. I need to see you pay for everything you've done."

He stands to his full height, his face now blotchy red with anger. "You bitches think you can pull me down with your half-baked lies and frame me?"

Carmen shoots back, "It's kind of hard to frame someone who likes to watch himself hurting others. After you've had a hard day at work or something's gone awry, you like to lock yourself in your library and make yourself feel better by exerting power over people you think are weaker than you. Small-boned young women."

"Get out!" he roars.

I cut in, smiling sweetly. "No, Don, you're the one who'll be getting out of this office, out of this company, and getting straight into handcuffs, by the look of things."

He glances from Carmen to me and to the chaos on the floor, his eyes wide with murderous rage and fear. He bends to the floor, and for an awful second, I wonder if he's bending to grab a weapon, but no, he's frantically picking up the spilled CDs.

"There's no need for that, Don. Like I said, those are copies; there's more out there."

"What the fuck do you women want? Money?"

"I told you. Justice," Carmen breathes, a satisfying smile on her face.

"And a little bit of revenge," I add. I check my watch. As if on cue, the door bursts open, and about a dozen armed policemen enter.

The next few minutes are a blur, and end with a thoroughly intimidated Don getting cuffed, being read his rights, then dragged off to the station, his face pale with fear.

"What a coward." I mutter. But I knew that already.

Carmen nudges me. "It's over."

"It's just starting," I think. "It ends with him in prison. Or dead, if Antonio's promise is anything to go by."

Carmen puts up her hands as if counting. "Forty different women. Antonio does have a point, after all."

I nod "True."

"I have to say, Stella this has been the most exciting couple of days. I almost don't want to go back to boring old Mendoza."

"Your twin babies will miss you."

"I know" she laughs.

"Carmen, what time are you set to leave?"

"Antonio should be taking me back later."

"Great, just enough time for a little treat."

"What is it?"

"You'll just have to wait and find out."

We spend the next couple of hours in Whirlpool for some spa time.

"About time you two returned!" Ryan's voice carries through the penthouse as soon as Carmen and I return.

"I know, baby, we couldn't resist getting some spa time after that nasty business."

Ryan pulls me into his arms and kisses me softly "How was it?"

"I can tell you there's nothing as satisfying as watching justice and revenge served in one steaming plate, then getting a full body massage to loosen the tight knots," I say.

The look in Ryan's eyes challenges me on that note. I incline my head and shrug in response, and he smirks.

"I still can't believe you chose to sit it out, Ryan," Carmen says, dropping onto the couch.

"I'd only end up getting charged for assault if I laid eyes on him. Besides, that was your moment. You two needed to see it through. Anyway, Antonio has been waiting for you for the past hour."

As if summoned by Ryan's words, Antonio emerges from the library.

"Hey Antonio," I call in greeting.

Antonio inclines his head in acknowledgment. "Mrs. Fairchild."

Carmen, seemingly unfazed by Antonio's aloof demeanor, approaches him with a smile. "Do we really have to leave so soon? Gina's on her way, and she'll never forgive me for coming to Seattle without seeing her. I won't forgive myself either. It's been four years," Carmen pleads, her fingers intertwined in a gesture of supplication.

Antonio simply nods his assent. "Okay. But we should be airborne in the next hour. Weather forecast," he explains gruffly.

"Oh, is there a storm coming?" I ask.

"If we don't haul ass out of here, yes, we'll be grounded here and I need to be back in New York by morning."

I'm not sure how he plans to manage that, considering Mendoza is at least a ten-hour flight from Seattle, one way.

Gina chooses that moment to walk in.

"At long last! Just the one person I've been waiting for." Carmen cries, hopping to her feet.

"Sorry guys I'm late! I was held up all the way across town with legal aid stuff... Where's Carmen—" She stops short as though suddenly walking into a brick wall.

A brick wall in the form of Antonio.

Antonio's reaction is no less shocked; he tears off his shades, his jaw going slack.

My gaze flies back to Gina, who has still not been able to close her mouth for the last ten seconds. I don't think I've ever seen anyone go so red in my entire life.

Oh, shit. These two know each other.

My gaze once again swings back to Antonio, witnessing his typically unflappable demeanor shatter as though hit by a wrecking ball. He runs shaky hands—*shaky hands!*—through his hair, only managing to stand the strands on end. He then replaces his aviators and settles back into his granite posture, the only remnant of the fit he just had being the reflexive twitching of his jaw muscles.

I stare back at Gina, who looks like she just ran a race. She's now throwing pleading looks back at me.

Dear Lord. They more than know each other.

"What the fuck?" Ryan's arms drop from around me. I hazard a look at Ryan, who is already sporting a thunderous expression.

"Baby," I begin in a placating tone.

"What the actual fuck, asshole?" Ryan roars, sending Antonio a look that could kill. "You have a fucking death wish?"

Carmen also gets what's happening and immediately grabs Antonio's hand. "Guys, there's a storm brewing. Gina, I guess we'll video call. Or Antonio here can bring you... that is, if he survives." She mutters the last part under her breath. "We should leave Antonio. Now."

Antonio doesn't need to be asked twice. He clears from the room like a shot and takes Carmen with him.

Ryan stares, stupefied, at the door for a full minute after Carmen and Antonio have left, while Gina and I remain frozen like statues, with bated breaths, waiting for Ryan to calm down... or lose it.

Ryan finally turns round, then in a seemingly controlled voice, he begins. "What the fuck did you do with that... that... tool?" Ryan demands from Gina, already getting worked up again.

"Ryan, Gina is a grown woman," I remind him gently.

"How does she even know him? How does a guy like that even get to speak to you, Gina?" Ryan booms.

Gina, apparently recovered enough to speak, chimes in with an epic eye-roll and a shrug. "I don't see what the big deal is. You've been pushing me to Chad for years, Ryan, what's another guy?"

"Chad is a lawyer who can't hurt a fly." Ryan snaps.

"And you're saying Antonio can?" Gina argues.

"Do you even know who the fuck that guy is?" Ryan jerks his thumb toward the doors Antonio just disappeared through. "Do you know what he fucking does?" He finishes on a near yell.

"He's a mechanic and races cars on the side. It's a bit on the dangerous side, I know, but—"

Ryan scoffs in disbelief. "Tell me you're not that fucking naive! Have you looked at his tattoos? Did you think to ask him what they meant?"

"I'll be honest, I was more interested in other parts of him," Gina says with a mischievous smile.

"Gina, so help me—"

I intervene, "Gina, don't wind him up. And Ryan, you need to tone down the caveman act. Gina doesn't need your approval to see anyone."

"Actually, Stella, Ryan's right to be concerned since I'm not just seeing Antonio." Gina takes a breath, then continues, "So you know that lawsuit the legal team went Vegas to squash? Well, as you know, Ocean Gate won, and we went out to celebrate. Long story short..."

She pauses for effect and I swear I hear drumrolls, or maybe it's the sound of my heart thumping as I hold my breath.

Ryan is likely feeling the same way because his eyes widen as saucers, mirroring mine. For the sake of everyone, I hope she's not about to say what I think she is.

"We got married last week," Gina announces with a twinkle in her eyes.

Epilogue

STELLA

SIX MONTHS LATER

I stare at the tranquil lake with the sun just peeking over the horizon, and I can't help but chuckle softly to myself.

Bonnie and Brooke swore that if they lived in a house like this, they'd never leave the bed.

But for me, it's the opposite. Now, I scramble awake just for this moment, to watch the sunrise. It's become a daily ritual that fills me with a sense of new beginnings.

My hand drifts to the mug of Gold Medal ginger tea on the ledge beside me, fingers circling the rim. I switched from coffee to tea last week, and going by my friends' strong recommendations, I chose ginger tea.

The door behind me creaks, and I recognize that step, the confident stride that can only belong to one person.

"Ready to roll?" I ask without turning, still tracing the rim of the tea mug with my finger, a small smile on my face. He usually leaves for work before six on days he's not taking Harriet to school.

I feel his warmth on my back before he slips his arm around my waist, pulling me against him in his signature embrace. I'm pleasantly surprised to feel his naked torso against my back and I melt into him, the age-old butterflies fluttering awake low in my belly.

"Good morning, baby." He presses a kiss to my temple then buries his face in my neck.

"You're not dressed for work." I raise my arms and link my hands behind his neck, then let my fingers trace his warm skin down to his shoulders and back up. "Did Harriet wrangle another drop-off day out of you?"

"Well, that little scamp Jack Adler stuck his tongue out at her again. He's getting a stern look."

"Baby, the last 'stern look' only lasted two days. I don't think it's working."

He drops light kisses on the curve of my neck. "I'm going to have to get more creative then."

"Actually, Harriet is going to have to come up with a more convincing story to get you to take her to school."

Ryan chuckles, "I don't mind."

"I know you don't. But what about your routine?"

"My routine is you girls. If you want me somewhere, I'll make it happen."

"Yeah, and Harriet definitely knows how to milk that."

He sucks on my earlobe, "Unlike her mom who still hesitates to bother me."

"She's wound you so tightly around her pinkie finger, you might as well be a ring."

He bites down on the flesh at the juncture of my neck and shoulder, and I shiver, the throb between my legs intensifying into an ache.

"And what about you, wife? What do you think you've done to me?" He cups my breast and pinches my tight nipple.

I moan and grind my butt against his erection. "Wrecked you perhaps?"

"Damn straight." Ryan suddenly places a rectangular box on the wide ledge beside me, momentarily distracting me from seeking my pleasure. "Happy anniversary, Stella."

I spin around to face him. "Oh, Ryan! I didn't even think you'd remember. I never imagined myself having a wedding anniversary."

"Neither did I," he confesses, then cups my jaw and murmurs against my mouth. "Yet here we are." He kisses me in a way that leaves me breathless with want, then lifts his head. "Well, go ahead. Take a look." His eyes are full of mischief and something tender that makes my heart race even faster.

I take the black velvet box, my hands shaking a little. "You shouldn't have," I say, but we both know I don't mean it. I turn back to the ledge, snap it open, and gasp. Inside is a necklace of tiny diamonds, ending in a large blue diamond pendant.

"My God, Ryan!" I gasp in shock. "It's the blue diamond. Again."

"You already have the earrings. It'd be a shame not to complete the set."

"But Ocean Gate's fortune was built on these very diamonds! They're the ones found by Aaron Fairchild in South Africa two hundred years ago."

"Someone's been doing their homework," Ryan teases.

"Well, I made Gina tell me when you just wouldn't. Ryan, these diamonds must have cost a fortune." While not the rarest in the world, they certainly are the most expensive to acquire from the family vaults. He would have had to give up a sizeable chunk of assets in exchange for them.

"Stella, you already gave me the most precious gift. You."

"Oh, Ry," I bite my lip as tears spring to my eyes.

He bends to my ear. "Too sweet and sappy? Shall I stop?"

"Don't you dare," I finger the cool stone, marveling at how it catches the morning light. "It's beyond beautiful."

He takes the necklace and clasps it around me. "Not as beautiful as you," he replies, his voice causing shivers down my spine.

I turn to face him, and words spill out. "I have a gift for you too. I was saving it for your birthday yesterday but you...ah, we got carried away."

He chuckles. "What is it?"

I hesitate. "It's not a gift per se, but it could also be, depending on how you look at it. I mean, I wouldn't necessarily consider—"

"Stella. Spill it."

"I'm pregnant, Ryan."

The world seems to halt for a moment. Ryan looks at me, then at then at the tea on the ledge and back to me, as if just putting it together. He never asked me why I switched to tea. A joy like I've not seen before spreads across his face.

"You're serious? We're... I'm going to be a father again?" His voice is thick with emotion.

Again. I nod, knowing it shouldn't surprise me because it's Ryan, but I can't help marveling at how deeply he loves Harriet.

"Yes," I say, tears welling up in my eyes. "You're the most amazing dad, Ryan. I'd choose you over and over again as the father of my children."

He pulls me into his arms, his embrace enveloping me, his strength surrounding me. "I love you, Stella. This... this is the best gift you could ever give me. A mini you. Another one like Harriet."

"What if it's a boy?"

"Then we'll call him Ronin."

"Not on your life!"

He laughs "I'm joking. We managed to drown that clause a couple of months ago."

"You're joking!"

"I couldn't very well look my daughter in the eye and tell her that her middle name will now be Ramonda."

"Fair point. So, would you like to see the stick?"

"Hell yeah."

"Just so you know, it's the same stick I peed on from a week ago."

"So? I'm demanding all kinds of evidence from you this time."

As if to make his point, he drags the hem of my night shirt– which is really one of his shirts with its sleeves rolled up. I'm not wearing any panties, so his fingers dive straight into my folds.

I moan as his fingers circle my clit. "I ah, distinctly remember you grossing out from the same last year."

"I'm well and truly domesticated now."

"Ha! I wouldn't use that word in the same sentence as you. Considering I was bound and gagged while you fucked me like a beast last night."

"You know we can't have you screaming the house down any longer."

Harriet and Mabel are the newest additions to our gradually growing family. It's a huge sound-proofed house but with the noises we make sometimes…

"You love when I gag you though."

My pussy clenches against his finger as if in answer. "Ryan" I moan.

He pulls down the band of his sweatpants, frees his cock and enters me in one smooth thrust.

"Oh God Ryan!"

"Be a good girl and keep your voice down." He thrusts hard and fast, expertly hitting my G- spot while his fingers circle my clit.

I'm mortified by how quickly my orgasm hits, but it's no less hard. It's blindingly hot and a scream is already working its way up my throat when he covers my mouth with his palm.

I'm still coming when he drops his face in the crook of my neck and bites down, triggering another series of spasms deep in my core. His muffled groans as he comes inside me are music to my ears.

We're still panting when his phone rings. We ignore it, letting it ring off, but it starts up again.

"Damn it," he mutters, moving to the side of the ledge and pulling me into him while I fight to even my breathing.

Once he gets the phone out and he sees who's calling, Ryan curses, "What the fuck does this asshole want now?"

I take a peek at the phone screen and then place a calming hand on his shoulder. "Baby, he's your brother-in-law."

Ryan throws me a look that clearly conveys his thoughts on that statement.

"Look, it's barely six o'clock, and he's calling. It must be important."

Ryan connects the call and barks "Fairchild."

"Ryan, it's Antonio." His usual clipped tone is softer which tells me that Gina is somewhere around there.

"I know that."

"Okay, I was just checking. As you are aware, Don is being sentenced today. Gina wants to know if you'd be coming to court?" Antonio has kept on top of the case and was a big support for Carmen during her testimony and cross-examination.

Ryan takes a steadying breath and grits out, "Gina very well knows that I have no plans to hop on a jet to hear the fucker's sentence, not when his days are numbered anyway."

Silence. Then, "They don't have to be."

Oh wow. Antonio is willing to spare Don? Gina must be doing a number on him. Even Alex had refused to "get involved in one of Antonio's revenge quests" when I'd mentioned the man's resolve to kill Don.

Ryan snaps, "Well, good for you. Was there anything else?"

I whisper, "Baby, he's trying. Cut him some slack."

There's another long silence at the other end. I shake my head at these two stubborn men.

"Hey Antonio, it's Stella."

"Hello, Stella."

"Could you remind Gina that Harriet is turning seven in three weeks? Or better still, bring her? Sometimes Gina gets lost in her work and forgets these things."

Ryan's jaw is tight, but he doesn't say anything.

"I'll be sure to, thanks, Stella."

He disconnects, and I look up to meet Ryan's gaze.

"Why did you invite him?" Ryan grumbles.

"Let go of the grudge already. Antonio's made it past the six-month mark. Besides, I think he'll fit right in."

"Stella," Ryan warns.

"Yes, his trigger finger might be a little twitchy, but you said it yourself, the man has a million other talents."

Ryan huffs, his jaw tight. "I don't like him."

"Well, tough. Gina loves him, and he loves her back."

"How? The grouch hardly speaks."

I have to laugh. "That's got nothing to do with anything. And it so happens that he's very well-spoken, baby. Gina says he can do perfect Scottish and Australian accents. And apart from English and Italian, he also speaks—"

Ryan shoots me a sidelong glance that makes me rethink gushing over the man.

I put my hand up in surrender. "Okay. But to be fair, Ryan, I didn't see you for the first two months of living with you. You hardly even looked at me, and wouldn't kiss me, and I still fell in love with you."

"Hey, I wasn't that bad, surely?"

"Like I said, I think I was already in love with you long before then, I just didn't know it."

A slow smile spreads across his face. "Since when?"

I roll my eyes. "Geez, I've told you this a thousand times, but yeah, since that first day in your New York office."

"You mean that very moment I called you my queen," He smirks.

Since Ryan's mood has lifted considerably, I press Gina's case. She's just as eager as I am to get the two men seeing eye to eye. "Anyway, I'm sure you'll find something in common with Antonio."

He shoots me a doubtful look, then heads back inside and toward our shared bathroom. "I'll always think he's a jackass," He tosses behind him but leaves the door open.

"Well, of course, he stole your baby sister's heart and then committed the ultimate crime of not being a choir boy." I follow him, leaning against the bathroom doorframe and watching him wash his hands. "I already feel sorry for Harriet's boyfriends, you know."

"Fuck. Don't even get me thinking about that yet."

He approaches me, leaning over the doorway and staring deep into my eyes. Slowly, he lifts the hem of my shirt high up, then palms my lower belly. "I can't wait for this to get swollen with my baby."

We stand like that until a musical "Daddy!" pierces the tranquil morning.

He gives me a quick kiss then straightens as the door opens and Harriet's curly head peeks in. "Daddy?"

"Here, pumpkin."

"Yay! You didn't go to work yet!" She bounds across the room and straight into his arms.

"No, we've got big plans at your school today remember?"

"Uh-huh"

"Now let's go see about your breakfast." Harriet is getting to that stage where she's picky with food.

"Mabel says I have to eat it all," Harriet grumbles. She spots me over Ryan's shoulder, "Morning Mommy," she greets as he carries her from the room.

"Morning sweetheart," I call after them.

"Well Mabel is right, pumpkin." Ryan coaxes, "But I can show you a cool trick to try with your cereal."

"Daddy, you're just going to make me eat it all..."

Their voices fade as they leave the room and I return to the bathroom mirror and immediately finger the necklace at my throat. The blue diamond twinkles and shimmers as it catches the bathroom lights.

The diamonds mean a lot to the whole Fairchild dynasty. True to Ryan's words, they are a 200-year-old expression for don't fuck with me. But for me, they tell me in two hundred ways that I found my family. It's not perfect, but it's forever.

THE END

Thanks for reading!
If you enjoyed this book, please consider leaving an honest
review on your favorite Amazon store

Want Ethan and Bonnie's story? Scan the QR code to start reading

SCAN ME

Sneak Peek: The Damaged Billionaire's Obsession

CHAPTER ONE

BONNIE

The raucous laughter around me grates on my already frayed nerves.

I'm sitting in the middle of a boisterous, half-drunk crowd, staring with a mixture of excitement and trepidation at the large, very male hand on my thigh.

Although I'm no stranger to entangled limbs, I'm particularly fascinated by the contrast between this tanned, muscled forearm with its thick, coursing veins and a generous dusting of silky, dark hair against my smooth thighs.

We're at a wedding reception in Cancun, Mexico. A wedding I had no business attending since I don't personally know the bride and groom, but my friend Sabrina and her husband Jordan, practically dragged me here all the way from New York.

I'd just concluded a four-week project where I had built a website for a client and was bitching about how stressful it had been when Sabrina invited me to tag along with them and unwind in Cancun.

Only, never in my wildest dreams did I imagine that I'd be providing prime entertainment at the wedding reception.

"Ethan, you're not doing it right," a big, blond groomsman shouts. "Forget the hands man, get your head in there and use your teeth!"

The rest of the men heartily agree.

For an awful moment, I wonder if he'll do it. Usually, I would be enjoying this kind of public display, maybe even shouting suggestions of my own, only now I find it's not quite the same when *I'm* the one in the hot seat in front of a man I can't stand.

A man whose hand on my naked thigh is, quite unexpectedly, sending shivers of awareness up my spine.

Ethan somehow senses my discomfort and takes his hand away, but the rest of the groomsmen are having none of that.

They wildly egg him on, including, to my utmost annoyance, Maxwell, the hot guy who'd been on my heels all day and whom I'd actually been making plans to fuck tonight.

I roll my eyes in annoyance. If the man was bothered in the least about trying to reclaim the territory that Ethan is all but pissing over right now, I wouldn't be up here with goosebumps and a red face.

Could Maxwell not have insisted on doing it instead of Ethan?

Well, there goes your fun tonight, pal.

I look down at Ethan's bowed head, at the thick, dark locks of hair falling over his forehead, and I tell myself that the tightening in my belly is irritation and the tingles racing along my spine are due to the awkwardness of the situation.

I'm confused by my reaction, but I'm not about to break character and let him see how affected I am.

Ethan looks up, and a furrow appears between his brows. Being only 5'2", I've had to tilt my head way up to speak to him all weekend, even with my heels, so having him kneeling at my feet throws me off.

Our gazes meet briefly; from this angle, I can see beneath the reflective, tinted lenses into his eyes for the first time.

My mouth goes dry. They're light brown with specks of bright green and ringed with a darker brown.

It's so unfair that an asshole gets to have eyes like that.

His gaze is questioning.

Is he...asking for permission? To take the garter off of me?

I remain silent, watching him watch me.

When I say nothing, his hand returns and trails high against the skin of my outer thigh, searching for the garter, and fire licks at me. Why, oh why, did I have to shove that damn thing so high up?

For fuck's sake, Bonnie, it's not a tampon.

His palm presses flat, seeking the lacy fabric, and then his fingers finally curl around the edge of the garter. I can do nothing to stop the ripples of pleasure coursing through me. The elastic catches on the soft flesh of my inner thigh, and he palms my other knee with his other hand.

My breath hitches.

"Bonnie? Are you okay with this?" Ethan suddenly asks.

I was right, he was asking permission. And I think he just heard my gasp. Fuck.

I hate that he's reading me so clearly, and I feel stupid for reacting this way to him, for reacting this way at all. It must be all the testosterone oozing off the raunchy audience. I'm clearly embarrassed and out of my depth here.

Am I okay? *No, I'm not. I'm so fucking not. I need this wild strumming, vibrating thing to stop. Right now*

He's still waiting for my response. Why wouldn't he just yank off the thing and be done with it? Why is the man getting all polite and making it such a big deal?

Because you're uncomfortable, and he knows it.

I shut out the voice of reason, and with a snarky confidence that I'm so far from feeling, I say, "What's the matter Ethan? You're shaking like a leaf. What, the girls at Harvard never showed you their panties?"

His gaze narrows. I think he's angry. My confirmation is the tightening of his grip around my knee, then in a rough jerk, he spreads my thighs wide apart.

The men go wild.

You'd think they were a bunch of rowdy teenage boys, not some of the richest men in the country.

His eyes meet and hold mine again while his right hand snakes between my thighs, his rough palm grazing against the sensitive skin. His eyes are like hot coals, and I can't look away.

I feel a draft against my panties and realize that they're wet.

Geez.

My face pales in shock and mortification, and I catch a glimpse of my reflection in his glasses. I look like a deer caught in headlights. Suddenly, I want to rip those glasses off.

"Hurry the hell up, Harvard. Taking a garter off is not rocket science!"

He grabs hold of the seam and pulls, his knuckles sliding against my thigh on their way down. As soon as the garter clears my foot, I'm off the chair.

"Gentlemen," Ethan says, slowly rising and twirling the stupid garter on his index finger. He proceeds to give a speech about completing the mission, ending by thanking the excited audience for their unwavering support.

I can't watch anymore. I walk, more like stomp off, my face on fire. I'm more upset that I got so riled up. I never get riled up.

I need a drink, I think, settling back at my table, which is currently empty. *And where the hell are all my friends?*

It's all Sabrina's fault, I tell myself for the thousandth time. *I never should have come here.*

The wedding so far has been nothing short of interesting. The wedding planner suggested that instead of the groom tossing the bride's garter to the groomsmen, each bridesmaid was to wear her own garter, and the groomsmen would then select who among them would be taking it off the girl fortunate enough to catch the bouquet.

Great. Not that I really cared who did what to whom as long as I got to watch these sinfully hot guys do those activities. It seems unfair that men as wealthy as these would also look so good.

Sabrina being the only married bridesmaid, didn't think there was any point in joining the others to catch the bouquet, so she'd handed over her garter, urging me to put it on.

I'd agreed and worn it on a whim but made sure to stay well out of the way of the other women. I figured since I wasn't even part of the bridal party, I shouldn't steal the show from those who were.

I only came here for the view.

Of course, the bouquet had to come flying at me like a nuclear missile while the other women who actually wanted to catch the thing dove in every other direction.

Seriously, girls, how hard can it be to grab a huge bunch of calla-lilies hurled at you?

Realizing with alarm what was about to happen, I'd turned away at the last second, but the damned thing still landed on my back.

Technically I didn't catch it, I'd protested, but Nora the bride, declared that the bouquet caught me, which was all the same, if not better than me catching it. And there's no arguing with a bride on her wedding day, is there?

And so, there I was, sitting with none other than Ethan Hawthorne's hand between my thighs while a group of rowdy groomsmen shouted suggestive tips.

Crap. It was the worst possible outcome, considering that if there's been any dark cloud on this otherwise wonderful holiday, it's *him*.

Ethan is the one person I've heard so much about but somehow never got to meet until the rehearsal dinner yesterday.

He and Jordan, Sabrina's husband are close friends, and in the year that I've been friends with Sabrina, it so happens that Ethan and I never got to meet.

To hear how Sabrina talks about him, you'd think he was an angel fallen from heaven with halo and wings still intact, and I'd been looking forward to finally meeting him on this trip, but I have to say, it's turning out to be the worst anticlimax of my life.

Suffice it to say that he was *not* as Sabrina had advertised.

The only angelic thing about him is his face. And perhaps his body. Otherwise, Ethan Hawthorne is the rudest, most judgmental man I've ever met.

And let's not forget, the keeper of a giant stick up his ass.

And I can't imagine how on earth he'd think those yellow glasses are in any way flattering?

I mean, who wears yellow glasses? I'll tell you who: pimply, nerdy weirdos who fancy themselves an avatar in their favorite video game.

Only this time, nature must have lost the memo and dropped him into a ridiculously attractive body.

The moment I walked into the wedding rehearsal yesterday, the way the man's gaze had raked over me from way across the room like I was a homeless urchin had made me almost regret my choice of a tight, black leather mini dress and four-inch, thigh-high boots.

Almost.

When Sabrina eventually introduced us, I managed to hide my shock in discovering that the man who'd appeared to be shooting daggers at me through those *Terminator* lenses was, in fact, the famed Ethan Hawthorne.

He on the other hand, had his eyebrows flying up in obvious surprise before he schooled his features into polite curiosity.

What was that initial reaction supposed to mean?

Those raised brows, coupled with the fact that I couldn't see his eyes behind the reflecting lenses, irritated me to no end.

Usually, I welcome interest from men. Thrive on it, actually. But this time, I felt like a lab rat under his perusal.

His attitude rubbed me the wrong way, so I blurted the first thing that came to my mind about him being a poorly designed avatar for a Harvard professor. I knew as soon as it left my mouth that it was the wrong thing to say.

"I'm surprised you know what they'd look like in Harvard," he'd given me another slow, derisive once-over, his voice a deep baritone, smooth as velvet. "You don't seem to me like the type to have a clue about such things."

That stung.

Because I dropped out of high school. Twice.

By the time I eventually found my way into to college, I was already making too much money as a hacker to take school all that seriously. So, I gave up on college, too.

Sabrina immediately slapped him on the arm. "Ethan, come on, that was harsh. I'll have you know Bonnie is an amazing freelance cyber-security expert. She helped out the gallery when we ran into major problems with our online security. And she built my website from scratch."

The fact that he couldn't hide his shock at that piece of information disgusted me. It was those damn eyebrows.

What did you think I was a paid escort?

"I see. So, you're a hacker, basically." He murmured, his voice lowered so only I heard him clearly. He might as well have said 'hooker' for the expression on his face.

"You bet, Harvard. And if you piss me off, you might wake up to find your precious Acercraft all pwned up." I replied just as softly, referring to his multi-billion-dollar online gaming company.

"I highly doubt that, sweetheart." His almost whispered tone was condescending.

It was true; I was bluffing. I wouldn't do that to Jordan, who co-manages the company with Ethan. Besides, law enforcement would easily trace it to me after the threat I'd just made.

However, just the thought of bringing the proud man to his knees had me smirking in satisfaction.

Sabrina had then said something about starting the procession, and I realized Ethan and I were engaging in a little stare-off.

Well if you could call it that, since all I could stare at was my own reflection.

I felt his gaze though. Literally. It reminded me of the tingly warmth Nan's soothing menthol left on my skin those nights when I'd return home after being out for too long in the cold and rain.

If I didn't know better, I'd swear there were infra-red beams emitting from those lenses. Weird.

Weirdo.

I avoided him the rest of the evening. But I was to get another dose of Ethan prior to the wedding ceremony.

It happened this morning when I came out of my friend's hotel room, dressed in nothing but her fluffy white robe.

I'd run smack dab into a solid wall of muscle in the darkened hallway.

Strong arms had stopped me from falling on my butt, and upon looking up, I saw it was none other than Ethan, minus the glasses. It was too dark to see his eyes but I'd caught his scent, a delicious mix of spicy cologne and male skin, the same I recognized from the previous evening.

I hardly noticed he was still holding me against him despite having got my balance because I was busy suppressing the sudden urge to bury my nose in his broad chest.

And failing apparently because I'd just taken a nice big whiff of him. *Fuck he does smell good.*

I'd kill for his perfume.

Jesus Bonnie! It's Ethan fucking Hawthorne. Asshole. Remember?

Appalled by my insane reaction, I'd angrily shaken off his hands, suggesting that he find his eyes instead of fumbling around in the dark.

He'd cocked his head to one side, watching me for a few seconds as though trying to figure out a puzzle, then simply stepped around me, leaving me in the hallway without a word or a backward glance.

Somehow, that hurt worse than any scathing retort might have.

Like when no one else was around, Ethan couldn't even be bothered to speak to me?

I shake off my gloomy thoughts and focus on processing what just happened over there.

The man with the disposition of a monk took a stupid piece of clothing off you, and for the first time in ten years, you got wet, is what happened. My mind unhelpfully explains.

I should really get laid. It's been a couple of months at least because I've been busy with this last project. That must be it.

Maybe I ought to lower my standards and reconsider Maxwell.

Looking around, I see the man in question currently flirting with another wedding guest, who looks at him like she might tear his clothes off in two seconds flat.

Yeah, no, girl, you can have him; you seem way thirstier than me.

I scan the room frantically, looking for Sabrina, who I've named the root cause of this situation. I spot her across the room, practically in Jordan's lap, his hand on her bare thigh thanks to the high slit in her dress.

Which reminds me of where Ethan's hands were a few minutes ago. I drown that thought with a gulp of champagne, watching as Sabrina reaches for the bunch of grapes on their table and slowly starts feeding them to Jordan.

Gag.

Those two can be nauseating. I know their schedules are crazy, with Sabrina's highly successful art gallery and Jordan straddling two multibillion-dollar companies. I get that they don't see as much of each other as they would like, but still.

I decide to leave the lovebirds to fawn over each other and look around the room for my newly-made, and thankfully *still single*, friend Brooke.

Brooke and I met yesterday at the rehearsal dinner while Jordan, Sabrina, and Ethan were busy with whatever bridesmaids and groomsmen did at wedding rehearsals.

I'd been feeling a bit left out and still smarting from the unpleasantness of meeting Ethan when I spotted Brooke also sitting by herself.

We had such an instant connection that it felt like we'd known each other for years. Brooke came to Cancun as a plus-one for one of the groomsmen, a certified playboy she's crushing hard on.

By the end of the rehearsal dinner yesterday, she'd begged me to make up an excuse to stay the night in her hotel room because she couldn't trust herself not to end up in Xavier's bed.

And now, she's AWOL, and so is Xavier, for that matter.

Yep. They're most likely off having crazy hot sex right now. I did warn the stubborn girl that there was no point in fighting her attraction to the man.

I signal to the passing bartender for another glass of bubbly champagne.

Brooke's absence only leaves Sabrina. She will have to do then, provided she can peel herself away from Jordan for two seconds.

I'm reeling from what just happened, and I need to decompress.

I watch them, and the moment Sabrina catches my gaze from across the room, I glare meaningfully at her, swiftly cocking my head at my table.

Get your ass over here!

She gets the message, disentangles herself, straightens her long, champagne-colored, silk bridesmaid dress, and saunters over to me.

I grab another champagne glass from a passing waiter and hand it to her when she reaches me. "You guys are shameless, you know."

Sabrina only giggles.

"Seriously, doesn't it get old? You've been married for over a year now."

Sabrina looks back at her husband, and a flush steals across her cheeks.

I have my answer. "Ugh." I take a gulp of my drink.

Sabrina watches me in amusement. "Would you prefer a bottle instead?"

I give her the stink eye.

"No, really, Bonnie. You seem upset. What's going on?"

"What do you mean what's going on? Didn't you see what just happened?"

"You mean the couple's dance?" She motions to the newly-weds Alex and Nora, who are currently swaying to a waltz on the dance floor.

I wonder if Sabrina is being deliberately obtuse. "No, Einstein. What happened with the whole bouquet and garter thing you made me do."

"Oh, no, we missed the whole thing. Jordan and I were outside taking pictures. Which reminds me, Bonnie, the photographer is awesome. You should totally take some. You look hot. And the dress matches your highlights."

I'm wearing a plum-colored dress that matches the streaks of purple in my curly, asymmetrical pixie-cut.

"Thanks, babe."

"So, catch me up. Who caught the bouquet?"

I pin her with a hard, accusing stare. "Take a wild guess."

"What, you?"

I nod.

"Really! I wouldn't have thought you'd want—"

"Exactly. I actively avoided it. I couldn't have been further away from the bride if I'd stepped outside the room. But even with her back turned, it almost hit me square in the face. I wonder if Nora throws frisbees."

Sabrina chortles. "Wow, I would have loved to see your face when—wait a minute. Did you wear the garter?" She sees the expression on my face. "Oh, my God, so Ethan took it off you? Shit, how could I have missed that!"

"Hey, wait a minute, how did you know it was Ethan? You said you weren't there."

"All the boys—well, the single ones—had a game of poker this morning, and the loser was to take the garter off the woman who caught the bouquet. Jordan told me that Ethan lost the game."

"Wow, how nice for you to have insider information. If only you shared that once in a while with your buddies so they don't get blindsided." If I'd known Ethan was going to be taking off garters, I would never have agreed to participate.

"I did not for a second think it'd be you, Bonnie. I mean, couldn't you have thrown yourself on the floor to avoid it or pushed someone else into the way or something?"

"Right, put your two cents in, why don't you, coach?" I roll my eyes.

"Okay, sorry." She doesn't look sorry. "Anyway, how did it go? I know you two didn't get on too well yesterday. Maybe the icebreaker you guys need is something funny and ridiculous like this?"

"Uh, no. I think not. If anything, the Arctic has completely frozen over on us. Sabrina, that was one of the most awkward moments of my life!"

"Really? How so?"

I don't think she gets it.

"With all those guys gathered around us! And you won't believe how the jerk actually gave a victory speech afterward."

Sabrina again tries to look horrified, but I can see she's amused. The man can do no wrong in her eyes. "I'm sorry. The boys sometimes go overboard with their games. They work so hard in their careers but play like kids. Just be grateful it wasn't Ryan, though."

Ryan is the big, loud, blond guy who suggested Ethan use his teeth. Yeah, he seemed to be having the most fun out there, and from what I've seen since yesterday, he doesn't hold himself back from a good time.

"They might act like that because many of them were raised as heirs of huge legacies, and they didn't always get the chance to be kids." Sabrina glances back across the room at Jordan, who has joined the other groomsmen, now arranging themselves like a choir.

Led by the best man, a big tattooed guy with a man-bun, they start to sing offkey to the couple, and the bride goes beet-red, giggling.

I don't even want to know the lyrics of the song.

"Anyway," Sabrina continues, "what I'm saying is that once you get to know them, they're not so bad. They're great, actually."

I'm unsure how, or if, to mention my surprising physical reaction to Ethan, something even I am ashamed to admit to myself. Given the circumstances, I want reassurance that my reaction was normal or expected, but I also don't want her to think that there's more to it than a knee-jerk response. Besides, I can't risk it getting back to Ethan because Sabrina will tell Jordan, who might then tell Ethan, his friend.

"I think I may have overreacted," I begin.

"How so?"

"I don't know. I didn't find the whole thing funny, which is strange. You know I don't mind a bit of attention now and again. But this time, it felt um... really intimate. I didn't want to do it," I finally admit.

"Did you tell Ethan that? Because he would have never done it unless he was sure that you were good."

I don't say anything, remembering how he'd asked if I was okay and the way I scoffed at him.

"Are you alright, Bonnie?" Sabrina asks.

"Yes, I... it just caught me off-guard, that's all. Two days ago, I didn't even know I'd be here, yet here I am, taking center stage. It's a little weird, especially after standing out like a sore thumb yesterday. I felt like a zoo animal with the way people were staring at the rehearsal."

The way Ethan Hawthorne was staring.

"I did tell you to wear a dress."

"And I wore one!"

"Of course you did, and it was sexy, but leather will make you stand out in a formal gathering," Sabrina points out in amusement. "Although, your standing out yesterday wasn't all down to the dress."

I wait for her to say more.

She shrugs. "It's just you, Bonnie. I keep telling you that you have a certain... elegance to you. Class. It draws people in."

I try not to snort. A memory of me back in Clonmel, Ireland, clad in torn, dirty clothes and picking pockets, comes to me. I violently shove it back and change the subject.

"Anyway, help a girl out. It's raining sexy men here, so I'd like to meet someone. Now, I've just ruled out Maxwell—"

"The doctor?"

"Yep, he's out. Ryan, too. But everyone else is fair game. You know most people here. So, tell me, who would you suggest?"

She looks around, rubbing her palms excitedly. "Oh, there's so many to choose from. Let's see, what was your type again? Coloring, build, personality?"

"Muscles, a clever tongue, and a working cock would be a good place to start."

"Well, that simplifies things then! Shall we find out how much they're charging?" Sabrina and I are still giggling when Jordan and Ethan reach us.

From Jordan's grin and the thunderous look on Ethan's face, I know they overheard our conversation.

Geez, lighten up, man. Your virtue is safe.

Ethan folds his tall frame into the chair opposite from me and then collects a drink from a passing waiter.

"Can I steal this gorgeous woman beside you, Bonnie?" Jordan asks. He'd been whispering to Sabrina prior to him asking me the question, and he's now helping her out of her seat.

"By all means!" It's not even been fifteen minutes, and already Jordan wants his wife back. I resist the urge to roll my eyes.

Sabrina goes with her husband, and we watch as he spins her on the dance floor as she giggles like a little girl.

I feel Ethan's eyes on me. The silence grows heavy with what I know he wants to say, so I mentally steel myself for another round of verbal sparring.

No need to get a hernia restraining yourself on my account. I sure as hell didn't hold back my thoughts yesterday when we were introduced.

"So, Harvard," I say cooly. "I heard you lost a game of poker."

He shrugs. "I suppose you can't be great at everything, can you?"

Arrogant, aren't we? Why does every word out of his mouth irritate me so much?

"Well, I have to tell you, poker isn't the only thing you're bad at. You certainly weren't the man for the job tonight. I've seen elephants with better finesse."

I hate the way his eyes bore into me. "You'll have to forgive me. I'm not that much into showmanship, you see."

How dare he say that to me after the silly speech he gave? "And I am? You think *I* put on a show?"

He glances pointedly at my black curls with its dark purple highlights and my dress, which has no neckline to speak of, as it opens down to my amethyst belly button ring. I feel naked under his gaze.

And inexplicably achy.

His face swings back up to mine, shuttered and unreadable.

"Whatever gets you through the night, Bonnie."

What the hell does that comment even mean? "Don't presume to know or judge me."

"Why would I judge you Bonnie?" His tone softens.

"Oh come on! You've been doing that since yesterday. Especially this morning. Your expression said it all: the twist in your mouth, the stiffness in your spine. Oh, wait, that might have more to do with the giant baseball bat shoved up your ass, actually."

Still no reaction. "And you got all of that from the two seconds I was in that hallway?"

"It doesn't take long to recognize disdain. What exactly was your issue this morning, Harvard? Have you never seen a woman do the walk of shame before? Or maybe you've never had a one-night stand?"

I'm not sure why I said that. I'd spent the night in Brooke's hotel room. But for some reason, I want to shock him, ruffle his cold, contained demeanor.

"Is that what you were doing this morning then, Bonnie? A walk of shame?"

"What did it look like?"

"Like a drama queen getting her rocks off."

He's not smiling. He's not frowning, either. He just has this cold, bland, irritatingly contained demeanor. And the reflection from his glasses mocks me.

I want to break them.

I wish I could see his eyes. They were so expressive when I caught a glimpse of them as he knelt at my feet. I bet if I could see his eyes now, I'd know what exactly he's thinking.

"Maybe if you took that log of bias out of your eyes, you might see better, Harvard."

He doesn't respond, so I continue. "Speaking of, I've been meaning to ask, haven't you heard of this little thing called laser eye surgery? It's all the rave these days."

He's a billionaire. Why would he insist on wearing those weird glasses?

He adjusts them in response. "As it happens, I've heard of it. You on the other hand, might want to invest in a truth filter. And a sober stylist."

Before I can fully process what I'm doing, I grab for my drink. Only, my fingers narrowly miss the champagne glass I was reaching for as he deftly collects it, somehow already sensing I was about to empty the contents on his head. Still, with that bland expression, he drains the glass and carefully puts it back on the table.

"Evening, Bonnie." He stands and stalks off, leaving me helplessly fuming.

Want more of Ethan and Bonnie's story? Scan the QR code to start reading

SCAN ME

Acknowledgements

I want to say thank you to my absolute rock of a man, Shawn, and to Muskaan Khan, Jess Miller, and Angela Jogno.
I couldn't do this without you guys xx

Also by Judy Hale